LA DOROTEA

LA DOROTEA

Lope de Vega

Translated and edited by

ALAN S. TRUEBLOOD

and

EDWIN HONIG

HARVARD UNIVERSITY PRESS
Cambridge, Massachusetts, and London, England
1985

Design/Edith Allard

Library of Congress Cataloging in Publication Data

Vega, Lope de, 1562–1635.
  La Dorotea.

  Translation of: La Dorotea.
  1. Trueblood, Alan S.   II. Honig, Edwin.
III. Title.
PQ6459.D6   1985   862'.3   84-22371
ISBN 0-674-50590-5

To the memory of
A M A D O   A L O N S O
who years ago in his Harvard classes
communicated to his students his own love of
La Dorotea

PREFACE

One of the surprises of literary history is that *La Dorotea* should have had to wait three and a half centuries before being made available to the English-speaking world. This first English version grows out of the hope that the neglected classic—surely Lope's masterpiece—will be as fresh for readers Lope never imagined as for those he saw about him daily in 1632.

Although our acquaintance with *La Dorotea* goes back much further than the seven years spent in shaping the translation, the total process yielded a richer, more far-reaching appreciation and sharper perceptions of the work than we could have known when we started the project. In our epilogue the Conversation between us attempts to share with the reader some of these discoveries.

Worked at jointly and separately during its various stages, this version has been revised so often and so thoroughly that neither translator can now distinguish his original contribution. Except for the notes and glossary prepared by Alan Trueblood, it has been a totally collaborative enterprise and the product of our complementary roles—Trueblood's more intimately concerned with assaying the qualities of the Spanish source, Honig's with attending to matters of style and tone as the work evolved in English. Beyond a certain point, however, even such distinctions tended to fade when collaboration led to an actual commingling of voices—each voice blending and interchanging with the other and both with Lope's. To bring *La Dorotea* alive in a language, world, and time far removed from those of its origin, we allowed a certain flavor of English style and usage from the early seventeenth century to temper the tones and registers of today's flatter and harsher language.

We owe much to several institutions and individuals who helped us complete the project. The National Endowment for the Humanities and Dr. Susan Mango, director of its translation program, granted us a major subsidy to pursue the work in several places, and notably for a while in what once had been the kingdom of Valencia, Lope's refuge during his banishment in 1588. There our experience of the country offered striking instances of the continuity of Spanish life from his day to ours. We are grateful to the Virginia Center for the Creative Arts and to its director, William Smart, for the hospitality that carried us, in the spring of 1983, into the last phase of the project. Professor Edwin S. Morby deserves particular recognition and gratitude for his admirable edition of *La Dorotea* (Madrid: Castalia, 1968); this edition gave us a totally reliable text and notes in Spanish to work from. Professor Bruce W. Wardropper kindly read the manuscript and made extremely helpful suggestions. Dr. Carol Bergen's assistance embraced a wide area of linguistic and literary matters, including acute editorial perceptions. To Katarina Rice, of Harvard University Press, we are indebted for shepherding the manuscript in its initial stages, and to Ann Louise McLaughlin for taking over thereafter. Whatever deficiencies remain are of our own making and not ascribable to those who so generously offered us their assistance.

Alan S. Trueblood
Edwin Honig

CONTENTS

INTRODUCTION

Lope de Vega (1562–1635) is best known as an extraordinarily prolific playwright, the author of some four hundred surviving plays, who shaped the course of Spanish drama for a century to come. He is less known outside of Spain as an excellent poet whose lyrics issued forth in a steady stream for over fifty years without losing their freshness. Among them there are some sixteen hundred sonnets alone. Even less known are his narrative works: pastoral romances; a Byzantine romance; Italianate epics, serious and burlesque; and poems on contemporary history and mythological subjects. The neglect of these works is perhaps partly ascribable to Lope's own avowal that he did not find the writing of narrative congenial to his talents. *La Dorotea* (1632), which Lope called an "action in prose" (*acción en prosa*), constitutes a special case. It eludes clear-cut generic classification, although it was his fondest creation, the one he most wished to be remembered by. An acknowledged masterpiece, it has never before been translated into English.

Born in Madrid in November 1562 in modest circumstances, the son of a master embroiderer, Lope attended a Jesuit school and ultimately the nearby University of Alcalá. Though an indifferent student, he acquired a considerable literary and humanistic culture there. In

1583 he participated in the naval expedition which conquered the Azores for Philip II. Back in Madrid, Lope began in earnest his career as a playwright, soon finding his scripts much in demand by acting companies. In his half-century of playwriting, his influence was decisive in shaping and refining the *comedia nueva*—the new drama of Golden Age Spain.

The *comedia nueva* was a theater of broad popular appeal, whose formulas were flexible enough to admit the widest range of subjects while leaving unquestioned the values of the established social order—faith, kingship, honor. The Neo-Aristotelian unities of time, place, and action and the proscription against mixing comedy and tragedy were not allowed to interfere with the overriding concern of playwright and audiences for a briskly paced action rich in surprise and capable of maintaining suspense to the end. What did hold the best plays together was theme—articulated by the manifold relations between primary and secondary plots, and sustained by poetic imagery. Characterization was contingent on the requirements of plot and action; Lope was often content with a quickly recognizable typology. The plays were in three acts, with no scenic divisions allowed to obstruct the action. Lope originally had no thought of retaining the scripts, which he looked upon as ephemeral and expendable. Only when his career was well advanced did he consider giving them definitive form, orienting his craftsmanship toward density and depth, and publishing his plays.

In the initial stage of this long career—probably in 1583 on his return from the Azores—Lope had become professionally associated with Jerónimo Velázquez, a producer-director whom he supplied with play scripts. This is how he met and became the lover of Velázquez' daughter, Elena Osorio, married to an actor who seems to have been absent much of the time. The affair was no passing diversion. It deeply engaged the feelings of both parties and pursued its often tempestuous course over four years. During this time Lope frequented the Velázquez household, in which Elena still lived. A tacit understanding based on mutual convenience appears to have developed: Elena's favors were apparently taken as reciprocation for Lope's scripts.

It is this personal history, and especially its violent dénouement in 1587–88, which nearly fifty years later was to reemerge in *La Dorotea*. (The limited resurfacings in the intervening years, which attest to its continuing vitality, need not concern us.) The breakup of the affair led to an action against Lope for libel, landing him in jail on the charge, clearly well founded, that he had written vicious satirical poems against Elena and her relatives. He was sentenced to two years' banishment from the kingdom of Castile and eight from Madrid and its environs.

In February 1588 he left for Valencia to begin his exile, apparently persuading Isabel de Urbina—a young woman who became his wife shortly after—to accompany him. In May he was off to serve on a galleon of the Armada, resuming his residence in Valencia and his playwriting on his return in September. From Valencia he moved in 1590 to Toledo and later to Alba de Tormes in the retinue of the Duke of Alba, whom he served as private secretary until his return to Madrid in 1595, after the death of Isabel. Alba de Tormes saw the production of plays and a pastoral romance, *La Arcadia* (1598), all of which chronicled in veiled fashion the amours, intrigues, and pastimes of the ducal court.

We need not follow Lope's intricate comings and goings around Spain in subsequent years—his establishment of two households, in Madrid and Seville, each eventually with numerous offspring; his growing fame as poet and dramatist; his fashioning of plays for religious orders and for royal festivities—plays on the latest events of the war in Flanders or the chronicled deeds of Spanish monarchs, on the folklore of rural Spain and the lives of Spanish peasants, on imaginary romantic adventure in the Madrid of his day, and indeed all over Spain and the New World.

Lope's dramatic resourcefulness was inexhaustible, but it did not bring him financial security. Even when, early in the 1600's, he became private secretary to the Duke of Sessa, a position he retained the rest of his life, his economic situation was scarcely alleviated. Rather than bringing him a fixed wage, the post made him humiliatingly dependent on the capricious benefactions of his patron. Moreover, it created deep moral conflicts, since he was obliged to act as scribal go-between in the Duke's pursuit of women. Schemes for remedying his situation, like the efforts to have himself named royal chronicler, which began in 1611, were repeatedly rebuffed. As he approached fifty, Lope became a prey to spells of melancholy and intervals of painful soul-searching which led him to seek ever closer ties with the Church. In 1609 and

1610 he joined two separate religious sodalities and in 1611 became a member of a penitential order of the Franciscans. After losing, in successive years, his favorite child (the seven-year-old Carlos Félix) and his second wife, he was ordained a priest in 1614. Though these particular losses contributed to his spiritual crisis, it had deeper roots in an overwhelming sense of guilt for offenses against God, brought on by episodes of anger and lust which instilled the need to do penance before it was too late.

This urgency notwithstanding, the deepest and most enduring passion of Lope's life still lay before him: his attachment to Marta de Nevares, whom he met in 1616 and who died shortly before *La Dorotea* appeared in 1632. As always, Lope astonishes us by his capacity to live and function in situations fraught with moral and emotional conflict, and his ability to muffle effectively the voice of conscience. It was Marta who, after Elena Osorio, left the deepest mark on *La Dorotea*. She was twenty-five years Lope's junior—about thirty in 1616—and had been married for some fifteen years to one Roque Hernández, whom she detested.

Lope became inordinately jealous of Roque, heaping scorn on him in letters to the Duke of Sessa. He was jubilant when the husband died in 1620, freeing him from the legal and financial entanglements into which the situation had led. But the underlying conflict remained. Earlier at intervals, and after Roque's death more insistently—as the correspondence with the Duke reveals—Lope's vows of priestly chastity rose up against the passion for Marta. As many compositions of this time attest, the conflict led Lope, with increasing earnestness, to attempt a Neo-Platonic sublimation of his love. This he seems to have achieved when his advancing years and Marta's failing health undermined the physical basis of the relationship. In this way Neo-Platonic idealism, long after its Renaissance flowering, became far more than a literary convention: it was a matter which involved his innermost being. Still, no sense of conflict between Neo-Platonic spirituality and the orthodox channels of institutionalized religion arose to disturb him.

Lope's literary activity did not end with the publication of *La Dorotea* in 1632. Though he felt superseded in the theater, he went on writing effectively into his last years, when he also produced a nondramatic masterpiece, his *Rhymes Human and Divine of the Licenciate Tomé de Burguillos* (1634). Assuming the persona of a penniless law student in love with a washerwoman, Lope brought together a collection of engagingly humorous and burlesque takeoffs on well-worn poetic conventions. The work also contained a mock-heroic epic, *The Battle of the Cats* (*La Gatomaquia*). The collection epitomized the subtle artistic control Lope sustained to the end over his innate ludic tendency—both his seriocomic sense of play and his accesses of pure playfulness. This ludic strain, already evident in the transcript of the libel hearings of 1587–88, came into its own in *La Dorotea.*

In his maturity Lope became painfully aware of the flawed and brittle character of the world of his time—indeed, peculiarly sensitive to the ephemerality of all human time. In *La Dorotea,* a youthful work made over in mature years, he shows us the actions and reactions of characters who have lost their grip on disappearing values. (The predicament will surely be familiar to twentieth-century readers.) If two crones playfully juggle thoughts of human evanescence in the opening dialogue, a more disquieting note of world-weariness is soon struck in "To solitude I go," the first poem presented in the work.

While Lope takes pains to relate this particular poem to himself, in his own name, he also is concerned to account for its inclusion as a choice of the character who performs it. Throughout he displays much versatility in finding ways to bring poems into the dialogue, in song or recitation, as reflections of character and mood on the part of their performers. The selection of poems is not random. On the contrary, the verse might be viewed as functioning in the dialogue in the same way that the operatic aria relates to the recitative that surrounds it. At times the poems reflect a character's nostalgia for the past they evoke, leading him or her to relive vicissitudes of once shared experience. At other times they acquire a new dimension by being set against a present state of mind or feeling, in the process revealing sensibilities or exacerbating them in performer or listener. Sometimes, too, the justification of the verse is its display of a much prized virtuosity in poet or composer, speaker or singer.

One character, the bawd Gerarda, although the possessor of a fine nonliterate ear, has no particular use for poetry except insofar as it can be pressed into the service of her matchmaking ends. Like Lope himself, a person advanced in years and *Lebensweisheit,* she is endowed with the kind of attachment and detachment later vouchsafed to the omniscient narrator of the developed novel. Nevetheless, she could not have been conceived without the precedent set in a work of over one hundred years before, *The Tragicomedy of Calisto and Melibea* of Fernando de Rojas, sometimes viewed as the direct forebear of the Spanish novel. Representing in fact an indeterminate form between novel and play, the *Tragicomedy*—soon popularly named *La Celestina* for the dominant character—established this character, the bawd, as the dynamic center of the fictional action. This is clearly not the case with Gerarda, despite her restless activity. Lope is at liberty to invent for her an ingenious and far from traditional role. Gerarda's bawdry spends itself as willingly on language as it does on people, a trait essentialized in her use of the proverb. Celestina wielded proverbial wisdom strategically; in Gerarda, however, Lope turns the proverb to ludic purposes never dreamed of by his predecessor.

Similarly innovative is Lope's handling of other aspects of style and rhetoric. Here, too, he carries in new directions tendencies only adumbrated in *La Celestina*. A reader who comes to *La Dorotea* with the traditional hierarchy of styles in mind may be surprised to find characters of uncertain social status adopting the speech of learned and highborn ladies and gentlemen. Any character appears capable of both ordinary bluntness and a brand of magniloquence sui generis. In a word, speech styles, varyingly based on the contemporary idiom, become an index of individual character and personality. It is the contemporary idiom which is stylized, though the oblique reflection of the realistic thus achieved is distinct from the self-conscious or programmatic realism practiced two centuries later by a Dickens, Balzac, or Galdós. A poet more rhetorical than vatic, Lope makes free use of the literary rhetoric of his time. He is well qualified to reproduce the stylistic heterogeneity of contemporary learning and of a literary culture which has lost its bearings.[1]

It may be useful to turn in conclusion to the remarks Lope himself makes about *La Dorotea* in his Dedication and in the Prologue addressed to the "audience." Although the latter is ascribed to a younger colleague, Francisco López de Aguilar, a manuscript in Lope's hand

---

1. For a fuller discussion of these and other aspects of *La Dorotea*, the reader may consult *Experience and Artistic Expression in Lope de Vega: The Making of "La Dorotea,"* by Alan S. Trueblood (Cambridge, Mass.: Harvard University Press, 1974).

justifies the assumption that it is Lope's. Two main questions concern Lope: the stage of his career to which the composition of *La Dorotea* belongs; and the generic and formal characteristics of the work, its literary ancestry.

La Dorotea, he says in the Dedicatory Note, was written early in his life, left unpublished, lost when he took ship with the Armada, recovered later, and trimmed of its "rampant growth"—and, dedicated to the Count of Niebla, it is now being published. In the Prologue, Lope makes early composition the justification for referring in passing to contemporary worthies (the writers listed at the beginning of scene 2 of act IV, for example) and to the type of dress then in fashion. It is noticeable that Lope refers to his revision as a mere pruning. His term, *lozanía* (rampant growth), is figuratively made to apply to both his own youth and the temper of *La Dorotea.* The implication is one of licentiousness trimmed away. The inference is that the atmosphere and tone were originally closer to those of the society reflected in the legal proceedings of 1587–88 than is the case with the present text.

While it is safest to take Lope at his word, we find it impossible to place the first stage prior to his departure with the Armada. One cannot conceive of the impetuous and tormented young dramatist of 1587–88 writing *La Dorotea* originally as a commentary on still unfolding events of his life. Lope would have been incapable then of attaining sufficient distance to write the "action in prose" as it now exists. More than likely, for Lope, writing as late as 1632, the first stage of composition and the inner time of the action, 1587–88, tended to coalesce. A persuasive hypothesis is that the original version took shape during the relatively tranquil years of Lope's residence at Alba de Tormes, 1590–95, when a decisive break with his Madrid past would have begun to give him a longer perspective. The present text is so evidently mature, and so thoroughly an amalgam of early and late, that it becomes pointless to attempt any specific discrimination between the two. Even the few straws in the wind that may point to particular moments of what appears to have been a long process of gestation, may be touches inserted from hindsight.

As for the second stage of composition, Lope in 1632 does not place it at all with respect to time. A series of prior references made by him to the coming work shows he was closely occupied with it from the early 1620's right up to the time of publication. The second version, it is safe to assume, became not only a thorough revision but an expansion of the earlier.

In classifying *La Dorotea* with reference to other works of the period and of antiquity, Lope seems first of all anxious to claim for it the status of poetry, despite its being written in prose—a possibility stressed, on the authority of Aristotle, by every commentator on the *Poetics* from the mid-sixteenth century on. The work, Lope insists, is an "imitation of truth"; this, not metrical form, is the major criterion of poetic art. All the same, he adds that the prose medium of the dialogue has particular significance in this case because the work is based on "history"—that is, personal history. Having the characters speak in prose (as live prototypes would have done) sets them apart from the dramatis personae of the author's stage plays, creatures of fiction whose verse utterance and stage costumes were accepted conventions. Prose dialogue, furthermore, is well suited to the nature of this particular drama, which is intended for private reading, not for delivery by actors on a stage. But, to relieve the reader and to achieve the beauty afforded by variety, the author has inserted verse to be recited by the characters.

Although Lope does not intend *La Dorotea* for the *comedia* stage, he still links it with Greek and Roman comedy, clearly not thinking of it as a tragic work. Indeed, he does not even mention in the introductory matter the most obvious model for the work's external form, the tragedies of Seneca. *La Dorotea* follows them in its disposition in five acts, in the presence of choruses more decorative than functional, and in the inclusion of the prophetic dream and the messenger who brings baleful tidings. (In the last instance—act V, scene 2—the *Hippolytus* of Seneca is specifically alluded to.) The careful subdividing of each act into scenes has no equivalent in Seneca or in the few tragedies of the Spanish sixteenth century written in the sensational Senecan manner. Lope has in mind, and in fact alludes to, another tradition, which he considered especially Spanish, or Iberian: that of nonstageable prose dialogue, of which Rojas' *La Celestina* (1499) and *La Euphrosina* of Jorge Ferreira de Vasconcelos (1555) are the outstanding examples. From the former he took his own version of the go-between and from the latter a structure of five acts broken into scenes which gave a certain order to a rambling and highly variegated dialogue and a very slight action.

As for Lope's designating *La Dorotea* an "acción en prosa"—perhaps, recalling schoolboy experience, he took the label from the term *actio* used by writers of Latin plays for Jesuit schools to cover every type of drama. With it Lope continues to stress both the fundamentally dramatic character of *La Dorotea* and its distinctness from any given type of drama. The phrase "in prose" adds an emphasis peculiarly his own. The dialogue clarifies the meaning: authenticity of a personal kind as against the invented fictions of his verse plays. Perhaps, finally, he felt prose to be a step in the direction of Cervantes' immensely successful novel, a possibility explored in the Conversation between the Translators.

LA DOROTEA

ACCION EN PROSA.

DE FREY LOPE FELIX DE VEGA CARPIO DEL HABITO DE SAN IVAN.

AL ILVSTRISSIMO Y EXCELENTISSIMO SEÑOR DON GASPAR ALFONSO PEREZ DE GVZMAN EL BVENO, CONDE DE NIEBLA, PRIMOGENITO DEL EXCELENTISSIMO SEÑOR EL GRAN DVQVE DE MEDINA SIDONIA.

Año *Exi de Theatro Cato,* 1632
Adhibe mentem Cicero.

EN MADRID,
En la Imprenta del Reyno.

A costa de Alõso Perez Librerode su Magestad

Dedication

To the Most Illustrious and Excellent Gentleman Don Gaspar Alfonso Pérez de Guzmán el Bueno, Count of Niebla

I wrote *La Dorotea* in my early years, and when I abandoned my studies to take up arms under the banners of that most excellent gentleman, the Duke of Medina Sidonia, Your Excellency's grandfather, Dorotea went astray in my absence, as often happens with such wayward ladies. But now that Dorotea has been restored, or misprised (a fate not infrequent when the bloom of youth has wilted), I have trimmed the rampant growth she flaunted in my own rampageous youth and, having taken counsel with my love and obligation, I am returning Dorotea to the most illustrious house of Guzmán, in whose cause I had lost her. There, if Dorotea still proves appealing, let her serve as an ermine on your most noble coat of arms; but if old and ugly, take her as the serpent facing the celebrated dagger on the crowned blazon of your glorious crest. Your Excellency bears the name of Good by nature and as successor to so many princes who have been good. In so stating, I do but give greatness its due, since the title has been passed down from God Himself. May He preserve Your Excellency many years.

Brother Lope Félix de Vega Carpio

To the Audience

by

DON FRANCISCO LÓPEZ DE AGUILAR

Music and song arouse such soft delight in our soul that some have called the soul itself harmony. Hence the ancient poets invented the mode of meters and feet for prosodic measures, so that they might thus more sweetly incline men's spirits to virtue and good conduct. Thus one sees how boorish and barbaric he must be who fails to esteem this art, which includes all the others, an art respected by the ancient theologians, who used it, unenlightened though they were, to laud and glorify their false gods; and now by our own, who use it to laud with sacred hymns the one true God. But the poet may also set forth his subject without versifying, proceeding by way of appropriate likenesses, for this mode of feet and measures is to poetic art as beauty is to youth, and finery to the shapeliness of well-proportioned bodies: the ornament of harmony is there as accessory and not in and of itself.

One who imagined that poetry consists of measures and rhymes would deny that it is a branch of learning. Lope's *La Dorotea*, although written in prose, is poetry, because, being so surely an imitation of truth, it would not be such, he felt, if written in verse like the rest of his plays. Nevertheless he has included some verse for recitation, to allow the reader respite from the ongoing prose, and so that *La Dorotea* should not be lacking in variety, his wish being to make it

3

beautiful, even though verses are rarely inserted in Greek, Latin, or Tuscan dramas.

In my judgment he has fulfilled his intention, surpassing many ancient and modern dramas (be it said with all due respect to the fervent admirers of their authors), as the reader may see for himself. For paper offers a freer theater than that in which the public is at liberty to pass judgment, friends to applaud, and envy to sink its teeth. The emotions of two lovers will be found true to life, the cupidity and scheming of a go-between as well, the hypocrisy of a profit-seeking mother, the pretentiousness of a man of money, the power of gold, the comportment of the servants, and, as a necessary moral, the disappointment of them all in the diversity of their pursuits, so that those who love with appetite and not with reason may learn what end awaits their vain pleasure and their foul, misguided actions.

Plautus puts most felicitously the consequence of such actions in his *Merchant* and Terence in the *Eunuch*, for all who write of love show how to avoid it, not how to imitate it, since this sort of appetite—as Bernard says—admits no moderation, modesty, or counsel.

If there is any flaw in the craftsmanship—especially from the inclusion of the interval of an absence—may truth be its jusification, for the poet preferred to follow truth and not be bound by the irrelevant laws governing time and place in dramatic fictions. The subject was an actual occurrence and this is also the reason for its being written with such truth to life. I am myself the occasion of its publication, taken as I am with the argument and the style.

Let anyone who thinks me mistaken take up his pen and use the time he would spend upon reprehension in proving that he can produce his own more perfect imitation, a truth of his own better appareled in witticisms and colors of rhetoric, with learning more suited to its context, humor more entertaining, sententiousness more serious, and with so many components of natural and moral philosophy that one is amazed the author could treat them so clearly in dealing with such a subject.

If one demurs at the persons referred to in passing, let him understand that they belong to the period in which the work was written, and the dress as well, both so different from those of the present that even language changes have made our nation a different one from the Spain that was. That was the custom then and this now—as Horace puts it, born but two years before the Catilinian conspiracy. The plays of Aristophanes, Terence, and Plautus are of greater antiquity and they are still read, with their depictions of the Greek and Roman customs of the day. And among our works, closer to our own day, the same is true of the Castilian *Celestina* and the Portuguese *Euphrosina*. Moreover, what is shown in *La Dorotea* is not characters in costume but actions imitated.

Lope has also been forced to publish this fiction because he has seen how freely the book merchants of Seville, Cádiz, and other places in Andalusia are issuing various volumes in his name, pretending they have been printed in Saragossa and Barcelona, using the names of printers of those places, and including in the volumes plays, written by ignoramuses, that he never laid eyes on, let alone composed. It is surely a great pity and a sign of little conscience to compromise his reputation with such shoddiness. And so he begs well-born and well-spoken men of understanding, on whose lips praise dwells and whose pens have never been stained by vituperation, not to believe these men who are forced into such impudence by sheer money-grubbing, and to read *Dorotea* as his alone, likewise paying no attention to those ignoramuses whose satires mirror their own failings, and who spare neither age, nor nobility, nor the cloth, neither honors nor high places. Of books, such men know nothing but the titles, and thus part with books as something bought for purposes of deception and sold because they have no use for them, men detested by all, the scum of the earth, envious of all virtue, gnawed inwardly by the glory others achieve through study. St. Augustine compares them to fens whose mud breeds serpents and foul creatures, and sees them as inducing princes to laugh at the expense of honor, although divine, princely minds could not possibly believe (to the detriment of virtue's study) the barbaric tongue and pen of ignorant envy, a beast whose teeth turn golden when she sinks them into fame and glory, although the envious relish the thought that their teeth are being stained by innocent blood.

Dramatis Personae

DOROTEA, a lady [by aspiration—playing Laura to Fernando's Petrarch—more than by station]

TEODORA, her mother [impatient of literary role models and not averse to exploiting her daughter's negotiable charms]

GERARDA, the latter's friend [an octogenarian bawd playing with gusto a role whose antecedents she knows to be literary as well as social]

DON FERNANDO, a gentleman [playing to the hilt the young man as poet, whatever the cost to others]

JULIO, his governor [combining, in one, protector, right-hand man, and servant]

CELIA, maidservant to Dorotea [sharp-tongued confidante determined not to be supplanted]

FELIPA, daughter of Gerarda [who for a while supplants Celia as Dorotea's servant and confidante]

CÉSAR, astrologer [friend of Fernando's, wary of running afoul of the Inquisition]

LUDOVICO, a friend of César and Fernando [trusted by the latter in matters both sentimental and artistic]

DON BELA, an overseas Spaniard [one, that is, just back from a lucrative stay in Spanish America]

LAURENCIO, his manservant [hard-bitten, protective]

MARFISA, a lady [who preceded Dorotea in Fernando's affections]

CLARA, maidservant to Marfisa [quick to pin down the foibles of her mistress]

Fame

Chorus of Love

Chorus of Cupidity

Chorus of Jealousy

Chorus of Revenge

Chorus of the Moral Ending

ACT · ONE

Scene 1

TEODORA · GERARDA

Gerarda. Love and duty oblige and absolutely compel me, Teodora my friend, to tell you how I feel.

Teodora. About what, Gerarda?

Gerarda. About Dorotea, your daughter.

Teodora. She is not the culprit you claim her to be.

Gerarda. I speak out because of our long-standing friendship and my love for her.

Teodora. Which is evident from the affection you have showered on her since we began to speak.

Gerarda. No greater misfortune may befall a child than to have parents derelict in their duty, either from the great love they bear it or their carelessness in rearing it.

Teodora. Should Nature be blamed for the love of one's own flesh and blood, or nurture for one's indulging its tender charms, from the first gurgle to the clear speech of reason?

Gerarda. Nature should, when punishment is required.

Teodora. As for Nature, that would be like smashing a mirror because it reflects oneself; the innocent glass merely returns what it is given. As for nurture, only beasts and fowl receive such treatment, being nourished the whole year through and slaughtered in a day.

Gerarda. If a child reflect the parent in behavior, it may be forgiven since it imitates. Otherwise, one may as well smash the mirror for failing to reflect one's image. When you were young, that is what you did if your mirror failed to give you a pleasant look.

Teodora. That allusion to when I was young was uncalled for. I still am.

Gerarda. If you start thinking you're a spry young thing, I despair of making you understand why I've come—you will only indulge your daughter's faults the more. After all, no judge has the heart to pass sentence if he is guilty of the same crime, and at your age there's little sense in starting to live when coming close to death.

Teodora. Do I look that old to you?

Gerarda. Believe me, you'd outscore the highest bid of any gambler.

Teodora. The favorite pastime of this world is reducing one's own years and increasing other people's, but that's sheer nonsense, since we all see through the increase and everyone sees to his own reduction.

Gerarda. What reduction can you charge me with?

Teodora. Look here, Gerarda, if you wish to make yourself intolerable and frighten off your friends, you'll think of nothing better than to go about pronouncing on people's ages, for the secret they most mind having revealed is their true age, and I know for a fact that some are so inquisitive about the affairs of others that, for no reason, they hunt up their baptismal records and keep slyly mum about the parish where they themselves were baptized. God be praised, I have a full set of teeth, give or take a few.

Gerarda. 'Crony, you're the picture of grace, except for that slash across your face.'

Teodora. My high spirits outweigh any defect.

Gerarda. That's 'locking the stable door when the horse has fled.'

Teodora. I happen to know that my complexion is the envy of all my friends.

Gerarda. It's envy makes people play the fool.

Teodora. Never having touched cosmetics, my skin, you see, was never stretched and broken by harsh astringents—any more than the God-honest truth ever was.

Gerarda. Be thankful that time has not dug furrows in a field it can claim for its own.

Teodora. I'll grant my color is somewhat higher than it was, but that indicates I shall enjoy a second youth.

Gerarda. 'Merry mules and widows: both stout, both gadabout.'

Teodora. Any gray hairs may still be plucked from the rest, and I always did have moles. Moreover, not having a few gray hairs in due course shows insensitivity.

Gerarda. You always were so sensitive.

Teodora. 'Gray in the hair: spots on the moon.' And why should women not be allowed what is perfectly permissible for men? Come to think of it, you cannot be so young and spry yourself, for unless I am mistaken, it was you who helped me take my first steps in my parents' house.

Gerarda. I should never have spoken a word about "when you were young," you lay it on me so. Now if you scolded Dorotea that way, you would not have the neighbors talking and you'd have a better reputation in town. But you'll tell me, 'He who trims the cloth removes the cock's crest.'

Teodora. What exactly has Dorotea done that should incense me?

Gerarda. You feign ignorance, like the well-trained husband. How can you expect to convince me you know nothing, as in the business about your age?

Teodora. Next you'll tell me Don Fernando is courting her, and what a terrible crime that is! Was this why you came here, Gerarda, bursting with dictums and loaded with advice?

Gerarda. 'So the light begins to dawn!' My friend, I am no fancier of picnics, little gifts, card games, and coach rides down to the river, nor can anyone accuse me of catering to the tastes of others. What fine blouses or beaded skirts do I have to show for it? What girls have I purveyed? Who has ever seen me in salons, gazing at the portraits, or whispering with the houseboys? Only two things have brought me here: to serve God, and to serve your honor.

Teodora. You mean to say I haven't any, because that foreign gentleman once favored my daughter. That was a great honor and included a true prospect of marriage.

Gerarda. 'Great oak and small pine—both are kin of mine.'

Teodora. He went back home. What is so unusual about that? Did not Aeneas leave Queen Dido, and King Rodrigo violate La Cava?

Gerarda. You don't imagine that's what bothers me, do you, Teodora? Surely we all know enough to 'let bygones be bygones.'

Teodora. The byword of evil tongues has always been hypocrisy. Don't all petitions at the outset claim as their motive the remedy of some offense to God, while what is truly behind them is spite or jealousy? Heavens, Gerarda, you're like that little black boy in *Lazarillo de Tormes,* crying out in alarm, "Mama, the bogeyman!" when his father comes in.

Gerarda. How does that apply to me? You mean I'm the pot that calls the kettle black? My daughter Felipa is married now, and if she were not the respectable women she is, whose business would that be—mine or her husband's?

Teodora. 'Praise an ass, bear a child eating grass.'

Gerarda. We parents, Teodora, resemble the birds: when the fledgling takes wing, the wind will support it and its own bill fend for it. Now your Dorotea, who is still under your wing, who returns daily to the nest, and whom this boy these five years past has reduced to helplessness, body and soul, leaving her so impoverished (since delicacy or fear prevents her from offending him) that yesterday she sold a friend a fancy cloak and now pretends a pious vow makes her wear a goatskin habit, she who used to go about trailing Milanese passementerie and Neapolitan fabrics after her. What good is there in her going about dressed like a cloistered nun for the sake of a fop whose entire worldly goods are his needlepoint breeches and amber-scented leather waistcoats? This by day—and by night his buckler and sword, without a scratch naturally, a gold-trimmed cape, all befeathered and beribboned, a guitar, lewd verses, and harebrained billets-doux? And she with her head in the clouds because the whole town sings of her foibles as well as her charms. What a perfect Petrarch to her Laura! What a Don Diego de Mendoza with his famous Phyllis! Come now, Teodora, tell me: is beauty the pier of a church or an ancestral seat up north in the mountains, to resist time, against whose ravages nothing mortal can be protected, or is beauty a carefree springtime from fifteen to twenty-five, a delightful summer from twenty-five to thirty-five, a late dry spell from thirty-five to forty-five? Beyond that, what earthly good is winter? You know quite well that women do not last like men.

Teodora. You've scored more fives than a game of bowls.

Gerarda. Well, never fear, they all overshoot the mark and lose the game. Now, men at any age discover ways of enjoying themselves. They find suitable occupations and positions of honor, increasing their means along with their reputations. But a woman's only good is to furnish the stuff out of which men's children are made; once that function ends, what post do we acquire in the commonwealth, what governorship in peacetime, what command in time of war? Return to your senses, Teodora. Do not permit this miserable youth to finish off Dorotea's beauty by mishandling it. You know well enough how lilies that fester smell far worse than weeds. Now then, I have learned that a Spanish gentleman just back from the New World has been panting away ever since he laid eyes on her at the recent bullfights, where he occupied a balcony nearby. And I know someone he told—because that someone was me—that he'd give her a necklace with a jeweled pendant worth a thousand *escudos,* and another thousand for household silver, and a sumptuous tapestry from London to grace her house. Not only that, but also two mulatto slave girls, thrifty and hard-working, fit for the King's own service. The man is about thirty-seven years of age; the touch of gray in his hair comes from the rigors of life at sea, but the city breezes will soon take care of that. Besides, I saw a sign the other day which said, "Lotions For Gray Hair Sold Here." His bearing is handsome, there's a bright look to his eye, white teeth gleaming under his black mustache like a string of pearls against smooth velvet—the most cultivated, alert, and charming of men. In a word, a man of substance, and not one of those tiresome striplings who make off with a woman's fine flour, leaving her nothing but the chaff—and you know what she's good for then.

Teodora. 'Cheer up, children, wine's going down: half a crown today, tomorrow a crown!' If that was your commission, Gerarda, what need was there for all the rhetoric? What did I tell you! Your petition starts out in the name of God, and ends up in the devil's service.

Gerarda. My dear friend, it is your welfare and reputation I have at heart as well as this poor girl's, who will wither like the rose tomorrow, with you searching high and low for the wherewithal to restore her. Because that's just where this little Don Fernando will leave her—unlike the munificence and life support of the overseas Spaniard. For every eventuality, choose men, Teodora, men, and not boys whose mustaches sprout out of women's saliva. And now I'm off to La Merced for a word of prayer, since I do not intend to go home without placing your affairs in the hands of God.

Scene 2

DOROTEA · TEODORA

Dorotea. What a fine talk you were having with that saintly Gerarda! You thought I wasn't listening! Well, even though I was doing my hair, I had ears for her words more than eyes for the mirror. How can you put up with such talk and permit a vile woman, who's been bribed, to tell you straight out to receive a man into your house to be my lover!

Teodora. Easy now, milady. If I am not shown proper respect, only milady is to blame.

Dorotea. I to blame? You can't be serious. Has anything I did ever seemed right to you? How quick you were to take Gerarda's word! How easily convinced of what you wished to hear! A fine judge you'd make, swallowing the first testimony you heard and dismissing all the rest.

Teodora. Can you deny a single thing she said, or find one fault in a respectable woman whose only thought is to serve God and our honor? I suppose you think she is now on her way to collect her reward from that overseas gentleman. The truth is, she has gone to La Merced to pray for us, and she's a woman on whom the prisoners, the needy, and the sick all rely.

Dorotea. Yes, the lovesick, the needy with an itch, and the prisoners of their appetites.

Teodora. Such a woman, and you find fault! What a sweet little tongue you've developed! How true it is that when honor goes, shame never lags behind. Does a day go by when Gerarda fails to light a candle to every holy image in the capital before dinner? Has she ever missed devotions at a church festival? Has a Saturday passed without her walking barefoot to the Virgin's shrine at Atocha? Has she ever failed to find a girl a good mate? Or restore a wife to her

husband's confidence? Or leave a widow unconsoled, a child un-
cured of the evil eye? Has any infant ever failed to thrive after she
blessed its swaddling clothes? Is there a prayer she does not know,
or any cure the equal of her own for our womanly complaints? Any
herb she is unfamiliar with? Any congestion she has not relieved?
Any secret birth she has not been summoned to? In a word, for any
house to prosper, the perfume of her presence suffices.

Dorotea. Why so quick to sing her praises? All those charms you list
are double-edged, and, if not actually ironies, are not to be taken literally.

Teodora. Listen to our little pedant trot out her lover's jargon. She's
well stocked with palaver. Is this what he teaches her? Then she is
sure to be *literally* rich in *ironies.* Or did she take them from his
sonnets? Ignorant girl, to waste the flower of her youth on such inanities, and to top it all, be celebrated in a pastoral romance or
praised in some new-fangled ballad—Amaryllis, if it's Christian, or
Jarifa, if it's Moorish, the lover being Zulema.

Dorotea. How powerfully the opulent physiognomy of the rich New
World Spaniard has battered the bulwark of your brains! As if such
men ever were munificent the way old Circe depicted him! And
how well she managed to diminish and belittle Don Fernando's attributes! How liberally your praise rewards her for the pleasure she
has given you! After such a testimonial, who would not find her
saintly, her prayers genuine, her medicines miraculous? Add to
those herbs she knows, the beans she casts her spells with, and instead of her blessings, remember her black magic. As for the evil
eye, you can be sure she's contrived more than she ever exorcised. It
was through her you met the count. Let her find fault with Don
Fernando; her only real reproach is that he's poor. But are there
riches greater than his person, his mind, and charm?

Teodora. Oh mad, unhappy girl, ruined and misled by another lunatic!
What good are his mind, person, and charm if you admit he's a
pauper? Have you ever seen sackcloth hemmed with passementerie?
How it turns your head to be called the divine Dorotea! I'll rum-
mage through your writing boxes, I'll burn up the notes you worship like idols and all that silly stuff you pore over to find words
you never dreamed of. If I have my way, there'll be no trace of him
left. Oh, how I'd love to root that stripling out of your heart! Why

are you looking at me that way? Make faces at me, will you? Upon your dead father's soul, I swear, I'll pull out a swatch of your hair so you'll have no need of curls. There! Now go and tell Don Fernando to write a poem about it: how I, a female Nero, sacrilegiously defiled the head of the sun, and how every gold thread I pull out shall turn into a thunderbolt against me.

Dorotea. Mock on, see if I care. Denigrate my feelings, slander my behavior. What men have you ever seen slain at our doorstep through a whim of mine? What woman complains her husband mistreats her because of me? What galas do I ever attend? What windows have you ever had to drag me from? What finery of mine sets tongues wagging when I go to Mass?

Teodora. What does that have to do with it? Pitiful creature—who are you doing penance for? Call yourself virtuous because that youth has bewitched you into doing what pleases him and will now be threatening you, as things always end up with men of that sort. Well, undeceive yourself, Dorotea, for you shall never speak to him again as long as I live. Could anyone imagine it: you a pauper, and I dishonored, you wearing goatskin a whole year through, and I nagged by my friends day in, day out? Make up your mind: either I cut your hair off and shut you away where even the sun will be loath to look at you, or else you give up this obsession, this mad ruination of yourself, this vile affair of yours. Tears? Go ahead and weep, but do not imagine tears will melt me, because my role here is not the jealous lover, but a mother bound by honor.

Scene 3

DOROTEA, alone

Dorotea. Oh wretched woman! How can I go on living? Why do I cling to this, the saddest life any slave has ever had to live? What woman of my years must face such turmoil and tribulation? Where is this perplexing love of mine leading me? What can be the end in store for this mad passion, so adverse to everything my heaven-sent gifts seemed to promise? Having spent my best years in this labyrinth of love, what shall be left me but repentance for those that remain, as the years I have thrown away take their vengeance?

Oh Fernando, I would not want my soul, now in your keeping, to tell you its present thought, one so wholly new I never imagined it could cross my mind. It is more than I can bear; surrounded by so many enemies, I cannot save my life without losing my mind. Yet if my soul should breathe some word of this inconstancy so unjust to you, may prudence guide your reason, not youth your love. Still, how can that first impulse to say what I am saying have entered my mind? Can I love anything which is not you? How can my years be better spent than in serving you? What more can I desire than to please you? What riches compare with listening to your voice? What time can I spend more pleasantly than in your arms? How shall I survive without you? Not to live means less to me than not to gaze into your eyes. Deprived of you, who will console me after the pleasure of our years together? Your manner, so irresistible, your vivacity, your manly grace, all those favors from your lips, on which this breath of mine brought forth the first traces of down—what New World riches can replace them, what gold, what diamonds?

Alas, unhappy woman that I am—this friendship of ours offends heaven, my family, reputation, and relations. My mother harries me, friends reproach, neighbors gossip, the envious preach at me, poverty has me at my wit's end. Fernando barely has the wherewithal to buy his fine apparel. When he looks at other women dressed in all their finery they must seem more attractive, since ornament and elegance add to beauty and high esteem, while a woman's shabbiness day after day only sets the eyes to wandering. Variety brings novelty and incites desire. This intimacy cannot last forever, and since nothing is more public than a love affair, though lovers never think so, it is bound to end disastrously for life or honor, and, more ominously, for the soul as well. Why should I wait for you to find me tiresome and hateful, to favor the garments other women wear, while this goatskin of mine feels like haircloth in your embrace, becoming a form of expiation in your eyes? Why should I await the end to which all love is destined, certain that the greater the love, the greater the enmity it breeds? Lest we become enemies later, we had better agree to be friends now, for an affair which ends in concord may well continue in friendship without re-crimination, with mutual good will free of apprehension.

Celia, Celia: fetch my cloak and tell my mother I'm off to Mass—my mind is made up. Why do I delay? Good Lord! Do I stumble over love? Ah, love, do not stand in my way. You let me make this choice, now let me leave, since women find resolution difficult, though acting on it simple.

Scene 4

DON FERNANDO · JULIO

Julio. You've wakened out of sorts.

Fernando. I tossed and turned the whole night through.

Julio. You had no sleep at all?

Fernando. Very little, and troubled at that.

Julio. It must have been the heat.

Fernando. No, it was something, I dreamed early on.

Julio. What was it you were dreaming?

Fernando. A confusion of many things.

Julio. Can any dream be so clear as not to be confusing? Heavy sleepers sleep peacefully and do not dream, as the Philosopher says. Since you did dream and your sleep was troubled, your mind was not at ease. The only reason people think they see what they dream is that the intelligence remains calm and undisturbed. This happens with a light sleep, not when sleep is driven inward because of excessive heat. We dream what we have done or wish to do, and our hidden desires bring on thoughts and imaginings as well. This is why the Philosopher believes virtuous people dream of better things than people who are evil, corrupt, and perverted in their ways.

Fernando. There you go, plaguing me with your philosophies. Leave me alone, Julio.

Julio. Oh, come now, tell me the dream.

Fernando. I tell you again, leave me, Julio. Do you presume to intepret it? What an ideal Joseph for a prison mate!

Julio. Amphitryon was the first to interpret dreams. That is according to Pliny, who also says that if a man places the left flank of a chameleon on his chest, he will dream of anything or anyone he wishes.

Fernando. That's Pliny for you!

Julio. Cornelius Rufus dreamed he was losing his eyesight and woke up blind.

Fernando. The devil take you and your pedantic instances, trying to squeeze the reason for my torment out of me. I dreamt, Julio, that the sea had pushed its way clear up to Madrid from the New World.

Julio. That would save a large portage fee between Seville and Madrid. Go on.

Fernando. The water was rushing wildly at the bridge.

Julio. Poor Illescas!

Fernando. In a vessel bravely decked and fully rigged, with sails unfurled, stood a single man, tossing silver bars and gold ingots from the poop deck into a boat.

Julio. Ah, to have been in that boat!

Fernando. In it was—how this hurts to tell!

Julio. Tell me and stop shaking.

Fernando. Dorotea.

Julio. And was she taking the gold?

Fernando. With both hands.

Julio. Quite rightly so. But would to God that I'd been there with her, because in all my life I've never had such luck, even in a dream. Oh, if what you dreamt came true, think of all the women of Madrid who would go down to the sea, especially if gold were being tossed out.

Fernando. You think there'd be many women going?

Julio. More than go to the Prado. But what happened about the sea? Because you look sadder than if you thought you would drown in it.

Fernando. What happened was that Dorotea and Celia disembarked, loaded with gold, and when I went up to speak to her, she passed me by without a sign of recognition.

Julio. And that's the reason you're so sad?

Fernando. Isn't that a good reason?

Julio. Well, what did you expect from her? Some of the gold?

Fernando. No, just any word at all.

Julio. You look for answers in dreams, do you?

Fernando. Shouldn't I? Since I complained of her slighting me, she might at least have spoken to me.

Julio. I will now interpret the dream.

Fernando. You've been reading Artemidorus, no doubt.

Julio. Impelled by the desire to give Dorotea what you do not possess, you were prompted to dream that she was rich.

Fernando. May love confirm it as the correct interpretation.

Julio. Be thankful that you have made her rich.

Fernando. Place no trust in dreams.

Julio. I don't know what to say, because I always dream I'm poor and when I wake up I still am poor.

Fernando. Will Dorotea succumb to gold?

Julio. You couldn't blame her.

Fernando. Ovid says that gold does more harm than the sword.

Julio. He must have had a grudge against gold, whose virtues I'll not mention since you dread it so. But who ever died of it, aside from Croesus, and he had it served to him melted, out of sheer greed? We do know that liquid gold can prolong life and that it is used, of course, in making electuaries from kermes.

Fernando. Had I gold, I'd never eat it, though my life were to be prolonged a thousandfold.

Julio. What would you do with it?

Fernando. I'd give it to Dorotea.

Julio. She's already been given enough from the New World. But ask her for a few ingots today and we'll produce the potable kind, made according to Leo Suabius' instructions, to wit: take an ounce of gold leaf or gold dust and dissolve it in as much distilled vinegar as necessary. Then keep distilling it until no taste of the mixture remains. Then pour the mixture into five ounces of brandy, let it stand and settle for a month, and take a sip of it now and then.

Fernando. By wanting to know something about everything, you know nothing about anything in the end. What philosopher ancient or modern ever failed to speak against gold?

Julio. Gold is like women: we all speak against them and we all desire them. In a word, gold is the sun's progeny, the very image of its brilliance and life-giving powers.

Fernando. That's not why it is yellow.

Julio. Well, why then?

Fernando. Because it fears having so many in pursuit of it.

Julio. What dusty old balderdash! Diogenes forgive you!

Fernando. Gold is older.

Julio. True, and silver is the gray in its hair.

Fernando. A gold bed brings the sick no relief, nor does fortune make a fool wise.

Julio. Socrates forgive you as well!

Fernando. Pass me your instrument, expert deflator that you are.

Julio. I'm past master of that and of philosophy as well.

Fernando. The treble string has sprung.

Julio. From the bridge no doubt, though no water flows beneath.

Fernando. I heard it last night.

Julio. Lying awake?

Fernando. Thinking of Dorotea.

Julio. Not of going down to the sea after her?

Fernando. Whoever said it would be convenient to buy ready-made letters and trimmed beards should have added tuned instruments.

Julio. That would be impossible. The substance strings are made of, you see, causes them to slacken with moisture and tauten with excessive heat. In other words, like some women, strings always need tuning.

Fernando. Which is why they are worked on so much—to bring them up to the pitch of the tuner.

Julio. Many break.

Fernando. Look only for the genuine and discard the false. That's what musicians do.

Julio. Which brings up something curiously à propos.

Fernando. Namely?

Julio. That as they undo the skein, they flip it with one finger, holding the end of the string between the teeth, and if the string casts two shadows, they discard it as faulty and go on to the next. The same applies to trying out a woman; if she casts shadows in two directions, change her for another.

Fernando. I have done my tuning.

Julio. At my expense, since I was listening.

Fernando. Listen now to a ballad of Lope's.

Julio. I am with you there.

Fernando.

> To solitude I go,
>> from solitude return,
>> what company I need
>> my thoughts provide.
>
> What is it about this town,
>> where I live, where I will die,
>> that the self I've known
>> seems so far away.
>
> My moods are neither up nor down,
>> but in my mind I know
>> that man, who is pure soul,
>> lives captive in the body.
>
> Knowing all I need to know,
>> still I can't divine
>> how a conceited simpleton
>> puts up with himself.
>
> With no trouble I ward off
>> annoyances of every sort,
>> but I have no defense
>> from a fool's onslaught.
>
> He'll say I'm the fool,
>> but his reasoning is flawed:
>> how can one turn out
>> both modest and a fool?
>
> On observing him and me,
>> I see this difference:
>> in arrogance, his madness;
>> in humility, my disdain.
>
> Nature must have grown
>> wiser in our day
>> or our brilliant wits
>> are all self-proclaimed.
>
> "I avow that I know nothing,"
>> a philosopher once said,
>> recognizing humbly
>> how little greatness is.

I lay no claim to wisdom,
   misfortune is my meat:
   those estranged from happiness
   never hope for wit.
They say this world can't last.
   That's true undoubtedly;
   it rings like shattering glass
   about to break in bits.
Judgment Day must loom,
   since we are losing ours:
   some acting overbold;
   some, not bold enough.
In ancient days they said
   truth had fled to heaven:
   attacked on every side,
   it's not been heard of since.
We live in different ages,
   non-Spaniards and ourselves:
   they in the age of silver,
   we in the age of brass.
How could the true Spaniard
   fail to be alarmed,
   seeing man no whit better,
   while valor is no more.
Everyone dresses lavishly,
   groaning about high prices—
   from the waist up, princes all;
   from the waist down, tramps.
God told Adam he must eat
   his bread by toil and sweat,
   as penalty for breaking
   the law his Maker set.
And now some men, ignoring
   natural shame and fear,
   auction off their honor,
   and look the other way.
Stumbling like blind men,
   philosophy and virtue

cling to one another,
beg and weep their way.
On two poles the earth turns
back and forth forever:
advancement by good connections;
via blue blood, money.
Hearing the tolling knell,
I ask: for living or dead?
The same cross that marks a grave
adorns the soldier's chest.
Looking at the tombs
of eternal marble made,
I see a silent mocking
of mortals there interred.
Bless the tombstone maker—
he provides a place
where the humble of the earth
lie level with the mighty.
Envy's a hag, they say,
but I confess I envy
those who never know
a next-door neighbor's name.
Lacking books and paper,
they tally no tale or toll.
If ever they need to write,
they find an inkhorn and quill.
Neither rich nor poor,
they stick to hearth and garden,
untroubled in their sleep
by lawsuit or advancement.
No gossips of the great
or tramplers of the lowly,
they send no gifts, like me,
or greetings ceremonial.
My envy thus confessed,
with all I leave unsaid,
to solitude I go,
from solitude return.

Julio. How is it you did not sing of Dorotea?

Fernando. Because the thought of her gold weighs so heavily on me.

Julio. But why should she not have taken it?

Fernando. Because, like the partridge which recognizes the falcon that is going to kill it, I sense that gold will be my undoing.

Julio. There's a natural affinity between gold and women. Nothing is more flattering to them than to be told they resemble a gold pine—not because they are tall and graceful, but because the taller the tree, the more gold involved.

Fernando. I think I hear the sound of clogs.

Julio. They say that that and wine aswish in jars are the best sounds you can hear.

Scene 5

DOROTEA · CELIA

FERNANDO · JULIO

Dorotea. Knock good and hard, till your hand hurts.

Celia. If Don Fernando has been out gallivanting, he'll be sleeping as usual, turning broad daylight into night.

Fernando. Julio, go out and see who's breaking the door in.

Julio. Someone must have come crashing down the stairs, or else it's some deaf beggar. Who's there?

Celia. Open the door, you good-for-nothing.

Julio. It's Celia, sir. Celia. That means there's a nice little letter for us.

Fernando. Is that all you can say, you heartless wretch?

Julio. Stop rushing, you've smashed the guitar! Where are you off to?

Fernando. To welcome my rainbow, harbinger of all the gods, my sun's aurora, springtime of my years, nightingale of my days, to whose dulcet tones the flowers waken, opening the petals of their eyes.

Celia. I am not alone.

Fernando. Who is with you? You distress me. Good God! Is it Dorotea? My darling! Holding your cloak over your eyes? Come in, come right in! There's something amiss—you're stumbling. Celia so serious, and you hidden in that cloak! There's some comet abroad. The

Prince of Love is ailing. Still not a word? Sit here, my lady, please. You've lost your breath climbing the stairs. Some water, Julio.

Julio. Do I bring something to go with it?

Fernando. What, you're still standing there? Dear lady, whatever is the matter? Why do you slay me so? Has someone been talking against me? It's your mother no doubt, spreading tales to make you leave me. I swear to heaven that, if ever I've glimpsed, seen, heard, or even imagined one thing in God's creation other than your beauty, may the sea I dreamed of last night drown and bury me, and may the gold you were given win you.

Julio. Here's water in a *búcaro* and some sugar cordial.

Fernando. Eat, and drink it, or else take my heart's blood. What's wrong? She has fainted! Celia, what does all this mean? I am slain! My life is over. Alas, my love! Alas, my Dorotea! Alas, my best and final hope! Ah, love, your arrows all are broken; sun, your light is all eclipsed; spring, your flowers all are faded; the world plunges into darkness.

Julio. Celia, shouldn't I light a flare?

Celia. Quiet, rascal, you're not on stage.

Julio. Take hold of her hand, she's tearing at her face.

Fernando. Oh alabaster Venus! Oh jasmine dawn still untinged by the fuller hues of day! Oh marble Lucretia, oh sculpture by Michelangelo!

Julio. Now I can swear she's chaste.

Fernando. Oh Andromeda, by Titian the great! Look, Julio, look at those tears. Like the pearls of dawn on a madonna lily. Brush her hair aside, Celia. Let us gaze upon her eyes, since the sun permits us to view it through the clouds of so mortal a swoon.

Dorotea. Oh God! Oh death!

Fernando. Everything you let fall to pieces, now falls back into place. Love slays again, sun sheds light again, spring once again is rainbow-hued, and I am returned to life. But how can your first words name, of all things, the two most powerful: God and death?

Dorotea. Because I beseech God to deliver me from myself, and death to end all misfortunes that assault my stricken heart and waning spirit, for the strongest woman is but Nature's imperfect handiwork, a prey to fear and a well of tears.

Fernando. When Nature, striving for greatest perfection, ran out of substance and fell short of her goal, which is man, she fashioned numerous exceptions to woman's common frailty.

Julio. Don Fernando puts it well, and thus we see such paragons as those Artemisias of memory, Carmentas of charactery, Penelopes of constancy, Leënas of secrecy, Portias of coals calefactory, Naaeras of loyalty, Deborahs of governance, Laudomias of love, Cloelias of courage, and such Semiramises of arms as she who, with comb in hair, went out to gain victories greater than Alexander's with his mighty helmet.

Fernando. Include amongst them, Julio, the perfection of Dorotea's beauty, her sweet-smelling comeliness, her gracious elegance, her excellence of mind, topping that of any other woman. And may this be proclaimed not by my eyes nor by my love, nor yet by what my mind actually knows; let bias be silent and envy speak, for there is no greater satisfaction than to leave praising to the envious.

Dorotea. Oh, Fernando! No charactery prevails against disaster, no governance against fortune, however favorable, no loyalty against the insuperable, no coals calefactory against the inevitable, no courage against the stars nor love against brute force, no secrecy against tyranny, no constancy against envy, nor any arms against betrayal.

Fernando. What is this, my treasure? Why must you draw my blood drop by drop? Tell me, "Fernando, you are slain"; Julio will have me fetched away, but do not thus prolong my suffering with perplexity, for fear is harder to endure than calamity; because once imagined, one keeps dreading it; but having once arrived, one thinks of how to set it right.

Dorotea. What is there for me to say, oh, Fernando, my very own, but that I am no longer yours?

Fernando. What? Has some letter come from Lima?

Dorotea. No, my lord and master.

Fernando. Then who has the authority to remove you from my arms?

Dorotea. That tyrant; that tiger that bore me (if I can be kin to anyone who does not adore you); that Egyptian crocodile that weeps and kills; that serpent who imitates shepherds' voices, calls out their names, then eats them alive; that hypocrite, forever counting her rosary beads, never her sins. Today she berated me, today she vilified me, today she told me that you have been the ruin of me—my honor, my estate, my prospects—and that tomorrow you will leave me for another. I retorted; my hair paid the price. Here before you are the locks you prized, that you called sunbeams from which love fashioned the chain that bound your soul—the locks your verses called the nets of love, whose color you hoped to match before the down appeared upon your cheeks. These are the locks, my dear Fernando, which paid the price. Here, I have brought the hair she pulled out, since what remains is to be yours no more; she reserves it for another, a Spaniard from abroad to whom she is presenting me. Gold has conquered her, Gerarda arranged it all; between them, they plotted my death. Oh cruel decree! She found out I had sold the passementerie of the cloth skirt last month, and the skirt in the flowering print the day before yesterday. She says I did it to give you money to gamble (as if you gambled), when your besetting sin is books—books in every known language; she claims you beguile me with verse, and, like a siren, lull me with your voice toward the seas of old age, where disillusionment will be my tomb, and repentance my punishment. Oh God! Oh the pity of it all! Let me destroy these eyes, since they are no longer yours. They deserve respect no more. The person she has in mind shall not have his way with them and me, because in their pupils he'll discover your likeness, which will find a way to defend them. Oh God! Oh death!

Julio. Back to the old refrain.

Fernando. Why, Dorotea—to carry on so about so small a matter! Let your eyes grow fair again, hold back those pearls, which hang like earrings from their inmost darlings, their pupils. Let not your roses wilt, do not disturb the harmonious cast of your countenance with dissonant emotions. I assure you, by the love I have had for you, that you almost took my soul away.

Dorotea. "Have had," Fernando?

Fernando. Have had and do have, for love is no mere shadow, vanishing when the body is removed. I thought that you were in flight from some jealous slander, or that your mother had succumbed to that female complaint which an excess of acidity causes, or that your husband was returning from the New World. But such a burst of grief for such a flimsy reason! Come now, into this heart restore the joy of seeing you which the sadness of listening to you had removed. And so, Godspeed, you may depart, since I expect a friend about a certain matter, and it would be unseemly for him to see you here. For ladies—and such beautiful ones at that—may be found without reproach only in the homes of magistrates and jurists, not in young men's lodgings filled with nothing but fencing foils, trunks of clothing, and musical instruments.

Dorotea. I don't think you understood me.

Fernando. Have I repeated the lessons so badly that you imagine I failed to take it in?

Dorotea. But when I tell you that our friendship is over, how can you accept the fact so lightly?

Fernando. As you yourself did when you told me.

Dorotea. My heart is broken.

Fernando. Had your heart been broken at your house you could never have reached mine.

Dorotea. Do you think I've been joking with you?

Fernando. How can I think so, if there's no joking about that Spaniard from the New World? Now please leave, my dear, it's late.

Dorotea. You even mean to put me out of your house?

Fernando. Well, why should you want to stay, if you say you don't intend to see it again?

Dorotea. Why won't I see it again?

Fernando. Because you're bound for the New World, and a sea lies between.

Dorotea. The sea of my tears.

Fernando. Women's tears are mere laughter turned inside out. No summer cloudburst dries so quickly.

Dorotea. What have you done for me all these years to oblige me to feign the love that I have had for you?

Fernando. You are also saying "that I have had for you."

Dorotea. And that's just what I mean, for no one deserves my love who doesn't mind losing me.

Fernando. You're mistaken. Losing me is what you have done, quite on your own.

Dorotea. You men will always be foreign to us.

Fernando. Rather, we are the native-born. In you women is our first dwelling place and from you we never depart.

Dorotea. Come, Celia, let us leave. No doubt this gentleman by now has found for himself precisely what Gerarda said he would.

Fernando. It's you who have found what Gerarda said. Why, if it weren't for you, I might be married and possess more gold than was brought to you. But I'm not yet twenty-two.

Dorotea. Am I five hundred, then?

Fernando. Is that what I'm implying or that, God willing, there's still good life left in me to make use of? You know that at seventeen I came into your life and Julio and I gave up our studies, leaving thoughts of Alcalá farther behind than the soldiers of Ulysses ever left Greece.

Celia. What a stick of a man, mouthing myths at such a time. God help us!

Dorotea. Let him be, Celia, he has his reasons. I knew all the while he was engaged elsewhere. He's found another woman. Otherwise he'd never be so hardhearted and so stony-eyed.

Julio. Oh Celia, Celia!

Celia. What is it, Julio?

Julio. You at least speak to me and don't deny me one last embrace, unless the servants of the returned Spaniard have brought you some letter from the New World.

Celia. Let me follow my mistress down, she is leaving all alone.

Fernando. Close the door, simpleton, and look out the window to see if Dorotea is glancing back.

Julio. The thought never entered her head.

Fernando. I'm dying, Julio. Close all the windows, let no light reach my eyes, since the light of my soul is doused forever. Remove that dagger from my sight, for the flesh is a thing of the devil, habit hell, love madness, and all are urging me to turn it on myself.

Julio. Easy, sir. Show some control. How can you be so blind?

Fernando. Let me be. My soul is like a swollen reservoir that bursts its dam and seeks to vent its fury through the eyes. Oh this poor life of mine! Those lost hopes! Julio, let me be. Since you were no prudent adviser at the start of this affair, don't play the meddlesome friend now.

Julio. The balcony isn't the best way to the street; you had better use the door.

Fernando. May my soul open a door in my chest and let my misfortunes out. What shall I take to kill myself? What poison will be quickest? Corrosive sublimate is for slaves, but I was slave to Dorotea, so I'll let it kill me ignominiously. Noble poisons are for Caesars.

Julio. Let's read Nicander. He'll have poisons for us.

Fernando. How false that laughter is!

Julio. How fussy your folly.

Fernando. Go find a bloodletter, hurry. I'll have my heart's vein opened and when he's gone I'll remove the bandage. For if love starts by diffusing those subtle spirits from atom to atom, infecting the blood and settling where it is purest, then by drawing blood, you'll draw love out with it. A known medical aphorism has it that failure of nerve sometimes requires bloodletting. Now what case could be more applicable than mine?

Julio. The argument does not impress me, for if love is equivalent to blood, no similar can expel its similar. As if heat could expel heat and cold, cold—it's impossible.

Fernando. Idiot, that may be true in itself but not in exceptional circumstances. Philosopher, indeed! You know full well that in this case they are contraries.

Julio. All I know is what that great physician Dryvere says in his *Method:* that proper conformation of the head indicates the temper of the brain. Yours has never seemed to me well shaped. Added to which, excessive heat warps its functioning, and this, brought on by misguided love, prevents your attaining the reasonable balance shown by sensible men on such occasions. If you do not summon up some prudence, I deem you done for, without dredging up prognoses from the *Nosomantica* of Moffett. For on this subject I am better informed than Hippocrates. What are you doing in that writing desk? What are you after? What is that you're tearing up? Leave those love letters alone, let the portrait be. What has that divine painting ever done to you? Respect the brushstrokes of the acclaimed Felipe de Liaño on that card. It's not right to deprive art of this miracle of his, nor thus satisfy the envy of a nature which resents such imitation of its perfections and such improvement on its flaws.

Fernando. By God, if I don't kill you!

Julio. Kill me, but you shall not touch the portrait, for it is blameless.

Fernando. Then I must go away.

Julio. Where to?

Fernando. To Seville, since to remain here where I behold my death is to suffer it every second of the day.

Julio. Wouldn't it be better to avoid the cause?

Fernando. That's impossible without some distance in between.

Julio. I'm not against your going off, but what about money?

Fernando. Marfisa, whom I have always belittled—though I was brought up with her—and wrongly dropped for this heartless creature, will come liberally to our aid.

Julio. On what pretext?

Fernando. Some trick or other.

Julio. Good idea. Let's go and see her.

Fernando. Put the letters and portrait away where I won't see them.

Julio. Poor fellow! He is losing his mind. But how can he lose what he does not possess?

Fernando. What did you say?

Julio. That losing Dorotea is tantamount to losing everything.

Fernando. Oh Julio, how right you are. And you should see the mind she has along with all that beauty!

Julio. The mind cannot be seen. It differs from sense in that the latter is a certain power that apprehends outward things without actually taking them in, except insofar as sense may be receptive to forms; whereas, through the mind man apprehends neither the thing itself nor any of its parts or corporeal attributes, but by virtue of receiving in the mind the idea of what it apprehends.

Fernando. Scholastic beast, is this a time to throw my words back at me? Am I in any state to understand what I say? Next you'll drag out that old chestnut about Aristotle disagreeing with Plato's view concerning the truth of things, which Aristotle thought the mind created. You know very well what I mean: that by what men speak and write you can gauge the quality of mind, and in her letters you can see and appreciate Dorotea's mind just as you can those of Laura Terracina or of the Marchioness of Pescara in their *Rhymes.* Now to make up for what you said, bring me her letters.

Julio. What? Take them out now? You're not very eager to get to Seville.

Fernando. Listen to this one: "Dearest Fernando, what's the use of so many apologies? Those you made last night suffice; then your tears melted my anger sooner than your words do now, for no rhetoric so prevails on angry hearts as such meek gestures do. Your youthfulness alone makes me uneasy, lest falling in love be due to your tender years rather than your feelings. If I praised Alexander for being gracious and handsome, no comparison with your person was intended; it was simply a silly inadvertence on my part. You laid a hand to my face. The offense consists in acting from jealousy; if from love, there'd be none. But you'll reply that one grows out of the other—and we'd best believe it, my face and I. If you wished to brand me so everyone might know I was your slave, what made you think I care to have it generally known? Rest assured that when that slap in the face echoed in my soul, the latter humbly said: suffer it, Dorotea—your offender is also your avenger, for his remorse will be greater than your pain. Now, such loving meekness is all very well, but please note that this is not a jest which a self-respecting woman accepts a second time. If this example shows us both what being completely forthright comes to, there's no need for another demonstration. Because, although they say a woman is an animal that thrives on punishment, not all may be relied on not to throw their riders and run off out of reach. Let me only ask you now to come and see the face you struck and determine which is more inflamed: yours with shame for what you did, or mine with the imprint you left on it."

Julio. I remember that night and how madly you acted.

Fernando. Oh, if only I had killed her.

Julio. Mind you, sir, it's getting late to talk to Marfisa.

Fernando. This piece is in my own handwriting, and it's in verse. I remember now: she returned it for me to sing to her. I have a notion to read it.

> On your honor, shepherdess,
>> tell me if you love me,
>> for though I shan't forget you,
>> I mean to fall but lightly.
> When I gazed into your eyes,
>> living pearls of love I saw.
>> When I looked in them again,
>> hate flashed lightning bolts.
> Only you can know the truth,
>> fear makes me uncertain,
>> for if fondness may be feigned,
>> tears can lie, for certain.

Since your weeping casts a spell,
   I'm divinely taken,
   as my eyes imbibe from yours
   drops of pearly poison.
Your tears are reassuring,
   your looks say, be not sad;
   while I bask in your favor,
   your jealousy drives me mad.
Granting this, how can it be,
   if it's true you love me,
   the slightest provocation
   makes you turn and leave me?
Forsaking me three days ago,
   you sought fields and fountains;
   in my eyes are deeper wells
   full of your reflection.
In what better mirror
   can lovers see love swell
   than upon a flood of tears
   where the soul must dwell?
Either love me or forget me;
   why return if you've forgotten?
   Why enjoy my suffering,
   if indeed you're smitten?
Can my guileless word or two
   greeting mountain lasses
   rouse you to such vengeance—
   you whom none surpasses?
When your green eyes leave the dance,
   thousands try to claim them,
   blameless all, and goodness knows
   I'm the last to blame them.
But you blame *me,* though wronging you
   never crossed my mind;
   before I'd look at other eyes,
   may weeping make mine blind.
Shepherdess, my only joy,
   returning, you would gladden me;

but if you come, come back with love,
   your hate will only sadden me.
Once you and hope desert me
   I'll know how to die;
   you'll be free, but for my dying
   you must answer and not I.

Julio. Now what good is repeating this sweet nonsense? If you have
   second thoughts about leaving, there's no need to put up a brave
   front with me.

Fernando. Ah, Julio! Seneca said it so well: as long as the mind is uncertain it keeps changing, impelled this way and that by conflicting
   thoughts! Was it I who determined not to see Dorotea? Impossible. Yet how can I see her when I am still aggrieved? It would be a
   greater misfortune to stay here and see her. Courage, oh despairing
   heart—it has never yet been forced to suffer hardship it could not
   bear.

Julio. Shall I tie up the letters?

Fernando. Not yet, we'll look at this one only. Can you guess what it
   says? Do you remember that day we went down to the brook?

Julio. As if it were yesterday.

Fernando. She is replying to some lines I wrote about her verve and
   charm, which utterly delighted me.

Julio. I know the lines by heart and could recite them for you.

Fernando. Then do it, Julio, and with due ceremony let us mark the
   imminent separation.

Julio.

   A pair of golden slippers
      fastened by white bows
      set off two small feet,
      the very hands of love.
   A pair of tiny slippers
      which might be said to be
      the white gloves of her feet,
      captives briefly prisoned.
   White stockings letting show
      just so much, lest more
      be taken as a hint
      she'd step out of bounds.

White hands catching up
  a rainbow petticoat—
  pins of ivory glittering,
  fingernails of sun.
These won my heart one day
  as, risen on her toes,
  the beauteous Amaryllis
  skipped across a brook.
The crystal waters laughed.
  I wish they'd had a voice,
  to tell of their delight
  and never breathe the cause.
Bless you, mountain maid,
  God grant you years and years
  to be the sprite of nimbleness
  skipping over brooks.
And many joys betide
  that lucky shepherd who,
  having won your person,
  wins your love as well.
When you glide in slippers,
  I'm told by many a bloom
  your footfall is so light
  it never crushes them.
No dawn makes its way
  so swiftly through the fields,
  but the flowers are offended:
  they claim you leave no print.
Footfalls you deny them
  my own heart will bestow
  which, envying the flowers,
  comes to greet you, too.
For years now, Amaryllis,
  my eyes have glimpsed your soul,
  but no imagination
  has ever beheld your feet.
When putting on your shoes,
  your hands take greater pains

finding the feet to fit them
than I take in their praise.
One day, no doubt, your slippers
—and right they'll be—will think
your feet have vanished utterly
or both are only one.
One thing now concerns me
(lovers' fears are constant):
that feet so light and airy
might be borne away.
Oh, mountain maid, who'd think
(and do not say I do)
that feet so insubstantial
could shape the darts of love!
Thus spoke to Amaryllis
a swain who chanced to spy
her leap across a brook
which babbled on forever.

Fernando. I was about to expatiate upon Dorotea's beauty and charm, her verve, her spirit and lightness of heart (that quality so indispensable in a beautiful woman), as shown by her that day. Ah, but Julio, this only sets up obstacles to my leaving. Better to assume I have died and my soul is now going off on its own to Seville. Come, Julio, bear up.

Julio. I have not heard such comic folderol from you since this affair began. Whatever gave you the idea that the souls of absent lovers go to Seville?

Fernando. I was thinking of my own, Julio.

Julio. To underscore their feelings, lovers who must absent themselves are wont to say they are leaving their souls with the beloved, claiming the soul lives where it loves more than where it has its being. To which they add that, though removed from the body, the soul does not perish or cease to be subject to the material world. Since they feel bereft of life, lovers convince themselves that their soul is not inside them and, still immortal, remains wherever they have left it.

Fernando. I'm half-inclined to believe that.

Julio. Only a madman could be forgiven such a notion, and in this connection, let me tell you what I think of those critical caterwauling Catos who, on seeing some tenderhearted gallant on the stage, assume the dramatist is imitating his own behavior; such a judgment, which makes miracles out of something perfectly ordinary, is unworthy of sensible men. In fact, the only thing being imitated is a wild youth who gives free rein to his appetites, and the better the poet depicting him, the livelier the feelings will be, and the truer the actions. Claudian said that, though his writings were licentious, his life was virtuous. But, coming back to that monstrous notion of yours—imagining that your soul has remained with Dorotea (although I'm convinced you don't really mean this, despite the wild extremes you are being driven to by the power of this overwhelming passion)—let me say that lovers and witches are alike in that they think they are proceeding bodily to where they are actually being borne in fantasy. They can see their ladies' actions in this manner and thus credit their own jealousy.

Fernando. I must admit, Julio, jealousy is what dominates my susceptible nature and most impresses it.

Julio. Every cause of limited effect will function more tellingly upon matter susceptible to it than upon matter which is not.

Fernando. And what will it do when the effect is unlimited?

Julio. Exactly what your headlong folly shows.

Fernando. I am simply doing what honor requires of me.

Julio. Honorable love—when it's illicit?

Fernando. Not all honor is subject to laws.

Julio. If not so subject, there's no honor in it.

Fernando. Men make of honor whatever they wish.

Julio. To be honorable, a man should desire what is right.

Fernando. It's right to remove yourself before you lose honor, isn't it?

Julio. You wouldn't lose it if you removed yourself from Dorotea and not Madrid, would you?

Fernando. With provocations on every hand, there's a clear and present danger. I'll try leaving town, though my heart isn't in it.

Julio. In following you, I'll be acting out of friendship, not obligation.

Fernando. I looked, I fell headlong, and error still keeps me in its thrall, as Virgil's Damon said.

Julio. Love is the root of all passions. From it spring dejection, pleasure, happiness, despair.

Fernando. It's despair that drives me away, with or without a soul—
who knows?

Julio. Love's entrance is easy, its exit always hard.

Fernando. It will be hard enough to shake off the force of habit.

Julio. So a poet said:

> Deck it out in motley like a fool,
> and say it's habit but not love.

Scene 6

MARFISA · CLARA
DON FERNANDO · JULIO

Marfisa. Clara?

Clara. Ma'am.

Marfisa. What time did Don Fernando come home to bed?

Clara. I heard the door—it was misgivings woke me more than the
noise—and before I slept again it struck four.

Marfisa. What a Godforsaken man!

Clara. Youth is his excuse.

Marfisa. Do you know what I think?

Clara. You're always thinking—I know that.

Marfisa. Dorotea has him bewitched.

Clara. You call a five-year affair bewitchment?

Marfisa. He should have *wearied* of her by now.

Clara. Only if they were married; the words almost rhyme.

Marfisa. She's not as pretty as they say.

Clara. Where have you seen her?

Marfisa. In La Merced one day.

Clara. Well, you're mistaken; she's a handsome girl with a genteel
manner, a certain air about her, and a good figure. Her eyes are very
beautiful, although somewhat bold.

Marfisa. That's how men want them.

Clara. Until they've won them. Once they have, they prefer modesty.

Marfisa. It makes me laugh! Laying siege to women, they like them
free; afterward they want them saintly.

Clara. Her eyes say yes before they're asked.

Marfisa. By nature or design?

Clara. Both, as the guest told the servant when asked if he wanted red or white wine. Her mouth is pleasant and she doesn't mind laughing, even with no reason to. She's on the thin side, though her face isn't.

Marfisa. Her cheeks are full. What about her coloring?

Clara. Darkish.

Marfisa. Her hair?

Clara. Rather curly—it goes with such color.

Marfisa. The signs of bluster and cowardliness in a man.

Clara. Who told you so?

Marfisa. I've read it.

Clara. Her mind, remarkable; her nature, affectionate; in disposition, rather forward; in speech, soft and slightly lisping, so that everything she says is rimmed in gold, as if the pearls of her teeth were not enough.

Marfisa. Curse you and your fibbing fabrications! How you lay it on! Don Fernando couldn't have put it better in his verse.

Clara. That's where I picked it up—not with my own two eyes, certainly.

Marfisa. May you never know happiness! Though you're so stupid, the curse won't even take hold.

Clara. I've still to tell you how she sings and dances.

Marfisa. To excuse herself, the crude, crass, ignorant, pretentious girl goes babbling on without the slightest idea of what she's saying. The ninny has to take her Don Fernando's side, of course!

Clara. More yours than mine, he is.

Marfisa. When was he ever mine? Why, even though we were brought up together his regard for me never went beyond the stage of dispensing with formalities.

Clara. He and Julio, his servant or his ruination, are rushing up here right now, and his friend Ludovico is keeping watch at the door.

Marfisa. What on earth is the matter?

Fernando. I don't know how to tell you. Go over to the window, Clara, and keep an eye out for the constable.

Marfisa. Misery me, what have you done?

Fernando. Last night . . .

Marfisa. Go on.

Fernando. . . . last night, between one and two, I was talking with—I don't know what to call her.

Marfisa. I'll tell you in case you have forgotten. You were talking with Dorotea.

Fernando. With that devil, Marfisa.

Marfisa. With her or me? You link the devil with my name and that's what I always seem to you.

Fernando. Let me be, I beseech you in the name of God. This is no time for reproaches. I was talking with her, I say, telling her all sorts of idiotic things I had dreamt about the sea, the New World, galleons, and pieces of silver. Two men came along, a gentleman and his servant; they loitered more than the hour warranted. I withdrew from the grille, told her to close the window, and sat down against one of those stones used for hitching horses and by outdoor suitors both—it's all the same. The men were rude enough to come up and peer at me, sticking the face-flaps of their capes up against mine, especially one with gilt edging to his cape. Then came I nimbly to my feet, not differently from the bull who has been lying beside the cow when, down the path that traverses the meadow, he catches the barking of the dogs of the huntsman who, trusting to his bullets, has no fear of him. "What do you want?" I asked.

Marfisa. That's not what the bull would have said.

Fernando. You seem to be making fun of me.

Marfisa. Well, what do you expect, seeing how poorly the simile matches the sudden alarm? But those are leftovers from your versifying.

Julio. Sir, don't forget the present danger.

Fernando. I won't, Julio. Now, Marfisa, please listen. They replied, "To find out what you're doing at that window." "I was inquiring," I said, "if any man so stupid as to ask would come by at such an hour." I dropped my buckler to my chest, because it's too large and does more harm than good, keeping me from seeing; and immediately on drawing our swords, I ran mine through one of them in fine style.

Julio. What about me? Wasn't I right there?

Marfisa. Don't blow it up so, for heaven's sake. I shudder to think what comes next. Tell it quickly. You certainly can, since you've come through alive.

Fernando. I killed one and wounded the other.

Julio. What about me? Was I peeling a medlar pear?

Fernando. Valor like mine the world has never seen.

Julio. What about me? Was I sitting at home?

Fernando. Julio did his part. What's the matter? Are you weeping for me or for the victim?

Marfisa. I'm weeping for you both.

Fernando. Do see if you have something to give me. I'm off to Seville until this storm blows over, because I fear they'll find me out or the survivor will identify me.

Marfisa. Except for my jewels, I've nothing to give you, unhappy woman that I am. But what loss are they to me, since I am losing you, my most precious jewel? There are ten diamonds in these ear-rings.

Fernando. Marfisa, don't take them off.

Marfisa. What good are baubles to ears that shall no longer hear your words? I'll go fetch my gold necklaces and whatever else of value I find.

Julio. You're acting very blindly; nothing is forcing you to leave.

Fernando. I cannot help myself; no force avails against the influence of the stars and man's free will. My, how she swallowed it!

Julio. That's one of women's failings.

Fernando. Have you seen to the mules?

Julio. The traveling bags and cushions are already on their backs.

Fernando. What did you put in my bag?

Julio. Some black apparel and linen in a green portmanteau that Ludovico lent me.

Fernando. What about the boots?

Julio. Only one.

Fernando. I said the boots, not the bootleg.

Julio. Mine's made of leather, too. But when it comes to wineskins, the spur is thirst.

Fernando. We'll be going down Dorotea's street; I want her to see with her own eyes how I feel. You'll make a noise to bring her to the window.

Julio. That won't be necessary. When she realizes there is someone looking up, she'll come on her own.

Fernando. Heaven help me! To think of all I've gone through between nine and twelve this morning!

Julio. I wish some dinner had gone through me.

Fernando. We'll have dinner along the way in Getafe.

Julio. Obliged, I'm sure, but I'd settle for some in Madrid right now.

Fernando. Didn't I tell you the dream would come true?

Julio. Hush, here she comes.

Marfisa. I've ransacked my jewel boxes, and anything of gold that I could find is wrapped in this kerchief for you to take.

Fernando. The soul I leave is my security, and as an earnest of your great trust I leave the memory of me. I will write upon arrival, and on my heart shall be inscribed the instrument of your receipt, which you may collect, if God grant me sight of you again, as your eyes are my witness. Tell me what form you wish my signature to take.

Marfisa. What better signature than your embrace?

Fernando. Weep not, Marfisa my own, or you make my leaving impossible. Nothing is so daunting to the soul as the tears of one adored.

Marfisa. I imprint them upon your face, desiring you hereafter to recall how my eyes poured them almost into yours, to create the illusion that they were yours indeed.

Fernando. A few of mine have commingled with them, and I swear those shed upon me trace across my face the letters of your name. But what slave has ever worn letters made of diamonds? I take my leave.

Marfisa. Your leaving is my dying.

Julio. Say, mistress Clara. What message have you for Seville?

Clara. Give my greetings to La Giralda.

Julio. Haven't you a farewell gift for me?

Clara. This jet ring.

Julio. Something of value, I mean.

Clara. When love is delicate, it prizes things of scant value. Valuable things are prized without love.

Julio. Love is also proven by coming to the aid of one's beloved.

Clara. Whoever told you I loved you, that I should come to your aid?

Julio. Let me have that necklace. I swear, you look better without it. Such snow needs no adornment beyond its own beauty.

Clara. I'll catch cold if I remove it.

Julio. I'll give you a neckcloth instead.

Clara. I'll look like a horse with a band around its neck.

Julio. What are you carrying in that handbag?

Clara. A few pieces of scented earth for my mistress to nibble at. Have some, they taste of amber.

Julio. I don't fancy the Portuguese variety; I prefer mine cured like those of Garrovillas.

Clara. My mistress is weeping; I'll go and comfort her.

Julio. That's more than you've done for me. However, some day . . .

Clara. Well, what did you expect? That I would be as great a fool as Marfisa, who pays with her jewels for his jealousy of Dorotea? Be off now, Julio; there's nothing noble in buying dear and selling cheap, dressing up clowns and not paying servants, and a woman's giving to a man what she needs for herself. Unless of course they expect our prerogatives as women to apply to them, along with everything they steal from our wardrobes. But if they go that far, let them take our frills, our curls, our dress patterns and our mirrors, but leave the wheedling up to us, since we acquired full rights to it when the world began, the franchise being renewed century after century through all of time down to the present.

Scene 7

TEODORA · GERARDA
CELIA · DOROTEA

Gerarda. Blessings upon this model of motherhood, honor of widowhood, gracious mistress of courtesies, charitable benefactress of the helpless, albeit not so lucky herself, who by rights should be a Transylvanian princess.

Teodora. You're something special today, Gerarda, speaking in both modern and antique styles. How is it you have coupled *albeit* with *gracious,* the latter the epitome of maidenhood, the former, of decrepitude?

Gerarda. Our language has become a brew of white and red vintages.

Teodora. Which is why you speak it with such gusto?

Gerarda. 'A jackass among apes is the butt of their japes.'

Teodora. For goodness sake, don't take it amiss. Where have you come from?

Gerarda. I've come from where I was born and I'm going to where I shall die. At La Merced I performed some of my devotions.

Teodora. 'If the preacher starts coughing, a good sermon's in the offing.'

Gerarda. The truth is, I've come not to preach but to be edified by your virtue.

Teodora. 'May my life taste as fine as partridge with limes.' All I truly want, Gerarda, is to have this girl emerge with great morigeration from my nurture.

Gerarda. Such nice little words—where did they come from, Teodora? I always said talk is as contagious as the itch.

Teodora. 'Follow your palate in food and drink, follow fashion in dress and speech.' Did you pray for us as you promised?

Gerarda. I was on my fifth rosary when who should turn up, to my delight ... You tell me, Teodora. You'll never guess.

Teodora. You mean that self-mortifying penitent who goes about exhibiting the iron bracelets on her wrists?

Gerarda. Yes, of course. 'Coming from the grave, she asks about the dead.' Who but that very New World gentleman I told you of this morning, the one who has his eye on Dorotea. There he was, praying like a lamb. He must be utterly guileless—and remember, friend, not all men eat the quarry they kill. There is such a thing as guileless love, arising from some special sympathy, or sympathony, as those say who know little Latin and much Greek.

Teodora. 'An old woman dancing kicks up lots of dust.'

Gerarda. For heaven's sake, don't be so witty—be sensible. Is it better having Dorotea wasted on young Fernando? He's worth his weight in gold, 'a down-to-earth chap with hair on his chest,' exactly what you need to make her stop doting on these sonnets and these new *décimas* or *espinelas* now in vogue. May God forgive Vicente Espinel, who brought us this novelty and the fifth string on the guitar, so that now people are neglecting the nobler instruments and ancient dances for the wild gesticulations and lewd movements of the chaconnes, so offensive to the virtue of chastity and to a lady's decorous reserve. Alas and alack, oh *allemande* and *pie de gibao,* who for so many years dignified our soirées. Ah, the mighty sway of novelty!

But, to come back to Don Bela—he told me it was not his intention to make love to window grilles and give women down the street reason to talk, but with due reserve and propriety to wait on Dorotea and lavish splendid gifts upon her, and those were his very words.

Teodora. 'When the pie was opened, the birds began to sing.' Look here, Gerarda. It's not sound policy to pull my daughter out of one mudhole only to deposit her in another. I admit this house is needy and in debt. But even if the debts were larger, it's not right to rip the silk in order to remove the stain. That New World gentleman, I realize, would be a solution for Dorotea, but a very costly one.

Gerarda. 'Three things help men prosper: learning, the sea, and the king's service.' My good woman, you're not sailing that sea; the returned Spaniard has already crossed it. Taking one dishonor with another, let's exchange the useless for the more profitable one. You are shrewd; think it over and sleep on it. It might happen that this gentleman would marry Dorotea, just as many of higher quality, though his is considerable, have married persons more disparate in rank and less deserving.

Teodora. That's when love and fortune, drunk as lords, toast one another's health, raising up the fallen and bringing down the high and mighty. But if this should come to marriage, now that we have it on good grounds that her husband Ricardo has died in Lima (God bless Lima for eliminating that obstacle), how is Dorotea to be put in readiness and repair for a decent bridal bed?

Gerarda. Truly such a difficulty calls for Hippocrates, like lacework so fine it has to be held up to the light and requires eyeglasses. As if glasses sharpened the bridegroom's vision, especially with falsehood playing understudy to blandishment and overconfidence to deception. Truthfully, I think more than sixty-five such accidents have gone through these hands and no bridegroom ever complained to this day. Dorotea is not so simple-minded as not to stick the white of a squab's feather in her hair, when the time comes, so as to color artfully what would be impossible to color naturally.

Teodora. Gerarda, not another word. She and Celia are outside and I think they're coming in.

Gerarda. I'll leave by the other door.

Scene 8

TEODORA · DOROTEA · CELIA

Teodora. Where are you coming from at two in the afternoon, Dorotea? What church is open at this hour? What pieties can excuse you? A fine way to get household tasks done. You began embroidering that hemp cloth for the ottomans two months ago. 'Give her an inch and she'll take a mile.' No doubt she's been informing the Knight of the Burning Sword of my anger. How he must have laid into me! No Don Diego Ordóñez can have uttered such threats against Zamora, that well-walled city. Look at the state she's in—all flushed and rumpled! Please God I may be wrong.

Dorotea. Now this is all I needed.

Celia. Be patient—it really matters.

Dorotea. Rather than patience, what matters is for me to put an end to my unhappiness once and for all.

Teodora. What are you two talking about? Taking turns mocking me, are you? 'Mother scolds and I laugh up my sleeve.' Bernarda, bring me something to eat. Milady will of course have had something— that poor gentleman would not fail to provide pastry and fruit. He has ample income when it comes to such delicacies. What is that black girl doing? Why doesn't she come out of the kitchen? I'll have to do it all myself. These ladies will want to go in and reflect upon some sonnet.

Celia. Let her go, don't retort.

Dorotea. What noise is that out in the street?

Celia. Some gentlemen in traveling clothes, and I believe I recognize Julio from his way of speaking.

Dorotea. You make me fear the worst! Let me look. Oh, unfortunate woman! Isn't the one wearing the plumes and gold chain Don Fernando?

Celia. He's turning his face this way.

Dorotea. There's no doubt of it, it's he. He's going away because of what I said. How can I call him back?

Celia. There's no way, he's riding too fast.

Dorotea. How explosive jealousy is; this will be the end of me. This awful thing I've done. My Fernando is going away—why should I live?

Celia. What are you doing, ma'am? What is it you've put in your mouth? Good heavens—she's swallowed the diamond ring to kill herself. Madam, madam!

Teodora. What is it, Celia?

Celia. Dorotea is dying.

Teodora. Oh, child! Oh, my precious! Dorotea, Dorotea! What caused this calamity?

Celia. It will be no small one if she dies. Oh, woman more resolute than Portia and nobler far in death! While the Roman took her life with live coals, this woman chooses diamonds.

Chorus of Love

Love all powerful on earth and in heaven,
warfare most sweet to our senses,
wastrels aplenty with uneasy lives,
    fall under your sway.
With hollow delights and foolish attachments,
desires inflamed and fears cold as ice,
pleasurable pangs and alluring deceits,
    you squander our years.
Tyrannical force of our youthful days,
you promise us good but thrust on us evil.
You seek to undo all those whom you favor—
    so barbaric are you.
Flee his deceptions, show some resistance
to such devastation, foolhardy lovers.
Like the snake in the grass with venomous sting
    are his hollow favors.
Temper the arrows in Lethean streams,
love nobly born in all moderation,
come, let us sing your heavenly praise
    in hymnody Sapphic.

ACT · TWO

Scene 1

GERARDA · DON BELA · LAURENCIO

Bela. I do not simply mean the gold I've promised—why, *all* the gold the sun brings forth in both the Indies appears paltry, even if you include the diamonds of China, the pearls of the South Seas, and the rubies of Ceylon. As for you, clever Gerarda, to whose skill this victory is due, I trust you will accept these *escudos* for the time being.

Gerarda. Heaven grant you the long life your munificent hands deserve. I do not understand all the talk about stingy overseas Spaniards. Either you are an exception to the opinion generally held, or one single wretch gave all a bad name, as with nobles from Calabria, which is said to be the fatherland of Judas, the most infamous man of all.

Bela. Laurencio.

Laurencio. Sir.

Bela. Give Gerarda the beaten-silver bowl so she can make chocolate, and one of our two boxes to make it with.

Laurencio. In short order these hussies will have stripped my master bare! I'll wager we go back to the New World without the shirts on our backs, like the prodigal son. Here you are, aunt.

Gerarda. I shall take the bowl, but you may keep the chocolate. My sort of chocolate is made out of grapes from these very shores, in Coca and San Martín.

Laurencio. Coca and Crocked are kith and kin like Manzanares and La Membrilla.

Gerarda. The silver of this bowl is paper-thin!

Bela. It is the capacity that counts, not the weight.

Gerarda. Nothing made of silver was ever the worse for weight.

Bela. True, but pour my good will into it and see how heavy it grows.

Gerarda. I shall give it to Dorotea.

Bela. Oh, no, heaven forbid, Gerarda—you will ruin me. Come here, Laurencio.

Laurencio. Sir.

Bela. Hand me that gilded *búcaro* with the Cupid taking aim at the sea god.

Laurencio. What did I say? Blast me if there isn't sorcery afoot here.

Gerarda. The rascal's grumbling; I'll win him over.

Laurencio. Here is the *búcaro.*

Bela. Take and give it to Dorotea. Once her ruby lips touch it, they'll transform it into a diamond worthy of the ambrosia of the gods. And should you wish to make her up a fable about these figures, tell her she is the Cupid and I the sea god, who crossed oceans to be assaulted by the arrows of her eyes.

Gerarda. How clever, how amusing, and what a pretty moral! Ah, wit—what a delectable quality of soul! Dorotea will go into ecstasies over you; she's dying to be thought clever. No gift is apt to win her more than a conceit, nor treasure bind her to you than a pretty moral. What does this writing say?

Bela. Omnia vincit amor, which is a hemistich by a Latin poet.

Gerarda. Heavenly God, Don Bela, it's a match already; she is wild about hemistichs.

Laurencio. Then they must be made of gold. Crafty crone!

Gerarda. If there's anything of the poet in you, her soul is yours. For, as flattery turns the heads of women, verse being so supremely flattering drives them right out of their minds.

Bela. For her I'll come up with hyperboles and *enargias* the likes of which no Spanish writer alive can hope to utter.

Gerarda. Say no more. Once she hears you mention hyperboles and *enargias,* she'll walk into your arms like a child reaching out for anyone who fusses over it. Why, let her hear a fancy word, and she'll write it down in a notebook, then willy-nilly drag it into everything she says. What were those two words again?

Bela. Hyperboles and *enargias.*

Gerarda. They sound like New World fruits, like bananas and avocados. Well then, I'll give her this *búcaro* and buy her some toques with these *escudos;* for as the girl is virtuous and her mother miserly, she goes about the whole year through with her hair hanging loose. And such hair! When she has it combed and spread out, she is the very image of Magdalene in the wilderness. It takes both my arms to hold it.

Bela. Under no circumstance, Gerarda. Keep your *escudos;* take her these doubloons, and let her buy the toques herself.

Gerarda. Magnanimous gentleman! Oh noble heart! Give me those hands of yours; I'll devour them with kisses.

Laurencio. Yes, you and that damsel will devour him all right. Was there ever a sorceress as wily as she?

Gerarda. On the way I'll buy some shoes and stockings for her. Shoes, did I say? Shoelets, and even at that, not nearly diminutive enough. You should see her—she barely takes size three, though her calves are shapely. It's all her own flesh, too, and not your padded kind of stocking.

Laurencio. Devils, that's what this sorceress has inside her. She'll get more gold out of him, I swear.

Bela. Don't buy the stockings, Gerarda—I'll send her some today, along with passementerie and enough watered silk for a long cloak.

Gerarda. Well, if you go to the market at the Guadalajara Gate ...

Laurencio. I'd be happy to give *you* the gate.

Gerarda. ... don't forget this poor old woman. Why, the nun's cloth I wear is more tattered than the cassock of the prodigal son.

Laurencio. The very one my master takes after!

Bela. I'll see to a cape and a dress of nun's cloth for you.

Gerarda. Yes, but I wager you won't think to buy one of those long cloaks of light wool or of Cuenca cloth. At the Gate you will find them ready-made. No need to wait for the tailor's markups: "So much for the tow," "More silk needed," and other superfluities they gouge a person with.

Bela. What color do you favor?

Gerarda. Each and every one of them, my prince. When young I was partial to green because 'Dressing up in green makes faces bolder seem.' But now, sinner that I am, no color suits me like a sheltering garment, especially when I see the tile roofs being repaired, the surest sign of winter. Poets depicting winter surprise me when they declare the winds do roar, the fountains groan, the birds seek sanctuary from frosts to come; they never say, "Now the title roofs are being mended and the braziers cleaned."

Laurencio. I'll frost her and her wheedling prattle, the old hag!

Bela. You shall have your long cloak, Gerarda, as a roof against your winter.

Gerarda. May the good Lord cover you with his grace and shelter you in his glory.

Laurencio. The sermon must be coming to an end.

Gerarda. I can see in your eyes you'll make it a gold-trimmed one . . .

Laurencio. And she asked for a plain woolen one!

Gerarda. . . . for, though I'm an old woman, I don't mind being told I have good foundations, which afford a person a certain standing and a cleanly aura. A poet once said that pages and lackeys are the foundations of a gentleman; if poorly attired, they diminish his standing. There is no gallantry without good feet and legs. No house stands solid without a firm foundation; mud respects new things and sticks least to them. In short, of the three acts that constitute a woman—namely, face, waist, and feet—her lower extremities make up the third act. A woman's best feature, like a man's, is good carriage. With poor footgear, anyone is bound to carry himself badly, and scarcely do you glance at the face of a passer-by when your eyes drop down and examine his feet. If they are not as I say, no matter how pretty the peacock, he soon furls his tail. God be with you, this afternoon you may look in on Dorotea, who is up and about again.

Bela. Mistress, what is this I hear about a ring?

Gerarda. Sheer slander, simply the jealousy of married women, the pure envy of single ones, loose tongues of loose tarts. Ah, poor beauty! Heaven's gifts always exact a price.

Bela. What is it I was told about some gentleman going off and Dorotea trying to kill herself?

Gerarda. Kill herself! As if the time were ripe for such a thing! As if the soul did not exist and a person would not be called to account by that righteous Judge of the living and the dead.

Bela. Is that why you are crying?

Gerarda. I am so devout that when I mention the Almighty my tears begin to flow.

Laurencio. It's the wine that does it.

Bela. Mistress, do not weep.

Laurencio. Tears straight out of the wineskin.

Gerarda. I'm going off for a bit of prayer—I have certain pious obligations to fulfill, plagued as I am by damsels dying to be wed and all the sick dying to be well.

Laurencio. She'll work miracles, no doubt.

Bela. Remember, at three I shall be at Dorotea's door.

Gerarda. I will be there expecting you.

Laurencio. Sir, are you in your right mind, throwing all this money around?

Bela. Simpleton, these are but the entering wedges of love. First take the fortress, then withdraw the artillery.

Laurencio. What's the use, if your ammunition's gone before you withdraw?

Bela. I know myself.

Laurencio. And I, this Court city.

Bela. It's too late to dissuade me. Serve and keep still, Laurencio. I brought you as a servant, not a counselor.

Scene 2

DOROTEA · CELIA

Celia. How enchanting you appear in that convalescent habit! While drawn looks leave other women listless, your pallor gives you charm, not to mention the harmonious composure of your features.

Dorotea. I must look quite ugly; perfect flattery is always founded on flaws.

Celia. Impossible, where you're concerned, for I have heard it said that heaven is not subject to alien impressions; by the same token, your face will admit of nothing unbecoming.

Dorotea. How erudite you've become, thanks to our good Julio, tutor or guardian to that absent gentleman.

Celia. For such things I need no books of theirs. I'd been aware they were learnèd, but have learned more from you than from them, since you know more than either.

Dorotea. One thing I do know when I hear you praise me so is that I do not look as you say. An untruthful compliment lays on not praise so much as a palliative for one's shortcomings—as when an elderly person is told he does not look one day older. Which is no more than the truth, because the days seem to have abandoned him and he seems to manage without them.

Celia. Say what you will, you've never had a better day in your life. Because, besides that blue scapular on the white habit, your air of injury makes you look about you with such provocative gentleness that you arouse love and sympathy, two effects inciting a desire halfway between pity and seduction.

Dorotea. I'm satisfied simply to be alive. Give me a mirror, for on being praised we women love to see the object of that praise, not because we disbelieve it, but in order to gloat in sheer vanity.

Celia. Here is the one you call your Felipe Liaño, because it provides so marvelous a likeness. Consult it and see if it does not agree with what I say.

Dorotea. It tells the truth and you are lying. Here, take it, put it back, for it has deceived me neither now nor earlier this morning. Mirroring the features of the soul, my face reflects precisely what is lodged in it. No indisposition of the blood made me ill, but distress of spirit. Alas, how foolishly I behaved when, showing so much disrespect for love, I spoke such mad nonsense to Fernando!

Celia. For heaven's sake, let's drop that subject or we'll have you fainting again. And if the first illness spared you when it found you robust, the next will not, for it will catch you weakened and off guard.

Dorotea. What do you suppose my darling is doing now?

Celia. He's surely in Seville, that great city, the Babylon of Spain, consoling himself most likely in a new affair, for one with the urge to change his locale will have spirit enough for a change of heart. Little do you understand men's inconstancy.

Dorotea. They learned inconstancy from us.

Celia. They came first.

Dorotea. We came from their sides.

Celia. Which is why they look sidelong at us.

Dorotea. There are two reasons for that, and neither is any fault of theirs.

Celia. What, pray tell?

Dorotea. Our being unfaithful to them, or being unlucky from the start.

Celia. And how faithful are they to us?

Dorotea. Well, they're men, remember.

Celia. So they're men! I'd like to see the dispensation Nature grants them for the freedom they assume.

Dorotea. Do you think it was granted for nothing?

Celia. I certainly do—they're only flesh and blood, like us.

Dorotea. You forget they are responsible for the feeding and clothing of us, and for our protection as well.

Celia. And what about everything women go through to bring them up? Surely that's no trifling matter! Not to mention all the unhappiness they themselves cause. But to see them first so helpless, saying "Mama" and "Daddy," playing with their mothers' nipples, and their poor mothers calling them monarchs, popes, and emperors, and tickling them to make them laugh! And to see them later on, becoming lions, cursing and swearing, behaving so cruelly, and, what is more lamentable, often bloodying the very breasts that suckled them.

Dorotea. Celia, I have no wish to defend them. I am a woman. But as with us there are good and bad, so also with them. It's not the good or bad in men that pains me now, but the absence of one I loved which tortures me. He was good enough for me—that much I know.

Celia. As he will be for another woman now.

Dorotea. Don't rouse my jealousy! It's the beginning of estrangement. Say he still thinks about me, cherishing the memories of all we shared together, no respite by night nor pleasure by day. Say he is sick of friends, finds women ugly; say his fancy carries him back and forth between Seville and Madrid more incessantly than the ticks and tocks of time itself. For when trust is lost, desire comes alive and makes forgetting impossible. I admit I have little cause for hope, since I brought this deception of his upon myself, and I subscribe to what Luis de Camoëns put so gracefully, as indeed so much else he wrote in his native Portuguese, complaining of love:

Que não pode tirarme as esperanças,

Que mal me tirará o que eu não tenho.

Celia. How adorably you speak the Portuguese tongue! Is there anything of beauty you would not enhance?

Dorotea. It is such a soft language, the softest of any for poetry.

Celia. For your own sake, apply that excellent mind of yours to banishing all thought of him. And since you say no hope remains, compel yourself to retain no memory of him, or only memory of the wrongs this object of your unwarranted suffering now inflicts upon you in his anger or simply because it is his nature.

Dorotea. Think no such thing, Celia. Men are never more incapable of offending us than when they are wronged. When they are satisfied we love them, their self-assurance returns.

Celia. Oh, yes, of course, that's what Seville is meant for. That's what they say about the beauty of its women with their come-hitherish mouths and teeth so flashing that, just as pearls are brought to Spain from the New World, so they could be sending pearls back overseas. And, as for the Guadalquivir, it cannot help but be the river of oblivion. Remember that into it flows the Guadalete, that river in the "Star of Venus" ballad. Why, when I asked Julio what this river was which people sang about even more than our Manzanares, he told me that was where the ancients located Lethe. *Lete,* you see, is Lethe, while *guada* means river in Arabic, as in Guadarrama, Guadalquivir, Guadalajara. And then all the stories they tell about its boats, with orange boughs for awnings, floating across to Triana and the shrine of Nuestra Señora de los Remedios.

Dorotea. May God never give you any remedy, silly girl! What remedy is there for me, when my love might speak those famous lines:

For now my misery has reached

the final stage of suffering.

Celia. There, that's all Don Fernando has left you: a few lines of verse, some marginal notes, and the newfangled words used by people who pride themselves on speaking like no one else.

Dorotea. Is there greater treasure for a woman than to find herself made immortal? Since beauty comes to an end and no one seeing her thereafter believes she ever possessed it, the verse in praise of her bears eternal testimony, living on in her name. Montemayor's

Diana was a lady from Valencia de Don Juan, close to León. And with the Ezla, her river, she will be immortal, thanks to his pen. The same is true of Montalvo's Phyllida, Cervantes' Galatea, Garcilaso's Camilla, the Violante of Camoëns, the Sylvia of Bernardes, the Phyllis of Figueroa, the Leonor of Corte-Real. Love is no mere daisy for cattle to crop. It requires subtlety of mind, abhors ulterior motives, walks naked, is not for base folk. Even after her death, Petrarch loved and celebrated his beautiful Laura. Fernando loved me in Madrid and will love me in Seville. And should he forget, my soul will go forth to remind him.

Celia. Madam, I desire only to entertain you. Do not look for hidden meanings in this brief canvas of Seville I have sketched and brought to life for you. Did you think the Betis was like our Manzanares, a river all sand and gallstones, which that famous Cordovan, Don Luis de Góngora, described as water made by one jackass in winter and drunk up by another in summer?

Dorotea. The Manzanares makes no claim to depth; it is like a courtier's wit, all glitter and clamor along its banks, but harmlessly shallow. It's not treacherous as other rivers are, exacting thirty drownings every summer, like that Minotaur who devoured youths and maidens. And any one of its St. John's Eves, with vervain, poplar, and mint, is worth all the days you speak of with their boats decked in orange boughs. Besides, if silver ships ascend the Betis to the Gold Tower, pearl and diamond coaches go up the Manzanares in the glitter of a thousand lovely women, whose persons are the appointed destination of all the New World produces.

Celia. Yes, but how can you not reprove the Manzanares when, at its lowliest in summer, it admits droves of all sorts of men and women like a Valley of Jehoshaphat? The license of this Court city—oh the pity of it—so often decried by those who value modesty in women, and in men, the shielding of it from public gaze. Liñán de Riaza, the distinguished wit, referring to the clothes the river washes, wrote that the Manzanares was

Rich in print of foot,
but in water sorely lacking.

But there was more sting in what another poet said:
Not all those standing in the water
are denuded poplar trees.

Dorotea. Leave me, Celia, go and do your sewing. I'd rather be alone than with one who puts caustic on my wounds to kill me.

Scene 3

MARFISA · CLARA
DOROTEA · CELIA

Marfisa. The door is open and that's the dais facing us.

Clara. This door lets you out the back way. The front door opens onto the next street, which runs parallel to this, but all the doors must be intended for quick escapes.

Marfisa. Ladies, might there be a spare jug of water for a woman arriving from the country and not in the best of health?

Dorotea. May God Himself bestow one on a demeanor so charming, a figure so fetching, attire so tidy, and face so lovely. Do come in and sit down to drink. You may then repose and, if you so desire, I shall send for a sedan chair to take you home.

Marfisa. Words entirely befitting the beauty of their speaker. Body matching soul as the cordial its fine-spun glass.

Celia. Here is one with water. How cool it is I cannot vouch for; cellars do not keep things cold nowadays.

Dorotea. Do not drink without eating something, or it will disagree with you. Bring some chocolate, Celia, or go see if there are any of those wafers left which my confessor sent me.

Marfisa. I am greatly in your debt; the water is all I want.

Dorotea. Do not drink so much at once.

Marfisa. It tastes good and loses nothing by the fragrance of the *búcaro.*

Dorotea. Take it with you, and some others, too, made of the selfsame earth.

Marfisa. So many favors! I'll take this one only because it comes from you. Here, girl; it's too large for my sleeve, where I would have carried it as a token of esteem, and if it were smaller, I'd wear it on my bosom.

Dorotea. You'd be giving more than you received, even if my gift were all gold.

Marfisa. As is everything else in your house. So tidy and spotless! This chamber's like a mother-of-pearl, with you the pearl inside it.

Dorotea. Since your entrance, it may well appear so.

Marfisa. Putting compliments aside, what lies behind that nun's habit of yours?

Dorotea. A vow.

Marfisa. Have you been indisposed?

Dorotea. Yes, most dangerously so.

Marfisa. One would not think it, to look at you. What was the trouble?

Dorotea. I was punished.

Marfisa. What for?

Dorotea. An act of boldness.

Marfisa. That sounds as if the trouble were love, as it surely must be in your case.

Dorotea. I spoke without thinking; then, thinking of what I had spoken, sought to take my life.

Marfisa. I seem to have heard that a certain Don Fernando killed some second gentleman at your door.

Dorotea. Who told you such a great lie? Why, he himself, no doubt.

Marfisa. I do not know him, but I do know a lady quite close to him to whom he said as much.

Dorotea. A lady quite close to him?

Marfisa. So she claims.

Dorotea. Celia.

Celia. Madam?

Dorotea. Did you hear that?

Celia. Someone must have deceived that lady.

Marfisa. That is always possible. Forgive my tactlessness if this gentleman means something to you, or perchance is lord over your house.

Dorotea. He means nothing to me and lords it over no one here, but I have a friend he has been deceiving and I am distressed on her account.

Marfisa. Deceiving in what way?

Dorotea. With courting and caressing, with passionate idolatries and clever little billets-doux and love poems, with all-night vigils at her door, with bursts of jealousy and tears.

Marfisa. Do men cry?

Dorotea. This one was so flattering he claimed that he had ceased to be a man; that, having turned into his lady, he'd yielded up his nature and could not be blamed for being tearful, any more than women are, for whom tears represent compassion, beauty, and a recompense—the inherited recompense for their imperfection.

Marfisa. If you were the reason for his tears, he needed no excuse. You are an angel, and now especially, with that white dress as your alb and the blue habit as your stole.

Dorotea. I was not the reason, never fear. Had I been, I'd not have given him grounds for leaving.

Marfisa. You mean he is not in Madrid?

Dorotea. He's gone off to Seville. But I must say your questions make me suspicious. If you come for information, why did you ask for water? By rights I should be the one to do so, since you are meting out the torture here.

Marfisa. I have not come to cause you any, nor do you merit it. I happened along and, since conversations between strangers take strange turns, misunderstandings such as this arise. But that should not surprise anyone who knows how customary it is among men, when one takes out his sword to show off its sharpness, for all those present to draw theirs. And so with us women: if one divulges confidences, the others must all unsheathe those they treasure most. You may be sure that never in my life have I seen Don Fernando.

Dorotea. Well, if you want to see him, you soon shall! Celia, hand me the little writing box with all the hocus-pocus in it. Don't let the word I use upset you. I am not a sorceress, really. I call it that because of the bagatelles inside—*that* word comes from an Italian gentleman who gave it to me in return for an instrument of mine he coveted.

Marfisa. You must have been the instrument yourself, because the box is the finest I've ever seen—and I myself have two very good ones.

Dorotea. After such praise, I should give it to you, but I cannot since I value it so highly.

Marfisa. What's inside this drawer?

Dorotea. Letters.

Marfisa. May I see the handwriting?

Dorotea. You're not jealous, are you?

Marfisa. I only asked thinking it was yours, so as to see your handwriting. If it matches your speech, it would be superb indeed, since you are so gifted in everything.

Dorotea. I am good at neither. This is the portrait.

Marfisa. Is this gentleman as young as that?

Dorotea. It was done when his beard was beginning to show. He has a mustache now, although rather sparse.

Marfisa. How good-looking!

Dorotea. He is not handsome, but by and large an attractive man.

Marfisa. Forgive my asking: how do you happen to possess the portrait if he himself is not yours?

Dorotea. As a token of Felipe's fine craft, which is prized by everyone.

Marfisa. Would you let me have it, since the sitter is of no importance to you?

Dorotea. Since you say you've never seen him, why do you want his portrait?

Marfisa. To see if it mattered to you.

Dorotea. At the outset I told you this writing box was full of hocus-pocus.

Marfisa. A plausible excuse.

Dorotea. Whereas you have none to ask it of me.

Marfisa. I've already told you why I was eager for your friendship, and would hope that from the start you'd keep nothing from me.

Dorotea. On the basis of what acquaintance do you seek such ready access to my private thoughts? The truth is, yours are showing, for all you're doing to conceal them.

Marfisa. I am acting for the friend I mentioned and it is her case I plead. Have you had letters from this gentleman?

Dorotea. You seem more intent on judging than on pleading. Take fewer liberties, for since I am still convalescing and you are dragging me uphill, I grow weary.

Marfisa. Is that a spinet?

Dorotea. It is a spinet.

Marfisa. Have you a harp as well?

Dorotea. If you play, I'd be pleased to listen.

Marfisa. My only accomplishment is wishing that I had some. Now that I am your friend, I shall come and listen to you play when you are stronger and in better humor.

Dorotea. The humor in which you leave me is such that I doubt I'll manage to oblige you.

Marfisa. It's not I but your indisposition that's to blame. Come, Clara, and mind you don't break the *búcaro*.

Clara. What a fine portrait of Don Fernando!

Marfisa. Would you expect anything else from such a painter? If only I could have taken it from her!

Clara. She's completely unhinged. How cleverly you managed it!

Marfisa. Jealousy is rarely very clever.

Dorotea. What do you say to this visit, Celia?

Celia. That she played false with us from the start.

Dorotea. Fernando—a lady friend! And especially one like that! I now see why he took so lightly what I said to him.

Celia. Then why did he leave in such a hurry?

Dorotea. He must have planned his journey ahead of time. So that was it, traitor! You may be sure, Celia, I had no impulse to give in, either to the overseas Spaniard or to his New World, until I learned of the present treachery from this lady's very lips.

Oh faithless man, deceiver, gentleman unworthy of the name! Ingrate, is this your way of treating a woman of my gifts who for your sake has renounced everything available to beauty, charm, and wit in this Court city? Is this how you repay my faithfulness, my surrender to you, my trials and tribulations at the hands of mother and relatives, the privations besetting me which I so honorably resisted and overcame? What Penelope was ever more besieged? What Lucretia more hard-pressed? What Portia more steadfast? And there was I, slaying myself for your sake with a diamond sword, since no impression could be made upon my strength by any death less potent! Repaying such a valiant spirit with treachery, were you? Filling your arms with other pleasures while my eyes filled with tears at the violence wrought by an indignant mother? Enough of such wrongs, love—enough. Today Fernando quits my bosom, like a spirit obedient to the conjuring of that woman. Obviously it's she, no doubt of it. Her words provide the evidence, her questions the confirmation. And the self-assurance of those words! Going so far as to ask for the portrait! I was wrong not to give it to her. No, better to give away the one in my heart, which my righteous truth and his criminal untruth will dislodge this very day.

The copy shall remain here and be held up to scorn and struck at a thousand times each day.

Celia. Simply with your lips, I fear.

Dorotea. Mine, Celia? I, put my lips to that? The day I do such a thing, may God glue them together.

Celia. On the card.

Dorotea. Yes, yes, how this jealousy does melt me! No, not jealousy at all, which comes from what's imagined, but from proven things. Just wait and see what happens. I'll prick his eyes out with a needle.

Celia. Your own will protest.

Dorotea. Then I shan't look at him.

Celia. Then how will you see where to prick him?

Dorotea. I'll call a painter and have a rope painted around his neck.

Celia. Poor Fernando! Remember, ropes are not for gentlemen. The way of executing men of birth is to slit their throats with a knife, because of its association with the sword, which noblemen profess. But do me a favor.

Dorotea. What is it?

Celia. Give him the opportunity to confess before killing him. Let him come here, and question him.

Dorotea. He'll tell a pack of lies. Come, come, give me the writing box again; today I am Julia holding aloft the Roman orator's head.

Celia. Was it you standing up for men before? 'The cock clawed the ground and a knife he found.'

Dorotea. I never thought I'd find one in such a handsome sheath.

Celia. Jealousy magnifies everything, which is why it is compared to eyeglasses.

Dorotea. Now, to my sorrow, I believe his praise of her.

Celia. To tell the truth, she's not so pretty, and for a lady, her complexion is a bit ruddy.

Dorotea. What does that matter if she's beautiful?

Celia. It's becoming in a wet nurse.

Dorotea. You are not saying what you really think.

Celia. I am not trying to comfort you. You've found your own consolation, that foreigner to whom you are ready to surrender your rebellious spirit.

Dorotea. No Spaniard is a foreigner, even if he lives in China.

Celia. As a man, he seems gross compared to that sensitive youth of yours who's gone off.

Dorotea. Indignation makes the impossible seem easy.

Celia. You must be imagining that with time Fernando's love has grown whiskers, of which our Don Bela is so fond he wears them crupper-fashion, one overlaying the other.

Dorotea. Certainly Don Bela is a good-looking man.

Celia. Don Fernando won't hear you say that nor can I tell him.

Dorotea. Write it to him, Celia.

Celia. What for? He'll say the same of the first lady he runs into.

Dorotea. Will he find a lady so quickly?

Celia. 'In Toledo, abbots for a song; and in Salamanca, for a farthing.'

Dorotea. There'll be someone to tell me.

Celia. Why, if you're to love Don Bela?

Dorotea. I have my reasons. I am saying I want them to return promptly and have Julio tell me all that happened while they were away from me.

Celia. I'll see to it he keeps mum about anything disturbing to you that Fernando may have done.

Dorotea. I'll find a way to make him tell.

Celia. Haven't you heard that proverb about bad judges? Well, commit this to memory.

Dorotea. How does it go?

Celia. 'Once the justice drinks it pure, taverners' wine is safe and sure.'

Dorotea. I don't care a whit about Don Fernando any more.

Celia. You seem to be out of your mind.

Dorotea. I am going over to the spinet for some diversion.

Celia. And I, to listen to you.

Dorotea.

> To the murmur of the rills
> 　　from flower to flower birds sing
> 　　of love, most heavenly thing,
> 　　and jealousy, hell's worst ill.
> In these delightful groves,
> 　　to the waters' melodies,
> 　　birds chant antiphonies
> 　　of jealousy and love.
> 　　As veins of ice relent,
> 　　their sweet crystal flow

makes music as they go,
on Nature's instrument.
To the murmur of the rills
from flower to flower birds sing
of love, most heavenly thing,
and jealousy, hell's worst ill.
Heavens of love reside
in every narcissus and pink;
but pansies and violets think
jealous thoughts, casting love aside.
Waves break on one another
along the water's strand,
and glimpsing fine-grained sand
beneath their crystal cover,
to the murmur of the rills
from flower to flower birds sing
of love, most heavenly thing,
and jealousy, hell's worst ill.
Streams that gossip and purl
of promises gainsaid
cast up pure silver thread,
webbing flowers with pearl.
All's jealousy, all's love,
and as love bids me weep
lost hour upon hour of sleep,
which jealous torments rob,
to the murmur of the rills
from flower to flower birds sing
of love, most heavenly thing,
and jealousy, hell's worst ill.

Scene 4

GERARDA · DOROTEA · CELIA

Gerarda. Peace be unto this house *et omnibus habitantibus in ea.*
Celia. From the Latin I can tell it's Gerarda. That old woman is the
very devil.

Dorotea. Mistress, welcome to you.

Gerarda. And to you, a fine life, my little angel, my bunch of posies, glass of fashion, treasure of tidiness, picture of comeliness.

Dorotea. All those compliments for me? Every one?

Gerarda. Well, what would you have me say, never having had a welcome from your lips? You always greet me with a different face, never the one God gave you—and what a face that is! His blessings on you! Here's to you—I'd like to be a fig tree with a thousand and one figs for you on every branch. Oh, what a girl—the apple of Cupid's eye! A girl to snatch his bow and give him two thousand lashes with it. Since he's always shown naked, you wouldn't have to pull his breeches down. What are you laughing at? He's only a little boy. Don't think he's a man like those great ruffians who go down to the river and stand there stark naked in front of everyone, looking for all the world like culprits lined up for a public lashing. When I had a husband, he never let me attend such diversions, and that lesson I've never forgotten. I go to the hospitals and take along my biscuits and little jug of wine. True, I sample it before going in to make sure it won't harm them if it's still green. Every time I hear that ballad sung that starts, "Love left me in the lurch," I think of our river in Madrid and all that goes on there in the month of July. They could easily charge an entrance fee to those baths; unchaste eyes wouldn't mind paying it.

Dorotea. Mistress, women can perfectly well find a private place where men will not be seen, or chastely avert their eyes when they go by.

Gerarda. Ah, child, I don't know what it is about the imagination: when we do not want to look, it always seems to tell us, "Now look at him, look at him!" Here are a few more figs to ward off the evil eye; however many I toss your way, your beauty still cries out for more. How elegant you look in that habit! Who would not become a friar to join such an order! Upon my word, if Cupid saw you, he'd never say what he told Venus when she proposed taking the veil in the Roman temple of the goddess Vesta: 'That'll be the day, Mother, the day when I turn friar.'

Dorotea. Gerarda dear, I am so unhappy.

Gerarda. Be still, you little ninny, mistrustful child, you who set the world on fire in that snow-white habit the blue scapular goes so well with—like the sky the astrologers depict, with the band of the zodiac across it. What do you suppose I brought you? Look, look at this lovely *búcaro!* Here's young Cupid; he's just your age, the cunning little lady-killer. Here, take it and whip him for the pain he's caused you. He well deserves it. But no, upon the soul of my confessor, you must give me something first.

Dorotea. How pretty it is!

Celia. Let me see, madam.

Dorotea. Let it be, Celia, you'll soil it. But what would you ask in return, Gerarda?

Gerarda. Simply that you take it. Say, "I take him."

Dorotea. Is this a marriage?

Gerarda. Well, I'll have you know I was given a thin silver bowl which left me none the thinner at lunch today, because it holds three pints—though, truth to tell, I'd already taken its measure.

Celia. That would make six, mistress.

Gerarda. 'I'll take you with me when heaven's beckoning, you're so good at final reckoning.' For you I requested shoes and stockings, and a watered silk cloak is being made, and some passementerie with gold thread, the likes of which Cleopatra never wore, she who ground pearls to drink Mark Antony's health, which shows you how silly the ancients were, since it would have made more sense to toast him with a salty rasher of bacon.

Celia. Mistress, there are no Garrovillas in Egypt for bacon to come from.

Gerarda. Come, come, don't be a donkey! Those who were led out of Egypt sighed for the stewpots they left behind, and there's no stew without pork in it.

Celia. If you stand on Holy Writ, who will contradict you?

Gerarda. In my day you had your Holy Scripture in the vernacular, and it was quite properly withdrawn, by pious decree. Because we women are such terrible chatterboxes and there are ignorant men aplenty.

Dorotea. And what makes you think I'll accept that cloak?

Gerarda. As I knew you'd take this *búcaro.*

Dorotea. The *búcaro* is but a toy. There's Love on it and, though the offended party, he hasn't told me not to take it.

Gerarda. Everything is going very well; clog and scissors did not deceive me. There is a difference in Dorotea today.

Dorotea. What are you mumbling about?

Gerarda. Your charms and years—how I envy them! What magnets you have in those eyes of yours, to attract desire and gold. And all the more now as they laugh at the thought of the cloak! There is no pedigree allowed women by Nature to equal beauty; it will draw the heart and *escudos* out of that overseas Spaniard. He has desk drawers full of them. To be honest, child, he gave me I don't know how many, which I won't show you because I have them put away for my funeral. They will be discovered together with my ashen habit. I am not touching them because the important thing, child, is to think of the end and to fear death. For a strict reckoning will be required of us by the Lord who can read our very minds, and there's not a single hair we won't have to answer for when we all meet in the Valley of Jehoshaphat.

Dorotea. How quickly you give way to tears!

Gerarda. Dorotea, I am a sinner, and I fear there'll be no place to hide on that dreadful day. As you are young, your mind is on your wardrobe; for, though they say that 'the young can die and the old cannot live,' the truth is that everything follows Nature's laws. And any old man who persuades himself that he can live longer than the youths he sees around him is a fool. For if that were the case, he would not have reached his present age.

Dorotea. What's the rustling in your sleeve, aunt?

Gerarda. A bit of paper that was on the magnificent gentleman's table. It looked like verse; and while it's true I prefer one small skin of Alaejos wine to Juan de Mena's three hundred stanzas, I stuck it in my sleeve on the chance it might be of use to you. Go ahead and read it to me.

Dorotea. "Recipe for putting a snooping husband to sleep."

Gerarda. That's not the one, child! Hand that over—I've mixed them up. This must be the one.

Dorotea. "Fabulous syrup for delivering a pregnant woman within nine months, after keeping everyone at home in the dark."

Gerarda. That's not it, either. I think it's this one.

Dorotea. "Prayer for St. John's Eve."

Gerarda. I do believe you're doing it on purpose.

Dorotea. I'm reading what you give me, aunt. You've got so many slips of paper in that sleeve, you need a table of contents to find any.

Gerarda. These two are the last. You see, this pouch belonged to a grandmother of mine; there are some scraps of Latin things in it, which would have had to do with her devotions.

Celia. Her powers have come down to you, Gerarda.

Gerarda. If only I were like her, what more could I ask? Sometimes she'd go into a trance for three days.

Celia. Awake, mother?

Gerarda. No, asleep.

Celia. Extraordinary powers indeed!

Dorotea. "Set of rules to guide a Spanish gentleman from the New World in this Court city.

"First, he shall put up in decent lodgings and see to it that no one knows the location.

"In all conversations he shall say that he is stopping with a friend.

"Under no circumstances shall he entertain anyone.

"He shall give his servants short rations.

"He shall act poor, and always tell how his silver went down with the galleons, or was seized by the Queen of England's navy.

"His menu, a hen every other day; his stewpot, enough to feed himself and two houseboys.

"He shall have no housekeeper; they're always prying and their tongues are never still.

"He shall form no close friendships with gentlemen, so as to avoid being asked for loans.

"When it comes to ladies, let him be free with words, but not risk pointless expenditures. He is not to fall in love; nothing was ever gained thereby in this Court city, and anyone deceives himself who thinks otherwise.

"The moment gossiping begins, he should say he has business elsewhere and be off.

"He is to be neat and decent in his attire, and should attempt to speak little, however hard that may be.

"He should not retire at night without having said or done something flattering where persons of influence are concerned (for such is the courtier's firm rule), nor should he arise without reflecting upon how to keep what he possesses.

"If he goes out on winter nights, the air of Madrid being harmful to the head, let him wear the cap with earflaps known as the Roman bonnet.

"And if he wishes to appear the gentleman, let him not pay what he owes, or at least put off paying until his creditor dies from sheer frustration."

Is this the man you are holding up to me, auntie? All a glazier needs is a cat to cavort through his glassware!

Gerarda. Look here, Dorotea; this set of rules was given him by one of those know-it-alls who go about with instructions for greenhorns, imposing on the innocent and dispatching bulletins and newsletters to every corner of the globe. They're the first to learn what time of day the Sultan died in Constantinople, when the post goes off to Cairo, what new scheme is afoot to make Madrid as large as Paris by joining Getafe to it, what the news is out of China, and other pointless particulars of that ilk.

Celia. Aunt, have you never thought up any scheme of your own?

Gerarda. A unique one, whereby a single soldier inside his stronghold might prevent the Dutch from landing in Florida or any other New World port.

Celia. A single soldier! How?

Gerarda. Listen to this, Celia: he would have one of those large jars filled with olive oil, and a syringe, and when he saw the Dutch coming ashore and marching up the beach, he would simply take oil and spray the first few. To avoid spotting their uniforms, they would doubtless withdraw, and warn the others of the oil barrage; whereupon all would reembark and sail for home.

Celia. You must have been athirst for lamp oil, to dream of it.

Gerarda. Read this other sheet, Dorotea; you can see it's all verse.

Dorotea.

>Thus Fabio sang
>>on Tagus banks,
>>to listening waters,
>>weeping nymphs.
>Lazy evening
>>in fleeting shadows
>>dropped from hills
>>in its own embrace.
>Vagrant birds
>>lay hushed in nests
>>as night supplanted
>>waning day.

Churning mill wheels
   splintered stillness
   with glassy disks,
   spokes of water.
Herding sheep,
   with whistling sling,
   he urged them on
   toward knotted folds.
Now Fabio lies
   alone and silent,
   sighing and wakeful,
   in his hut of thatch,
stirring and thinking
   thoughts past doubting,
   past dying, dead—
   though memory lives.
The tears of dawn
   woke the spice-pinks,
   who saw her pearls,
   thought them laughter.
Plucking his lyre,
   this song he sang
   to listening rocks,
   rebounding echoes:
"Amaryllis, to love
   any beauty of yours,
   any wit and grace,
   I shan't call love.
Love decrees
   what's right and fair:
   to love you for
   your soul alone.
My eyes, in loving,
   ask no return—
   yielding to yours
   is but their duty.
Hope by hope, I watched
   all hope depart;

now hopeless love
makes me unique.
Desire for beauty,
I've been told,
is the source of love—
frightening thought!
As you are beauteous,
the rule is nought;
love and desire
merge as one.
That such effects
are wrought by beauty
may seem unlikely—
but the soul says no.
To deny you beauty
would be wrong—
but not to desire you
seems more wrong.
This firm commitment
the soul has made:
subdue desire,
love your true worth.
To merit your love
(if I am favored)
I keep all fancy
reined in tight.
My soul declines
all thought of loving
with imperfect love
a being so perfect.
Which is why this song,
Amaryllis, transmutes
the pangs of love,
and so refines it:
'I ask you no favor
for this pain—
to be its cause
is favor enough.'

Such is the love
    my love requires:
    never to think
    of love in return.
    Thus passion itself
    uniquely finds
    its own reward
    in loving you:
    'your being its cause
    is favor enough.' "

Gerarda. What have you to say to that?

Dorotea. I am impressed.

Gerarda. You may be sure that our Don Bela is not one of those poets who belong to a clique. He stands on his own.

Dorotea. He belongs to you, mistress. This acquaintanceship is not like an order of friars, where everything is held in common.

Gerarda. That was not my meaning. It was his wit I was praising. Minds are like instruments, you know: they must be played on to display the harmonies they possess. And if yours, which is extraordinary, should play on this novice at Court (that's what newcomers here are called), you may be sure the hidden veins of gold would surface.

Celia. That would suit you, would it not?

Gerarda. I meant the gold of his mind.

Celia. And I, that of his coffers.

Dorotea. He makes a great show of being a chaste lover in this verse, but all men follow such a line. They begin by saying they desire to look; they look and say they desire to listen; they listen and say they want to bed down; by that time, since we haven't thrown them out at the start, we might as well believe them.

Gerarda. Dorotea, Dorotea, while young be as covetous as a crone. When you're old, no one will offer you what a girl is offered. Put aside all your mad thoughts and think of the cloak promised you. Why, I can see you wearing it now, like Don John of Austria glittering in his armor at the naval battle, surrounded by all those bold captains that brought their nation so much honor.

Celia. Strange, this old woman. Listen to the non sequiturs she strings together.

Gerarda. Those were the days when doughty swords were needed for stalwart hands, not shameless curling irons for perfumed heads and beards.

Dorotea. Mistress, try to set the world aright, and you will lose your friends. Fashion cannot emasculate a Spaniard, for his manliness of soul is innate. But tell me, were you at the naval battle?

Gerarda. Promise you won't tell a soul? Three of us girls went there, for the fun of it.

Celia. Airborne or in a coach?

Gerarda. We always have a few tricks up our sleeve.

Celia. Then how did you go?

Gerarda. Some captains took us with them.

Celia. With claws on their feet?

Gerarda. What do you mean by claws, Celia?

Celia. Only that you must have been a young hen, to go riding with the rooster.

Gerarda. Ah, and what a young hen! In all of Italy there was not another Spanish girl as lively.

Celia. And from what vantage point did you view the battle? What window did you rent? Or did you jump about from topsail to topsail, like St. Elmo's fire?

Gerarda. That St. Elmo's fire is a little star, bright as a diamond.

Celia. Gerarda, I'll wager Uchalí and Redbeard were your boon companions in those days.

Gerarda. Are you making fun of me, Celia? Stop asking questions and see who's at the door. The timid knock makes it sound like a suitor.

Celia. Good Lord, madam. It's Don Bela.

Dorotea. That Spaniard from the New World?

Celia. The same.

Dorotea. Why, how dare he take such liberties? Say I am not at home.

Gerarda. Oh, child, such cruel treatment for a gentleman of such attainments!

Dorotea. Gerarda, it was you who concocted this call.

Gerarda. What are you asking? If he's brought the cloak and all? Why, certainly! As if he'd neglect to!

Dorotea. I'm simply saying the two of you are in collusion.

Gerarda. You ask if there's passementerie in profusion? As if there wouldn't be! And all shot through with gold an inch thick.

Dorotea. That's not what I said.

Gerarda. Alas, child, I am so gone in the ears with age! I put rabbit fat in them last night.

Celia. She hears well enough when she's given something.

Gerarda. Look here, Celia, I now behave as dogs do. When they see an outstretched hand, they come up to it, and when they see a hand raised, they retreat, knowing that one means bread and the other a beating. But, my precious, don't be discourteous and let a caller who has been knocking stand waiting in the street. This gentleman won't devour you the first time he sees you.

Dorotea. You'll make my mother scold if she finds him here when she returns.

Gerarda. I have her permission. Come in, Don Bela, come in; it's not a big step down. What are you afraid of? We're three women here, a hundred and twenty-five years all told, and by myself I account for eighty.

Scene 5

DON BELA · LAURENCIO
GERARDA · DOROTEA · CELIA

Bela. Don't pull at my cape, Mistress Gerarda; a person coming of his own free will needs no coercing. God preserve such beauty as evidence of His power, however many lives it may cost.

Dorotea. Bring a chair, Celia.

Bela. Don't leave the dais, Mistress Dorotea. I am not so exalted as to merit your leaving the platform. Go back to your cushion.

Dorotea. Only when you are seated. And do forgive my not venturing further forward; your coming has so taken me by surprise that my heart can find no way to regain repose.

Bela. As long as it is yours, it will be restless, wondering who may be worthy to receive it.

Dorotea. I should hope it would always be mine.

Bela. The heart has portals through which it risks being stolen.

Dorotea. Even if it has, a guard will keep it secure.

Bela. Eyes have no guards.

Dorotea. Indeed they do, and many—such as virtue, modesty, and the duty to one's honor.

Bela. By the time such guards have moved from heart to eyes, the observing will already have taken place. That shepherd in Ovid had one hundred eyes and Mercury put them all to sleep with his spellbinding music. That is why peacocks, on whose feathers Juno set them, now spread their tails as if beseeching the eyes to stay awake, and if they hear singing, grow alarmed, thinking someone is coming to kill them.

Dorotea. With you at any rate, there would be no reason to guard the eyes, since you could easily steal any heart through the ears.

Bela. My mind could never attain such bliss as to find your attention favorably inclined to the music of my words.

Gerarda. May I be permitted to step in, though I'm bound to get the worst of it? Peace, gentlefolk; let us assume you are in agreement. Now what is Laurencio toting in? He has a heavier load than a convent jackass.

Bela. Only a small bolt of cloth and some passementerie.

Gerarda. Open it up, open it and let us see—unwrap yourself. How snarled up you are! This cloth is harder to pull from your arms than from a tradesman's shop. What a lovely thing! Is this Milanese cloth? Blessed be the hands that fashioned you.

Dorotea. It *is* exquisite.

Gerarda. Were more flowers ever seen in a meadow painted by springtime or imitated by a poet?

Dorotea. The green goes so well with the mother-of-pearl in these rose carnations.

Bela. If only two hearts' desires were matched as well as these two colors are.

Dorotea. The green is hope and the incarnadine, cruelty.

Bela. Cruelty is evidently your color, and hope is mine. But who can ever make them match if they are contraries?

Dorotea. Contraries, yes, but not enemies.

Bela. Well spoken, for enmity is one thing and contrast another.

Dorotea. Another thing about such hope: it's enameled with flowers, which hold out more than a promise of fruition.

Gerarda. You could not have said anything more fitting.

Dorotea. Just a moment, Gerarda. Almond trees that bloom out of season are often lost.

Gerarda. You've gone and spoiled everything, my child. You should have said: since blossoming may be a matter of fine weather and not any boldness of the tree, to merit punishment by frost.

Bela. Since frost was always an inclemency of heaven, it is no great feat for the wind to strip bare a poor almond tree that trusts the sun and bursts into bloom. There would be more valor in stripping a hardy mulberry.

Dorotea. They call the mulberry wise, because of all trees it blooms the latest.

Bela. I would call it unfortunate to be so ill favored by the sun.

Dorotea. It is no misfortune to ensure the good which one aspires to.

Bela. That which comes late is not a good, since hope long deferred may turn into despair.

Dorotea. Hope has merit only insofar as it is long-suffering, and to possess none is so gallant an effect of love that for some time now the very word has been banished from the great houses.

Bela. I have always held Platonic love to be a snare and a delusion, wholly unfair to nature. Why, the world could have come to an end. Plato calls him a poor lover who loves the body more than the soul, on the ground that he loves something impermanent. Since beauty fails or withers with age and sickness, it follows that love must fail or decline, which would not happen were it love of the soul.

Celia. Now the pompous bore drags Plato into it! He's heard that Dorotea is mad to be thought learned.

Bela. To which argument I reply that if the body's beauty is the visible part through which the invisible makes itself known, the love of each part deserves indulging, the former by caresses, the latter by way of the ear.

Celia. I have always heard that these overseas Spaniards talk a great deal, though that has its good side since the climate produces rare and subtle wits. But what's Plato got to do with this except to put a silver plate in front of Dorotea?

Bela. Pray, what is your response?

Dorotea. I am most sad.

Bela. In Greece something took hold of the maidens so that they were all doing away with themselves. So Plutarch writes.

Celia. Another philosopher!

Bela. To put a stop to it, the Senate decreed that any woman who had killed herself was to be exhibited stark naked in the marketplace and kept exposed all day to public view; thereupon the suicides ceased, to avoid the embarrassment of being seen by everyone.

Gerarda. (Poor old Gerarda—but these sophistries are her bread and butter!) Dear child, only glance at this passementerie, which the sun itself would deem fit to embellish the costumes of its planets.

Dorotea. It's more gaudy than tasteful.

Gerarda. You are even ungracious toward the passementerie because the sight of handiwork reminds you too much of hands. Has anyone asked for yours so far? And what a pair of hands for someone to ask for, to desire and to extol! As you are convalescing, you have left them unadorned. Don Bela, upon your life, lend her those two rings a moment; you'll see how they look against that snow.

Dorotea. Don't be such a ninny, Gerarda. Lord, and what a ninny you are! Please, sir, withdraw your hands.

Bela. Do not look upon these diamonds with disfavor—they bear some resemblance to you, after all. Allow me to place them on your fingers.

Gerarda. Stop dawdling, child. Why do you withdraw your fingers? Such discourtesy! Were you not born in this Court city?

Bela. They do not fit this finger—they go better here. Give me your other hand.

Dorotea. Honoring one hand is sufficient.

Bela. The other will complain if I do not treat it equally, and I desire that nothing in you complain of me.

Dorotea. I yield them up to your favor then, since I would not have Gerarda scold me.

Laurencio. He's faring nobly, this master of mine. He has fetched up between Scylla and Charybdis. These two women must be the riptide of the court. It's a perfect case of toilsome earning and reckless spending.

Bela. These rings are so becoming on you. On your hands the diamonds look like stars.

Dorotea. Well said, since the hands are night.

Bela. Night, madam! Were the hands of dawn ever so crystalline? I must confess I never thought I'd see stars out at noon until I glimpsed these diamonds on your hands.

Dorotea. I have kept them on long enough—ample time for you to see the hands adorned. Take back your rings.

Bela. Oh, that slight is undeserved! Do not remove them, fair Dorotea, for no hands in the world would be so bold as to wear rings that had touched your own. Nor would the rings allow it; for Alexander's horse, Bucephalus, would let no one mount him but his master.

Laurencio. Ah, if only women were like that! But would any dumb animal have spoken as my master has? What does Alexander's horse have to do with Dorotea's diamonds? It reminds me of what some writer says—that the flesh is like the Cid Ruy Díaz; that actually appears in print.

Celia. That's the sort of thing they put in print.

Laurencio. And not the sort of thing that sells at all badly.

Celia. What everybody can understand, anyone will buy.

Laurencio. If a person fails to make himself understood, why write? If it's intended for the learned, they have no need to learn what he happens to know.

Celia. There's always more to know than one man can know.

Laurencio. Right you are, and take my word for it: as there's an infinite amount to learn, and life is short, the most learned man knows next to nothing.

Celia. Has this master of yours ever studied anything?

Laurencio. Enough to show off what he knows, like the bachelor of arts—the worst breed of courtier to deal with. Because if he talks with men of learning, they can see how much he doesn't know and they lose patience with him for thinking himself learned. If he converses with the ignorant, they shun him because, holding them in low esteem, he looks down on them. In any case, this business of lecturing is for the classroom, not for chitchat.

Celia. You acknowledge this and still eat his bread?

Laurencio. As he eats up my service.

Celia. What you imagine is behind this affair with Dorotea is irksome to you, isn't it? We servants all are jealous, and the more so the more loyally we serve.

Laurencio. It's not his love makes me jealous; it's his money.

Celia. I shouldn't think he needed a counselor; he's stingy enough, hailing as he does from across the seas.

Laurencio. My master is extremely bounteous.

Celia. Oh, we've seen the set of rules he intended to follow in this Court city.

Laurencio. Mother Sponge will have put you onto them. She has already sucked the rings off him, and I fear his breeches come next.

Celia. Don't be so grumpy, silly.

Laurencio. And you keep your hands off me, know-it-all.

Celia. Don't you appreciate a love pat?

Laurencio. Only ladyfriends and barbers have the right to fiddle with my face.

Celia. How do you know I don't want to be your ladyfriend?

Laurencio. If I don't know, what makes you think you can be?

Celia. Did you bring much silver with you?

Laurencio. If you have read the set of rules, how is it you don't know we're expected to act poor?

Dorotea. Be good enough to take back the rings, sir.

Bela. I do not take back what I have given. That is the trouble with the ocean, among other things: it takes back the rivers that once came out of it.

Dorotea. If in days of yore rings were considered prisons, my hands now become prisoners of your munificence.

Bela. How could they be prisoners of one whose liberty rests in them? But let me give them a thousand kisses for a favor so huge I can do it justice only by going mad with joy. Bring on the stockings, Laurencio. There are only a few pairs because Gerarda did not tell me which color most entertains the favor of your taste.

Dorotea. The mother-of-pearl are superb.

Gerarda. The color leaps to the eyes.

Dorotea. Not the eyes but the taste; a better color for the eyes is green, which preserves the eyesight.

Laurencio. What dreadful pedantry!

Gerarda. They'll go better with the long cloak.

Dorotea. Nonsense, nothing can go better with what stays unseen.

Laurencio. Some damsel we have here! This art of loving puts Ovid's to shame. Don Bela's gone mad, indeed.

Celia. These white ones are very pretty.

Gerarda. Not for ladies—they make legs look like a corpse's. Ever since John of the White Hose, they have infringed the standards of good taste.

Celia. Yes, but they do plump out the legs.

Gerarda. For those that need plumping, not for this girl, who has no need to purchase any; not cotton but bountiful nature has been her plumper.

Dorotea. We might have done without these purple ones.

Gerarda. They'd look good on a bishop.

Dorotea. And these golden ones, aunt?

Celia. For a soldier of the Royal Guard.

Gerarda. You take them, Laurencio.

Laurencio. I'm off guard-duty by now.

Gerarda. These nice purple ones will be for me, since no one else wants them.

Bela. I did not bring shoes, as they had none small enough, nor should feet be shod in shops, which only the sun should shoe.

Laurencio. Now the sun has shoe soles. What exquisite idiocy!

Gerarda. Only a touch of amber is required for her slippers; indeed, the madonna lily would go best on such a foot.

Laurencio. Says the old hag! And the girl will still wear regular size thirteen, like anyone else, giants notwithstanding.

Bela. Do you mean you've seen the lady Dorotea's foot?

Gerarda. What a question! These are the very arms that raised her. There is no better witness to her perfections than I. Believe me— though this may make her blush—in my time she has had a few spankings from these hands. But, Don Bela, sir, what about this poor old woman? Has she not been provided for as well? Are loyal retainers not to be included?

Bela. A black woolen nun's cloth is on its way to your house. And the long cloak was bought ready-made because that is what you wanted.

Gerarda. I wager you forgot the ornamentation.

Bela. I am not so neglectful of my friends. Three embossings of gilt velvet adorn it.

Gerarda. You guessed my color. A clever man thinks of everything! You thank him, little dear; it's because of you that this most open-handed prince has clothed me. May the merciful hand of God clothe him. What a great work of charity it is to clothe the naked!

Laurencio. And likewise give counsel where it's called for.

Gerarda. What a fine and full and meritorious account shall be yours on Judgment Day when this nun's habit and this cloak are weighed in the balance! Nor shall I leave my Don Bela unaccounted for. I promise henceforth to say a rosary each day for him and for the souls of his dear departed, being so particularly devoted as I am to the purgation of souls.

Laurencio. Of purses, you mean.

Bela. Lovely Dorotea, as soon as I entered I noticed that harp. I'm told that among your many graces are singing and playing. Do not be disobliged if I beseech you to favor me with some lines of whatever your pleasure may dictate.

Dorotea. The one thing about being a musician I shall not do is ask indulgence for all my deficiencies. Give me that harp, Celia. Why the sour look?

Gerarda. There is good reason for it. She has not been given any stockings.

Celia. Am I an orphan?

Dorotea. Take these white ones.

Celia. I thank you for the thought, not the stockings.

Bela. You deign to honor me in so many ways! How those strings enhance your hands!

Gerarda. Like the diamonds they wear, sparkling in all directions!

Laurencio. And pitching us penniless into the dark.

Dorotea. Forgive the tuning—governing this commonwealth of strings is such a task.

Bela. Two sets of strings make the chromatics easier.

Dorotea. You must know music.

Bela. I *am* fond of it.

Dorotea.

> Abindarráez, prisoner
>> of Antequera's warden,
>> in his cell lay pining,
>> and there lay sighing.
> Don Rodrigo asks him
>> the cause of all his sorrow;

        after all, misfortune
        tests a strong man's valor.
    Ah my good Narváez,
        if my grief's sole cause
        were being taken captive
        and your defeating me,
    I'd put aside misfortune,
        since to be Abencerraje
        is far less noble,
        than to be your slave.
    Today I'm twenty-two,
        and all these years one lady
        has been for me the soul
        to give my senses life:
    Jarifa, born with me—
        you must know her well,
        since your sword's renown
        is her beauty's peer.
    To say I'm twenty-two
        is trifling; before our birth
        Nature bade me love her
        as a pure idea.
    To say the stars stood sponsor
        to this love offends
        the heavens; it took no star
        to draw me to her beauty.
Bela. Eight excellent lines! Who wrote this ballad?
Dorotea. A gentleman residing in Seville at present.
Bela. What is his name?
Dorotea. Listen to the rest of it.
    Raised as brother and sister,
        how could we be lovers?
        Neither hope nor patience
        ever would avail.
    Separated once,
        the error came to light,
        though one hour's absence
        always proved tormenting.

By letter we agreed
  I should come this night.
  I donned these wedding clothes,
  I was not armed for battle.
When you approached, Rodrigo,
  you heard the happy song
  I sang to my fortune,
  not thinking it could change.
I resisted all I could
  but how can any man
  oppose what fortune wills?
  I'm captive, and she waits.
There's many a slip, they say,
  between the cup and lip.
  Longing for her arms,
  I'm held in Antequera.
The sympathetic warden,
  hearing this tale of love,
  freely gave his blessing
  and sped him to Jarifa.
The Moor told his story
  as the dawn was breaking,
  for stories are unwelcome
  when love is in the making.

Bela. Ah, too happy Moor! For such he is to this hour, in having his happiness sung by that celestial voice, which has abstracted me from myself all this while.

Gerarda. Did you notice that *abstracted,* Dorotea? Didn't I tell you how clever he was?

Dorotea. Mistress, the life I lead is so solitary and sheltered, I shall ever be ignorant. Don Bela has seen a great deal of the world.

Bela. Yes, but nothing in it to equal you.

Dorotea. Here, Celia, take the harp. That response places me under too great an obligation.

Gerarda. No, child, upon your life, do not be so quick to put it aside. Don Bela, do beg her to sing something else. If you had anything to oblige her with, you would already have repaid her for the pleasure she has bestowed upon you. She is not often so free

with her talents. But your kindness merits all this, and much
more.

Bela. I could offer her this wedding of the ruby and the diamond.

Gerarda. 'Not everyone has the guile to wheedle.'

Laurencio. Oh, the wily crone!

Dorotea.

> A gentle stream once flowed
>   at dawn, between two valleys;
>   the valleys took pearls as bond
>   and lent it emeralds.
> White blooms and red
>   bathing by its banks
>   were narcissi repeated
>   in watery reflection.
> Field flowers mirrored
>   dawn's retreating colors:
>   jealous flags, her blue eyes;
>   white jasmine, her hands.
> In green bows decked,
>   roses pink and white
>   gave envy its revenge:
>   beauty one day long.
> The birds left off swooping,
>   imagining the water,
>   dazzling in the sun,
>   had turned to sheets of silver.
> Meanwhile our Lisardo
>   came forth from his cabin;
>   how could he be sad
>   in such a world of joy?
> His cattle before him
>   on trails still wet with dew,
>   browsing along, lapped ice
>   for food, and frost for drink.
> Then stepping toward him came
>   the cause of all his sadness,
>   lovely as herself alone—
>   for she's beyond compare.

She reads a little ditty
   Lisardo wrote one day,
   moved more by love than hope,
   on the stars in her eyes.
Seeing his wonderment,
   she unties purple ribbons,
   taking instrument in hand
   to flatter him to death.
From two strings of pearl
   framed by two carnations,
   she sang to the gentle breeze,
   repeating these words:
"Oh Mother, those two eyes
   so lovely, gay, and green—
   I'll die if I can't have them,
   yet they do naught but tease!"

Gerarda. Only from you would I put up with a ditty beginning with "Mother," because after all you do have one and you are still young—but not from one of that bewhiskered company who start out with: "Oh Mother mine—my locks ..." Though men nowadays may be better able to say it than women.

Dorotea.

"In their skies her pupils
   undergo a change
   from the green of hope
   to blue of jealousy.
Mother, in those eyes
   I read my life and death.
Oh Mother, those two eyes
   so lovely, gay, and green—
   I'll die if I can't have them,
   yet they do naught but tease."

Bela. What a delightful refrain! Who wrote the melody?

Gerarda. The person singing it. Is that a question to ask?

Bela. Oh, how wrong of me to ask! One whom heaven has endowed with so many talents could not be lacking in any skill.

Gerarda. Why, should you ever see her set hands to a spinet, you'd think a crystal spider was running over the keys. And when it comes to writing script, she can copy royal grants, and as for speed, she'll take down sermons verbatim.

Dorotea.

> Who'd ever think that green
>   would play so false with me,
>   yet who'd not be mistrustful,
>   if he were free of love?
>   "Mother, I'm lost in them,
>   in them I must be found.
>   Oh Mother, those two eyes,
>   so lovely, gay, and green—
>   I'll die if I can't have them
>   yet they do naught but tease."

Bela. It's excellent, but I'll take the Moor.

Dorotea. Why so, Don Bela?

Bela. Because once you bring in shepherds, everything is always murmuring streams and riverbanks; and they're forever singing, or their shepherdesses are. I'd like for once to see a shepherd sitting on a bench, and not perpetually perched on a rock or beside some fountain.

Gerarda. Gracious, how amusing!

Bela. Although it *is* true that Theocritus and Virgil—one Greek, the other Latin—wrote bucolics.

Gerarda. Didn't I tell you, child? See the learning that goes with the fine figure he cuts. With such a mind he might easily have been ugly.

Bela. Do be good enough to let me have the Abindarráez ballad. I should like to see your handwriting.

Dorotea. I'll do as you request, and will oblige you by singing it another time. Perhaps it won't appeal to you as much.

Bela. What are you doing, mother? Why are you fumbling about in my pockets?

Gerarda. Seeing you in such transports over Dorotea's voice, I thought I'd play a trick on you.

Bela. As well you might, for I was in ecstasy, listening to Orpheus himself.

Laurencio. As anyone would know, seeing how he draws the wild beasts after him.

Bela. Oh happy Moor—happier being celebrated by lips of yours than for being allowed by the generous warden to return to his Jarifa! That was subtle of the poet to say that Abindarráez already loved her before he was born, in Nature's ideal imagination.

Dorotea. Poets are overreachers. All their stock in trade consists of things impossible.

Bela. And of high-minded maxims when they write of serious things. I'd like to appropriate that conceit and say I loved you before I had any being.

Dorotea. If you do, I'll think your love is all poetical.

Laurencio. It will soon be historical, and I pray God it be not tragical.

Dorotea. My mother is knocking at the front door. Go out this way; and you, remove all this, so she won't see it. Otherwise I'll have no way of meeting you again.

Bela. And when shall that be, dear madam?

Dorotea. Gerarda will let you know. Now I cannot.

Gerarda. This overseas Spaniard does have a way with him.

Celia. When it comes to giving you his fortune.

Dorotea. So it seems. I've taken more than I expected.

Gerarda. Think of all you're going to take. This much you already have.

Scene 6

TEODORA · DOROTEA

GERARDA · CELIA

Teodora. What were you doing, Dorotea?

Dorotea. I was here with Gerarda.

Teodora. With Gerarda? Miracle!

Dorotea. A miracle? Why?

Teodora. Because I have never found you very eager for her company.

Gerarda. I was telling her that in my nuns' distribution of saints for this year, I had been assigned St. Agnes, and was moved to tears by her martyrdom, and I was telling Dorotea the story of her life. Where have you been?

Teodora. Visiting a friend in labor.

Gerarda. Why didn't you take me along? I could have placed the rose
   of Jericho on her, and my pouch of saints' relics.
Teodora. She already has given birth to a dream of a baby girl. But the
   child doesn't look like its father.
Gerarda. The woman must have been thinking of someone else. Not
   everything that happens has to be someone's fault.
Teodora. She had a mole exactly like one I've seen on a friend of her
   husband's.
Gerarda. What did I tell you? She could have been looking at him
   that day and the image took effect. That woman is as innocent as I,
   and my every errand today has been in pursuit of my devotions.
Dorotea. Mother, your cloak is covered with mud.
Teodora. One of those gentlemen who go around staring the soot off
   the windows spattered me. Give it a good sunning in the garden,
   Celia.
Dorotea. Something is always happening to you when you go out.
Teodora. The other day I stumbled into a cellar.
Dorotea. Why not support yourself with a cane?
Teodora. Because you are the support of my old age and you refuse to
   walk with me.
Dorotea. You walk so slowly.
Gerarda. You seem tired, Teodora. Ask for a little nip of something, if
   you are still sore from the other day.
Celia. 'You ask first, so I can slake my thirst.'
Dorotea. Mother, it would be best to have Gerarda stay for dinner.
Teodora. What has come over you?
Gerarda. God reward you, child. My stew can wait until tonight. The
   truth is, in my haste to go to Mass, I forgot to put in the chickpeas.
Teodora. Oh! What is this *búcaro* doing here?
Dorotea. I obtained it from a woman friend in exchange for that cloak
   you claimed I had sold, and out of pique I didn't show it to you.
Teodora. Although I spoke to you that way, Dorotea, I'm well aware
   you are a decent and virtuous young woman. What a lovely *búcaro!*
Gerarda. If you start talking about this girl's virtue, you could go on
   endlessly. If this were the age of myth, she would be stone by now,
   like Anaxarete.
Celia. Here's the food.
Teodora. Be seated, Gerarda.
Gerarda. I shall be your chaplainess. *Benedicite . . .*

Dorotea. Dominus . . .

Gerarda. . . . *nos et ea que comituri somos, benedicat Deus in corporibus nostros.*

Teodora. Less fruit, Dorotea—you're still convalescing. Leave the grapes alone.

Dorotea. What harm will they do me? I'm all well again.

Teodora. Have some of these figs, Gerarda.

Gerarda. I shall take one for your sake, though I wouldn't do it for my own father. But you must understand that every fig requires three drinks.

Teodora. Who wrote that?

Gerarda. The philosopher Alaejos. You didn't think it was Plutarch, did you? First I split it open. Now, pour me the first one, Celia.

Teodora. You drink without eating it?

Gerarda. Now I put a little salt on it. Pour me the second.

Teodora. That makes two. What comes next?

Gerarda. Closing it up. Now pour me the third.

Celia. Drink, and good health to you. Mind you, though, it's strong.

Gerarda. 'Not as strong as Samson, and love conquered him.' Blessings on your vintner.

Teodora. You throw the fig out the window after such elaborate preparations?

Gerarda. You think I'd let it go down inside me? Such joy it will never know.

Teodora. Don't touch the bacon, Dorotea. Eat your chicken; you're not well enough for such things.

Dorotea. Must I give up everything? Chicken, chicken! Even chestnuts in Lent would be less of a bore.

Gerarda. Oh what lovely bacon! Fill my glass, Celia; you're neglecting me. And truly I do not deserve it of you because, while you go about your work, not even thinking of me, I am studying my nominative cases so as to denominate your husband to be. And on St. John's Eve I saw great things in a glass urinal. And believe me, anyone abroad at such a time was not just larking about. "Your husband will come from La Montaña," quoth the Hornèd One.

Celia. One of those water vendors, you mean?

Gerarda. What do you expect? That he'll have ancestral acres, keep his own regiment for the King's service? Fill my glass, I'm parched.

Celia. So soon, aunt?

Gerarda. You call that soon? That's a good one, I swear. 'Take a little and see how little little is.'

Teodora. Take some of that hen, child.

Dorotea. I can't; boiled hen turns my stomach.

Gerarda. Eat up, Dorotea; 'a toothless head revives the dead.'

Dorotea. And whose head are you calling toothless?

Gerarda. The hen fowl's, child; they make you nice and plump.

Celia. When the old girl spouts proverbs, she's feeling no pain.

Teodora. You have the right idea, Gerarda—talk and eat.

Gerarda. 'Give me a child not loath to eat and suckle both.'

Celia. There goes another proverb. How flushed the old girl is! Lit up like a strawberry tree and her nose like a carrot!

Gerarda. My Nuflo Rodríguez, when I start to think of him at table . . . How he did go on! What jokes! What stories! It was from him I learned the prayers I know. He was a real lamb, he would never in his life hurt a flea. When they made a spectacle of him and lashed him in public, it was because he was entirely too honorable ever to tell who took the Canon's plate. I can see him right now on the Calle Mayor. That face of his as he rode along on the donkey! You'd have sworn he was riding to his wedding. And since his beard was so handsome, it added much to his aplomb as he spurred the sluggish beast along. I had reminded him above all not to forget the spurs.

Teodora. Gerarda, don't drink any more, and curb your tongue. Anywhere else people might take you at your word. What are the tears for?

Gerarda. Because it was sheer cruelty packing him off to the galleys.

Celia. You call that curbing the tongue?

Gerarda. God ordains that truth be told.

Teodora. Not at the expense of someone else.

Gerarda. What's the harm in singing his praises, Teodora, or in refreshing memories of good things past?

Celia. You mean, in refreshing good drink downed.

Gerarda. The first time he caught me at that prank with the student he was wonderfully forbearing. It was wintertime and he threw a pitcher of water over both of us in bed, saying with that kindliness he was so proud of, "Scoundrels must be soaked."

Teodora. There, Dorotea, now you see the ill effects of wine.

Dorotea. Entrusting your secrets to it—that's the first ill effect.

Teodora. Oh, most infamous vice, no less contrary to honor than detestable to temperance!

Dorotea. With every swallow a secret dribbles out.

Teodora. Wine remembers being trampled, so it flees the feet and goes straight to the head.

Celia. Why are you motioning to me, aunt?

Gerarda. So you'll ask me why, ninny! How much do you wager I'll have to rise, since you don't take my meaning?

Celia. A mosquito's fallen in.

Gerarda. Never fear, it won't crack its skull. Don't take it out, Celia; they are the spirits of this liquid, like atoms of the air. Wine sires them and no one has ever found his offspring ugly. 'And when you give your master wine, don't hold it in the light.'

Celia. 'Willy-nilly, the donkey must go to the fair.'

Gerarda. 'Weigh it fast, I'll take the quarter for the half.'

Celia. 'The cup is brimming full, it's not a sack of wool.'

Gerarda. Wine is old folk's milk. I don't know who said it. Either Cicero or the Bishop of Mondoñedo. Oh, my good old Nuflo Rodríguez!

Teodora. There she goes again.

Gerarda. He never minded mosquitoes. You should have seen him, he would just slurp down whatever came along. He considered water gross, because it bred frogs. And one of the ways he convinced me not to drink it, when I married him, was to tell me they would start singing in my belly. He put such fear in me that since then, praise God, I've never touched it. And for the time that's left me now, I'll manage with His help to avoid that risk with ease.

Celia. Watch out, aunt, you're falling asleep.

Gerarda. 'It's the same old trouble I beweep—once I'm full I fall asleep.'

Celia. 'Since you know the trouble, avoid the cause.'

Gerarda. 'The knife that cuts my bread cuts my finger too.'

Celia. 'Needlepoint or saddlebag, it's all a matter of stitches.'

Gerarda. The first time I left my Nuflo, I was not gone five months from his house. I can still remember how delightfully he received me when I returned: "Madame, I suppose, was expecting me to come after her?"

Teodora. Mother Gerarda, eat more and drink less; you're over-toasting yourself with the salt of your wit.

Dorotea. I am sorry now you ever invited her.

Gerarda. Ah, Dorotea! As you're a girl you have no need of wine, nor any idea of its virtues.

Dorotea. Now you'll start to chronicle them, I suppose.

Gerarda. My physician once told me that wine that's more than four years old is warm and dry to the third degree.

Dorotea. What do you call degrees, aunt?

Gerarda. Child, all the things one has to learn to get along in this world! I'd say degrees are something like quantities. Anyway, the older the wine, the warmer it gets. The exact opposite to our natures, which keep cooling off the longer they last. The best wine will have the most bouquet, strength, and spirit, with no tartness nor any trace of vinegar, since it must appeal to all the senses. And the kind that keeps dancing in the glass is the liveliest, you can be sure of that.

Teodora. 'Bread full of eyes, cheese with no eyes, wine that leaps to the eyes.'

Gerarda. The wine I speak of helps evacuation, dissolves harmful humors, does away with flatulence. It's good for those with a touch of irritation in their veins and elsewhere.

Teodora. It's no wine for youngsters and it's poison in the summer. In winter it should be good for phlegmatic old men. It's a sensible wine, but must be drunk in moderation. That way it cheers the heart and fortifies the spirit.

Dorotea. To avoid the harm done by wine, one should avoid eating sweetmeats and anything appetizing.

Gerarda. How free I am of such problems!

Teodora. If before breakfast you had taken seven bitter almonds or some such astringent, the wine would have no ill effects.

Gerarda. Come, Teodora, don't talk nonsense! There's nothing like seven slices of bacon. Seven almonds for me? Give them to the seven princes of Lara. I'm over twenty-five and know what's good for me.

Celia. The old girl is hopeless.

Dorotea. What's the best kind of water, aunt?

Gerarda. Child, the kind that falls from heaven because no one drinks it.

Dorotea. They say it's the clear and subtle kind that rises out of the East and runs over the ground, without touching stones.

Gerarda. Let it run where it will, you needn't worry, I'll not go out of my way to look for it.

Dorotea. I don't see why they say that wine benefits the tongue, and that some people, to pluck up courage to talk to princes, depend on it. Because I can see, Gerarda, that your tongue is getting thick.

Gerarda. Sleepiness is the reason for that, not wine.

Dorotea. And what's the reason for the sleepiness?

Gerarda. Having put one's intrin ... trinsic parts at ease.

Dorotea. You had a hard time getting that word out.

Gerarda. Why is Celia taking so long to refill my glass? You fill it up, pickaninny. Celia is annoyed with me because I scold her when she's naughty.

Celia. Your pickaninny is in the kitchen.

Gerarda. Well, then, you give me a draft, young lady, and forgive me, I know I have worn you down going back and forth.

Celia. Madam says no.

Gerarda. 'That son of yours goes honeyless and moneyless, between vinegar and wine-lees.'

Celia. Wine-lees are what you have in those bloodshot eyes of yours, from weeping.

Gerarda. 'The blotches at your temples are not gray hairs but moles.' Pour me another while they're looking the other way.

Celia. You have had nine drinks.

Gerarda. 'Nine lords a-leaping.'

Celia. You'll need neither lover nor cover tonight.

Gerarda. 'A body is no colder than the clothes it wears.'

Teodora. Look here, Gerarda, it's bad for you. Celia and the pickaninny are laughing, and though Dorotea is your friend, she can't condone it.

Gerarda. 'When the prior plays cards, what won't the friars do?'

Teodora. Take those olives away from here, pickaninny.

Gerarda. It's about time. I've been sucking one pit for at least an hour, hoping for something better.

Teodora. Clear the table, child, and give Gerarda some of those black gumdrops.

Gerarda. Take your old gumdrops to Guinea! I'd sooner burst than have one enter my body! You'll find no eater of sweets in my family tree. All my life I've kept away from baptisms, for fear of seeing marzipan and sugared almonds. When I'm on the street, I make for the tavern and avoid the pastry shops, and when I see a man eating a slice of orange, I look twice to see if he has blue eyes. As for raisins, a pox on the creature who ever sunned them or soaked them in lye.

Celia. Watch out, aunt, you're tottering.

Gerarda. 'If the gallows had mouth as well as ears, you'd hear it calling far and near.'

Celia. One ends a meal with proper prayers.

Gerarda. Don't remove the cloths. Since I said grace, I'll give the benediction.

Teodora. Go on, we're listening.

Gerarda. Quod habemus comido, de Dominus Domini sea benedito, y a micos y a vobis nunca faltetur, y agora dicamus el sanctificetur.

Dorotea. She's amusing, that can't be denied. And many I know who claim to be learned have less Latin.

Gerarda. I always tend to my devotions after supper. Take me to the oratory, Celia.

Celia. To bed would be better, aunt. Don't lean on me so, you are very heavy.

Gerarda. 'Placed in its hinges, the heaviest door has no weight at all.'

Celia. You've tripped over the chair. This way, aunt.

Teodora. What a bump she's given herself! Feel your way carefully with her, thoughtless girl.

Celia. What do you mean, "feel"? She can't feel a thing.

> *Chorus of Cupidity*
> Love, your forces vigorous
>   are cowardly and weakliest,
>   for subjects the loftiest,
>   to conquer most difficult.
> For wealth most glittering
>   seductions are easiest,
>   thanks to gold Dalmatian
>   and to diamonds Scythian.
> Giving, prodigal artifex,
>   makes honesty adultery,

for not all are Eurydices,
   Evadnes, and Penelopes.
Pyramus is now no suicide,
   nor are all Daphnes treeified
   against the sacred majesty
   of golden coins imperial.
What Rhodope, what Caucasus,
   what solid marble Ligurian,
   will not like wax be liquefied,
   when gold coins come a-jingling?
When he saw naked Venus lie
   in that brute satyr's brawny clasp,
   Love bewept her bitterly,
   shedding tears most pitifully.
A goddess, yet most shamefully
   she snubbed fierce Mars indomitable,
   and bright Apollo Delphian—
   for what? A faun ridiculous!
Love need not hope, solicitous
   of Herculean victories,
   to write its histories tragical
   in everlasting porphyries.
For I have apples Hesperidian
   to outdo all his trickeries,
   and win triumphal victories,
   surpassing Roman emperors'!

ACT · THREE

Scene 1

DON FERNANDO · JULIO

Fernando. Julio, I have scarcely arrived and I am already wishing I had
not come. How well that poet put it:
  Oh perfidious pleasure of love,
    most flimsy and lightest of dreams,
    in fancy bulking so large—
    once enjoyed, how slight it seems!

Julio. Well, what ails you now? And why the haste? Is this why you
kept saying time had stopped? And why you woke me before the
birds ever knew it was growing light? And was it for this you promised the coach boys all that money to bring you to Madrid on a set
day?

Fernando. Why are you so surprised, Julio? Don't you know that desire grows more urgent the closer one draws to its source? Others,
returning from long absences, assuage their feelings when they see
the object of their concern, but, alas, why have I come if I am not
to see Dorotea?

Julio. What stands in your way?

Fernando. The very love that leads me on.

Julio. Take your mind off what's on it.

Fernando. How can I take off it what's on it?

Julio. By putting something else on it.

Fernando. Hand me a book.

Julio. Latin, French, or Tuscan?

Fernando. Give me Heliodorus, in our own tongue.

Julio. There's a prayer book to cure you, all right! Here.

Fernando. This is what it says: "Theagenes and Chariclea remained alone in the cave, taking as a great boon the postponement of the hardships anticipated; for, finding themselves free, they embraced lovingly." Is this what you'd have me read?

Julio. You asked for it, not I.

Fernando. This is more inflammatory than entertaining. Oh, pity me, Julio! What can that cruel Dorotea be doing?

Julio. Good Lord, stop making things up to torture yourself.

Fernando. Bring out the chessmen, we'll play a bit.

Julio. Fine idea. Here, I'll set them up.

Fernando. Are they set up now?

Julio. Can't you see? You start. What are you doing?

Fernando. I've knocked them over so I wouldn't risk losing the queen. Bring out the fencing foils.

Julio. I'll wipe off the dust they've gathered since we went away.

Fernando. Carranza says all wounds are inflicted by an angular thrust. What angle must love have assumed when it inflicted mine?

Julio. Ask Dorotea, she supplied the bow.

Fernando. That was a great thrust you just made; it's the only way to hit home. Oh, Dorotea, I have no protection against stabs from you.

Julio. Why throw down your sword?

Fernando. So Alciato won't say it's in the hands of a madman.

Julio. A gentleman you know has lost his lady. Let me entertain you with some of his verses in the piscatory idyllic style.

Fernando. I have two poems by him, and I have set them to excellent melodies.

Julio. Well, then, first listen to these, which are just as good as the ones you refer to.

Fernando. Go ahead, if you remember them.

Julio.

> Ah, wasteland of longing
> for my dearest belovèd

where no one will listen
   but waves and wild beasts!
The waves as they foam
   strew snow upon rocks
   to make them seem softened
   by the impress of grief.
The beasts, although roaring,
   grow ever less fierce.
   In their hearts they subside
   to my echoing moan.
Bereft of my soul,
   on this strand I collapse;
   can I hope for daybreak
   when my dawn is dead?
Or must I, lamenting
   the dark void she's left,
   hope for two dawnings
   when her soul meets mine?
Though stars pierce the dark,
   my star never will;
   for stars return nightly,
   but her night's eternal.
Oh Venus, kind goddess,
   leading the way
   for the dawn and the sun
   at morning and evening,
on this night only
   defer to my star;
   in pureness and light,
   admit her as peer.
Forlorn little boat,
   wearing black mourning
   from stem to stern,
   on riggings and sails,
no awning shall deck you,
   no sea fennel crown
   your festival riggings,
   but deadly rose laurel.

The sedges and rushes
   which once wove a fringe
   on these very shores
   with flag flowers golden,
with bay clusters green,
   turning dry as salt cedar,
   with their uselss leaves
   will reflect my lost hopes.
Oh cabin abandoned,
   by shepherds disdained,
   may you be razed
   and strewn on the ground.
No more on the mizzen
   shall your streamers appear
   silk serpents in air
   and taffeta comets.
The blades of your oars,
   bereft of gay colors,
   shall darken the foam
   as they cleave and dip.
Unfurling your sail,
   you'll see no naked nymphs
   lifting their heads
   near the well-caulked keel.
May hurricanes raging
   drag you seaward and back,
   since all Spanish tides
   must yield to their sway.
Come, all you boatmen
   with wives safe at home
   so comely and bright
   in each of the hamlets:
now in friendship attend
   this mournful lament
   as waves scale the rocks
   and come crashing down.
Since fishing is halted
   and boats kept ashore,

assist with your sighing
my piteous dirge.
The quickest way home
from any far voyage
is to sail the salt seas
of my lachrymose eyes.
No man of gladness
should ever approach me;
one glance and he'll turn
unhappy forever.
Cut cypress for mourning
and join my grief,
come swell with your sighs
my doleful laments.
The best rhymes written
for funeral rites
of a wife so belovèd
shall garner these prizes:
two oaken goblets
whereon I have carved
Daphne disdainful
and Leda delighted.
Daphne sprouts laurel,
Leda feels the soft down
of the covering swan
who fathered Helen.
Two nets so close-knit
that one counts their knots
as if counting my sighs
while I, the sea sands.
Nymphs of the ocean,
the hills, and the groves,
will peer from the waves
or the greenwood edge,
crowned some with coral,
some with vervain,
to redouble the tears
this tragedy sheds.

Say, friends: "She is dead,
  a sprinkling of earth
  hides Amaryllis.
  our glory and honor,
hides one whose green eyes,
  with love ever sparkling,
  were celestial musicians,
  like Orpheus, drew souls;
whose limpid pupils
  of queenly hauteur
  under canopied forehead
  black eyebrows defended;
whose mouth, when she smiled,
  could teach ocean seas
  how corals are made,
  teach dawn to make pearls;
who never could utter
  one word that strayed
  from humble virtue
  and the honest truth;
whose hands were composed
  of fresh orange blossoms,
  snow in pure whiteness,
  and crystal to see through;
whose feet would have found
  Easter lilies their rivals
  if lilies grew smaller
  to gain greater beauty;
who sang so divinely
  she'd match any siren;
  from whom no Ulysses
  could find defense;
who gave Parnassus
  its muse most perfect,
  virtue and wit,
  beauty and charm.
It was beauty that slew her,
  so envy no longer

might hear her praise spoken,
  or gaze on her grace.
Come and console me,
  I die of this grieving—
  but, oh, boatmen, come not;
  I will cling to my pain.
For life, by not ending,
  is bound to bring forth
  more death while it lasts,
  more life than death could.
With instrument broken,
  strings, ribbons gone,
  let tears now extol
  what voice once sang.
I invoke a sweet name—
  alas, to my sorrow
  an echo that mocks me
  sends my words back.
By my own voice deceived,
  I start in pursuit;
  I strain for the echo
  slipping farther away.
Deluded by love,
  I see her there waiting;
  fancies beguile me
  and turn to ideas.
As they rise before me,
  I strain to grasp them,
  embrace my imaginings
  in hopes they'll turn real.
But alas, to my sorrow,
  so great is the difference
  that my arms deluded
  drop undeceived.
How gaily her answer
  with laughter would open
  her mouth, spicy pink,
  in double half-blossoms!

And I, her sad mate,
   tongue tipping her lips,
   picked from those petals
   the laughter and pearls.
Ah, she answers no longer,
   my dearest belovèd;
   from silence eternal
   replies never come.
Her memories have left me
   grieving alone,
   seeking her footprints
   on strand and stone,
and finding so many
   (was there ever such folly?)
   I choose the most tiny
   and say they are hers.
Each tree in whose shade
   she would take siestas,
   I clasp with my plea
   for the shade it denies.
In this desolation
   of lonely longing,
   I avoid her portrait,
   though yearning to view it,
for eyes cannot bear
   to think she is dead
   whose exquisite form
   the painter has caught.
What I seek most I shun,
   and shudder to find
   how much less enduring
   is Nature than art.
When her eye meets mine
   and she still is silent,
   I become convinced
   this cannot be she.
Since Franceliso's brush
   has preserved her likeness

on the wall of my cabin,
  I've no greater wealth.
If it chance to happen
  I glance at the likeness,
  my eyes are soon blinded,
  the tears alone see.
She will never complain
  that my eyes have beheld
  lovely things, even flowers,
  and not found them ugly.
So sad is my life
  all things are torture;
  death will not take me,
  life won't run out.
When I see fellow boatmen
  forgetting dead wives
  (when alive so beloved),
  feeling happy again,
I avoid them completely,
  for full well I know
  that time cannot cancel
  her memory in me.
If aught could console me—
  even something once hers—
  I know I'd offend her
  and I cast it away."
So Fabio lamented
  by the salt-sea shores
  his lost Amaryllis,
  his death in hers,
till, brought to a standstill
  by strength ever ebbing,
  heartbroken with anguish,
  tears tied his tongue.
Love, who was listening,
  spoke: "This is the age
  of Pyramus, Leander,
  Portia, Julia, and Phaedra.

Our age will not know
　any love so steadfast:
　death cannot cure it,
　nor time heal its wounds."

Fernando. You read those verses so expressively, Julio, that you brought tears to my eyes.

Julio. No doubt because your resistance was already low.

Fernando. Oh, how I enjoy sad things! God bless that steadfast and fortunate man!

Julio. How can a man who has lost the things the poem speaks of be called fortunate?

Fernando. Would to God that I were mourning Dorotea!

Julio. In your wish you remind me of that tyrant who, on leaving for Rome at Caesar's command, arranged with a friend to kill Mariamne, his wife, if Caesar did away with him. In this way, the one he loved so much would never belong to anyone else. Afterward she became the mistress of the very friend in whom he had confided.

Fernando. That lover Fabio is better off than I, Julio. Ah, if we could only trade misfortunes! Because he is lamenting what he has lost, and I, what someone else possesses.

Julio. Don't say such things. That's impossible.

Fernando. Since it is possible, as indeed it is, why do you doubt it?

Julio. Either you love Dorotea or you don't love her. If you love her, think well of what you love. If you don't love her, don't think so much about someone you don't love.

Fernando. I love her, and I hate her.

Julio. That can't be.

Fernando. Aristotle writes that lovely Helis had an Ethiopian lover and bore him a white daughter, but afterward that daughter's son was born black. And thus Dorotea's beauty brings forth my love white, then from the same love later brings forth my hatred black.

Julio. Does the Philosopher give the reason?

Fernando. Simply that the likeness recurs after many generations. Consult him in the first book of *The Procreation of Animals.*

Julio. I'm afraid you contradict yourself. Because if Dorotea's beauty brought forth your love white, which of you was the Ethiopian to engender your hatred black?

Fernando. Jealousy, Julio. Never yet was love engendered without it.

Julio. A clever answer!

Fernando. If the consequence is inferred from the position of the antecedent, the syllogism is perfect.

Julio. Why do you love Dorotea?

Fernando. Because she is worthy of being loved.

Julio. A thing must necessarily be a good in order to be loved.

Fernando. There's considerable distance between being *a* good and being *good.* I am well aware, from the Philosopher's *Ethics,* where he speaks of friendship, that anything absolutely good is to be loved and sought after. But he says love resembles affection, and friendship, habit.

Julio. I wish you had read, in the first book of the *Rhetoric,* the reason why lovers stay happy in the midst of their sorrows.

Fernando. What are you getting at?

Julio. He says that, as sick people take heart at the height of a fever from the thought that they are going to drink, so lovers, when they are separated, when they correspond, and when they are filled with longing, find cheer by turning their thoughts to the fulfillment of the good they are anticipating.

Fernando. I understand you now, Julio. You mean I am hoping to see Dorotea. Well, how does that thought pertain to mine if I love her because she's beautiful and don't see her because I hate her?

Julio. Rather than reply, let me entertain you. Listen to the second declaration of that same lover:

> My poor little sail,
> > to keep you from sinking,
> > misfortunes shall serve
> > to ballast your hull.
> But how will you bear
> > so heavy a burden?
> > Were your cargo hope,
> > it were lightly borne.
> All is gone with the wind;
> > you now see what ensues
> > from trust in great oceans
> > pretending they're calm.
> Caressing the shores
> > with soothing waves,

they comb the sands
with smooth undulations.
Serene in appearance,
they lead boats astray,
lulling the oars
to distract them from warning.
But on the horizon,
they outdo a giant
in scaling the skies,
as thousands groan.
Beware of such waters,
let no sail trust
so fickle a nature,
so quick to serve winds.
First topsails are lifted
within reach of heaven,
then broken keels scraped
against ocean floors.
My poor little sail,
for so many years
butt of the waves
from Charybdis to Scylla,
it's now time to rest,
to give up the ocean,
be lashed to this tree trunk
as madmen are lashed.
Don't seek new planking
or challenge the wind,
for ravaging time
admits no repair.
Till you hang, an ex-voto,
prepare to prevail
over insults and wrongs
with triumphs of patience.
On your broken stern write,
having shed all illusions:
"There's no human force
can overcome time."

Not for you storm warnings
   in cries of seabirds,
   the angry wind rising
   and whistling through trees.
No heed shall you take
   of ships outward bound,
   nor envy brand-new ones
   taut sails and fine riggings.
The great lofty ships
   of imperial Philips
   point sea-roving prows
   toward far-distant climes.
Sweeping on southward
   to new worlds of treasure—
   Orient's diamonds,
   amethysts, sapphires—
let coats of arms
   with lordly escutcheons,
   amaze mountainous waves,
   make foreign lands gape.
But you, who aboveboard
   bear nothing but sky,
   cease tempting the waves
   that have spared you till now.
Flee flaming Troys;
   against wrathfull Achilles
   set Aeneas' silence,
   Anchises' virtue.
When you saw our mistress
   come down to this beach
   to greet you and me
   as we stepped ashore,
dawn still had not shown
   its outlines pure white,
   in lilies its laughter,
   in gillyflow'rs, tears.
When, proud as a swan,
   you sailed after trophies

down pathways remote
    of the Nereids' realm,
you never feared storms
    nor Circes bewitching;
    like Ulysses, my love
    turned deaf ears to sirens.
The crystalline eddies
    even saw me at times
    go diving for pearls
    and spying out fish.
Oh, the catches I brought her—
    when night wreathed in shadow
    the shapes of these mountains
    that rival my love—
in woven rush baskets,
    and not silver plates,
    for where souls commune,
    to display wealth is vile.
For two hearts that share,
    the soul holds dearest
    things truly chosen
    and simply displayed.
But now dreaded fate
    indifferently pacing
    the mansions of nobles
    and hovels of paupers,
robbing earth of her beauty,
    has sealed forever
    those green eyes of hers,
    the rainbows of heaven.
Those emerald eyes
    that rival the sun
    in beauty and light,
    in other skies glow—
eyes ever smiling,
    serene, ever showing
    virtue's own soul,
    and never bold seeming.

No more may brooks echo
   her voice's cadenzas,
   nor nightingales match
   her soprano so sweet.
Amaryllis divine,
   who died first—you or I?
   Which one is dead,
   which now alive?
We surely changed souls
   the day you departed,
   for I know that yours
   now dwells within me.
Lying prone on this strand,
   I, sobbing, repeat
   your own sweet name
   to solace my grief.
The waves, my companions,
   send sad echoes back
   from opposite shores,
   and say all I say.
There's no rock so stubborn,
   when it sees and hears me,
   will not crack and cry,
   and melt in pity.
The dolphins and seals
   lift heads and listen
   to my bitter sobs,
   my phrases bereaved.
"Do not wonder," I tell them,
   "that this poor boatman
   whose joy you once knew
   should sigh now and weep,
that one so illustrious
   he was crowned with laurels—
   as the fame that follows
   on learning, assures—
now burdened and bowed
   by myriad misfortunes,

his humble brow
  with sad cypress wreathes."
The joy her sight brought
  leaves me bereft;
  in her death I now live
  and shall to the end.
That lyre I loved,
  on which I sang wonders
  of feats unsurpassed
  and wept at misfortunes,
I yesterday smashed
  against these green willows—
  which the boatmen discovered
  and gruffly reproved.
One, picking up fragments,
  tried restoring the lyre,
  but what use are strings
  when their muse is dead?
One sang its praises;
  a third, to protect it,
  hung it high on a bough,
  like a Thisbe transformed.
But nothing erases
  your beauty from memory,
  and I tearfully countered
  their every reproach:
"I shall never be happy
  till Italy's waters
  join waters of Spain
  and Tagus meets Tiber;
till meek little lambs
  frolic with tigers,
  and learning is free
  of envy's pursuit.
I shall weep till my soul
  suffuses the air,
  rejoined to hers
  in the union we shared.
I know such weeping

will end in my death—
then sweet thought of her
revive like the phoenix.
In bronze everlasting
love limns her memory,
disdaining lines penciled
by lead on soft paper.
Oh light that has left me,
in what fullness of time
shall my soul regain you,
my life be restored?
Pity one so lonely—
but ah, where you dwell
in sweet peace, you but smile
at foolish desires."

Fernando. Give me a copy of the two elegies, Julio. If only they were short, I'd memorize and sing them.

Julio. The other two you have are more suitable.

Fernando. Such love! Such delicacy! And how genuine, how forlorn! The only thing that lover failed to do was to drink the ashes of his Amaryllis.

Julio. I once saw, at the feet of idols in India, some golden urns. And when I asked what was in them, I was told they contained the ashes of certain Hindus who, being assured they would be placed at the feet of the idol, let themselves be burned alive by the priests. I gather you'd like to occupy some urn of that sort at the feet of Dorotea.

Fernando. Nothing of the kind, Julio. Just remember that poetry appears to have been invented to ease the cares of those in love.

Julio. And to banish fears and melancholy from the mind, as you will have observed in Horace, where he says that in the muses' company he has no fear of relentless care.

Fernando. A cure for love—that's what Theocritus calls the muses in his "Cyclops." It must be because they relieve love's pains by lamenting them, not because they cure love. And the verse you recited is a case in point. If only one's sufferings could be tossed to the winds, as Anacreon says! But neither composing verse nor singing it will calm the stormy oceans of my thoughts.

Julio. Since running away proved no cure, how can returning prove one? It went better for you in Seville. I thought you'd surely fall in love with that dark-eyed lady.

Fernando. Oh, Julio, that was mere plaster over an old wound.

Julio. Not that she lacked beauty.

Fernando. Or brains.

Julio. Then what was missing?

Fernando. Have you never known a man who wrote poorly and wanted a master to teach him how to write well, and the master had a harder time ridding him of his old ways than teaching him new ones? Well, in similar fashion a second love can teach nothing until the first lets go.

Julio. I should like to recite some lines I heard in a play, apropos of your jealousy, your travels, and this Don Bela who torments you— since I imagine that *bell* alarms you more than Dorotea's grace and beauty.

> Enamored, the bird in the underwood
>> sings to its mate, not seeing the hunter
>> lurking and listening there below
>> in the brush, with flexed crossbow.
>
> He aims, he misses, the bird flies away.
>> Anguish freezes the song in its throat.
>> Flying back, it flits from branch to branch,
>> staying near its beloved mate.
>
> So tranquil love sings in the nest,
>> but once stung by jealousy's dart,   ·
>> fears of desertion rise in its breast.
>
> Then it flees, but keeps watch from afar,
>> and not till the man it fears departs
>> will it cease flitting, thought to thought.

Fernando. We're here now, Julio. There's nothing for it but to be patient and take a walk in the country for some distraction.

Julio. It would be more to the point to look at other things possessing beauty, and strike up a conversation.

Fernando. And where can beauty be found outside of Dorotea?

Julio. In everything possessing proportion, for beauty is exactly that. As Leo Hebraeus says in his *Philography:* that form which best informs matter makes the parts of the body, one with another, more proportionate to the whole, and unifies the parts with the whole.

Fernando. And where can such unity and kinship be found?

Julio. In many women, for Nature did not curtail her handiwork with
  Dorotea.

Fernando. It's occurred to me a thousand times that, out of what was
  left of the substance from which she wrought Dorotea, Nature
  made the rose and the jasmine.

Julio. So that we now have Dorotea antedating the rose?

Fernando. No, Julio; simply that, when time had used up the white
  and purple of the jasmine and the rose, they were restored with
  remnants of Dorotea's colors.

Julio. Poor wit! It's wiser to leave you than to reason with you.

Fernando. Julio, be patient with me; you'll fall in love someday.

Julio. A peasant once sent some nag to a grandee who coveted it for
  the hunt, with a letter saying: "The accompanying nag is skinnier
  than when your lordship saw him because he is in love. And so I
  beseech your lordship to treat him as you would wish to be treated
  if you were a nag."

Fernando. You're tiresome, and dense as well.

Julio. What I tell you is for your own good.

Fernando. And I'll tell you what Ovid says, that nobody in love can
  recognize it, and what Seneca says in his *Hippolytus,* in that portion
  Garcilaso took from him: "Albeit I know the best, I but choose the
  worst."

Scene 2

DON BELA · LAURENCIO

Bela. Laurencio, I am pleased to have won the favor of Dorotea's
  mother. Until now, she and I have had nothing but apprehension
  and worry, with mine necessarily the greater.

Laurencio. What could you not win, with diamonds as general and
  gold for an army? Simply tell yourself that while you stayed in Madrid they went to the New World.

Bela. Anything spent is a pittance compared with what Dorotea
  merits.

Laurencio. Whatever she merits, she is quite expensive. Beauty is a remarkable trade. Let anyone Nature favors with it engage in no other.

Bela. It is not a trade but a distinction bestowed.

Laurencio. One can trade in distinctions.

Bela. They're called endowments of Nature as opposed to those bestowed by Fortune.

Laurencio. The endowment of your fortune is slowly being bestowed upon Dorotea's natural endowment, and she'll end up having both. You can see for yourself the trade they're all in, and how right I am to say they have no need to go to the New World.

Bela. Those unable to enjoy beauty are irked that it should even exist.

Laurencio. And those who can enjoy it are sorry they have done so, when they've paid the price.

Bela. No one could ever regret enjoying such pleasure.

Laurencio. There is no pleasure which does not give way in the end to displeasure; even day, beautiful and pleasant as it is, must finally yield to night.

Bela. No riches from the New World are more precious than the privilege of seeing Dorotea.

Laurencio. Nor she more precious than when she deprives you of them. I recall a story I once read in the history of the Sherifs, in which the clever Moor was told that some gold mines had been discovered in the Montes Claros, on the far side of Morocco. He quickly ordered them filled in, directing that no one should mine the gold on pain of death, because if the Christians found out, they would no longer go to the New World to look for mines, but come to his country.

Bela. Suppose I do own one; revealing it has not harmed me a bit. Dorotea is taking it from me by her beauty, not by main force.

Laurencio. Beauty always was the strongest of forces because it has so often conquered the stronger. Omphale downed Hercules, Briseis downed Achilles. When it comes to wise men, Aristotle worshiped Hermia and wrote hymns to her (as the Greeks commonly did to the gods) until it reached such a point, that, being denounced by Demophilos and Eurymedon, he was banished from Athens.

Bela. Then, is it excusable?

Laurencio. Loving her is, lavishing gifts is not.

Bela. You cannot be loving without giving.

Laurencio. Nor giving without going poor.

Bela. Why does God bestow gifts on men?

Laurencio. Because He loves them.

Bela. Then may one in love not present gifts?

Laurencio. God cannot grow poor. If that were possible, we would say that when He had nothing left to give, He gave himself.

Bela. Tell me, Laurencio, was Plato a wise man?

Laurencio. He was called divine.

Bela. Well, he said that everything good is beautiful. It then follows that everything beautiful is good, and whatever is good is worthy of being loved; nor can one who loves what is good be reprimanded.

Laurencio. What a remarkable tautology! Really, though, sir, I think the little learning you and I have acquired has done us much harm. But, God preserve you, do lend an ear to Marsilio Ficino's explanation of why the ancients depicted the god Pan as half man, half beast.

Bela. How did he explain it?

Laurencio. Since Pan was the son of Mercury, they indicated by his two forms the two ways of speaking: when truly, as a man; when falsely, as a beast.

Bela. A neat way of calling me one.

Laurencio. That wasn't my meaning, only that you make little use of the higher faculties in your arguments.

Bela. Dorotea's beauty needs no defense from me.

Laurencio. No, only your money.

Bela. Phryne was a woman of Boeotia who, when hauled into court as a result of a fortune she'd acquired, undressed before the elders, who, on seeing the perfection of her body, let her go free. Quintilian said that, even more than the efforts and the sponsorship of her advocates, it was her beauty that worked in her favor.

Laurencio. The judges looked at her with an eye not to the law but to their desires. Octavian would have set them a better example; he listened to Cleopatra without looking at her face. But why should I mind, if you do not.

Bela. How could I mind, now that Teodora, Dorotea's mother, is on my side?

Laurencio. How? Very easily, because whereas before you had one leech sucking your blood, now you have two. And I see you behaving like a bull in the ring: set upon by a mastiff, he uses his free side to defend himself; but when they set another on him, he gives in, and with equal strain drags them both along, dangling like pendants from his ears.

Scene 3

GERARDA · DON BELA · LAURENCIO

Gerarda. 'Where there is good will, don't knock—there's a welcome waiting.'

Bela. Ah, my dear woman, you may be sure of one from me.

Laurencio. But not from me.

Bela. First of all, how is my Dorotea?

Gerarda. She is in bed. It is her bad time of the month.

Bela. To help her through it, put a gourd on each breast. That's not my idea, it's Hippocrates'.

Gerarda. You mean to say that *Aphorisms* man went into this? He'd have been our salvation. Although as far as I'm concerned, it makes no difference now. Nature has seen to that. Thank God, I'm free of it—that and the toothache.

Laurencio. How could your teeth ache when you haven't any?

Gerarda. 'How is it your master isn't cranky? Because he is not married.' See here, Laurencio, those which are no more were pearls once, and in my day I've seen many a sonnet penned to my teeth. Did you expect me to be like that Moor in India who lived three hundred years and every hundred sprouted a new set of teeth, while his hair changed from white to black?

Laurencio. We do just as well right here, without Nature's help. But nobody lives that long.

Gerarda. All that Nature gives is on loan.

Laurencio. On short-term lease.

Gerarda. 'A pig on lease, a good winter and a bad summer.' Those of us who frolicked in the spring will have a hard time in the autumn.

Bela. Why, mother, your health is good and you look fit.

Gerarda. 'There's no mending a cracked bell.' Have no fear, I'll not imitate that Moor.

Laurencio. Despite all you have in common.

Gerarda. 'Peter was married to May; he's a scoundrel, so is she.'

Bela. Mother, in order to fortify your native faculties, I would like to reveal a secret to you, which will supply any affected and morbidified part with strength and vigor, although you won't be needing it to remedy dizziness due to Venus.

Gerarda. And what is the secret? You New World Spaniards are the very devil.

Bela. Take a piece of gold and put it red-hot in wine. It makes a miraculous potion.

Gerarda. You've been infected by that frilly language: *potion, native, affected,* and *morbidified.*

Bela. Don't you see that these are the exact terms? Do as I say with the gold, then drink the wine.

Gerarda. I should be glad to have the gold in order to buy the wine, since that salutary drink needs no help from elsewhere. It's strong enough as it is.

Laurencio. You might try it out by using some of those doubloons you now have.

Gerarda. 'One eye on the frying pan, the other on the cat.' Brother, what Don Bela has given me is for my funeral. I don't intend to go to the parish cemetery with one sexton droning *Kyrie eleison* off-key, as if he were crying up the loss of some jackass. I mean to have my sodalities, and the best tomb will be mine, for I have no desire to be rained on from the open sky.

Laurencio. You despise water even when you're dead?

Gerarda. We're not on the best of terms.

Bela. There are natural aversions and oppositions. For just as you find sympathies, so too antipathies; as between animals, so too between men, and even between planets, in either malevolent or benevolent aspects. The stag and the snake hate each other, swan and eagle, bull and wolf, partridge and crow. And so with men, the poorly educated detest the better educated; young disciples, trying out their wings, the masters who taught them. By the same token there are naturally mysterious friendships, the reasons for which many philosophers have stated.

Gerarda. I don't know why you are exercising your rhetoric and chit-chat upon me—it's like selling honey to a beekeepers. Give me something for wine, since you are not giving me any gold.

Bela. How much will satisfy you?

Gerarda. As the proverb has it, 'A pint sinks in the wink of an eye; a half-gallon shrinks, I can't tell why; a gallon unkinks you valiantly.'

Bela. Give her eight *reales*.

Gerarda. The strings are going out of tune. I'm not surprised. 'In tourneys and love, there's no part like the start.' Well, as a matter of fact, I plan to mortify myself where thirst is concerned. You know, the first day you visited Dorotea, I dined with mother and daughter and, if you'll forgive me, I made so free with the bottle—since I rarely slip between cup and lip—that I spent two whole days in a pantry, thinking all the time I was in the oratory.

Laurencio. Your dreams must have been beatific.

Bela. Now tell me, Gerarda, why have you come? Is this a visit from you or from Dorotea, with you as the angel Gabriel?

Gerarda. From Dorotea. I do not come here for myself simply to rattle on pointlessly. The tailor brought this list of the materials it would take to make the tawny-colored dress.

Laurencio. May tawny-colored lions tear into you.

Bela. Is there to be gilt?

Gerarda. 'A decent stew needs meat too.' Just a few hatchings and some braid on the doublet.

Laurencio. I'd give them all a good upbraiding, and with a whip, too—mother, daughter, and go-between.

Gerarda. What are you mumbling there about her mother, Laurencio? Is she not a most honorable and virtuous woman?

Laurencio. I was not referring to her, but to the easygoing ways of her household.

Gerarda. You find that so remarkable, you simpleton? Have you not heard the saying 'Every family has a skeleton in the closet'?

Bela. I've examined the list, and everything will be purchased as Dorotea directs. Nothing is too good for her.

Gerarda. This Laurencio of yours, meddlesome steward that he is, always wears a sour look on his face, and that must be because Celia will not respond to his advances.

Laurencio. I set eyes on *her?* Yes, of course. So you have found your swooning mooncalf, haven't you? 'Don't be a baker if your head's made of butter.' I'm handy at proverbs too, you see. And she's such a dainty morsel to be courting. A fine brown sorrel she'd make, and spotted all over, too!

Gerarda. She has her admirers, all the same. 'There's no pot so ugly it doesn't have a lid.' 'If our son-in-law is any good, the rest is understood.' So 'let nobody dare say, I'll never walk this way.' For times have a way of changing.

Laurencio. 'Changing times, the idiot chimes.'

Gerarda. 'Even in Salamanca the moon's round and the moon's white.'

Laurencio. Look here, Gerarda, 'a woman and a garden want but one owner,' since 'maiden and hawk, keep out of the sun.'

Gerarda. What can anyone say against Celia, and such a retiring girl, too? 'Since the first slip, I've been a virgin.'

Laurencio. 'See no evil, hear no evil, speak no evil.'

Gerarda. 'I catch the words but not the drift.' For 'a blow with a frying pan leaves a smudge, if not a scar.'

Bela. At the bottom of this list, mother, I have written a few lines. Best let Dorotea do the shopping herself. I'll have the coach brought round for her.

Gerarda. What a Sly Boots you are! To save giving me a little something, you want Dorotea to go herself.

Bela. What do you need?

Gerarda. A cloak.

Bela. I'll put that down.

Laurencio. 'Drop by drop, the sea dries up.'

Gerarda. 'Fear not, ladies, the sparrow hawk from Alcaraz has not got bells in an uproar.' Brother Laurencio, 'if you want a dog's trust, toss him a crust.'

Laurencio. Mother, they also say, 'And if he draws blood, it's all to the good.' And remember this, too: 'Who'd be rich in a year, will hang in six months.'

Bela. I've set down a cloak for you.

Gerarda. May the King set the red cross of St. James on your chest.

Laurencio. A red fox would suit your foxiness better.

Gerarda. I'll be going—I must drop in on a young maiden who has need of me.

Laurencio. Being a maid can't be much to her liking.

Gerarda. Brother Laurencio, 'it's never too late to do a good turn.' The poor thing is upset. The wedding is tomorrow and I believe she slipped up with a page.

Laurencio. It wasn't the first and it won't be the last.

Gerarda. She is pure gold. She wouldn't do badly for you, since Celia's not to your liking. She can steal out easily enough a day or two after the wedding.

Laurencio. 'It's the slender one dances at the wedding, not the fat.'

Gerarda. You can thank me for one thing: I've taught you to pump out proverbs. Goodbye, Don Bela.

Scene 4

LUDOVICO · DON FERNANDO · JULIO

Ludovico. I decided you were staying on in Seville.

Fernando. Oh, Ludovico, how good to be welcomed by your embrace!

Ludovico. Permit me to move from it to Julio's.

Julio. I esteem yours as much as the one you relinquish to honor mine.

Ludovico. I never thought you would stay away so long.

Fernando. Heaven knows all it's cost me in anxiety, heartache, and despair.

Ludovico. In that case, absence can hardly have proved the true Galen to cure you of love.

Julio. We left Madrid three months ago. And if Don Fernando's love affair were part of a play, we would have had to throw the rules out the window, since the playwright's craft allows only twenty-four hours, and leaving the locality is an inexcusable blunder.

Fernando. Which makes mine a true story. And no worse a crime than for Aristophanes to introduce frogs and for Plautus to bring the gods into his *Amphitryon.*

Ludovico. I did all you asked the day after your departure.

Fernando. Did you slash Gerarda's face?

Ludovico. No, because I knew you'd regret having asked me to, as I now see by your expression you do. And because one night, as I was waiting for her to leave for the house of a neighbor of the same calling, she looked out the window and said, "Go back to your house, muffled gentleman; I shall not leave mine until the sun tells me to and there are people about, to protect me."

Fernando. What are you telling me, Ludovico?

Ludovico. Simply what happened between us.

Julio. But you'll now agree she's a sorceress and soothsayer?

Ludovico. No crime justifies the slashing of a woman's face, for it is the sole fortune and only pedigree bequeathed her by Nature.

Julio. If at least the legacy were permanently secured . . .

Fernando. Better that it not be, since this makes possible our revenge.

Julio. No revenge could be sweeter for those they've made fools of.

Ludovico. You mean you'd not hesitate to take such revenge on Dorotea?

Fernando. Never could I abhor her so completely as to desire to see her ugly, so sweet will the memory of her beauty be to me always. Nor will my soul suffer time to convert a Dorotea so beautiful into one so ugly to my eyes, nor can I imagine that the years would dare tarnish so great a miracle of Nature.

Julio. Many retain their beauty a long time.

Fernando. The Queen of Rhodes, jealous on her husband's account, had Helen of Troy killed at the age of sixty.

Ludovico. I carried out all your other commissions. And since you did not receive my letters because you went to Cádiz and Sanlúcar, for which reason they were lost, know, Fernando, that I took yours—I mean, the ones you gave me—to Dorotea. I found her in bed, and not out of danger, because she had tried to kill herself with a diamond the night you left. Her servant Celia took the letters. She spoke little, but that little was of your unjust decision, and not without a tear or two, which, despite her efforts to conceal them, she could not withhold from me. Because it was with her as with the sun shining through the rain: though the cloud is not visible, sun and shower are. I departed, and many days later went back to see her, by then recovered from some bouts of fever, the gravity of which had left her emaciated. I'd always known that the sufferings of the soul affect the body, since the two are neighbors and close friends. Dorotea convalesced; a crutch appeared, a low headdress, a wimple encircling her face the first few days, and, afterward, the hair showing a bit, as if by accident. With this transformation there came a blue and white habit. Then one day I saw her here—I would not wish to reopen your wounds.

Fernando. Can't you see they're still fresh?

Ludovico. No woman more beautiful was ever painted by Titian, and that includes Rosa Suleiman, the Sultan's favorite.

Fernando. Could you not have said Sophonisba, Atalanta, or Cleopatra?

Ludovico. They were not painted by Titian.

Fernando. Touché! We've all seen that portrait of his.

Ludovico. Peasant women are wont to carry in their wattle baskets pure white curds, on which a few rose petals will drop from the nosegays they also carry. So in her face you must imagine bastard color against legitimate snow.

Fernando. Evidently you write verse, a habit leading you to carry that style into your prose—or else you're trying to drive me mad.

Ludovico. Restrain your delight; you're bound to lose it when you hear the sequel.

Fernando. In that case you would be doing me an immense favor, since my life depends on hating her.

Ludovico. I went back several nights to see if there were any Moors lurking offshore, and spied some figures wrapped in capes, like servants waiting while their master paid court. I was not mistaken. Would that I had been! A man stood at the window grille. Dorotea recognized me, and laughed repeatedly. I had the impulse to run them through, then reflected that her closing the window promptly was a sign of respect. Latterly, I paid her a call a week before you returned—having since been to a novena in Illescas, I could not see you until today. I noted a rich tapestry and a new dais. These gave me such a start I asked for water, whereupon I observed new silverware and two very well mannered mulatto girls, one bearing a tray and the other an embroidered hand towel which, as if being fresh were not enough, was most exquisitely redolent of a floral lozenge. I drank an asp in a gilded *búcaro,* but did not dare question her, because to inquire of a charming young woman the provenance of her domestic adornments and appointments is to deny her beauty and offend her honor most discourteously.

Fernando. Did she inquire after me at all?

Ludovico. This time she said nothing.

Fernando. Well, there you'll find the explanation of what you refrained from asking, and a key to the mystery behind the wealth you observed.

Ludovico. My dear fellow, I must tell you the truth: there has been talk of a Spaniard from the New World.

Fernando. Stop right there. Why did the ancients paint Love holding a fish in one hand and flowers in the other?

Ludovico. Because Love is master of both land and sea.

Fernando. He should have been painted with a bar of gold.

Ludovico. Ah, the enormous potency of gold!

Fernando. Let my misery speak to that.

Ludovico. No, since Arnaldus de Villa Nova does so in his *Book on Preserving Youth and Delaying Old Age*. To renew and restore the skin covering us, you make, as he has it, a drink concocted of the purest unalloyed gold. It has neither moistening nor drying effects. Instead, it blends smoothly with the humors of our temperaments. This drink is suited to the human constitution, and restores to lasting balance everything in it that begins to run down; it helps a cold stomach, gives a coward courage, fortifies the substance of the heart, and expels every harmful impression from it.

Fernando. You needn't go on about the powers of that potion. If it possesses the last one alone, it will tear this pernicious love out of my heart, and therewith restore what it took away, assuming gold was indeed the cause of my losing Dorotea.

Ludovico. The ancients were so secretive about how to perfect the potion, I doubt there is anyone in Spain who could prepare it.

Julio. It would suffice if someone still possessed it.

Fernando. An infallible example confirms the excellence of gold, to wit: as I was occupying Dorotea's heart, making her uneasy, I was dislodged therefrom by that gentleman who gave her gold in a takable, if not potable, form. Of the cuttlefish it is written that it moves up the line from the hook, stings the fisherman's hand, and, affecting the heart, kills him.

Ludovico. It must have cost the gentleman dearly.

Fernando. Not so dearly in gold as it cost me in heart's blood, and no gold can equal blood.

Julio. Plato observed that metals possess a spirit, and from him Virgil adopted the idea in the sixth book of the *Aeneid*—this, according to Leo Suabius.

Fernando. Spirit it must possess, at the very least, in order to produce such effects.

Ludovico. In the nature of things there are two fixed elements; from them, according to Levinus Lemnius, all types of metal are engendered in the innermost bowels of the earth. The elements are sulphur and mercury. The latter in the role of father, and the former, of mother, produce first gold, then the less noble silver, and then the other metals. So it should come as no surprise, Fernando, that the originator of them all should be so powerful.

Fernando. Damned stuff, to do me so much harm—for though so cold in itself, mercury engenders the gold that sets me afire! I am well aware of its utter inconstancy and also of its usefulness, recalling both the fickle and garrulous nature of women, and their being so necessary and important.

Julio. It has been observed of mercury that, when a man who had been treated with it for the French disease was being bled, it came out through the open vein, mingling silver and blood in those tiny globules that resemble pearls.

Fernando. Oh, Julio, having Dorotea lodged so deeply in the marrow of my bones, I believe, after suffering contact with her, if I were bled at my heart's vein, she would emerge from the incision like mercury!

Julio. What you need is to be bled from the vein of your head, so that both the hot air and Dorotea would come out at once.

Ludovico. In my opinion, this rage of Fernando's is not love, nor is his obsession with Dorotea an effect of it; rather, as a compass touched by a magnet always points north, so his former passion touched by jealousy of this New World Spaniard forces him to keep his fancy-ridden mind continually fixed upon her.

Julio. That being the case, it must have happened with him as it commonly does with concave mirrors. Set facing the sun, they throw off a refracted fire which easily kindles any suitable matter exposed to it (as is related of the mirror with which Archimedes set enemy ships on fire). Because when the sun's rays are focused upon a single point, such conflagration is the result.

Ludovico. So that the sun is Dorotea, Julio; the overseas Spaniard, the mirror; and Don Fernando, the matter set facing against it.

Julio. Dorotea's beauty is deflected by the glass of jealousy to Don Fernando's love, which would not be so ardent if her beauty had not been so deflected.

Ludovico. You are correct in your notion, Julio. Because any love brought to bear upon a focal point of jealousy will set the hardest-frozen Scythia on fire.

Fernando. Alas! When I was away, things went badly for me; now I am here, still worse. My life has not long to run.

Ludovico. And how have you been spending it since you returned?

Fernando. At night I read out of some storybook or poet. I lie down fearing I shall not sleep, and I am proven so right that I may be counted on to keep time like any clock. And if, in sheer fatigue from battling my thoughts, as Petrarch says, I do happen to sleep a bit, I conjure out of the shadows such prodigious fantasies that I would do better to stay awake.

Ludovico. Such are the effects of melancholy.

Fernando. At dawn I go out on the Prado or down to the river where, seated on the bank, I fix my gaze upon the water, offering it fancies to carry off, that they may never return.

Ludovico. What a silly way to waste the day!

Julio. And understand, Ludovico, with this goes so much misery that he will often fall into my arms half-dead from such amorous fits of swooning. I tell him (since he claims his sufferings are in a good cause, or so he says in a ballad he sings) that there is no valid reason to be sad. Yesterday, when we were down in the grove by the river, I wrote him a sonnet to this effect in a notebook.

Ludovico. In Latin or Castilian?

Julio. Why, Castilian. No one appreciates Latin anymore, which is a great pity.

Ludovico. Not so. For in my view, the poet should write in his native tongue. Homer did not write in Latin, nor Virgil in Greek, and each of us owes it to his own tongue to write in it. Camoëns did so in Portugal and Tasso in Italy.

Fernando. Sannazaro wote his long poem and eclogues in Latin.

Ludovico. But also wrote his *Arcadia* and other works, just as Bembo, Ariosto, and Petrarch did.

Fernando. Did Ariosto write any poetry in Latin?

Ludovico. Muzio Giustinopolitano cites an epitaph of his on the Marquis of Pescara, which stands in direct opposition to every other one ever written.

Fernando. Recite your sonnet, Julio. Let us not overlook it.

Julio.

No merit lies in growing sad with love.
    Let love's pangs freely be invited,
    for if one places the affections wisely,
    losing the heart's the same as winning heaven.
Possession should not be the goal of love.
    The loved one gains esteem by being wary
    and too much hope entails the risk of loss,
    while silence is the surest way to win.
Jealousy will give clear cause for sadness
    if love is placed where it does not belong.
    Confidence never can exist with care.
If one is sad, his choice was no doubt wrong,
    for when a worthy love finds out the heart,
    the lover never knows a moment's sadness.

Ludovico. You ended it skillfully, not like some I could name who begin a sonnet and then drop off in style and thought till in the end they say nothing. And what about you? Haven't you written anything on this separation?

Fernando. These lines:

Oh harshest of states,
    perfidious absence,
    you split the soul,
    but not life itself.
Death-in-life you are called,
    as well you may be;
    you quicken desire
    but put out its eyes.
Why not show mercy
    at this separation
    by taking my life
    as you've taken my soul?
Manzanares, humble stream,
    beside your green banks,
    that crown you with elms,
    and festoon you with ivy,
a shepherd girl lives,
    so divine in all things,

she does the Court honor
and brings the town glory.
Cascading waters
   are singing her praise
   to listening birds,
   attentive flowers.
Her beauty unrivaled
   envies only itself—
   she might stop to reflect
   she makes the sun jealous.
No peer can sun find
   along his gold band,
   on his way to Spain,
   and beyond, to the Indies.
If she loved me not,
   when she looked in her mirror,
   the glass would make her
   a lady Narcissus.
Allowed to love her—
   oh, luck of the bold!—
   my greatest delight
   is to suffer for her.
Not doubting a moment
   I'd see her and serve her,
   I'm deprived of such joy
   by force overwhelming.
For their selfish ends,
   men plot my death,
   at the moment my hopes
   flourished the greenest.
So the flower of Apollo,
   when he drops in the west,
   entombs its red disk
   beneath it green leaves.
So the yellow carnation,
   when rudely trampled
   by grazing cattle,
   loses its fragrance.

So the vine embracing
  with frail caresses
  the poplar felled
  by pitiless blows,
feels its strength ebb away,
  its soul come undone,
  and, undoing its clasp,
  releases its tendrils.
If bodies are forced,
  leaving souls behind,
  to seek other skies—
  God in heaven, the woe!
Were my love not pledged
  to purest trust,
  the pain of this parting
  would work my death.
To heal such pain
  would be a disservice,
  since what makes me love
  is the cause of my sorrow.
Oh mountains, capped
  and clothed in snow,
  defying the clouds
  with your lofty brows,
if my love scaled your heights,
  would its fiery flames
  burn your snows away
  or be frozen by them?
In the end I'll prevail
  and my shepherd girl,
  through sighs and throbs,
  will hear my voice sing:
"Oh thoughts of my sweet,
  traveling with me,
  the breath of my sighs
  will waft you home.
Having come with me,
  you must leave me now,

with a following wind
    to hasten you home.
Persist as you may
    in staying with me,
    why comfort yourself
    by slaying me?
Thoughts of my sweet,
    traveling with me,
    the breath of my sighs
    will waft you home."

Julio. You'll have to find some pastime, master Ludovico, for Don Fernando. If he continues to go mad at this rate, he will soon reach the point of ending it all, which must be what he wishes.

Fernando. On the contrary, I neither fear additional suffering nor do I seek relief from what I now endure.

The insidious pain is not the foe
whose cruel assaults I combat to my sorrow—
to pain inured, there's none I don't know.

This is from a sonnet by that renowned Andalusian, Fernando de Herrera, and really, though it may seem to Julio that my obsession will lead me into more desperate straits, he is mistaken. Because I'm less in danger of going mad without Dorotea than with her.

Ludovico. Which speaks well for her beauty.

Julio. I am certain that if she were his, he would not love her half so much.

Fernando. The argument from privation is foolish in this instance.

Julio. Well, if not that, jealousy suffices.

Fernando. How can I love her for the very thing that makes me abhor her?

Julio. You do not abhor her. Rather, you fear she will abhor you.

Fernando. As you well know, I have wished her dead.

Julio. Reading the third book of Xenophon, I discovered something which amazed me, not unrelated to this subject.

Ludovico. If it impresses you, it must be noteworthy indeed.

Julio. Armenius told Cyrus that husbands, on discovering them with adulterers, did not murder their wives because of their part in the offense, but out of fury at their wives' having withdrawn love from them and attached it to someone else.

Ludovico. Curious notion! And when you stop to think of it, that seems the original impulse for killing them, as many have shown who were content to suffer the indignity as long as their wives were not in love.

Julio. Proof indisputable.

Fernando. On loving and hating, consult the same source. For Cyrus replied that he was of two minds when people thought it impossible he could leave the lovely Panthea. And you'll discover there that one feeling was love and the other hate.

Julio. Which is why I fear for your sanity and would prefer that you either love or hate, once and for all.

Ludovico. This illness, which doctors call *erotes*, is melancholia arising from amorous proclivities or from losing possession of a beloved whom one has enjoyed. The cure is baths, music, wine, and theater.

Julio. Wine Fernando does not drink; as for music, singing makes him all the sadder. For he is like the chameleon, which assumes the color against which it is placed—sad against sad, gay against gay.

Ludovico. Pliny gives the reason for this, but it does not satisfy me. For, he says that, being the most timorous animal in the world, the chameleon loses color the fastest; but this should be attributed, rather, to transparency, as in the case of glass.

Julio. There is an herb called *centum capita* by the Latins ...

Ludovico. That name would best fit the common herd. Woe to anyone exposing the sum of his learning to their vitiated judgment and benighted taste!

Julio. The herb in question has a hermaphroditic root, and its effect depends on whether it is applied to male or female. But let that falsehood go the way of all the other fables.

Ludovico. The same author asserts that possession of the root was what made the great poet Sappho love Phaon Lesbius so much, the subject, you recall, of one of Ovid's *Epistles*.

Julio. If Gerarda has discovered this root known by her ilk as mandrake, and Dorotea now possesses it, what theater, what music, what wine better than herself "to allow my darling convict some surcease"?—to quote that ditty everyone is now singing.

Fernando. I'd sooner die a thousand deaths.

Ludovico. Then you don't intend to see her?

Fernando. May that be the last day of my life.

Ludovico. Plato in his *Banquet of Love* says the gods reserve their laughter for lovers who break their vows.

Julio. They did once laugh at Pallas Athena's piping, since it contorted her face so.

Fernando. I might have seen Dorotea often since my return, yet, contrary to every desire, my disenchantment prevailed, for honor is ever obdurate.

Ludovico. Then follow some respectable calling.

Fernando. I have no inclination to the hunt, nor have I ever gambled.

Ludovico. Write a poem. You know it will be a great distraction.

Fernando. Love deprives me of all wit.

Ludovico. Love has given wit to many who lacked it.

Fernando. And taken it from those who had it. What would you have me write about?

Ludovico. Some lofty subject; there are so many Spanish captains to provide you with a theme. Consider those most excellent soldiers, the Duke of Alba, on land, and that most felicitous Marquis of Santa Cruz, on the sea: the former, invincible scion of Toledo; the latter, illustrious Bazán; the former obeyed by earth; the latter by water. And dedicate the poem to one of their children.

Fernando. Such an undertaking is beyond my years.

Ludovico. It won't be after you finish it. You have a long way to go between first sketch and final polishing.

Fernando. More appropriate for my untried hand would be an amorous subject, such as the beauty of Angelica.

Ludovico. That would never distract you, which is my aim. It should be something serious.

Fernando. I'll start tomorrow.

Ludovico. You'll be halfway there already.

Fernando. Beginnings are always difficult.

Ludovico. Exitus acta probat—endings bear out all that went before, as Ovid says. Because the ending is not only what everything else leads up to, but the best part of all, according to the Philosopher in his *Physics.*

Fernando. I must prepare for the ending at the beginning. But why exhaust myself, since I know perfectly well that, except for a few mournful ditties I might sing, this jealous passion will leave room for nothing else, and like a cloud-curtain will snuff out all the light of my mind?

Ludovico. I shall see you tomorrow and bring you a subject of my own poor devising to write about, which dressed up in your style of verse will look admirable. God keep you.

Fernando. What do you think, Julio, of the turns my fortune takes? I swore to Ludovico I'd never see Dorotea again, and I am dying to break the oath.

Julio. Have you already forgotten what he told you about the laughter of the gods?

Fernando. That's exactly why I won't succeed in not seeing her, but I will in not speaking to her.

Julio. If you see her, you will speak to her.

Fernando. Do not believe it for a moment.

Julio. No, I won't, since I ready do.

Fernando. What have we to lose by going tonight to see those doors through which I used to pass into such a paradise? That's not seeing Dorotea; Dorotea is no door.

Julio. That's an easy syllogism.

Fernando. How so?

Julio. Every door is wood, every woman is flesh; therefore, woman is not a door.

Fernando. The devil take you, you've made me laugh for all my misery. What a ridiculous syllogism!

Julio. At least the one the overseas Spaniard is composing with Dorotea is in the *Dari,* or Donor, form, and if there were a *Recipient* form in her logic, you'd find her syllogism there, the conclusion being inferred from the two propositions, to wit: love doing the giving and gold, the digging.

Fernando. Now, by way of precaution, we'll take two bucklers and two nags, in case we should need to make use of the fencing lessons of Paredes.

Julio. A superb master, though he goes into mourning after every lesson.

Fernando. Tonight let us at least view the jewel case our gem inhabits.

Julio. Shall I take the instrument along?

Fernando. Bring it. If there is occasion for swordplay, it won't much matter if it's lost.

Julio. What could be more lost than you?

Fernando. Be still, Julio; as some writer of sacred verse once said, the tongue of love sounds barbarous to anyone not in love.

Scene 5

DON BELA · LAURENCIO · FELIPA

Bela. Entering this street, I seem to be going down another one in the noble city of Valencia in April.

Laurencio. What do you mean?

Bela. Its fragrance is like no other.

Laurencio. I hold that to be impossible, when you consider the orange trees from which such different blossoms issue forth at this hour.

Bela. Ah, Laurencio, remember how Plautus says of lovers that they flatter even their ladies' dogs.

Laurencio. Your fancy has lighted on the sweet scent of Dorotea, and the closer you come to her house, the more fixed it becomes. People in love shift all their senses to the imagination.

Bela. This is the window grille. By day I like these blinds; at night they irritate me.

Laurencio. Why is that?

Bela. Because by day they keep Dorotea from being seen, just as I wish. And at night they prevent me from seeing her, my sole desire and purpose in coming.

Laurencio. Think of all the ardent entreaties that have passed through the bars of this window.

Bela. Can there by anything to compare them with?

Laurencio. How could there not be?

Bela. Then with what, Laurencio?

Laurencio. With the very inanities addressed to her.

Bela. In my case, just call it madness. What can Dorotea be doing?

Laurencio. Making plans to bilk you further, no doubt.

Bela. Spoken like a menial!

Laurencio. Just ask the shopkeeper.

Bela. I've already told you: considering her merits, nothing is too good.

Laurencio. Someday you'll consider it all too bad.

Bela. Beautiful as she is, she'd not be worth a farthing if she weren't expensive.

Laurencio. True enough, since men are more attached to what they've put their money into than to their ladies' charms.

Bela. Why is that?

Laurencio. Because, like gamblers, they are bent on recouping their losses.

Bela. Someone has opened a window.

Felipa. Is that you, Don Bela?

Bela. It is, Felipa.

Felipa. Teodora has not yet retired.

Bela. What is she doing?

Felipa. She is at her rosary, and her head keeps dipping like a mare's with every bead she prays.

Laurencio. Is she mounted sidesaddle or astraddle?

Bela. What about my Dorotea?

Felipa. She is composing a ballad to send you.

Laurencio. What did I tell you? How much do you wager the ballad addresses the shopkeeper and the jingle your pocketbook?

Bela. Keep your voice down, idiot.

Felipa. If you could only see how delightfully she minces at the conceits—her hand with the pen vying with the paper, being made the whiter by the black one dispensing the ink.

Bela. From the horn, Felipa?

Laurencio. What a compliment! Tell her to go a-blacking till she's blue in the face.

Felipa. Fido is loose. I must have him brought in. Go for a stroll, meanwhile, and I'll let Dorotea know you're here.

Bela. Give her this note. Love has turned me into a poet too.

Felipa. Why are you wearing amber-scented gloves? They only rouse suspicion when you go by.

Bela. Here, you take them and they'll be out of danger.

Laurencio. My prophecy comes true.

Bela. How do you mean?

Laurencio. I always said these ladies would skin the hide off you. Tell me if I was wrong, since they are now peeling off your gloves, which comes to the same thing.

Bela. You must mean I have skin like Alexander's, of whom it is reported that he sweated pure amber.

Laurencio. That's writers' flattery for you.

Bela. I'm well aware that the fame of princes rests upon the report of pens, for better or for worse.

Laurencio. Assuming that is true about Alexander, Nature favored him as she does certain animals, for Eastern monkeys smell of musk and civet is extracted from cats.

Bela. Dorotea's scent is naturally sweet.

Laurencio. Say she's a cat in clawing at doubloons, not in giving off perfumes.

Bela. What an unconscionable fool!

Laurencio. Because I never learned flattery.

Bela. Shall I demonstrate the error in your thinking?

Laurencio. I'd much rather see none in yours.

Bela. Tell me, is Dorotea beautiful?

Laurencio. That I cannot deny.

Bela. Is she cultivated?

Laurencio. In every respect.

Bela. Has she natural charm?

Laurencio. In everything she says and does.

Bela. Have you heard of anyone suspicious entering her house?

Laurencio. No one.

Bela. Does she behave lovingly toward me?

Laurencio. You know she does.

Bela. Is she clean and wholesome?

Laurencio. What does that mean?

Bela. I wish to remain healthy.

Laurencio. I acknowledge it all.

Bela. Does she deserve to be loved?

Laurencio. She does.

Bela. Then what is my crime?

Laurencio. What you're spending.

Bela. What am I spending?

Laurencio. Time and money.

Bela. Isn't it all mine to spend?

Laurencio. Money is, time is not.

Bela. Where should it go, then?

Laurencio. Into the business at hand.

Bela. What does Dorotea keep me from in that regard?

Laurencio. From attending to your own advancement.

Bela. On the contrary, she alleviates the insufferable discouragement of the replies I receive, always having to listen to the same thing.

Laurencio. Who seeks preferment and has no patience, should seek no further.

Bela. So you also frown on my seeking?

Laurencio. No, of course not. But the pursuit of high preferment does not sit well with indulgence in low diversions.

Bela. Preaching at me, are you?

Laurencio. Come now, sir—human ambitions demand superhuman effort.

Bela. I do nothing if not exert effort.

Laurencio. One effort you never make.

Bela. You mean giving up Dorotea?

Laurencio. That only stands to reason.

Bela. How can I do so, when she loyally responds to my attentions, and I am so much in love?

Laurencio. You can, indeed, once you recognize she would leave you, should something better come along.

Bela. No, she would not, since she's a woman of principle.

Laurencio. Yes, but still a woman.

Bela. Ladies of her quality transcend the sex.

Laurencio. Of what quality?

Bela. Her noble birth and the responsibilities of rank.

Laurencio. Just say she's the lady of Dorotea's house, as people now put it.

Bela. But surely there are lords of houses and manors?

Laurencio. Many. But some have the unspeakable effrontery to use the appellation on no other basis than their family name. And, as no one challenges them, they get away with it. However, one who is the legitimate possessor of his name ought to take pride in it and should be honored for his lustrous lineage. But for common men to claim estates and vassals when they have neither positions nor occupations of honor is both scandalous and ridiculous.

Bela. Beauty is always a mistress of vassals.

Laurencio. Particularly if you regard as such anyone laying claim to it.

Bela. What difference does that make, if their claims fail?

Laurencio. Remember how you staked your claim to her beauty?

Bela. How could I forget it?

Laurencio. What instruments did you use?

Bela. Gold and Gerarda.

Laurencio. Has she shown you favor?

Bela. What a question!

Laurencio. And if another staked his claim, would he not use the same instruments?

Bela. No, because here I stand blocking his way.

Laurencio. So did the one you supplanted.

Bela. The law says that possession and ownership are two separate and distinct things.

Laurencio. Then what ownership can you claim where there is no entitlement to possession?

Bela. I am convinced, Laurencio, that all the gold in all the world would be powerless to conquer Dorotea now.

Laurencio. I am not referring to your high merit, which she recognizes. But gold has always been gold, and Gerarda will always be Gerarda.

Bela. Against gold, more gold; against Gerarda, steel.

Laurencio. If it brings more trouble, it's no remedy.

Bela. If what brings more trouble?

Laurencio. Laying hands on a wretched old woman.

Bela. It would mean one troublemaker less in the world.

Laurencio. And what good would that do when there are so many left who, by tongue and pen, deceptive letters, ugly words, are constantly depriving others of the honor which they themselves do not possess?

Bela. You appear to be out of sorts this evening. Go home, Laurencio. You've grown impertinent.

Laurencio. I cannot obey you. It would not be right of me to leave you alone.

Bela. If you are to stay with me then, be still.

Laurencio. I was wrong to speak up as a friend would, when I should have kept quiet as a servant does.

Scene 6

DOROTEA · FELIPA · CELIA

Dorotea. To whom were you speaking, Felipa?

Felipa. Don Bela.

Dorotea. Has he left?

Felipa. I told him Teodora was uneasy, saying her prayers, peering about, and grumbling.

Dorotea. And what did you say about me?

Felipa. That you were writing a ballad to him—and Laurencio kept muttering something.

Dorotea. What was he muttering?

Felipa. That the ballad must be something prosaic on the subject of your wardrobe.

Dorotea. You've all guessed wrong.

Felipa. What do you mean?

Dorotea. You can't possibly imagine.

Felipa. It wouldn't be a letter, by any chance?

Dorotea. I couldn't bear waiting any longer for Fernando to remember me.

Felipa. And I would never have expected him to wait so long, considering the great love he bore you.

Dorotea. Men are so strong-minded!

Felipa. Particularly when offended.

Dorotea. I gave him no ground for offense.

Felipa. You told him you were bound to offend him.

Dorotea. If he had not gone off, I would not have done so.

Felipa. What can you possibly have to write him about, with Don Bela so blissfully installed?

Dorotea. Fetch the candle here and listen.

Felipa. Celia is jealous of my becoming your confidante.

Dorotea. She should be, so as to avoid growing conceited and puffed up. A master is wise to neglect for a while servants he's fond of and so make them fearful they have been forgotten. Always treating them as equals is not to use but to be used by them.

Felipa. You are right to shuffle us about like a deck of cards. Having the same one turn up over and over undercuts one's position and misprises one's hand.

Dorotea. Listen to some lovelorn nonsense of mine.

Felipa. If it concerns love, it cannot be nonsense.

Dorotea. "Who would have thought on the night before you went away, Fernando my love, that so great a misfortune could befall us both that I would be pressed into giving you cause and you would have cause for departing? Cruel as we both were, you were more so with me, in view of your greater strength and understanding. Woman's nature is so timorous, and the slightest threat so quickly uncovers her cowardice, that there the blame for my audacity must lie. You may say, how could my love fail to counsel me that it was better for us both to die than to separate, or that my mother could never be so stern a judge of me as I was of myself? Here I have no excuse to offer you, except that my mother seems to have deprived me of my wits along with my hair. I went to your house all in tears, so blind and dazed, the last thing to cross my mind was the thought you might abandon me. For if I had thought you had another love which left you free to choose a way out of your troubles rather than a way to avenge your honor, I would sooner have yielded the rest of my hair to my mother than have gone to you with the handful she had already pulled out.

"I was thinking as I went along that I would find consolation in your distress, and I found greater cruelty at your hands than at hers. For she was punishing me because of you, and you me because of her. You responded so sternly and with such asperity that my soul was forced to enforce my natural weakness, lest it lose honor, for there is nothing more destructive of honor than the scorn of one beloved. This you cannot deny, for Julio and Celia were present, more astonished at your reply than at the unexpected turn of those events I had been recounting. What beast could be so hardhearted as to inflict in one instant and so implacably a punishment so great upon five years of love? The ancients, with their catalogues of men's ingratitude—what record would they not have left of your cruelty, had you lived then? All you could do to comfort my tears was to lay the blame on me for your not being married, never stopping to think that you are still only twenty-two years of age. Consider, heartless one, how many years still remain for you to marry, and how much in my debt you are for this very reason, since the five years we have known each other I have saved you from incurring regrets. Your coldness froze my tears; your asperity, my heart; and your words, my will; for unjust replies inflame humility, cloud the understanding, and shake the serenity of the spirit with storms of anger.

"In a word, you had sufficient spirit to depart. Yet that is not the greatest cruelty, when I measure it against three months of neglect, during which you must have thought it would demean you to let me know, by writing, that you did remember me. What could you have lost in self-respect by inquiring about the body whose soul you had carried off, having left me that night in such a state that, as I had no sword with which to kill myself, I resorted to a ring you had given me so that the poison of its diamond would serve as one? But it declined to work my death, in deference to the heart wherein you lodged, for since that heart always melted to wax at your pleasure, the diamond, like a thunderbolt, disdained to crush a thing so feeble. Oh, how perfectly you encouraged me to suffer, without offense to you, such a desperate absence! Oh, how splendidly you kept alive my hopes of seeing you again, so as to save me from succumbing to any temptation to forget you! But you did well to disabuse me of your love so that mine would not torment me. I shall not reproach you for all the sacrifices I have made because of my esteem for you—in health, in reputation, and in estate. I shall, though, for my poverty, which drove me to the extreme of looking unbeautiful in your eyes, for want of anything to clothe me.

"But why do I reproach you with such things, when you must think I drove you away in order to obtain them? And if by chance this reaches you, and you share it laughingly with some woman who derides my tears and glories in having made you cease loving me, you will both be in error because you will not be out of love and she will not have supplanted me. And all this, not from any arrogance but from an obvious conclusion: you cannot have forgotten me, since I have not forgotten you. For, according to what you men think, say, and write concerning us, we women more easily forget you. And despite all the reasons I have for hating you, and my being a woman, since I still love you, it follows that a man must still feel the same love for me he has always felt, all the more so because men have more to forget in women than we in them. For our perfections and our charms are always greater, to say nothing of our gentle, sweet, and loving natures, which incline your desires in our direction. I do not ask for your reply nor that you remember me; asking will not do what feeling does. I beg only that you not complain of me in your verses, lest, having compromised my reputation by praising me, they now destroy me altogether through obloquy. Yours, ever and again."

Felipa. The best thing in that letter is the close.

Dorotea. How does it strike you?

Felipa. As worthy of your love and your wit.

Dorotea. The former makes up for the failings of the latter.

Celia. If you have finished reading, I'll come and speak to you.

Dorotea. Don't be so peevish, Celia. I have no reason to withhold anything from you. This is a letter.

Celia. I should like to inquire for whom it is intended, since I am to be the bearer.

Dorotea. Is your resentment sending you to Seville, like another Don Fernando?

Celia. No, ma'am. But I must know if he's the one you are writing to, since it may be you have troubled yourself unnecessarily.

Dorotea. Oh God, Celia! Is that madman dead or has he gone over to the New World?

Celia. No, ma'am, God forfend. Only I think he is in Madrid.

Dorotea. Don't be silly—what are you saying?

Celia. Bernarda and the black girl have seen him come down our street muffled in his cloak, with Julio, that most worthy tutor and counselor of his. This they told me privately, I decided to find out, and there can be no doubt of it.

Felipa. What is agitating you so? Where are you off to? Restrain yourself, Don Bela is in the street. Leave it to me. If need be, I can speak for you.

Dorotea. Restrain me, love. Now with Fernando's return, better to feign indifference than to reveal concern.

Scene 7

DON FERNANDO · JULIO

Fernando. Dark night.

Julio. Befitting your purpose.

Fernando. I rely upon the darkness to assist me.

Julio. Virgil says that Cacus belched a smoke-filled night from his mouth. What would he not have said of this street?

Fernando. To me it seems the very Idalian dew which Pontano speaks of, along with the myrrh of the Orontes and all the aromatic herbs—Sabean, Arabian, Armenian, and Panchaean.

Julio. 'The dust of sheep is intoxicating to a wolf.' But Don Luis de Góngora said the streets of Madrid were simply muck laced with parsley and mint.

Fernando. I'd sooner sleep in this one than in the gardens of Cyprus, amid the roses of Mount Pangaeus, or Hyblean and Elysian flowers.

Julio. In his picture of Ariadne, Philostratos uses the term "inebriates of love" for those whose excessive love shows neither moderation nor restraint.

Fernando. Now tell me, Julio, is not the blood of youth more fine, more clear, hotter, and more sweet?

Julio. An astute philosopher weighs the meaning behind a proposition before formulating his reply, concession, or denial. Your meaning, I presume, is that once age dissolves the fine particles, the blood turns thick and sluggish, and with passing years grows cold and dry. Well, I am not ten years your senior, and if I remonstrate with you, it is not as an elder but as a friend.

Fernando. You seem to answer before you are questioned.

Julio. It is not your loving which concerns me, but your over-concern with loving.

Fernando. As the sun, great heart of the world, in its rotational movement forms light, which is diffused over lower things, so my heart, perpetually in motion, stirs up the blood, spreading such spirits throughout my being that they emerge as sparks from the eyes, sighs on the lips, and love-conceits upon the tongue.

Julio. I acknowledge that you have the extremely delicate blood of Dorotea transfused into your veins, as Lysias had that of Phaedrus in Marsilio's *Plato.* But all the ancient philosophers say that law is simply a rule of reason derived from the divinity of the gods, a rule which ordains what is virtuous and prohibits what is not.

Fernando. Am I perchance in love with a marble statue, like that youth who wreathed one in roses and tried to buy it from the magistrates in Athens, and when they would not sell it to him died in a most pitiful agony? Or am I in love with a painting of Helen, like the emissary of Caius Caesar, and not with a woman whose soul and infinite graces made the fashioning of her beauty the special study and concern of Nature?

Julio. In any case, for such troubles only time can be the Avicenna.

Fernando. Did it have to be a Moor? Was no other doctor to be found?

Julio. No, because it takes a barbarian to cure a madman.

Fernando. Ah, these walls, these doors! Ah, the bars of this beauteous prison of my liberty! You shall have a thousand kisses.

Julio. You are kissing the bars?

Fernando. Here Dorotea would lay her hand when these bars were the links of my chain and her hand a crystal loop encircling them.

Julio. As report has it, she can now make the bars golden.

Fernando. Is anything beyond the power of gold, that most excellent material of the element earth?

Julio. According to Paracelsus, every primary body is reducible to its element. Thus man to earth. And giving a philosophic twist to the fable of the nymphs, he reduced them to water. There was something else there about Melusinas, those creatures which he assigned to air.

Fernando. And the bearing of all this, Julio?

Julio. Only that he neglected the realm of love.

Fernando. What realm is that?

Julio. The element of fire.

Fernando. That, alas, he retained for the salamander of my heart.

Julio. Aelian and Pliny speak of an animal named pyralis which is engendered by fire.

Fernando. And that animal, oh Julio, am I, who live and die tempering with my tears the searing flame consuming me.

Julio. The poet Hesiod says somewhere that naiads are long-lived. By now your spirit must have turned into one. And the amphibian is a creature living half on land, half in water.

Fernando. All such fables are the moral figures for my sufferings.

Julio. Some persons claim they're true and cite witnesses. There's Draconet Bonifazio, who saw Tritons, and Theodore Gaza saw Nereids, and on one of those voyages of discovery in the New World, certain pilots saw an old man standing naked on a cliff, and upon their coming up to ask what land it was, the man suddenly threw himself off the bluff into the sea, and, amid swirls of spray, dived beneath the waves.

Fernando. Dove sounds better.

Julio. You might also say *took a dive,* which, though expressive, sounds slightly harsh.

Fernando. What a silly way to divert me! What can Dorotea be doing now?

Julio. She is probably lighting candles by the *bale* at your portrait, and praying for the return of its original.

Fernando. Oh, enemy of mine! Was it not enough to mock me without dragging *Bela* into it? Did you think the equivoque would escape me?

Julio. In no way was *bale* maliciously intended. That would be carrying subtlety too far. You will just have to believe me when I say that what happens to poets happened to me: a rhyme often leads them to say things they'd never conceived with their own wit, all the more so the closer they are to the laity, or, as they say, to lay brothers of Parnassus.

Fernando. What a misguided woman she is!

Julio. Very well guided rather, since the overseas Spaniard, though not so young, is said to be most accomplished. And in Guazzo's *Dialogues* you'll find that where simple-minded women love the body, wise ones love the soul. And·in a canto of his *Orlando,* Ariosto advises women to give their love to men of riper years, so long as they're not *troppo maturi.*

Fernando. Alas, for these twenty-two years of mine and their twenty-two thousand miseries! When will they ever end or else put an end to this wretched life of mine!

Julio. Is this any place to bring all that up?

Fernando. Oh, my treasure, my first love, my only hope! Oh, my belovèd mistress, Dorotea, my own! How could you be so cruel to me? How could you have spoken words that left me honor-bound to lose you forever?

Julio. For goodness sake, master, stop your ranting. Pick up your instrument and sing, if only to lift yourself out of such a black mood. I think she knows you're here, and perchance you will discover if any live ember still glows among the ashes of the fire, so that love, the phoenix, may rise to live again, in Lactantius' phrase, as "the *antistes* of the wildwood and the reverend priestess of light," after she makes her tomb or nest of tears of myrrh, wafting amomum, acanthus, and cassia.

Fernando. Try as you will, you cannot lift my spirits. Whether or not she knows I am here, I intend to make these strings tell Dorotea how unstrung I feel. And if she does not listen, it won't matter, because the soul delights in music naturally.

Julio. Thus spake the Philosopher.

Fernando. Ah, sunlight of my life! Break forth and hear me now, though you set me ablaze, being fire itself.

Julio. Heavenly bodies produce heat, not because they are themselves hot, but insofar as they possess luminosity and rotational velocity.

Fernando. But, sunlight of my life, how can you come out and hear me, though you possess my soul, which bids you to, when you also have the soul of Don Bela preventing you?

Julio. Quite impossible for a subject to have more than one form. If the soul of Don Bela inhabits Dorotea's love, where is there any room for your soul?

Fernando. Right there beside her.

Julio. It's also quite impossible for form to exist without matter.

Fernando. Who told you so?

Julio. Averröes, for one.

Fernando. Well, you and Averröes can both go hang; you've pummeled my brains long enough.

Julio. Then go ahead and sing, since you're finished tuning, lest someone come along and interfere.

Fernando.

> My poor little barque
>   split on the reefs,
>   sailless yet sailing

alone in the waves:
whither bound, off course,
　　heading out to sea?
　　No wish can be sane
　　where mad hopes prevail.
Like all those tall ships,
　　you bravely set forth,
　　turn your back on the coast,
　　plunge into wild seas.
Though you run equal risks,
　　with more to dismay
　　and less to protect you,
　　you challenge the waves.
Beware, for they hurl you
　　against the sharp reefs
　　of prideful envy,
　　that wrecker of honor.
When you would sail
　　skirting the coast,
　　you'd no cause to fear
　　the sea's stormy rage.
While safely sailing
　　along native shores
　　where water is shallow,
　　there's never great danger.
Yet virtue's more honored
　　abroad than at home
　　and pearls more valued
　　on leaving the shell.
You will say many vessels,
　　unlucky when leaving,
　　came back in triumph
　　on favoring winds.
Heed not their example;
　　remember the others,
　　how many were lost
　　for each that succeeded.
For venturing seaward,
　　you are too guileless;

you lack sails of falsehood
and flattery's oars.
Oh barque, who deceived you?
   Turn back, make for home;
   competing with galleons,
   you ask for trouble.
What riggings bedeck you,
   what elegant pennants
   go whipping the wind,
   and shading the water?
What crow's nest reveals
   a tall tree's crown,
   a prospect of land,
   empty fringes of sea?
What fair-weather clouds
   encourage soundings,
   when you've strayed off course,
   your bearings lost?
What price bright fame
   if you're buried in sand?
   The child of misfortune
   never reaches his goal.
What good to be girt
   by green and red branches?
   In woods of coral
   only salt grass grows.
Waterside bay trees
   reserve accolades
   for high-riding ships
   with riggings of gold.
Drop your arrogant airs
   lest they make of me
   Phaëthon of boatmen
   bewept by green bays.
The days are gone by
   when zephyrs billowed,
   caressing the roses
   and wafting their scent.
Now hurricanes wild

in arrogance rising,
spatter the stars,
besprinkle the sun.
Now heavy bolts
from Vulcan's forge
set fire to hovels,
sparing great towers.
When, pleased with our catch,
you rode up the beach,
I would step ashore drenched
but exult in my safety.
When dawn rouged her cheeks
with mother-of-pearl,
you'd list with more fish
than the pearls she was weeping.
The bright sun I worship
dried me off with her beams.
and a cabin gave us
a bed of strewn leaves.
Groom I was called,
and bride I called her,
while heaven's great torch
stood still with envy.
Without quarrel or suit,
death has divorced us;
oh, pity this barque
engulfed now in tears.
Stock-still on the strand
your sail ropes idle.
With no love to return to,
there's no need for sails.
Oh you, my boat's mistress,
while your steps everlasting
gild the fixed stars
and in peace you repose,
may I merit your asking
Him you joy in forever
to convey me to you,
more lovely than ever.

My love be your pledge,
    for no merciful god
    will turn a deaf ear
    to human entreaties.
Ah, you pay me no heed!
    But man's life is brief:
    while it lasts, all falls short,
    at the end, all needs cease.

Julio. Sir, I believe they have opened the window slightly. There's a shadow in the light. Can it be Dorotea?

Fernando. Simpleton, how could that be? The sun would never cast a shadow upon another light unless some body intervened.

Julio. It could be striking Celia, and she'd create the shadow.

Fernando. I believe I sang poorly because my voice was unsteady.

Julio. On the contrary, never in my life have I heard you produce such excellent trills and chromatics. And when your voice shifted to falsetto an octave or two higher, it sounded superb.

Fernando. You are still trying to lift my spirits, I see. A trembling heart rarely makes for a steady voice. I'll sing something else, now that I'm recovering.

Julio. Or at least now that there's an audience.

Fernando.

What do you want of me, joys,
    if you are bringing me cheer,
    since you can only endure
    till you learn you're mine?
Why try to convince me
    to welcome pleasure and joy,
    when no heart is left me
    whence they might derive?
Joys, how should I use you,
    beset by griefs so many,
    since you can only endure
    till you learn you're mine?
Denying sadness, one
    betrays a want of courage,
    since to suffer through love's sadness,
    is the heart's most noble pledge.
Joys, I have no desire

> to wait upon your pleasure,
>   since you can only endure
>   till you learn you're mine.
> I could bear the pains
>   of this wearisome life,
>   if you would but assure me
>   that another was your intended.
>   Say that you do belong
>   to one who will value cheer,
>   since you can only endure
>   till you learn you're mine.
> When all my days were joys,
>   alas, I learned to be sad.
>   So short-lived did they prove,
>   they soon eluded my grasp.
>   What are you, joys, but comets,
>   and I, but your light in decline,
>   since you can only endure
>   till you learn you're mine?

Julio. There's not the faintest sign of anyone addressing or summoning you. Only shadows keep moving back and forth past the half-opened window.

Fernando. Those must be my happy days, which were nothing but shadows in this house. Come, Julio, let's be gone.

Scene 8

FELIPA · FERNANDO
JULIO · DOROTEA

Felipa. Oh, sir!

Julio. Turn back, they're calling you.

Fernando. I do not recognize the voice.

Julio. Everything will have changed.

Fernando. And all to my disadvantage.

Julio. They change the staffs of office with each new magistrate.

Fernando. Who is calling me, and what is it you wish?

Felipa. A lady most delighted to hear your voice begs you to sing once more about that poor little barque.

Fernando. The owner may be unwilling, since he has never on the high seas encountered such danger as on coming into port. However, I will oblige you by singing of his present state of mind, which is not a very happy one. For I owed to this house the happiness I once knew, since here a lady lived, as sweet a subject of my affections as now she is a painful one.

Felipa. Lived, and lives still, for in this house she was born and she has known no other.

Fernando. I'd heard she had gone over to a new world.

Julio. Touché! Though not a subject for public airing.

Felipa. To a new world? Why, whatever for?

Fernando. Such are the changes wrought by time and the power of gold.

Felipa. Fortune, which may sway the body ruthlessly, cannot change the soul.

Fernando. A body cannot be swayed unless the soul is too.

Felipa. You are mistaken. For, without the company of the will, the body must proceed alone, as when someone with a lantern illuminates the street but remains in the dark himself.

Julio. I've never heard anything put so ingeniously.

Fernando. Your words have slain me.

Felipa. Why, what is it I have said?

Fernando. The emerging light must pass through the lantern door, which is made of such base metal it impugns the very name of honor.

Julio. How cleverly he indicated the horny material of which lanterns are made!

Fernando. But I shall do as you command, being thoroughly blinded by the lantern. Nothing is harder on the eyes if the bearer shows no consideration.

> Crystal giant, the sea,
>> was challenging heaven,
>> lifting white towers
>> of wind-tossed spray,
> while Fabio's poor boat
>> was tied to a trunk—

once the proud base
of canopied green,
stark remnant now
of a lightning's wrath.
Oars lay on the sand,
nets sprawled in the sun.
He cares little now
for boat or himself.
In memory's tight grasp,
a man's spirit fails.
The victim of fortune
misprises his life;
indifferent to all,
from all he withdraws.
To hold all in scorn
is humble conceit,
bespeaks sheer despair
and wisdom's default.
But regret for lost joys
entraps the soul
and leaves one indifferent
to living and dying.
Waves daring to mount
their ladders of glass
and carry by storm
the fortress of heaven,
split open a ship
from topmast to keel
and cluttered the waves
with riggings and lives.
Had you tied up
to shore, he said,
like my humble craft,
you'd have lived much longer.
How lucky I am
to be richly poor,
tempted no longer
to leave my home port.

It is not for lost galleons
   I waste away now,
   nor sky-filling mansions,
   but love's treasure lost.
When I see high fortune
   and tall ships founder,
   I take consolation
   in the mischance of others.
But regret for lost joys
   entraps the soul
   and leaves one indifferent
   to living and dying.
It is memory only
   sues for my death,
   for memories only
   sharpen misfortune.
For your sake alone,
   divine Amaryllis,
   when dawn spread its rays,
   I hauled in my nets,
scooping up coral
   which, flaunting its color,
   to rival lips, ruby,
   grew ruddy with choler.
In your lovely cupped hands
   I would also place
   in one single shell
   fishes and pearls.
My poor cabin walls
   which once had embraced
   your joys with mine
   now only sigh.
In this desolation
   of hope defeated,
   love still would feed
   on memories vivid.
But regret for lost joys
   entraps the soul

and leaves one indifferent
to living and dying.

Dorotea. Oh, Felipa! Who can that lady be? I'm aflame with jealousy.

Felipa. Be careful, he may hear you.

Dorotea. My heart is trembling. I have an impulse to call to him.

Felipa. Your mother recognizes the voice and, although she pretends not to notice, is observing how agitated and restless you are.

Dorotea. Oh, Felipa, Fernando and I are voice and echo. When he sings, I repeat the very last notes.

Felipa. Are you moving back and forth so he will see you?

Dorotea. Can his soul be unaware that mine is listening?

Felipa. He has replaced his broken treble string and is starting up again.

Fernando.

The day of your leaving
    is so fixed in mind
    that death in me lives,
    my life lives no longer.
Not for a moment
    can I put out of mind
    how I saw your blind eyes
    eclipsed by death.
So Easter lilies
    in summer heat
    feel white petals wilt
    above their green leaves.
So the purest red rose,
    having known at daybreak
    the dawn's sweet laughter,
    at nightfall fades.
So keen is my anguish,
    we share death alike:
    in your life expiring,
    my soul has died.
Vain consolation,
    I glimpse your image
    and hear your voice calling
    to beckon me on.

But regret for lost joys
  entraps the soul
  and leaves one indifferent
  to living and dying.

Felipa. Good sir, the author of this elegy certainly spins fine curls and curlicues.

Fernando. Combs them out, rather.

Felipa. These new terms exalt the language most tellingly.

Fernando. Are tellingly telltale, rather.

Felipa. Raised work is so admirable.

Fernando. If only it were understandable.

Felipa. One writes either poetry or prose.

Fernando. Like beauty and wit, grace and good sense go well together.

Felipa. I have no wish to contend with you. It would be bold and discourteous.

Fernando. I have never seen you in this house before, but now I am convinced that nothing but wit resides within.

Felipa. You flatter the owner. But do tell me why.

Fernando. So many have lost their wits here, the very slave girls must have acquired some for themselves.

Felipa. Surely that would not apply to your wit, since yours is so apparent.

Fernando. It is misfortune speaking, not wit, since the unfortunate are obliged to use their heads.

Felipa. Some unfortunates I have seen were stupid.

Fernando. Then they are stupid twice over.

Felipa. While I cannot see your person for the darkness, your attainments are so evident that I am sure you must be fortunate, at least in one respect.

Fernando. In what respect, pray tell.

Felipa. Being loved.

Fernando. Suppose that were true, and I had a few attainments, what greater obstacle could there be to having my love reciprocated?

Felipa. Tell me, are merits not the basis of love?

Fernando. If Fortune so decrees.

Felipa. Does not Fortune vie with Nature?

Fernando. No, since Fortune always topples Nature.

Felipa. What do you call Fortune?

Fernando. Wealth.

Felipa. But merit is invincible.

Fernando. But not forever.

Felipa. Anyone who of his own accord gives up what he possesses has only himself to blame.

Fernando. Because I do blame myself, my songs are sad. Still, I assure you I had no choice but to leave such a possession. Yet, that's no matter, since what I left behind has never left my thoughts.

Felipa. Still, if you should chance this way another night, leave your lamentations behind.

Fernando. I defy you to put an end to my sadness. The fact is, to increase it, I chose, among the poems I have memorized, only those most suited to my own memories.

Felipa. It seems to me the fisherman was grieving for some beloved who had died. How can that be suited to your feelings, since your love is still alive?

Fernando. Because if she is far away, she might as well be dead. Although not quite, since persons far away may offend, whereas the dead do not. And this fisherman was grieving for the most beautiful woman who ever graced the shores where she was born—the truest, most steadfast, and in faith and morals the most pure.

Felipa. Sounds like a censor giving approval to a book.

Julio. At the corner three men muffled in capes have been listening restively, and I suppose, from that sound of bucklers, they are sounding a knell.

Fernando. Then hand me mine and put this guitar over there by the grillework.

Scene 9

DON BELA · DON FERNANDO
JULIO · FELIPA
LAURENCIO · DOROTEA

Bela. This must be that man from Seville whose graces Dorotea is always holding up to us.

Laurencio. If his other graces are like his voice he must be perfection itself.

Bela. That's right, go on, make me more jealous than I am.

Laurencio. I have no wish to rouse your jealousy, only to allay it.

Bela. If jealousy is roused by the attainments of another, how can it be allayed by dwelling upon them?

Laurencio. By one's knowing enough to yield to their possessor, since he is being encouraged to display them openly.

Bela. The height of sheer cowardice! I mean to see what he looks like. Once his face and figure have gainsaid his voice, my jealousy will be allayed.

Fernando. What are you peering at? Can't you go by without staring? Courtesy, indeed!

Bela. I am not here to be courteous, but to throw you out of that doorway.

Fernando. If that's your purpose, you've come at the right moment.

Felipa. Good Lord, ma'am, they're at each other's throats!

Dorotea. Yes, and it's Don Bela and Don Fernando.

Felipa. Julio and Laurencio, too.

Dorotea. Shine a light out the window. My heart is bursting to help Fernando.

Felipa. What a thing for you to say!

Dorotea. And what a thing for him to fight that way! To his rescue, stout heart, or never call yourself my own.

> *Chorus of Jealousy*
> Oh jealousy, despotic king,
>   love's bastard, Oh most base!
> At war with sense, at odds with truth,
>   oblivion's messenger.
> Oh raging power, you blindly take
>   mere shadows for love's shape,
> ever afraid of being wronged,
>   fool's wisdom, wisdom's fool;
> in seeking out what you call truth,
>   your own worst enemy.
> A baseless fabric made of air,
>   the riddle of a sphinx,

you grasp at straws, you split fine hairs,
　　pursuing truth phantasmal.
Uneasy love, suspicion's prey,
　　cold fever, scorching blaze.
In ancient days you brought to pass
　　catastrophes untold:
fair Helen hanged; Antiope
　　relentlessly pursued;
Scylla to sea monster changed;
　　Procris by Cephalus killed,
moving white Dawn to tears,
　　on flowers like manna shed.
Time and again your dreadful shape
　　wrought tragedies untold.
Stay at the stage of mere suspicion;
　　offense, once sure, wants retribution.

ACT · FOUR

Scene 1

MARFISA · CLARA · FELIPA
DOROTEA · FERNANDO · JULIO

Marfisa. How lonely the Prado looks!

Clara. What do you expect, with daylight just arriving to keep it company.

Marfisa. Oh, the word-painting Fernando would have made of such a gilded morn!

Clara. With gilt straight off your jewels.

Marfisa. Gold is sired by Fortune, good wit by Nature.

Clara. We are the earliest arrivals at this school of ladies taking their constitutional.

Marfisa. Here come two others stepping boldly along.

Clara. As if all the young blades were gawking at them.

Marfisa. When a woman has spirit, she needn't worry about another thing.

Clara. They are coming our way.

Marfisa. Ah, Madam Dorotea, here to add another blossom to the scene? Or perhaps you require a constitutional, shall we say?

Felipa. You two would already seem to have wind in your riggings.

Dorotea. As for blossoming, the scene needs no other, since you arrived first. I have not returned that visit of yours since I did not know

your address, and your visit was a matter of pure chance, requiring
no return call.

Marfisa. Bless you, you're totally recovered. You look glorious! Such
peaches and cream! Such mother-of-pearl!

Dorotea. Your flattery I shan't return since the beauty you politely as-
cribe to me really belongs to you. I look no different this morning
than when I went to bed last night.

Marfisa. As in those verses:

> To win at love, observe this constantly:
>
> bed down, stay young, be spotless in your beauty.

And then these other verses written to a lady who consulted astrologers to discover if the man she loved loved her in return:

> Consult your mirror in the early light:
>
> if you require neither jasmine nor the rose,
>
> you'll need no horoscope to set you right.

Dorotea. I had no way of consulting a mirror, since there was no light
to see it by.

Marfisa. You are your own mirror.

Dorotea. And you the sun's, who rises earlier only to learn from your
face whether his own is more aglow in Spain or in the New World.

Marfisa. You're the best judge of that, since you've made yourself at
home in both.

Dorotea. You know a good deal about me. Don Fernando must be
your informant.

Marfisa. How could that gentleman know anything when he's been
away in Seville so long?

Dorotea. Are you pretending ignorance? He's been in Madrid for quite
some time now.

Marfisa. One can never trust a jealous friend. That friend of mine
who's so in love with him, never told me. She doesn't trust me,
evidently.

Dorotea. Now I know she isn't you, since you knew nothing of it.

Marfisa. You must be deceiving me, imagining I can give you news of
him. That means I am caught between two jealous women and
duped by both.

Dorotea. I have not seen him but have heard him in my street, talking
and singing, and in fact crossing swords with two men, one of
whom he wounded, though the man is out of danger now.

Marfisa. You must have been taken in by him, because he is quite the expert at feigning murders.

Dorotea. I'd be only too happy to hear that this one was feigned.

Marfisa. And I, to enjoy your company, but I am off to Atocha. I fear the hot sun if I am late returning.

Dorotea. Remember me in your prayers to the Virgin.

Felipa. A handsome woman she is, Dorotea, although she seems a bit heavy. She'd be more attractive, were she more slender.

Dorotea. Her hands were most impressive. Straight out of her gloves she drew them, as if expecting me to fall in love with them.

Felipa. That's the trouble with fine hands and teeth—they're forever on display, especially the teeth, gleaming so grossly and wantonly to catch the eye.

Dorotea. Talking to Doña Inez, Octavio was extolling a lady's hands, which she had draped around her coach curtains, as if the hands were on display in a dress shop and she were about to ask, "Anyone care for hands?" Jealous, Doña Inez drew hers out of her gloves and slapped his cheek, exclaiming, "Were they anything like these?"

Felipa. Oh, Dorotea! Pull down your shawl; I don't need to myself, since Don Fernando does not know me, but surely it's he and Julio there, just turning onto the Carrera.

Dorotea. Let us sit down here by the fountain. This upsets me, and, besides, I am less likely to be recognized if I am seated.

Felipa. Take this *alcorza*. If you need water, I have one of those Maya jugs from Lisbon.

Dorotea. Fernando used to say, in that hyperbolic way of his, that this must be a bit of paradise, where the fashioning of the first man took place.

Felipa. Here he comes—cover up well.

Dorotea. He walked by without so much as a glance at us.

Felipa. What peculiar melancholy!

Dorotea. I thought he was following that lady, but he's going straight up the Carrera. Call him, since he doesn't know you. Let's see what he has to say. I shan't say a word myself.

Felipa. Oh, you sir! Oh, sir!

Julio. See here, those women are calling to you.

Fernando. Forget them, don't be stupid; they're no cure for what ails me.

Felipa. Sir, do not be so disobliging.

Julio. They come here early to ply their trade, though these don't appear to be idle skirts. Do go and see what they want of you.

Fernando. You know I don't speak to women.

Julio. Then don't expect to be cured of what ails you. And you needn't take my word—take Petrarch's in the *Triumph of Love,* if you've forgotten the story of King Ahasuerus. My master says he does not speak to women.

Felipa. Even if I go after him, pull off his cape, and sit him down here, willy-nilly?

Julio. Sir, that woman means to drag you over there by main force. Remember, women pursue men who flee them, and she'll come after you simply because you do not want her.

Fernando. What is it you wish of me, madam? I hope you appreciate that you are the first woman I have spoken to in over four months.

Felipa. But why, fine sir? What have we done to you?

Fernando. Injuries and betrayals at the hands of one have caused me to detest them all.

Felipa. What a wonderful tale awaits me! Here, sit down beside us both, and thereby achieve two things most desirable: a rest for yourself and entertainment for us.

Fernando. Why is that lady not speaking?

Felipa. She's as disinclined to men as you are to women.

Fernando. If she hates the former as much as I do the latter, between us we'll have the makings of a poison to end the world. There, I'm seated.

Felipa. What brings you into the country so early in the day, if not to ogle little slippers and fine feathers?

Fernando. I never sleep a wink the whole night through, struggling with the most foolish and disillusioned love ever born of hopeless obstinacy since madmen of my kind first came into the world.

Felipa. Having obliged us by sitting down, and satisfied us that you hate women so much that you won't make advances to us, divert yourself by relating the events you now complain of. Persons having your malady are known to pay large sums simply to be heard.

Julio. Quite a little lass we have here! Now madam, is that shape next to you a woman or a stone? Because we could find a place for her on the fountain. Sitting beside her, I'm like someone hitching up

to a post. Lord love her, how sweet she smells! Nothing wrong
with that plump arm, either. She's not even asked me, "Who is
this, anyway?"

Felipa. Careful she doesn't do it with the file in her vanity case. But
now, be still. Your master's just cleared his throat—a sure sign he's
ready to start the performance.

Fernando. I, dear ladies—both speaking and nonspeaking—was born in
this city to noble parents, who were left by theirs with a pittance
for patrimony. My upbringing was not princely, but they still desired to see me instructed in letters and in virtues. At the age of ten,
I was sent off to Alcalá with this chap here present, who would
then have been about twenty, to accompany me as governor and as
friend, and so he has done ever since with rare loyalty and devotion.

Julio. Could anyone be more worthy of it?

Fernando. Julio, in comparing your tutelage with that given Achilles, I
find his Chiron ignorant. And as for true friendship, I wish I were
as good an Alexander as you a Hephaestion.

Julio. I shall forgo replying in kind so as not to break the thread of
your love story.

Fernando. At that age I had already acquired grammar, and was not unfamiliar with rhetoric. I proved reasonably talented, quick and receptive in any branch of learning. But it was at poetry that I proved
most adept—to the point of using the covers of my exercise books
to jot down my thoughts, which I often did in Latin or Castilian
verse. I began to collect books in every language and literature, for
besides acquiring the elements of Greek, I had much practice in
Latin, learned Tuscan well, and started French.

Julio. Are you offering this lady references for some position?

Felipa. Do not suppose me so ignorant as not to relish hearing of literary matters and amatory ones as well. We women, you know, when
we have no material interest at stake, are very easily entertained.

Fernando. My parents died, and a creditor collected all he could from
their estate, and went off to the New World leaving me a pauper.
The New World has always been my downfall; whereas others return home with fortunes, I saw mine taken thither.

Julio. It evidently amuses this lady to hear you speak of the New
World as your downfall.

Fernando. She can have no idea of my meaning.

Felipa. Quite true. I laughed at the amusing way he put it, not at his reasons for feeling so.

Fernando. And oh, such reasons! Would to God the place had never been discovered and Columbus never born!

Felipa. Are you so narrow-minded that, just because the New World deprived you of your fortune, you can wish it had not made Spain so rich and powerful, nor spread the True Faith so far and wide?

Fernando. You overshoot my meaning. I'm not surprised—no one could possibly grasp it.

Felipa. Refasten the chain of your story, lest a link or two be lost.

Fernando. I returned to this Court city, lodging with a rich and generous female relative, who fancied helping me.

Felipa. I applaud her fancy.

Fernando. At that time she had a fifteen-year-old daughter—I was seventeen—and a niece slightly younger than I. I might now be married to either, but ill fortune had another fate in store for me. My fashionable wardrobe and my idleness (cutthroats of virtue and hangmen of reason) soon diverted me from my studious beginnings, thanks in no small measure to Marfisa, on whom my eyes had fastened—she being the lady's niece, the lady herself Lisarda. Predictably enough, constant compansionship fed this love, but in the midst of the affair—which, owning to my consideration and guilelessness, did not catch fire—she was married to an older man, an advocate, though not the oldest of advocates, albeit very rich. The day the jurist I refer to took her off to his home, I tasted her lips so that she might not succumb to the poison of her distaste for the violence being done her, and behind closed doors we both wept, mixing words with tears to such effect that anyone observing us could hardly have told the tears from the words.

Felipa. You must be a tremendous weeper.

Fernando. My eyes were veritable crybabies, and my soul is Portuguese. But believe me, anyone born without a tender heart may become a poet, but not of the sweeter kind.

Felipa. There you go again, parading your profession.

Fernando. Love is to blame.

Felipa. How so?

Fernando. Because to love and to write verse are one and the same, and for its best poets the world has love to thank.

Julio. True enough, and what's more, no man in love ever failed to write verse, good or bad.

Felipa. What happened to the bride?

Fernando. What happened was that this wretched old husband, looking on her beauty and overlooking his age, stimulated his inadequacy artificially, and died in the breach, like a true knight.

Felipa. 'A short life but a merry one.'

Fernando. Marfisa was brought back home without a dowry, since he had taken her without one. There are some people who'd rather die for nothing than live for something.

Felipa. How you must have welcomed her back!

Fernando. No, nothing of the sort, because on her wedding day a good friend brought me a message from a lady of this Court city. I cannot find a name to fit her; there's a chill creeping through my veins. Her name, in short, is . . .

Felipa. Short or long, don't stop now.

Fernando. . . . Lioness, Tigress, Serpent, Asp, Siren, Riptide, Circe, Medea, Inferno, Paradise, Heaven, Hell—and Dorotea.

Felipa. All the insulting names that poor women has to carry ashore from the ocean of your wrath!

Fernando. They're not the half of it. But yes, they are, since I said Dorotea.

Felipa. Men would have their women behave like the downtrodden vassals of Aragon, subject to all sorts of treatment, good and bad.

Fernando. Women are worse than Aragonese; they never treat us well at all.

Julio. That particular dispute, if I may say so, began with the calends of the Silver Age. I only wonder that, with no other species in the world than man and women, we are never at peace.

Fernando. Our love for women is at the root of all the discord.

Felipa. Your love for so many women is what you mean.

Fernando. What about your loving so many men?

Julio. A point well taken.

Felipa. Naturally you'd say that, being a man, his governor, and his friend.

Fernando. Had Julio been less prone to defend women, I would not be in such straits now.

Felipa. He never reprimands you, then?

Fernando. Were I as docile as Alcibiades, I'd have found my Socrates in him.

Felipa. Leave off ancient history and get on with your own. What message did that friend bring you?

Fernando. To go and see Dorotea, because in certain conversations at which both of us had been present, my person or my manner or both attracted her. And such attraction caused more unattractive things to befall me than there are stars in the sky, if you need a comparison.

Felipa. Then you did go by and see her the very day Marfisa was married?

Fernando. I dressed up in my best, as fashionably as I could, and went to see her with all the niceties of a suitor—circumspection, scent, and toilette.

Felipa. In long hose, too, no doubt, and in an amber-scented waistcoat, letting a bit of gold chain show, and on the soft-spoken side, with an occasional lifting of the eyes skyward.

Julio. With such words from her who speaks, what may we not expect from her who speaks not?

Felipa. I've told you not to touch—she's not ripe and will set your teeth on edge.

Julio. Women are never better than when about to ripen.

Felipa. You have a governor's taste—I almost said a pedagogue's.

Julio. Do you know Latin, then?

Felipa. I've a brother who's a student and, when he trims his Latin, gives me these scraps. But pray tell, what's a woman like with a whiff of the nest about her?

Julio. A whiff of the sheepfold's worse. Nor will you deny that two twenty-year-olds are better than one aged forty.

Fernando. On Marfisa's wedding day I arrived, as I said, dressed impeccably, which reversed our roles, making me look the new husband, and the bridegroom the father-in-law.

Felipa. The only difference being that, whereas bridegrooms must trim their whiskers, you'd have had none to trim. But what touching concern you showed for the lady who'd been married. Oh, you men! How quickly he dried his tears and forgot the taste of lips behind closed doors!

Fernando. Well, what did you expect, that I'd go and grieve to death while she lay in her husband's arms?

Felipa. Be sorry for her, since it's such a miracle when a good match is made between assorted ages; disaster is usually the outcome.

Fernando. The reason for disaster is not the difference in age but in temperament.

Felipa. At any rate, you saw this Dorotea. Is she very beautiful?

Fernando. On that score, I'd rather not be questioned, since Nature seems to have distilled all flowers, all aromatic herbs, all rubies, corals, pearls, jacinths, and diamonds in order to prepare this potion for the eyes, this poison for the ears.

Julio. Nature must have been playing apothecary at that time. The only thing you missed was mixing those simples with tartar.

Fernando. Some star propitious to lovers must have been in the ascendant at the time, because we had no sooner beheld each other and spoken than we were completely slaves to each other.

Felipa. What about Marfisa?

Fernando. That was a minor affair; it took very little effort on my part, and Dorotea took even less. For I might apply what that excellent poet Vicente Espinel says of beautiful Hero's accessibility:

That's Hero you've been running down, no doubt,
she who, once approached, would not back out.

Felipa. How disrespectful men are! It's women's fault for not driving them frantic! But tell me, is this Dorotea really so beautiful?

Fernando. I have been speaking only of her outward guise; there are in addition her elegance of figure, her freshness and grace, her way of speaking, her tone of voice, her mind, her dancing and singing, and the different instruments she plays—I'd need two thousand lines of verse for all of those. Besides which, she is so fond of every sort of accomplishment that she let me leave her to take up dancing, fencing, and mathematics, together with other fascinating subjects, which, considering how blindly in love we were, showed our true mettle. At this time, the lady's husband was away and not expected to return; meanwhile, a foreign prince had won her favors. She dangled high hopes before him, delaying their fulfillment, and responding tepidly to the ardor she aroused. It was he I found holding sway over her affections when Dorotea and I proved such star-crossed lovers it seemed we had known each other always. With this great personage I have mentioned, I had a few narrow escapes, not through any arrogance of mine, for I well knew that anyone who pits his limited forces against the mighty must perforce fall into their clutches sooner or later. And so it was that, one night when I knocked more eagerly than wisely on Dorotea's door, he himself came to open it, despite Dorotea's and her mother's pleas. Having recognized my voice, and with dagger in hand, he lunged at me for what he assumed would be the so-called coup de grâce; but either because I hunched over or because luck so willed it, through a slit of my loosely worn white leather waistcoat he pinned me to the very door he had opened, slamming it shut. And this should not surprise you, because as I supposed it was a maid opening the door, I let desire lead me toward the jealousy lying in wait for me. Having to step down because the parlor on which the door opened was not level with the street, I bent forward and my waistcoat was swept up in the air.

Felipa. I listen to you aghast at the thought of the night your Dorotea must have spent imagining you wounded by so terrible and willful an act.

Fernando. I could not reach her, so each of us had to suffer alone.

Felipa. How did you survive the hazard of contending with one so powerful? You put me on tenterhooks.

Fernando. He would certainly have taken my life, since I had lost all fear of his might and of my dying. But at that point, the King happened to send him off on a mission befitting his high station and my good fortune; my own fancy could not have devised a more effective solution. Amusingly enough, he did everything in his power to have me brought along as his secretary, not that he needed one, or that I was of suitable age, but to keep me from Dorotea, who before daybreak had sent a maid to inquire about my physical condition, which we then proceeded to celebrate in bed together by way of congratulating ourselves on the outcome. And so, for the first time, we were able to steal a march on the vigilant jealousy of that powerful lover and take our revenge through love's sweet transgressions, ever the sweeter when shared desires have had to suffer such obstacles and privations. Eventually he departed, and I was left undisputed master of a possession so rich that I considered Croesus, though deemed the happiest of mortals, as poor compared with me, and the resplendent army of Antiochus Magnus, with all its harnesses and helmets glittering silver and gold, as lackluster compared to my simple dress and exalted emotions. But despite such wealth, I began, after several days, to be tormented and assailed by concern for my poverty, and by fear of being subjected, through no fault of my own, to some offense brought on by my impoverished state, such that our friendship would be unable to find nurture within the spheres of love's motion. Amid such fears, and despite the sheer number of rivals and relatives involved, since I had not been born with that sort of complaisance which—according to those who have read it—is found in the first chapter of the book of infamy, one indifferently embracing the good names of lovers and the honor of husbands, Dorotea read my thoughts, so easily betrayed by the sad faces of lovers begging to be asked what they wish were not revealed. To reassure me that she would be mine alone, she gathered together her finery, jewels, and silver service, and sent them to me in two chests.

Felipa. It was surely the act of a courageous woman.

Fernando. In this way our friendship lasted five years, during which time she was stripped nearly bare, having to resort to unfamiliar needlework simply to supply the daily needs of the household.

Felipa. What singular delicacy in one so beautiful and in her prime, in this Court city!

Fernando. That I do acknowledge, as well as the times innumerable when I experienced such shame and pity that, being unable to cover those lovely hands with diamonds, I bathed them in tears, which she deemed finer stones for rings than those she had scorned and sold.

Felipa. And what were your rivals doing meanwhile?

Fernando. Their attentions to Dorotea waned. For where fine clothes fail to catch men's eyes, beauty itself seems to play the coward. In a word, I saw her so reduced that, when I consider her sore need, I excuse her, but go mad when I consider how hopelessly in love I was.

Felipa. And so what did she do?

Fernando. One day she firmly told me that our friendship was at an end. Her mother and relatives, she said, were reviling her, and the two of us were the talk of the town, with me largely to blame for broadcasting in verse what otherwise would not have been so blameworthy.

Julio. True enough. Ladies should understand that if they take up with poets, they may find fame but no privacy.

Felipa. And you—how did you take such a sudden change of heart?

Fernando. At my house I made up a tale about killing a man the night before—and that was true, for the dead man was myself—and how, if I did not leave town at once, I would inevitably fall into the hands of the law. Marfisa gave me what gold she had, along with the pearls of her tears; with this I departed for Seville.

Felipa. You showed high resolve, indeed.

Fernando. As befits a man of honor.

Felipa. How did you fare then?

Fernando. Not well at all. Every league I traveled I kept wanting to turn back. But honor outweighing love (as honor has always been of all things most powerful—despite that age-old debate about wine, women, and truth), I pressed onward until at length I staggered into Seville.

Felipa. So there, what with the rich variety of the scene—ladies, gentlemen, foreigners, the New World galleons, the river, the boats, and Triana—Madrid and your Dorotea must soon have been forgotten.

Fernando. Forgotten indeed! No sooner had I arrived than, amazing as it may seem, the river became a very Lethe to me; the sails were souls; the women, their helmsmen; the galleons, mountains shooting tongues of flame, like Mount Etna; the hustle and bustle, the cries of the damned; in brief, that most beautiful and populous city became a nightmare of hell. I did not expect to survive the night, for bliss and despair are the last extremes which lovers reach, and having been deprived of the former I was inevitably headed for the latter. I left town to gain a view of the sea, which was all I desired then, after having died. I saw it in Sanlúcar, and addressed it in these words I had heard a poet say:

> Supposing I should drink it in,
> then weep it out again,
> not all the waters of the sea
> could quench the fire consuming me.

I journeyed thence to Cádiz, where a relative was a church dignitary. And seeing that I could not flee beyond the farthest point of land—occasion of the heroic shield of Charles V—I wrote some verses, of which I have retained this much:

> Since you share the way with me,
> do not call this absence,

    though it take the eyes away
    and leave the soul behind.
Am I ignorantly wise
    and taking needless pains
    to flee the bow whose shaft
    has pierced me to the heart?
Can changing earth and sky
    cancel fortune's frown,
    uproot envy from the earth,
    efface unlucky stars?
My sadness finds no boon
    whether I live or die—
    living puts me to death,
    dying restores my life.
I have grown inured to pain
    or pain is less than pain
    or Nature interanimates
    stones and men together.
Except for me, I find
    no likeness of what I am.
    Besides myself, the world
    holds no one else like me.

Felipa. I wish I had sufficient learning to praise your verse. I shall say simply, not to offend your modesty, that it is chaste and pure and free of that congestion some verse displays.

Julio. You've taken his measure well. And it was distinctly flattering of you to respect his modesty, for you will find among practitioners of his profession men who sing their own praises so fulsomely they leave no room for others to do so. These may be dismissed as mad but you will find others who, were Virgil to read his poetry to them, would not so much as part their lips to praise it. Theirs is a breed of discourtesy, which, if it does not touch on arrogance, betrays invidiousness.

Fernando. What brought me respite then, brings it to me now. Then my only consolation was to put my thoughts in writing; now it comes from repeating them.

Felipa. Then do not let my faulty understanding or inadequate appreciation constrain you, for this veiled lady both writes and understands them.

Fernando. In that case I beseech her, since I am not to be favored with her words, to favor me by listening.

Julio. She nods her head. If all women did the same, they'd be more yielding and less trying.

Fernando.

> Cares, why do you pursue me?
>> Pull in your reins awhile,
>> for you will not unsettle
>> my steadfast devotion.
>
> Between the world of love and you,
>> there's this world of difference:
>> love finds its bliss
>> in what you own as torment.
>
> If you think it's any favor
>> to rescue me from pain,
>> Cares, you are mistaken;
>> torment is my vocation.
>
> I need you for yourselves.
>> Could any lover want you
>> as surcease from pain,
>> or balm for jealousy?
>
> Amaryllis, in reflecting
>> how divine your beauty is,
>> I'd forfeit every blessing
>> for pleasuring in pain.
>
> Your disdainful glances
>> I welcome as a boon.
>> Love has now invented
>> a welcome for all suffering.
>
> I have come to such a pass
>> that I esteem your hatred—
>> in that way I'll discover
>> if love can feed on pain.
>
> Though I've put you in my debt,
>> I'd not have you know it,

since a lover who is true
takes pride in love alone.
But wait—oh chilling thought!
Your beauty while we're parted
no comfort can afford me
if I feel it unfaithful.

Felipa. Your poem leads me to believe you have Dorotea in mind.

Fernando. Heaven knows I wish it were otherwise. In the place I mentioned, madam, I spent several days—several years I should have said—during one of which, driven by my intense imaginings, I climbed those rocks, bearing a still larger one on my shoulder than Sisyphus does in the depictions of his everlasting torments. And, if it hadn't been for Julio, I do think I would have thrown myself off those crags. I bowed to his will, and in my memorandum book wrote down these lines, drawing on my recollections for their substance:

Seated high upon a cliff
which the sea in haughty rage,
sought to level to water,
though it proved the rock it was,
Fabio sat there watching
as the beach stole silver
from each incoming wave,
foam from waves withdrawing.
In them he sees the pains
of love, and love forsaken:
forsaken in their dying,
still loving in their lasting.
Forgetting won't erase
truths of love enduring,
nor men's efforts win
against disdainful wrong.
In vain do humble pleas
supplicate the gods,
for heaven only laughs
at oaths that lovers swear.
Love would fain forget
yet trusts it never will,

for love is never firmer
than when it seeks to change.
Persisting in your suit,
　　you harm yourself the most.
　　When luck abandons you,
　　persistence is in vain.
Let Nature sing the praise
　　of her well-tempered beauties
　　but desist from boasting
　　when they become despotic.
Plucking on his strings,
　　to mute rocks he confided
　　all his unstrung feelings
　　as if they would reply.

Felipa. What did he confide to them?

Fernando. That I didn't put in. But I want to tell you what I did in a fit of madness.

Felipa. Yes?

Fernando. I took out a card with that lady's portrait on it, which I kept wrapped in taffeta; thus I had more reason than unlucky gamblers do to say that I threw my fortune away on a card.

Felipa. But didn't you say you were poor and that she'd thrown hers away?

Fernando. What can the soul or anyone's life and liberty have to do with gold?

Julio. In fact, this gentleman carried with him not only that keepsake but other relics too, and over his heart he wore a tiny amber-scented slipper, like a twist of crimson silk, to soothe the heart.

Fernando. Julio, why call it amber-scented—it comes from Dorotea's foot, doesn't it? Something to self-evident should be taken for granted.

Julio. You may call it redundancy or amplification, like a figure of rhetoric. Still, amber does soothe the heart. The amusing part was that he wore it against his shirt on the left side, with the sole showing, so I called him my Commandant of the Order of the Slipper, and judging by the size, I'd say it was a full number thirteen in the Order.

Felipa. You should be saying the size was small.

Julio. Large enough to cover the whole heart.

Felipa. Is this gentleman's heart so large, then?

Julio. No, because he's so valiant, and those who are have small hearts, as proved by lions, whose hearts are smaller than those of other animals.

Felipa. He was wrong to wear the slipper as a balm to soothe his heart, for feet are trained to walk, and slippers with them, and so they would only make his heart more restless.

Fernando. No need for that with my heart, for it's only there that you'll find true perpetual motion. I resolved finally to rid myself of the cause of so much suffering, since it no longer brought me consolation, but despair, and so, taking out my dagger . . .

Felipa. Good lord! Did you kill Dorotea?

Fernando. . . . . I found a bit of spare earth between two rocks, and there I buried her portrait, having first composed these lines:

> Here, where no mortal foot shall ever tread
>> rudely upon your fair and shining face,
>> your tomb shall be, oh heavenly Dorotea,
>> nor shaft of porphyry shall mark the place.
> A fragrant pyramid my tears have raised,
>> to take the place of some Sabean urn,
>> lest phoenix be reborn to light of day.
>> So may its endless rest have no return.
> But all in vain, since love grants life unending
>> to this one miracle which it destroys
>> and sends it winging to an immortal sun.
> Of what avail this tomb among the rocks,
>> if in the soul love kindles from the ashes
>> a new phoenix supplants the dying one?

Julio. In the age of Claudius, if Pliny is right, a phoenix was brought to Rome. They say it was the size and shape of an eagle, gold neck glistening on its purple body, cerulean tail with roseate feathers interspersed, or perhaps a peacock's tail but with roseate eyes, and crown glistening with other more subtle-hued feathers, and shifting coruscations and iridescence. But now I should like to ask Pliny: if this was the only phoenix in existence, how were its successors bred?

Fernando. Julio, all I know is that phoenixes live six hundred years, but for mine that does not suffice. Alas, how was I ever able to return to Cádiz after committing such a monumental, though loving, act of madness! Oh if my tomb had only been the sea, as Dorotea's was the land!

Felipa. What most surprises me is that you should feel so deeply about forsaking a portrait when you were determined enough to forsake its subject.

Fernando. I did not forsake the subject; I brought her with me.

Felipa. If you had kept her in mind, you'd have tried to obtain news of her, and there's no trace of that in your account.

Fernando. Many were the times the thought crossed my mind.

Felipa. Why didn't you act upon it?

Fernando. So as not to add fuel to her vengeance.

Felipa. True love harbors no vengeance.

Fernando. Then what does habor it?

Felipa. Hating.

Fernando. That's what I hoped Dorotea would think I felt, as she would not have thought if I had written her.

Felipa. Wouldn't it be better if she thought you loved her?

Fernando. No, because she's forgotten me.

Felipa. What makes you think so?

Fernando. Because she's a woman.

Felipa. That's no way for a sensible man to talk. Not all women are fickle, nor all men faithful.

Fernando. My faithfulness would more than cover all men's.

Felipa. And Dorotea's would keep all women's reputations intact.

Fernando. How can someone who does not know her make such a statement?

Felipa. From what you've told me, I have no doubt she's the same person, who, as a woman friend reported, tried desperately to kill herself with a diamond ring the evening of the very day a certain gentleman, whom I take to be you, went off, putting her life in the balance a good long while.

Julio. This you may certainly believe, sir. Dorotea was not made of marble, to be proof against the cruelty of your leaving. Keep in mind the price she has been paying for you with her soul, her life, her honor. One who acts from love does not thereby lack discrimination, since between those who have it and those who lack it, the difference is this: the former love with their reason, the latter out of habit.

Fernando. You are quite right, Julio. My tender years betrayed me. I might have caused the death of Dorotea; I might have deprived Nature of its greatest miracle and the world of its beauty. I beseech you, madam, to pardon me; my heart and eyes are overflowing.

Julio. Oh, that pitiful man! Hold onto him, madam, or he'll break into a thousand pieces.

Felipa. Poor young man! Have you ever seen him in such a state?

Dorotea. I can bear this no longer, Felipa.

Felipa. Well, take off your veil then, Dorotea.

Dorotea. Oh, treasure mine! Oh, my Fernando! Oh, my first love! Would that I had never been born to cause such unhappiness. Oh tyrannical mother, barbarous woman! It was you who forced me, you betrayed me, you destroyed me! You shan't have your way. I'll take my own life, I'll go mad.

Felipa. Come now, Dorotea, you already are. Let your hair alone, let your hands be. Is this why you were so silent? Oh, love, how you ravage bright minds! Just see how a single dram of your fond tears brings Fernando to.

Dorotea. It is no use deceiving me, Felipa. My treasure is dead.

Julio. How true to form these lovers run! Now I am convinced that love and fear were twin-born!

Dorotea. Lay his head in my lap. I shall be the lioness, and with my roars blow life into him.

Felipa. Take his pulse, Julio.

Julio. Any sudden irregularity has always presaged great troubles.

Felipa. As to the irregularity, that's true; his color turns now pale, now red, and his hand feels now cold, now hot.

Julio. Two contrary effects may well proceed from a single cause. To wit: the sun's heat, softening some things and hardening others.

Felipa. Hand me that *búcaro* of water.

Dorotea. Whatever for, Felipa, with all these tears of mine?

Julio. Love having caused his fainting, I marvel that the tears do not bring him round.

Felipa. What shall we do? He shows no sign of reviving and people will start talking.

Julio. Let me prescribe a cure.

Felipa. What is it?

Julio. Take the herb Dorotea, remove all leaves from the New World, then rinse well in three solutions: love, new amity, complete confidence; brew it all with repentance of things past over the slow flame of injuries assuaged; apply same to Don Fernando's breast each morning of this month, without her mother knowing, and he'll be brought round, as prescribed by the doctrine of love restored, from the first volume of the book on reconciliation after jealousy.

Dorotea. If only love vouchsafed that remedy! I would see to its fulfillment as earnestly as you now are mocking.

Julio. Well now, observe the next phase of this eclipse, as the soul of Don Fernando hands him the key to open his eyes.

Dorotea. Are you alive, my treasure? Speak—delay, and my life departs.

Fernando. Dorotea, I live. As my dying lay in your hands, so now does my life.

Julio. So indeed do the ladies of Valencia nurture silkworms between their breats.

Dorotea. Say I had done you all the wrongs you have imagined—and aside from giving you fair warning, I did you none—the fright you gave me makes your vengeance greater than the offense.

Fernando. I did not seek vengeance.

Dorotea. Nor did I mean offense.

Fernando. I left because you desired it.

Dorotea. Because you no longer desired me, rather.

Fernando. My leaving showed my love.

Dorotea. It showed mere cowardice.

Fernando. What was I to stay for after being so disillusioned?

Dorotea. So that no one could think of taking me from your sight.

Fernando. What do you mean, Dorotea?

Dorotea. Killing anyone who made the attempt.

Fernando. I did not know your pleasure in this.

Dorotea. No matter; where love was involved, so was honor.

Fernando. Your counsel comes late.

Dorotea. Love and honor need no counsel.

Fernando. By refusing to compete with gold, I believe I acted wisely.

Dorotea. Steel is the metal of swords; and of love, madness.

Fernando. Against gold there is no steel. Because I could not be expected to kill the person who took it.

Dorotea. Had there been no one to give it, there would have been no one to take it.

Fernando. I did not see the one giving it, having left before it was given.

Dorotea. True lovers are like Germans: let them gain a foothold, there's no dislodging them.

Fernando. And true ladies are like Catalans: to preserve their rights, they'll die a thousand deaths.

Dorotea. In a book of fables I once read how Hercules and Antaeus, who was the son of Earth, were wrestling, and how Hercules with his great strength kept lifting him up. But each time his foot touched the ground his strength came back—and came all the greater, the more overcome he was.

Fernando. Exactly what do you mean?

Dorotea. That had you been present while love was struggling with self-interest, the invincible giant, each time my eyes alighted on you, I would have found new strength to defend myself. But since you went away, leaving me in the arms of Hercules, and would not stand by to help me, why then—whose fault was it?

Fernando. That's just like you women: not satisfied with wronging us, you must also blame us for the wrongs you do us.

Dorotea. My love never did you wrong.

Fernando. Love is as love does.

Dorotea. I was compelled to it.

Fernando. Don Bela was not king.

Dorotea. Kings are not the only ones who compel.

Fernando. You mean your mother?

Dorotea. Who better than she?

Fernando. How obedient of you!

Dorotea. You know how the coercion began—with my hair—then all of you joining against me: she reviling me, Gerarda with her spells, you leaving me, and a gentleman of wit with his suasion.

Fernando. Of wit, Dorotea? Let's go, Julio, before she sings his praises.

Julio. Don't jump up in a rage, she hasn't given you reason to.

Fernando. I know Don Bela is a fool.

Felipa. You've ruined everything. Why did you have to mention his wit?

Dorotea. To excuse my mistake in the way least likely to make him jealous. I didn't praise Don Bela's good looks.

Felipa. Come now, Don Fernando, sir—something must be allowed Don Bela.

Fernando. Let him have his silver, let him have his gold, let him have his diamonds—let him even have noble birth; but wit or good looks, never.

Dorotea. I pronounce him stupid, and the ugliest person on God's earth.

Fernando. Hold on there, Dorotea, you're overdoing it.

Julio. More people are coming by. We'd best leave the Prado, together, and you two can talk at home without fear of censure, and there look into these charges, free of witnesses.

Dorotea. If Fernando takes my hand, I will go with him. If not, you may count on it, I will shriek to high heaven, and stop at nothing, right here on the Prado.

Julio. Now, now, my pets, in the month of April on the Prado only nags may be frisky.

Fernando. So you heard all I said, Dorotea?

Julio. Comes the dawn at last, after all that anger.

Dorotea. Each word of yours was imprinted upon my soul. What keeps your hand from holding mine? Let me have it and I'll forgive the slap it gave me the day I praised that young man who was so dapper and so brave with the bulls. That was no slapping an unknown Chariclea by Theagenes; it was an offense you long regretted, and that very night handed me your dagger to avenge myself on the perpetrator of so unjust a crime.

Julio. The incredible inanities lovers speak and practice! I am sure he gave you the dagger knowing for a certainty you would not lop his hand off. With a love so imitative of Mucius Scaevola, who could have played Porsena?

Fernando. What can one deny you, who owes you his life?

Felipa. You two go ahead; people have begun to stare.

Julio. Were you not the one who would never speak to Dorotea again?

Fernando. But you see, my horoscope shows Venus squaring the ascendant, and today I observed her in Taurus and in Libra.

Julio. Men are always blaming the influence of the stars, as if stars had any power to compel, when in fact resisting them is the effect of using will power, as Scipio Africanus and the divine Plato both attest.

Fernando. I am neither Roman nor divine. But I do wonder what they would have done, soldier and philosopher as they were, had they seen Dorotea.

Scene 2

LUDOVICO · CÉSAR

César. Don Fernando will not be joining our session this morning.

Ludovico. He must be mulling over his poem; getting started is always so troublesome.

César. Let us hope the poem is not Dorotea.

Ludovico. He's made it a point of honor not to give in. Let me see the sonnet you brought along for him.

César. It's written in the new language.

Ludovico. No matter, I know a bit of Greek.

César. There are men of great talent decking out and enhancing the Castilian tongue in speech and in writing, in the church and in the academy, with new phrases and rhetorical figures, embellishing and polishing the langugage with singular propriety. To them all respect is due as master craftsmen, and to one of my acquaintance especially. They have expanded and dignified the language, enriching it with the luster of fine, uncommon terms. Such increase, richness, and beauty are applauded by all who understand these things. But there are others, who in seeking to imitate them, out of some brash, inordinate ambition, badly overreach themselves, and thus bring forth misshapen and ridiculous monstrosities. Witness this sonnet, which is pure burlesque:

Pullulating with *culto,* Claudio, my friend,
    a minotaurist am I, starting this morning;
    renouncing Castilian phraseology,
    may *The Solitudinous* bless me on my way.
Henceforth, as day's precursor, Lady Dawn
    by name of Joan the Baptist shall be known;
    Waterfly, the raucous frog shall be;
    gold mange, the wheat; and watered silk, the sea.
All out of sorts, I cannot slough off tedium.

Henceforth I'll say hose, not pantaloons,
as in Bandurrius the Shepherd's days of old.
These lines—are they Turkish or a Teuton's?
They're yours, oh reader-garblers of our tongue,
so gobble up this *culto* heap you're bred among.

Ludovico. Shall we comment on it while we wait for Fernando?

César. I would venture to say that the argument of the sonnet (God save the mark) is the conversion to this new poetic religion of some poor wit disavowing his own fatherland. Yet I would not wish it said of us that we are like roofers who from some rooftop go tossing down into the street anything they happen on: here a few balls of various sizes, there a pair of old hose or some cat's carcass dispatched by bird shot and buried under the tiles.

Ludovico. Many commentators are like that: anything they come upon, whether in Stobaeus or the *Polyanthea* or Conrad Gesner or other fat tomes of commonplaces, they immediately toss in, relevant or not.

César. Speaking dispassionately, I would say that many commentators are not worthy of praise, although I trust I'll be worthy of this sonnet. Because, while invention is the poet's main attribute, if not his whole stock in trade, and though invention and imitation are one and the same, you never find either in the commentator. Rather, they resemble props placed under tree limbs, which, though they hold up the branches, do not themselves produce leaves or fruit but simply serve as supports for fertility not of their own making, telling us, as if we would not see it for ourselves, "This is a pear, this a peach, and this a quince," like the painter who labeled a cropped lion, "Lion rampant."

Ludovico. Those who write commentaries and explications of Greek and Latin poets deserve all praise and reward, since those hoary poets are now so inaccessible and because this best reveals the different authors and languages the poets drew upon. I wish someone would write on Garcilaso; so far, no one has.

César. There are many serious poets these days, but they would rather see their own works published than edit someone else's. Diego de Mendoza, Vicente Espinel, Marco Antonio de la Vega, Pedro Laínez, Doctor Garay, Fernando de Herrera, the two Lupercios, Don Luis de Góngora, Luis Gálvez Montalvo, the Marquis of

Auñón, the Marquis of Montes Claros, the Duke of Francavila, Canon Tárraga, and there's the Marquis of Peñafiel, who wrote such lighthearted Castilian verse, as in the lines of that complaint of his—

In the face of wrongs,
what use to complain?
Where ears won't hear,
one has lips in vain.

—and then Francisco de Figueroa and Fernando de Herrera, both of whom have earned the name "divine," Pedro Padilla, Doctor Campuzano, López Maldonado, Miguel Cervantes, Rufo the jurist, Doctor Soto, Don Alonso de Ercilla, Liñán de Riaza, Don Luis de Vargas Manrique, Don Francisco de la Cueva, and the attorney Berrío, and this Lope de Vega just starting out.

Ludovico. And those are all there are now in Spain?

César. I've heard of these and of Bautisa de Vivar, a natural prodigy of improvisation, wondrously impelled by the muses, and by that poetic madness which Marsilio Ficino in his *Plato* divides into four parts.

Ludovico. What are they?

César. The first is poetic madness, the second hierophantic, the third vatic, and the fourth amatory. Poetry comes from the muses, the hierophantic spirit from Dionysus, the vatic from Apollo, and the amatory spirit from Venus. How all this transpires, you may discover in the aforesaid work.

Ludovico. It seems to me that so many more poets will eventually spring from these that in a single Madrid street there'll be more than you now say are writing in all of Spain.

César. Such is the promise held out by the fertility of their talent.

Ludovico. What have they published up to now?

César. Austriadas, Araucanas, Galateas, Fílidas, and various *Rimas.* Don Francisco de la Cueva, and Berrío, most worthy jurisconsults, whom one could describe as Dino and Alciato were described—namely, as the most learned interpreters of the law and the sweetest of poets—have written plays which were produced to everyone's satisfaction.

Ludovico. What has been the result of the examination of the plays?

César. His Majesty, God preserve him, to satisfy his royal conscience, had the question of their propriety examined. On final scrutiny they were found inoffensive in the judgment of the learned theologians, who pronounced them lawful. And so, henceforth, they are not to be calumnied and impugned. But this, let it be noted, is on condition that they satisfy all provisions relative to our holy faith and sound morals.

Ludovico. For this purpose there is a secretary with power of censure and a Royal Council with power of approval. To return to our sonnet, from which we have strayed, do say something about the term *culto;* I do not properly understand its meaning.

César. If I tell you that Garcilaso de la Vega was *culto,* it will be plain enough.

Ludovico. Was Garcilaso *culto?*

César. A poet is *culto* who so cultivates his poem that he leaves nothing rough or obscure, like a farmer his field. Culture is precisely that—although the *cultos* of today will say they take it to mean ornamentation.

Ludovico. The second law relating to those things that may be considered as never having been written says that what cannot be understood is no different from what has not been written at all.

César. I'm convinced that the term *culto,* properly understood, is equivalent to precision and clarity of sense, free of all obscurity. For a jumble of misplaced terms, with metaphor piled on metaphor, no more enhances style than does barbarous phraseology ineptly applied.

Ludovico. Viewed logically, that sentence is defective which is couched in dark and inappropriate language, and which obscures instead of clarifying the nature of the thing defined. And, if things which are essentially related to each other must be defined in terms of each other, what connection can there be between sail-bearing doves and ships, so as to define or describe the latter by the former? One might just as well call a galleon a sail-bearing kestrel or a frigate a sail-bearing stork.

César. How ingenious of Virgil to call an arrow a flying sword!

Ludovico. Yes, but that was Virgil.

César. Nevertheless, when he describes fire as liquid, meaning pure or glowing, Macrobius calls it excessive, while condoning him on the ground that Lucretius had used it first.

Ludovico. Aratus, translated by Germanicus Caesar, called the rain from heaven gentle lymph, and the great poet called fertile ears of grain joyous.

César. What an apt metaphor! It is like saying the water laughs its merry way.

Ludovico. Terms based on wrong etymology are completely barbaric, as, for example, the person who called *iron*smiths "those wielders of *irony*," as if that subtle rhetorical term had anything to do with their lusty trade.

César. A student who was eating blackberries answered someone who inquired what he was doing, "I am munching blacks," thereby transferring the fruit to the African race.

Ludovico. Naturally we are not referring to those great men who use elaborate language intentionally as a way of disguising philosophical thought—I mean those treated in his *Heptaplus* by Pico della Mirandola, that Florentine marvel, talented as are all his countrymen. For those of whom I speak have no conception of quality, no sense, namely, of manner, species, and order.

César. A demonstration, as our Philosopher says, is founded on true things. Because whereas from things false both true and false may be inferred, from what is true only the truth may come.

Ludovico. César, proof should proceed from what is most familiar; otherwise it leads to obfuscation and not proof. Proof should illumine, not becloud, the understanding.

César. Those propositions sound hypothetical; that is, they may or may not be true, depending on certain conditions that indicate which is the case.

Ludovico. Call them enigmas, rather; whereas Plato wraps his philosophy in dark conceits, poets should use the simplest words to convey their ideas. Indeed, I took this to be the reason why first sketches are removed as the form emerges.

César. The *cultos* do not believe it possible to elevate language without resorting to barbaric phraseology. And this belief is shown to be self-deception or lack of wit by the example of others who do succeed.

Ludovico. They'll claim that there are many experts of their persuasion, and state that a dialectical problem is a premise advanced by the two opposing sides of a question.

César. I wish that those men known locally as wits would take up such matters when they came together, taking their cue from those flourishing Italian academies. Coming together simply to denigrate others must be entertaining, though it smacks of envy and, in many instances, ignorance.

Ludovico. No one enlightens and everyone babbles there. It might be helpful to put up a sign saying, "Here wits gather," as if to say, "This is a tavern."

César. Have you not seen the tool booksellers use to cut the books they bind? Well, the term for it is *paper cutter,* which might apply as well to these, who chop and cut up words. But luckily for the printed page, they stay marginal and never go into the text.

Ludovico. Some persons maintain that natural logic suffices for disputation and rebuttal, and that Nature similarly suffices for the making of poems, without adherence to the rules of the craft.

César. The art of poetry belongs to rational philosophy and is thus included among the liberal arts. But although it is true that poetry originates in nature, is there anyone so ignorant as to be unaware that art perfects it? To be sure, we know of untutored geniuses, but their very limitations restrict their performance. For no sooner do they stray from their circumscribed orbit than they lose all control and spout nonsense. But to put an end to this unavoidable digression, let us return to the poem.

Ludovico.

Pullulating with *culto,* Claudio, my friend—

César. Columella will tell us what *pullulate* means here, since the term commonly applies to trees.

Ludovico. As you wish the muses to favor you, César, let us not be so earnest, since the sonnet is in jest. Forget your Columella and your commonplaces. Curse them all—they give me a headache!

César. As you please. But should some serious or scholarly matter turn up, you must forgive me. I would add, right now, that to *pullulate* with *culto* means being a catechumen of this sect. The construction using "with" is quite current, as for example, "I plunge with the ducks," "he talks with a stammer," "she gets away with murder," "he's been done away with," "he's someone to conjure with," "she has a face to stop a clock with," and other items along these lines. So don't say I'm trying to vex you with Columella and company.

And just see the divine metaphor *Ecclesiasticus* makes of *pullulate,* telling Caleb and the judges of Israel that their bones "pullulated in their graves," meaning that progeny and memories kept springing to life from them.

Scene 3

JULIO · LUDOVICO · CÉSAR

Julio. Hail and well met, Nisus and Eurialus, Pylades and Orestes, Damon and Pythias, Scipio and Laelius.

Ludovico. Ah, friend Julio, welcome! But how without Don Fernando?

Julio. An important piece of business keeps him at home. He sent me ahead to tell you he'd come as soon as he could.

César. I am sure the muses have kept him occupied.

Julio. The muse herself, rather.

César. How can that be?

Julio. I wish I could tell you.

César. The muse he has been invoking keeps away from Parnassus, and has other ends in view.

Julio. Virgil asked his muse why Aeneas had left Troy to go to Italy. The rhetorical figure for this is a sort of apostrophe or anthypophora.

César. You are expatiating on your own statement, not mine.

Julio. You wished to know who that muse is, and I am suggesting you ask her yourself, because not only is there the need for secrecy, but it's a long story as well.

Ludovico. Well, give us a *brachylogia,* as in the lines,
    Love fires Paris,
    Paris steals Helen, the Greeks take up arms.

Julio. Well, on that model, let me say,
    Fernando went away,
    swore false, tearfully returned another day.

Ludovico. Well put, with your usual pungency.

Julio. It's an induction at least, whereby one may proceed from particulars to universals.

César. Julio, you've not come ill-disposed for the discussion we were having, although Madrid never did succeed in undermining your education.

Julio. How were you passing the time?

Ludovico. While waiting for Fernando, we were trying to understand a sonnet.

Julio. Understand it?

César. Why so surprised?

Julio. Men as learned as you?

Ludovico. Here, read it yourself, then you can help us elucidate it.

Julio. In all humility, I shall read it.

César. This Julio is remarkably intelligent. He and his master are both perpetual students.

Ludovico. I don't see how Fernando can devote himself to love and to his studies at the same time.

César. That question is like the Philosopher's problem: how are hermaphrodites produced?

Ludovico. Ovid's fable of Salmacis and Trocus proposes an explanation.

César. In his *Tusculan Disputations,* the Roman orator remarks that no perturbations of mind are so overpowering as the madness of love. For how can a mind distraught lend itself to studies, which require the utmost tranquillity?

Julio. I have now read and duly considered this macaronic extravaganza. This far outdoes Merlin Coccaï.

César. We'd already reached the second line, but what do you make of the first?

Julio. He's addressing a friend of his.

Ludovico. Since we're doing a commentary, the word *friend* obliges us to bring in Lucian and Tully.

Julio. If I am to make any contribution, you won't find me citing catalogues of famous names of old—rather, the most rarefied poets, after the fashion of those moderns who think themselves erudite when they string names together without having read the books.

César. How does the second line go?

Julio.

A minotaurist am I, starting this morning.

César. It's perfectly clear he's spoofing; by making himself the minotaur, he confesses that the poem is a labyrinth.

Julio. A poor compound of man and bull.

Ludovico. The word minotaur derives from Minos and *tauros.* It was the name of the son of Pasiphaë, whom Ovid libeled in that tale about her falling in love with a bull. Of all the fables and moral tales of the poets, none so slanders women as this piece of bestiality, not to mention the horse of Semiramis. Because the swan of the lovely Leda and the shower of gold of the inaccessible Danaë were actual men, although the allegorical sense must have been that might, brute force, cupidity, and opportunity were overwhelming for many women.

César. Ausonius depicted opportunity magnificently.

Julio. In sum, the poet says he'll be a minotaur starting tomorrow.

César. In the labyrinth of the *cultos.*

Ludovico. May the golden thread of the celebrated epigram of Stigel come to his aid.

César. The Romans used to put the minotaur on their banners as a symbol of secrecy.

Julio. That could apply here, too. The language of the *cultos* strikes many as arcane.

César. Shall we not say a word about *morning?* The commentarors would never let something so clear go unnoticed.

Ludovico. Then say it's the successor of night, as night is the mask of day. And if you want something rather more rustic, bring in Virgil's *Moretum.*

Julio. How far from describing morning is that tag by the Bounder of Marseilles:

My first duty done at dawn
is doing it upon the lawn.

Ludovico. Where did you ever discover that poet, Julio?

Julio. Don't trouble to inquire. A writer who cites rare authors greatly impresses everyone, you know.

Ludovico. And even when the authors quoted are classics, a writer would do better to put it in his own words.

César. They would lack authority, since antiquity lends an aura to works which have in fact been surpassed in our own days.

Julio. That doesn't hold for women, since they are more appreciated when young.

Ludovico. They say it used to irk Michelangelo, the Italian sculptor, as memorable for his statues as Nature for her originals . . .

Julio. What was it irked him?

Ludovico. That people were always extolling the ancient sculptors, your Phidias, Euphranor, and Polyclitus, while he was not given the recognition he deserved because he was not of their time, although manifestly superior to them. And, in order to trick the invidious, always the bane of the living . . .

Julio. And of the dead at times.

Ludovico. He produced a fabulous statue, and when, with consummate care and perfection he had completed it, he removed a foot and buried the statue at night in a cardinal's vineyard (which Italians call a garden) then being laid out. A few days later, designers at the site discovered it. That brought all of Rome to view the marvel, some saying it was a work by Mentor, creator of the Capitoline Jupiter and the Diana of the Ephesians; others, that it was by Myron, creator of Minerva and the Satyr, mentioned by Juvenal; and some, that it was by Teladeus and Theodoros. In short, the sculptors said there was no man alive who would dare to fashion the missing foot. At this point Michelangelo had the foot brought out and, fitting it to the statue, told them, "Romans, I made it."

Julio. Now comes the line,

> Renouncing Castilian phraseology.

César. Renouncing is more than denouncing, because it means acting and not simply talking.

Julio. So it does. Which explains why Cosmic Birdbrain, that poet from La Mancha, most appositely says in his *Zarambaina:*

> In summertime, ladies start renouncing;
> it suffices not for you to be denouncing.

And because so great a renunciation would require help from above, he concludes the quatrain thus:

> May *The Solitudinous* bless me on my way.

César. The Solitudes would sound better, I should say.

Ludovico. Not at all, because proparoxytonic words make verse full-blown.

Julio. Overblown, I'd say.

Ludovico. Not only is it more *culto,* it's more crinkly.

Julio. The poet Bartleby Corduroy loved proparoxytones, and so, in his "Lavish Snack," he says:

> What provender could be more heavenly
> than food for bellies rumbling rav'nously?

But Cairasco outdoes him in the *Cadences:*

> And taking up a pair of spatulas
> he fashioned her a snout like Dracula's.

César. Now for the second quatrain—how does it go?

Julio.

> Henceforth, as day's precursor, Lady Dawn
> by name of Joan the Baptist shall be known.

It's a very fine figure, with the metaphor fetched from the River Jordan, and, if one wished, far-fetched from the River Amazon.

Ludovico. Julio has made me laugh and remember a play about St. Christopher, where the poet describes a procession in which one of the giants plays the saint's role and the dragon the devil's. The latter has two lines, repeated after each stanza:

> With all my might, and just like that,
> I'd sooner eat a cherub than my hat.

César. Superb hyperbole!

Ludovico. And how about this snatch of *cultismo* by the same poet: "Let blood be coral, flesh be snow." Or take this one, along the same lines: "Her crystal blood is let—a glassy snare."

Ludovico. Go on, Julio, and finish the quatrain.

Julio.

> Waterfly, the raucous frog shall be;
> gold mange, the wheat; and watered silk, the sea.

César. Absolutely remarkable!

Ludovico. You know, of course, that silk cloth may be flowered as well as watered.

César. I have both kinds.

Ludovico. Well, I'll have you know that for our *cultos* the earth is the flowered silk cloth, and the sea, the watered silk cloth.

Julio. Those expressions wouldn't be so bad if the sound of *silk cloth* didn't grate.

César. True enough, for many phrases of the *cultos* beguile one with their pleasing sounds, such as when they call the nightingale "that feathered lyre." By the same token, the lyre should be called "yon wooden nightingale." But the unpleasant sound of such words prevents their being used, though the meaning is the same. And so the beauty of *lyre* and *feather* makes one overlook the lack of propriety.

Julio. And what if they possessed both beauty and propriety?

Ludovico. They would be perfect, since the inherent form of the concept would find embodiment in the sound, as Leo Hebraeus in his *Dialogues* opines is essential for the consummation of beauty.

Julio. Liberties are of course allowed. As some poet says, "A man is forced by hardship into things he never meant"; the same may well be applied to rhyming. For even among naturally created things, some exist by contingency, others by necessity, as the Philosopher puts it. Quintilian likewise applied the term *poetic license* to this expedient.

Ludovico. The good poet should spare no pains. Let him ponder, blot out, reconsider, select, and reread what he writes a thousand times. For the origin of *rhyme* is *rimar,* which is to look into things and pursue them scrupulously. So thought Cicero and so did Statius.

César. So there's no merit in not revising.

Julio. Hear this reply and you'll see how neatly the whole matter is put. It's from a play in which a poet tells a prince who asks him how he composes:

> How does one compose? I read,
> and what I read, I imitate,
> and what I imitate, I write,
> and what I write, blot out,
> and then I sift the blottings-out.

César. Listen to this curiosity out of Suetonius Tranquillus. Speaking of Nero's poetry, and the common belief that he was passing off others' verses as his own, Suetonius says that after his death they found lines blotted out and written over, in his notebooks, and so were certain the lines were his own. So blottings are a proof of thinking, for if one does not think one does not blot. Wherefore, anyone using rhyme will come up with a perfect find, as if he'd come upon a treasure trove—and you know that a *trove* actually means a *find.* And this is why that poet says:

> God pardon Castillejo's antique lines,
> since he found good in my poetic finds.

Ludovico. That poet's works are still alive. He was secretary to the Emperor, and not unworthy of fame among the older poets; although another poet holding the same position earned greater fame: Gonzalo Pérez, as excellent a translator of Homer as Gregorio Hernández was of Virgil. Those were men of stature, who did not wait for Italy to transpose those ancients into her idiom. Their versions of the Greek and Latin came before we saw them in Italian.

Julio. You have touched on a point which has caused no little amusement among men of letters—men, I mean, of humane letters, now called "polite letters," I'm not sure why.

César. What is your point, Julio?

Julio. Just this: certain translations from the Latin, French, and Greek, lifted from the Tuscan, are passed off on us as originals.

César. That is no better than passing off as your own the labor of others and books pirated from their proper authors. But to return to the art of *rhyming* or finding, which is the same as invention, and which gives rise in Italy and Spain today to the term *rhyme* for individual compositions—the word itself makes clear the thinking that must go into rhyming. And such hidden power of seeking-out is what Cicero calls *inventing* or *thinking-up*. So consider the care it takes—why, even Aristotle deplores finding iambs and trochees in prose, and is cited by Cicero himself.

Ludovico. The reason poets writing prose fall into verse rhythms is that they are used to writing metrically; the practice greatly exercises the two philosophers, and understandably so. But a born poet will have trouble mending this flaw, unless he takes great pains.

Julio. The poet Symmachus overindulged in rhyme. But how can you be forgetting the sea, which our sonnet calls watered silk?

César. Even if those words were soft, the metaphor would grate.

Ludovico. Pico della Mirandola says that matter resides in the sea bed, in this sphere of ours where things are born to die.

Julio. Yes, but he doesn't say whether the sea should be of purple cloth or watered silk.

Ludovico. There is Solomon's admirable application of the ebb and flow of waves to the coming and going of generations.

Julio. I assure you that those waves wore neither fine royal cloth nor rough Cordovan goatskin.

César. Antonio Spelta, in his *Rhetoric*, frowned on anything far-fetched and grating. And for Quintilian, in a word, metaphor must be "beautiful and clear." What would he have called words lacking all

propriety, a charge he levels against Lycophron, Gorgias, and Alcidamas for their epithets and adjectives?

Julio. Listen to the raucous frog of the seventh line.

César. What does he call it?

Julio. "Waterfly."

César. What's the propriety there?

Ludovico. Both jar upon the ear.

César. Then would an oxcart, a mill hopper, an organ being tuned, a
flea that won't let up, all be flies?

Ludovico. That's why he calls the frog "raucous," so that the adjective
will specify its importunity. But what he overlooks is that Virgil
calls swans raucous, and Ambrogio Calepino absolves him, saying
the whirring of their wings is to blame.

Julio. In verbo flea—since you've brought it up—I'd like to recite a
song Master Burguillos wrote for a certain flea.

César. By all means, go ahead, Julio, and divert us from this implacable
sonnet, since it's too late now for Fernando to come.

Julio.

    Lascivious sprite,
      sealer of every lover's plight,
      like a jumpy atom gone astray,
      mustard-color with mustard's bite—
      you might at least alight:
      how can I paint you in bouncy flight?
    Since darkness shields your life
      from sleuthing fingers' nail-sharp knife,
      sweet goblin, prithee, stay.
      Don't always bite and run away.
      You're jealousy insectified—
      you nip and then fly off to hide.
    In tropic climes the wildest wight
      owns beauty a thing most sanctified.
      Why, even death will turn aside.
      But you, ears deaf and heart of stone,
      more Turkish than the sultan's throne,
      sow garnets in the pearliest hide.
    Elusive spot
      upon your victim's ample waist,

unnoticed dot,
    you murder slumber with impunity
    and then repair in no great haste
    to Aragonese immunity.
Is there one worthy you've not slain?
    One beauty you have not undone?
    What cloister will you not profane?
    What virtue not soil to have your fun?
    You raise a hive and then, to tease,
    elude the firmest finger-squeeze.
An elephant did once complain
    to Mother Nature of a flea:
    "What good is such great size to me?
    I'm envious of such as he,
    for while I sleep here in the dirt,
    this creature lolls in scented shirt.
The grass I munch is my sole fare
    while he sips purest human blood.
    On land, in water, in the air,
    all creatures else have their abode;
    he dwells in scarlet cloth and gold,
    whence smugly he surveys the globe."
Never did beast speak word more true.
    Even Columbus is outdone.
    For all the lands he thought he'd won
    in the Old World and the New,
    your fancy's mere geography
    excels in sheer hydrography.
Let pens expatiate on your puny size;
    can any man, king though he be,
    boast palaces like those you roam, o flea,
    or halls you promenade inside?
    And yet you're Justice wrongly used:
    once wrung you die, albeit abused.
Alcides' arrows slew, so goes the fable,
    those food-befouling fowl of Phineus' table.
    You, flea, have found what I aspire to:
    the highest table e'er desire knew.

Beware of looking down, lest you should slip
and end up squashed by jasmine fingertip.
Remember, living grain of pepper-seed,
　　red-hottest of the spicy Eastern breed,
　　you could meet your match in burning lamps,
　　you winged set of pinching clamps,
　　you wasp, without one ounce of money,
　　feasting one everyone else's honey.
Could any vengeance be so sweet
　　as catching you red-handed at your treat
　　and squeezing you with crystal fingertips?
　　Not a bad way to draw your final breath,
　　in emulation of fond lovers' death,
　　tight-clasped, a kiss upon their lips.
Don't go beating about the bush,
　　blemishing white virgin snow.
　　You're given the name of flea, you know,
　　because you'd flee a thumbnail's crush.
　　But thumbs are made for squelching fleas,
　　turning thumbs down to all your pleas.
How foolishly the gods above
　　behaved when drawn to earth by love.
　　They took the shapes of horse or bull,
　　of swans and roses, fountains full.
　　The thought ne'er seems t' have crossed their minds
　　that fleas, nor lynx nor Argus finds.
Phyllis is angry as she can be
　　that you should hunt so fearlessly.
　　Even in zones off-limits you sponge.
　　Beware her dagger-fingers' lunge!
　　Yet would I, were I in your place,
　　die happy 'twixt those ivory gates!
Flea mine, for us two something's awry:
　　I envy your bliss, you my human-being.
　　But if you continue biting and fleeing,
　　you may well find yourself loath to die,
　　so let's just effect a change of place:
　　I, dying of bliss, you, of human race.

At any rate, when you bite and spring,
>   you leave a tiny purple ring
>   for a blind man's dog to thrust himself through.
>   The blind man is Love (his vision a cypher),
>   the dog quite clearly has to be you,
>   and I, the one left to pay the piper.

Ludovico. Just what you'd expect from a poet so close to a subject of that order.

César. Has Master Burguillos ever chosen a more elevated subject for his muse?

Ludovico. If he were only with us, he'd settle many of our doubts concerning this terrible sphinx of a sonnet.

César. Where did we leave off?

Julio. At Virgil's reference to swans as raucous—believe me, it quite delighted me, since I am heartily sick of the sweet and dulcet tones in which they are said to sing.

Ludovico. But that's the basis of the attributes *melodious* and *harmonious,* which Propertius and others routinely apply to them.

Julio. And to every other bird as well, which is why the poet Filondango Snotnose said . . .

Ludovico. There's a poet for you!

Julio. . . . in his *Luciferiad*—borrowed, incidentally, from the Greek of Calipod—:

César. Listen to that wag!

Julio.
>   Let owls ululate and no lark sing,
>   doleful ditties do not to lyre ring.

Ludovico. Anything sui generis, applauded, and grand, though unforgivably outlandish, should be deemed a genuine achievement.

César. Ovid calls raucous the voices of the frogs or Lycian peasants transformed by Leto. He depicts them vividly, but does not call them flies.

Julio. In a peppery sonnet to a jowly fat lady with skinny legs, Don Carrot Snailshell wrote:
>   Phyllis, since I'm gross and yet compliant,
>   I want you as my frog and not my giant.

Then he calls wheat the "gold mange."

César. Can anyone possibly fathom that?

Julio. Why, it's quite simple. The mange has its grains and so does wheat. And to them he adds *gold,* for comparisons need not apply *in omnimodam rationem.* But the poet in his sonnet must have borrowed from the *Mangiad* written by Swifty Gerundive in a book entitled *Boarding School:*

> How sweet the liquid that I down
> when furiously I scratch my crown!
> I know, for all my later wails,
> I string gold grains between my nails.

Ludovico. Like clothing, metaphor should be cut to measure.

César. Aristotle mocks Gorgias for calling seeds "green things." What would he have made of what poets get by with today?

Ludovico. Virgil calls wheat "Ceres," as a metonymy.

César. See Quintilian on tropes, although Cyprian reduces them to eleven in number.

Julio. This is the first line of the tercets:

> All out of sorts, I cannot slough off tedium.

Ludovico. He says he is annoyed with himself for not having always followed the new mode, since living in the old-fashioned way and speaking in the language of today had seemed to him to make good sense. *Tedium,* as you know, is heaviness, a word the holy bard of Bethlehem uses in saying his soul is heavy with extreme tedium. The man of Uz, greatest of all the men of the East, said something very similar. And Cicero, to wit: there are men whose monstrous infamies do not weigh heavily upon them. *Slough* is an uncommonly significant word, although not much used. In effect, it means to shed something one is uncomfortable with, as a snake does its skin, and as lovers and husbands cannot do since they may not openly slough off their jealousy.

Julio. You'll find it in the poet Magalon Pestifery's commentary on *The Caticide* by Wormygut Magurnius:

> When your jealous scoffing puts me in a huff,
> off this long face of mine I'd like to slough.

And in the play *The Belle of Saragossa:*

> My one cure, when depression I cannot slough,
> is watching naughty ladies strut their stuff.

It is these *uff* sounds that are so strong and expressive in our language, and most impressive, too, as in *tough, rough, enough,* and the like. And, as for *tedium,* it has put me in mind of a lady's letter, the beginning of which I can quote for you: "I find myself sunk in such unaccustomed tedium, I fancy my heart is being strangulated by the gasps of my deprivation of your most amiable consolation with its exquisite delectation."

Ludovico. That is surely in a class with what the grammar master told the pupil he was whipping: "Compute the flagellations, wretch, and if you provoke me to iracundity, reiterating the lines on your bottomside, I shall convert them into a solfeggio of antiphonies on you, though you lacquer your hose with scarlet."

Julio. That's precisely where the next line comes in:

Henceforth I'll say hose, not pantaloons.

Pantaloons take their name from the comic character Pantaleone, or from some other loon, though in fact they derive from the Greek. While they are comfortable gear, hose go better with weapons. And I am of the opinion that Spanish hose were not of the variety called *leotards,* but rather any kind of half-hose, including those of steel worn by the Roman soldiers, which the French call *chausse de guerre,* or military hose.

César. Cicero, in his Fifth Epistle to his friend Atticus, indicates his dislike of them.

Ludovico. The *cultos* of our time must know a great deal about footgear, considering every blessed thing they wear on the feet: stars, flowers, clouds, nights, suns; they even put clogs on the moon, as if these were precisely the thing to go around in while seeking Endymion on Mount Lathmos.

Julio. Macarias Portulaca put it most wittily, after stealing his lady's shoes and stockings, having slipped out from behind some briars as she was bathing in the river:

The socks were more like stockings
and the stockings more like drawers,
and would have done as well
as casings for a pair of flutes.
How can I express to you
the chicness of her shoes?
They'll soon be requisitioned
as billets for the troops.

Ludovico. Get on with the sonnet.

Julio.

As in Bandurrius the Shepherd's days of old.

César. Never have I heard nor read of such a shepherd, though I have perused a fair number of Greek, Latin, French, and Tuscan poets.

Julio. Bandurrius is quite ancient. He invented the *bandurria,* or bandore, which still bears his name. It's a small instrument and, like others of the sort, once primed, will drown out an organ. Bandurrius was called the Rustic Orpheus because, when his lady died, he tried to go to the Elysian fields. And, acting upon this mad idea, one night, when he had reached the Gamenosa pastures near Cordova, where so many asphodels grow, the fancy seized him that some white mares grazing there were souls. Taking up his *bandurria,* he so affrighted the creatures that the boorish herdsmen, acting like Thracian bacchantes, beat him to death. And, although not mourned as Orpheus was in the elegant epigram of Fausto Sabeo, still he was not without an epigrammatist of his own:

Here lies Bandurrius, oh passer-by!

Halt your steps nigh.

Ludovico. You halt them. I am so sick of hearing about that passer-by, who has to be included in every epitaph, that I've sworn off any in which he appears.

Julio. And right you are. Because aside from the banality and triviality of the thing, it is an imposition for a poet to expect travelers going about their business to read what he happens to feel like writing, whether in praise or dispraise of the deceased. If the traveler is on horseback, how is he to dismount or who is to hold his mule? And if the tomb is in a church, the epitaph was clearly not written for coach travelers. If the traveler is on foot, why must he tarry for something of no concern to him, only to arrive later at his inn?

César. That tag and that favorite of the ancients, "May the earth rest lightly on him," both drive me to distraction. For what can it matter to the deceased if they shovel a mountain on him, or a fool—the greatest dead weight of all?

Ludovico. Exactly what that philosopher had in mind, who ordained that he be buried in the open. When the disciples objected that the birds would eat him, he replied they should put a staff in his hand. Their answer was: if he was not alive to scare off the birds, what

good would the staff be? And he in turn: "Well, if I am not alive to
scare them away, then what do I care if the birds peck at me?"

César. The heroic soul who had this inscribed upon his tomb gave little enough thought to passers-by: "Here lies Vasco Fernández, who
never knew fear." And the great Duke of Alba, when told of it, observed, "That man must never even have snuffed out a candle with
his hands."

Ludovico. A subtle way to imply he'd never put himself in a position to
be afraid.

Julio. The poet Snaky Know-it-all wrote an epitaph on Bonamí, a servant of His Majesty's, and a fine freak of Nature to boot, since in
the tiniest detail imaginable he was absolutely perfect, like the entire *Iliad* which one extraordinary writer put in a nutshell.

César. Give us your epitaph, Julio.

Julio.

> Your step here halt, oh passer-by,
> to see what you will hardly see—
> though should you have no time to tarry,.
> and on would haste, feel free—
> but if you have a mind to look
> at this atomic Bonamí,
> you won't be sure he lies here
> since he lies so tinily.

But without halting the passer-by, Master Burguillos wrote the following for the tombstone of a very tall and very thin lady:

> The Lady Mistress Roance,
> so tall and thin was she,
> she planned her tomb to be
> the inside of a lance.
> Yet this could never be,
> it was too short, you see,
> and, more troublesome beside,
> one quarter inch too wide.

Ludovico. That will do by way of digression. Let us proceed with the
twelfth line.

César. How does it go?

Julio.

> These lines—are they Turkish or a Teuton's?

Ludovico. Apostrophizing himself, the author inquires if they are written in the Turkish or the Teutonic tongue.

Julio. All you need say about the Turks is that Constantinople is swarming with them.

César. What astonishing news! Pray God forgive the Emperor Constantine.

Ludovico. Read Giovio.

César. Read him yourself. We Spaniards owe him nothing, unless his insults put us in his debt.

Ludovico. He was a venal writer and in the Sultan's pay.

César. In that regard he was more a streetwalker than a chronicler.

Julio. As for the Teutons, they live, as you know, in any part of Germany you care to name. I swear some writer would here drag in, to no purpose, selection of the emperors by consensus. In sum, the sonnet concludes:

> They're yours, oh reader-garblers of our tongue,
> so gobble up this *culto* heap you're bred among.

César. Reader-garblers here stands for *cultos,* as *Roma pro Romanis* and Ceres for wheat.

Julio. Garblers gobbling is a superfluity.

Ludovico. Then call it identity. But here comes Fernando.

Scene 4

DON FERNANDO · LUDOVICO
CÉSAR · JULIO

Fernando. Let no one blame me. I'd sooner have forfeited life itself than forgone the occasion which has kept me from you.

Ludovico. Whence comes all this joy? You seem transformed.

César. What can have happened to change you from the Heraclitean you were into a Democritean?

Fernando. It can't be told in two words. My tale embraces victories of love, miracles of resolution, wonders of will power, windfalls of the stars, shifts in fortune, happy conjunctions of the times, rewards of patience, triumphs of endurance, and joys restored to the joyless—

all bound up together. Join me in my study; reading you this experience will give me a head start on a poem.

César. What ails this man, Julio?

Julio. The same thing as usual, with an added dose of madness. He'll
give you a full account, although looks and behavior already suggest the cause.

Ludovico. Somewhere in Aristotle I once read of a woman named Po-
lycrata who died of sudden joy.

César. According to Aulus Gellius, the same happened to Phillipides,
that eminent playwright whom Guido of Bituria called "the nob-
lest of men," when he won a poetry contest.

Ludovico. And Sophocles the tragedian, whom Cicero calls "divine,"
died the same way.

Fernando. Your very Cicero, in the Fifth Book of his *Tusculan Disputations,* says that Democritus Gelasinus, who was always laughing,
lived to be a hundred and nine. So happiness does not always kill
everyone.

Julio. Evidently you aim to be another Old John of the Ages, the one
who, according to Gaguin, lived to be three hundred and sixty-one
years old, born during the reign of Charlemagne and dying under
Louis the Young.

Fernando. Unexpected happiness can make anything happen.

Julio. In Spain that same Old John of the Ages must have occasioned
the legend of John-Who-Waits-for-God, the Wandering Jew, with
his five pieces of silver.

Ludovico. Control yourself, wild man, and tell us, if you can, what has
happened to you.

Fernando. Do they not praise the piety of Pompilius, the constancy of
Regulus, the fortitude of Cato, the impartiality of Aristides, the
wisdom of Socrates, the compassion of Scipio, the clemency of Laelius, the perseverance of Fabius, the courage of Romulus, the judi-
ciousness of Seleucus, the continence of Curtius, the modesty of
Camillus, the humanity of Pyrrhus, the luck of Alexander, the pa-
triotism of Mucius, the daring of Brutus, the belligerence of Tully,
the splendor of Ancus Marcius, the raiment of Tarquin, and the
prudence of Servius? Well, in the annals of history, there alongside
all these titles to glory, shall stand the gratification of Don Fernando.

Julio. Remarkable string of Romans and Greeks!

Fernando. Is not Scipio called the African because he conquered that part of the world?

Ludovico. Just as their Caesars are called the Germanic or the Britannic.

Fernando. What name would you give to one who has overcome the disdain of Dorotea?

Ludovico. Fernando the Doroteanic.

Fernando. Well, such is my name, my joy, and my story. Be seated and prepare to learn the secret ways of fortune, and why I am constrained to pen her praises.

Ludovico. Do no such thing, for Tully says that praising fortune is folly and censuring fortune, conceit.

Scene 5

GERARDA · TEODORA

Teodora. That girl has not returned since she went out with your daughter Felipa this morning for her constitutional. I fear something may have happened to her.

Gerarda. Don't worry, she's old enough to find her way. Remember, 'she's no longer the little lass dragging her feet to Mass.'

Teodora. I've been disturbed no end since that young Fernando came back. Quite aside from his wounding Don Bela and company, which I fear spells trouble for us, we've enough putting up with his serenades.

Gerarda. You know very well how I feel and what I think you should do. But 'give advice to the old—you'll never win: you can't pick fleas from a black sheepskin.' Why are you always giving in to her?

Teodora. So as not to explode all at once.

Gerarda. 'Neither feast nor famine. Neither icing for bread nor hogshead for wine.'

Teodora. Celia has been misleading me.

Gerarda. 'Beware the black dog and the Galician servant.'

Teodora. She's full of praise for her mistress and the fatuity of Don Bela.

Gerarda. 'Come spring and the sap in the hack flows back.'

Teodora. If she takes that Fernando back, we're done for.

Gerarda. You needn't worry, since Felipa is with her.

Teodora. 'When the two Peters see eye to eye, then Alvaro de Luna goodbye.'

Gerarda. Well, what opinion do you have of Felipa?

Teodora. She's her friend, she's a woman, and a young one, too.

Gerarda. She is a friend of yours, a married woman, and no mere child.

Teodora. What do you expect an egg to be like?

Gerarda. I suppose you mean like any other.

Teodora. You don't say!

Gerarda. Have you such a bad opinion of me?

Teodora. Not an opinion; it's a certitude.

Gerarda. Gossip, I'll tell you a story. King John of Portugal was brought a bowl of whipped cream by a peasant woman with a plea that her husband be pardoned for killing a man. This during an absence of the Queen, who, sitting down to supper with him, ate a good deal of it. The woman threw herself at their feet, pleading with both for her husband's life. The King was for pardoning, the Queen against; whereupon, seeing her so wrathful, he said, "Just a moment, madam—wasn't that her whipped cream you consumed?"

Teodora. I take your meaning, Gerarda. Hush, here they come.

Scene 6

TEODORA · FELIPA

GERARDA · DOROTEA

Dorotea. You'll want to know where I've come from, no doubt.

Teodora. Why should I, seeing you've come back so flushed?

Dorotea. If I'm flushed, it's wrong; and if I'm pale, it's wrong. What can I ever do to please you?

Teodora. Come home at one o'clock.

Felipa. Oh, but that sermon we heard!

Teodora. It must have been little Father Fernando preaching.

Felipa. On my word of honor, it was a famous barefoot friar.

Teodora. As barefoot and threadbare as the gentleman in question?

Dorotea. Oh, Mother! If only you'd heard him you would have wept your eyes out.

Teodora. Such tears I have indeed shed at the pieties of that saintly preacher.

Gerarda. 'Up the ladle ships the cat and you know what she's at.'

Dorotea. You too, Gerarda! Don't you believe me when I say where I've been?

Gerarda. 'Been there and back—a likely story, that.'

Dorotea. Oh, the virtues of the elderly: malice and envy.

Gerarda. I'm talking to Felipa, not you, Dorotea. Felipa is my daughter—'the mare's kick never hurts the colt.'

Dorotea. We women all know proverbs, Gerarda. So, 'though the file has a bite, it sometimes breaks its tooth.'

Gerarda. Have I been attacking you?

Dorotea. Celia, fold up my cloak. These two ladies are feeling no pain.

Gerarda. Why, honestly, I've breakfasted only on my devotions.

Dorotea. Gerarda, Gerarda! 'Cry wolf and out come the dogs.'

Gerarda. Not at all. I've been doing my best to reassure your mother.

Dorotea. My mother never tires of accusing me. For myself I don't mind, but I do for your daughter. Felipa is a saint.

Teodora. 'Birds of a feather flock together.' Come, pickaninny, set the table here.

Dorotea. I don't want anything to eat.

Teodora. Naturally, since you've already eaten.

Dorotea. Yes, the poison you've been feeding me.

Teodora. 'A cat's claws under a bigot's cloak.' Go ahead and whimper now.

Felipa. Hush, Dorotea. Let's not make a scene and ruin everything.

Dorotea. Today, Felipa, I have no intention of weeping or quarreling, for though the peak of pleasure is the presage of pain, I will be wronging my own soul if I ever again spoil the memory of such happiness with sadness.

Felipa. People never consider past youth but only passing years.

Teodora. Dorotea's present company is not to my liking.

Gerarda. 'All morning she powdered and primped, but left her hair unkempt.'

Teodora. 'Let's at least hope the water is clean,' Gerarda.

Gerarda. 'Where there's little choice, don't raise your voice.'

Teodora. 'A nasty pair of scissors put out my father's eye.'

Gerarda. If Dorotea has good instincts, Felipa can hardly lead her astray.

Teodora. 'What have a pair of legs to do with the price of eggs?'

Dorotea. Oh, happiest of women, how blissfully you rose with this day's sun! Your longings have been fulfilled at last—at last you've seen the object of your yearnings, the center of your every thought, convinced that he adores you, convinced that he respects you. In his eyes, I saw Fernando's tears, when I least imagined that he cared for me. Mine he shall be, in spite of my old hag of a mother and that old witch who prompts her. No New World riches for me, nor shackles on my youth. My pleasure is my gold and diamonds. Oh, of all women, the happiest! I was not about during my mother's salad days. Now she's a widow and she's still trying to cut a figure. 'Blind man's wife, who are you primping for?'

Teodora. What are these fine ladies whispering?

Gerarda. Whisper what they will, they can only fault us on our years, which are no fault of ours.

Teodora. Your Felipa will be the ruination of Dorotea.

Gerarda. 'The pot calling the kettle black.'

Teodora. 'When I went out to gossip about, 'twas me I heard being gossiped about.'

Gerarda. Dorotea is clever, Felipa is not. So who's deceiving who?

Teodora. They say they've come from church.

Gerarda. 'Fish stories and lies improve with size.'

Teodora. What I'm afraid of, Gerarda, is that Dorotea has taken up with Don Fernando again. That youth has all the appeal of poverty, and she, all the foibles of vanity.

Gerarda. 'What good is a wedding ring, if it brings no profiting?' But if your fear is the reconciliation of these two lovers, my fear is that Don Bela will find out about it, which would be the death of us all.

Teodora. 'Our friendship fell asunder when the rug came out from under.'

Gerarda. Have no doubt on that score, he's not the man to put up with a senseless affront. 'No one can serve two masters' and 'three is a crowd.'

Teodora. Oh, Gerarda! Dorotea so jubilant, with no silk or jewel from the Guadalajara Gate—and this, at one in the afternoon! That means only one thing—the old affair has been patched up. This is the end of me!

Gerarda. 'A trip to the neighboring shrine, not much wax but plenty of wine.' Now just keep an eye on her, Teodora. You let her get away with anything she wants. And if she takes up with Fernando again, your house is done for, your subsistence gone. 'Money and reputation win your children high station.'

Teodora. 'What watch can you keep when the watchdog's asleep?' What good is my scolding Dorotea if she's in the company of Felipa?

Gerarda. 'Get yourself the right name, you'll win marriage and fame.' Look here, Teodora, it's not Felipa who is ruining her, it's her love for Don Fernando.

Teodora. 'There's none so deaf as one who will not hear.' You know very well what I mean, Gerarda. Young Fernando has his little friends, and your daughter, her little hankerings.

Gerarda. I challenge you to say a single word against the girl's virtue and sheltered life! What happened to her before she married has often happened to others. And do you think I stood idly by? The fact remains, her husband never noticed a thing, and he was no fool. A likely one to be leading others astray! Has she ever failed to weep at sermons? This past Lent the way she fasted during Holy Week I thought she'd never pull through. The rosary of knotted cord she has made to be buried with her stretches from here to Rome. Believe me when I say that on her wedding night six of us matrons still could not drag her into the bridal chamber. Imagine, such modesty! I could wish Dorotea had some of it.

Teodora. There's nothing easier than denying, nothing harder than defense. You've taken the easy way, and left me with the harder.

Gerarda. Hush, they are listening.

Scene 7

MARFISA · CLARA

Marfisa. If I haven't lost my mind, it's because I had none to begin with.

Clara. You've been so rudely betrayed, I'm at a loss to console you. Indeed, I am tempted to add further indignation to what you already feel, a course more desperate than effective.

Marfisa. Don Fernando in Madrid, Clara, and not come to see me all this time! Is there any doubt but that he's thoroughly smitten with that notorious Circe who has lulled his wits asleep? I shall not budge from this doorstep, though night overtake me here, and however much daylight and neighbors reprove me. That gentleman I spoke to is a friend of Don Fernando's. His attachment to Lisena, Dorotea's neighbor, led, through the fellowship of love, to their sharing secrets. He asked me how I had fared with Don Fernando since his return from Seville. I replied that Don Fernando had not returned, whereupon he divulged (as is the custom in this Court city) the reason for Fernando's leaving, namely, jealousy of a Spanish gentleman from the New World, received not unfavorably by the family, though tepidly by Dorotea. He said Fernando had not killed anyone, which indicated he had invented it all simply to extract from me what you already know I gave him so he could get away. Never have I purchased so cheaply the satisfaction of separating him from that damsel who, on account of his absence, is obliged by some vow or other to wear a habit—ironically, a chaste one. Only the blue scapular can be in earnest, since it's for jealousy. I don't know what Fabricio (that's the gentleman's name) wanted from our conversation. But can there be any doubt? The same thing all men want, coveting whatever they lay eyes on. He must have been trying to make me give up my love of Fernando, for he showed me this letter, which Fernando had written him on the road, along with some verse about his departure. The letter goes this way—

Clara. It will serve to distract us while awaiting him.

Marfisa. "Friend Fabricio, I journey without my soul, since I have left it behind, and without my life, since it seeks to leave me, and accompanied by so many thoughts that, like different poisons canceling each other out, keep me alive. I have not slept, although I've tried. So madness begins, and there's nothing I can do to stop it. Julio and I are more intent on Dorotea than on the road. We speak of nothing else from break of dawn onward and the same is surely not true of her. Ah, lucky womankind! At a lover's first rebuff they find another to court and woo them, amuse, spoil, and shower them with riches. Oh we unhappy men, whose only hope is to have no hope. These lines will tell you more about me than I realized when I composed them. If someone cares to sing them, I would not mind Dorotea's hearing them:

"Where are you bound, my Thought,
　having gone so far astray?
　How can you escape
　when branded like a slave?
What use is running off
　when a brand gives you away?
　It only allows your mistress
　to wrong you all the more.
One thing you must remember:
　the folly of ever thinking
　you'll cast off in a day
　so many years of bondage.
No such life can be borne,
　you thought, and off you fled,
　never stopping to think
　you'd left your life in her arms.
Did you believe her tears?
　You must know that shedding tears
　is writing off in water
　love's once plighted troth.
To expect success, my Thought,
　where others have always failed,
　you'd have to be a wizard,
　or be as mad as I.
Can you think you'll forget
　all the bliss you have known,
　with memory still retaining
　the subject of your thought?
Were I wiser than I am,
　and you, Thought, less impulsive,
　I'd not be in this quandary now
　nor would you now be fleeing.
You may say I can return—

I won't have yet been missed.
　　Don't you see such weakness
　　increases her revenge?
As for me, I'd rather die
　　than find that I've been spurned
　　since love, though honor-bound,
　　mistreats his vanquished foe.
To see so meek and humble
　　one who left in anger
　　will freeze or reassure—
　　a mistake in either case.
Love, my Thought, is uneasy.
　　Once it ceases to doubt,
　　if perchance it rise again,
　　it will never reach new heights.
Pretending this not true
　　is merely self-delusion,
　　since a ruse is given away
　　once to foe disclosed.
How could I trust in you—
　　it's so plain you've led me on.
　　I forgot how ardor thrives
　　on daily interchange.
Unless, my Thought, you think
　　of sounder remedies
　　we'll both of us be lost
　　and Amaryllis avenged."

Clara. That is so well written—if only it were as well intended.

Marfisa. Such a courtly style!

Clara. And so uncourtly to you! But tell me, ma'am, since when has this lady been called Amaryllis? Dorotilis is what he should have said; you being Marfisa, the name Amaryllis was always reserved for you.

Marfisa. Oh, Clara, he was deceiving us both. Poets invent Janus-headed verse, facing either way, like singers of popular ditties, which with a few little changes will serve for many saint's days.

Clara. Put the letter away. Here he comes, talking with Julio, his postilion.

Scene 8

JULIO · DON FERNANDO
MARFISA · CLARA

Julio. What's this—veiled women at our door?

Fernando. Some message from Dorotea, no doubt.

Julio. Her mother must have scolded her for being late. I can imagine the flutterings in the dovecote since your return.

Fernando. May I be of service to Your Ladyships? Should you care to refresh yourselves, be assured this is the house of a young man.

Marfisa. So young, in fact, that shame has not yet wiped the freshness from his face.

Fernando. Great God! Marfisa, my treasure, my queen! You, here at my door? How could I tell where you were? We'd scarcely removed our spurs when we went looking for you. Did we not, Julio?

Julio. Would fulfilling that obligation require witnesses?

Clara. No indeed, since you have the gall to swear falsely all by yourself.

Julio. Why, Clara, is that any way to talk to your long-lost, beloved Julio?

Clara. Why, Julio, is that any way to talk to your despised, long-forgotten Clara?

Marfisa. You've been in Madrid eight whole days, or should I say eighty?

Fernando. What nonsense! Ever since my return I've been hiding from Justice.

Julio. Keeping always to the remotest parts of town.

Marfisa. There he goes—the shadow of your deviltries, the cover for your insolence, Mercury of your embassies, cloak of your betrayals—trying to pull the wool over our eyes again.

Julio. This is the reward I reap for my salutary advice to him to show you his gratitude, and for spending the whole journey reminding Don Fernando of your beauty, charm, and wit, to such effect that he was even persuaded to compose a poem one night, expressing his pain on leaving you.

Marfisa. Scoundrel! The poem was written to Dorotea, that exceedingly glamorous mistress of his! She of the snow-white habit and sky-blue scapular, with her rich Spaniard from overseas, for whom she dropped this one, as he well deserved. Worthy, indeed, is *she,* of all those fine words, for being so constant, so devoted, so disinterested! For his jealousy of her I sacrificed my gold, yielding my innocence like the stupidly loyal woman that I am, the decent woman you've known since childhood. Oh honorable women, how little the love of such men becomes you! What they succumb to is not virtue and modesty but double-dealing, deceit, jealousy, rivalry, obstinacy, and scorn—these arouse their love. And all their plotting, their disastrous escapades, and slaughter of others turn out to be like the slaying of that man, God rest his soul, on whose account you went off to Seville. The way you plunged your sword into him! Oh, you're brave all right—in words. The plague take tender feelings, constancy, and all I've had to bear for your sake from my aunt and uncle and from my . . .

Julio. She has broken down completely. What are you staring at her for? Why don't you say something? Why don't you console her? Clara is weeping too, and even I have a mind to sob, if my beard didn't get in the way.

Fernando. Marfisa, I plainly see how right you are. So put out am I, so distraught and sorry for what I have done, that I would throw myself at your feet and give you this dagger to pierce my breast a thousand times, were we not in the street. Come in, my precious. You shall see, you'll be my own true love despite all my wayward follies, or else I forfeit honor and cease to be my parents' son. Please come in.

Marfisa. Not on your life—I know your tricks. Fernando, all the tears and hardships I've had to bear on your account, sweet enemy of mine! I have suffered too much to continue to condone so many wrongs. Still, I implore you, for the sake of the childhood we shared and the tenderness with which we pledged our troth (all come to naught through my miserable luck and your misplaced infatuation), if you should have any news of that sweet treasure you fathered, and my outraged family disowned, please let me know and allow me to reclaim the child.

Fernando. Wait, wait, madam. At least do not depart in tears.

Marfisa. Let me go or I'll scream.

Julio. Goodbye, Clara.

Clara. Julio, my little Caesar, though my nose is long and straight, I can still snub you with it.

Fernando. What do you make of this calamity?

Julio. That it's a pity you had to spurn someone with so much to be said for her. I'm aware of the love Dorotea has had for you and says she still has. But in any case she belongs to someone else and, since he's no husband who has to be endured, it's downright ignoble to play second fiddle and show deference where it's not due.

Fernando. I call upon Heaven and all creation to be my witness—which includes you, Julio, and my honor, and whatever wit I possess—that I will employ them all to wreak vengeance on Dorotea, who chose to dismiss me in the first place, and so pay Marfisa the legitimate debt I owe her.

Julio. Come, sir, don't be so hasty. I have a scheme for you, to make your love of Marfisa deliver you gradually from your love of Dorotea.

Fernando. Her capitulation has already delivered me.

Julio. Only started to, I would say.

Fernando. I tell you, Julio, it is all over.

Julio. So you suppose, after being in bed with her. But so great a love cannot possibly have expired, once the desire which should have increased it, was satiated.

Fernando. Dorotea no longer seemed to be the same as I imagined her while I was away—not so beautiful, so charming, so intelligent. And just as something is washed in order to cleanse it, so was I washed clean of desire by her tears. What inflamed me was the thought that she was in love with Don Bela; what drove me mad was imagining their love was mutual. But once I saw how put upon she was, how desperate and driven, how she disparaged him, found flaws in him, cursed her mother, denounced Gerarda, resented Celia, and called me her truth, her one and only thought, her lord and master, and her first love, the dead oppressive weight was lifted from my spirit, my eyes began to notice other things and my ears to hear other words, so that when the time came to separate, I not only did not mind, I actually was glad.

Julio. You'll drive me insane and make me say the world does not understand the philosophy of love. After so much amorous passion—

such swooning, yearning, folly, despair, such itching, jealousy, and tears—that all this should have withered away seems wholly impossible.

Fernando. Since Ovid among his cures for love includes meditation on infidelities, and resultant sufferings, and since I have taken this to heart, what is so surprising?

Julio. Nothing, any longer. But I do not want you making any mistake. Reassurance cools love; misgivings rekindle it.

Fernando. I am sure I have found my cure in the rose of Apuleius.

Julio. Meaning what?

Fernando. In Marfisa.

Julio. For her constancy and loyalty, she deserves your love. One cannot truly love, create a bond, and continue honorably, if one uses absence as an excuse for infidelity. For one lover to put up with another shows either cowardice or infamy.

Fernando. At least I can apply to myself what Catullus says to Lesbia:

Poisons of love and hate
I take in equal parts.
Ask me how I do it:
I'm truly of two hearts.

Chorus of Revenge

Having suffered offense and sought revenge,
   love, assured it is now returned,
   weakens its hold, disperses its ire,
   reduced to freezing where lately it burned.
The offending lover should never protest
   a change of heart was forced on him.
   Though he thinks meekness has won the day,
   the other is plotting revenge on him.
Being loved again after injury
   hastens forgetting in a lover aggrieved,
   who feigns his love, until he's avenged,
   making pleasure a pretense, just to deceive.
If you have given offense, beware
   confusing what's felt with what is spoken.
   Patching up is sweet, when jealousy ends;
   where wrong's been done, it's a worthless token.

ACT · FIVE

Scene 1

DON BELA · LAURENCIO

Bela. Go see what that servant of the count wants, Laurencio.

Laurencio. He's come to claim the horse you promised him for the jousting tourney during the holidays. He chose that horse specially, to make a spectacular showing.

Bela. Why didn't you tell him it had a nail in its hoof?

Laurencio. I did, and said you were extremely sorry.

Bela. I feel utterly dejected. I don't know what's come over me of late. I cannot throw off this mood.

Laurencio. Your dejection stems from Dorotea's.

Bela. I thought she would soften toward me when I was wounded for her sake; since then I think she detests me.

Laurencio. If this love affair of yours comes to an end, many could tell you why she might.

Bela. Then you suspect something?

Laurencio. Nothing definite.

Bela. Since I promoted you from manservant to friend, you have given up behaving like the ordinary servant who tells all. But as you're my friend now, at liberty to reprimand, feel free to disenchant me.

Laurencio. If you look closely at Dorotea's unhappiness, it will all come clear. For if there is any danger, it's evidently being kept secret, although for days now nothing remotely suspect has crossed her threshold.

Bela. In that case, unhappiness, why do you pursue me and, jealousy, why do you provoke me? Laurencio is my servant and my friend. As the one, he holds his tongue; as the other, he will not disabuse me. Hence, Dorotea is not to be blamed for my suspicions. Hand me those papers. Last night, from the smatterings of my school learning, I wrote a madrigal. I wish now to make a clear copy of it.

Laurencio. Here are the papers. Much is blotted out.

Bela. I once knew a highly gifted poet who blotted out so much that only he could read his manuscripts, and no one could copy them. So, you see, Laurencio, a poet who does not blot a line cannot be serious. The madrigal reads:

> Lady, on ideal beauty once I gazed,
> love guiding me aloft on turning paths
> of all the heavens nine.
> By such grandeur there transfixed,
> I then returned to gaze upon the form
> of things ideal in human veils.
> And here, in your form sensible
> descrying the intelligible divine,
> I saw the copy was so true
> to its own primordial form,
> and I so loved your beauty,
> reflection of that light divine and pure,
> that when I look upon you now
> discretion overwhelms desire.
> Thus, if discretion guide me totally,
> love all soul will be, everlastingly.

Laurencio. Very well written indeed. But I confess I do not understand it, and doubt that even Dorotea's subtle mind would.

Bela. See here, Laurencio, all Dorotea need gather from my pen are my letters of credit to merchants for her wardrobe. Only *I* need understand this piece.

Laurencio. I would like to also.

Bela. As divine beauty, glowing in the eternal and inexhaustible light of the Supreme Artificer, diffuses its rays and sheds them through all bodies, to illumine the Angelic Intelligences and embellish the

Universal Soul, ultimately descends into Nature's material bodies, where the heavenly spheres revolve in smoothest harmony, the sun beams, the stars twinkle, fire keeps burning in its own purity, the air in its serenity rejoices, the restive waters enjoy their perpetual flowing, the earth bedecks herself with myriad flowers, trees, and plants, and lastly man marvels at the selfsame rays of that divine beauty shining forth more brightly in the beauty of women than in any other being here below, so, step by step, love teaches our understanding insofar as it can follow its aspiration to such lofty contemplation, to form a particular idea, and love it, without letting the mind stray beyond the bounds of reason.

Laurencio. What do you mean by idea?

Bela. Exemplary knowledge of phenomena.

Laurencio. Do you mean to tell me that you love Dorotea so Platonically that you have derived the contemplation of her beauty from the supreme beauty of ideas?

Bela. I should hope at least to love her with that in mind, for I seem to recall reading in the Philosopher that there are two ways to love, and to love her with the soul alone is the truer kind, and for her the surer way.

Laurencio. I don't know what's come over you this last week—you seem a different person. You—devout, contrite, melancholy! If the impulse is divine, as heaven grant it may be, I shall consider well spent all the time I have taken going back and forth from Dorotea's house. If it is an access of jealous melancholia, then beware of hypochondria, lest you lose your mind and your friends.

Bela. Oh, Laurencio! How could any man of God-fearing mind fail to acknowledge his mortality? Pleasures are shadowed by conscience; those who have murdered another in cold blood feel his weight upon their conscience wherever they go. Dorotea is so uniquely beautiful, so cultivated, and so variously talented that if the golden thread of reason does not deliver me from this labyrinth, I believe we shall have to say, with that king of Great Britain, when life comes to an end: "We have lost everything."

Laurencio. In the name of God, do not give in to melancholy; acknowledging the need for it puts you well on the way to amendment. Here comes Gerarda, just when we need her. Her old wives' jabber, not to say her wheedling, will cheer you up.

Scene 2

GERARDA · DON BELA · LAURENCIO

Gerarda. 'When the King is out, he's not about.'

Bela. Have you been looking for me, mother?

Gerarda. Have I, indeed! Ask any of those servants of yours who stay at home. I relieved your butler of the toothache yesterday, and he raving like a dog in midsummer.

Laurencio. You mean, of his teeth, don't you?

Gerarda. Look here, Laurencio—barely am I inside the door and you begin to bait me? What do you take me for—a tooth-snatcher?

Laurencio. No, mistress, though certain ignorant women say they help in casting spells.

Gerarda. 'Tell it to your grandmother!' Truly, I never believed any good could come of the dental furnishings of those unlucky enough to preach their last from the gallows, as their clacking heels deliver the closing blessing.

Laurencio. Now listen, mother—when you are so certain that I am mocking you, I am in fact lauding your abilities. And don't you do the same when we fetch Dorotea's costumes, accusing me of conniving with the tradesman for my share?

Gerarda. 'When the monkey's up the wall, all mock him and he mocks all.' Laurencio, my lad, 'two wrongs don't make a right.' How can Don Bela remain silent while my venerable person is treated with such disrespect? Of you I might almost say, 'A mean little lout deserves a hussy's clout.'

Bela. Mother, you're so quick to tears. Such weepy eyes I've never seen. Laurencio, give her four *reales*.

Gerarda. 'My words cannot come *near* my love for you, my dear.' There's not enough here for a stew and I've a friend coming to dinner.

Bela. Is she young?

Gerarda. Between us we share three teeth and one hundred forty-five years. How now? You were not about to shortchange Dorotea, were you? God preserve me from such skullduggery! Always keeping poor Dorotea guessing—letting that scoundrel Laurencio cover up for you and hoodwinking her into the bargain.

Laurencio. I, mistress? How can you have such notions when Don Bela, my master, leads such a quiet life and I such a retiring one?

Gerarda. 'Pimple or bump, it's still a lump.' Do you think I was born yesterday? But let's get back to that guest of mine; here's our stew: a pound of mutton, fourteen *maravedís;* a half-pound of beef, six— that makes twenty; four for bacon, four more for charcoal; two *maravedís* for parsley and onion, and four for olives—that comes to a whole *real.* Now, three *reales'* worth of wine for two self-respecting women hardly wets the whistle—just a swallow and a half. Increase the sum, so may God increase the sum of your life.

Laurencio. Three *reales* for wine, when you can get half a gallon for twelve *maravedís?*

Gerarda. Brother Laurencio, 'in a bad year, let sieves be sturdy, and strainers clear.'

Bela. Give her four more *reales.*

Gerarda. 'With a skinny cow, use tongue and hoof somehow.'

Bela. Mother, where did you learn so many proverbs?

Gerarda. My boy, they're the quintessence of all the books in the world—by usage contrived, by experience confirmed.

Bela. Indeed, many are so true and expressive, they teach in their laconic way more than heaps of books by the old philosophers discoursing endlessly. But come, Gerarda, tell me what brings you here.

Gerarda. Dorotea says she wants no rented balcony to watch the bullfights from. She's out of sorts, as they say in Valencia, and moreover, she has no wish to amuse herself simply because others are doing so.

Laurencio. I have a solution.

Gerarda. What's that?

Laurencio. Drive a bull into her balcony.

Gerarda. Hilarious! God repay you! Here, take this.

Laurencio. The solution doesn't satisfy you?

Gerarda. 'As May told April to her face: it's funny to me in any case.'

Bela. Dorotea sad and not going to the bullfights—something is surely upsetting her.

Gerarda. What else but the jealousy you arouse, great gawker that you are? You think she didn't see you ogling those nymphs in La Merced? Oh yes, indeed, they're all beauties! Upon my life, if I were a gentleman in hose, I would not waste a silk ribbon on them—all primped and painted, full of fancy talk, and with those little mincing steps of theirs.

Bela. Mother, do those girls use face paint?

Gerarda. No, they wouldn't dream of it! There's not one of them would do without it—pale complexions trying to be paler, dark complexions ... need I say?

Bela. I'd say they're quite mistaken, because it's better to look youthful longer than beautiful a short while. Corrosive sublimates destroy the teeth and coarsen the complexion. Moreover, cosmetic is like time: it takes so little away each day, you're not aware of it. And, for that matter, Dorotea doubtless uses it, too.

Gerarda. There's an exception to every rule, Don Bela. You should not conclude that every woman uses it; and face paint is not something you can hide. If a woman appears one way when she goes to bed and another when she rises, how can the man beside her help but notice? But to get back to those nymphs you gawk at, what do they have to rival Dorotea's serene hauteur? With her patrician poise, she'd pass for a Venetian aristocrat, quite aside from her noble bearing on the dais; her virtuous demeanor in the street; her piety in church, her free behavior in the country, and ... well, 'everything comes to one who waits.' If you could only see her now, the siren at her harp, her nimble fingers gliding over the strings, which seem to be laughing as if she were tickling them; her tresses loosely falling over the harp, which sometimes enviously wish they were strings she might play on. And, indeed, I think the strings were resonantly telling her tresses not to meddle in their affairs, since as strings they didn't try to interfere when Dorotea was dressing her hair.

Bela. Mother, you are waxing poetic this morning.

Gerarda. The truth is, I've had nothing for breakfast but my devotions, because I had to go and comfort a young woman who has just had a child and cannot decide which the father is. She wanted my advice and I told her to choose the stupidest of the four.

Bela. What an edifying occupation!

Gerarda. Giving advice when needed, my lad, is an act of charity.

Bela. What was the song Dorotea was singing?

Gerarda.

> Watch yourself or 'tis of no *avail*
> to watch the castle deep in the *vale,*
> when night over daylight casts its *veil.*

How do you like those allusions to your name? And she also supplied stanzas to this refrain. Now think how beautifully she sings, think of all she knows, think how grateful you should be.

Bela. Give her four more *reales.*

Gerarda. Ah, yes, my friend! 'In like a lion, out like a lamb.' You're one of the old beaux all right! All of you, starting out with a burst of bounty, and ending up wanting your suppers free.

Bela. Gerarda, Gerarda—let's be truthful. I am not so simple as to be unaware of Dorotea's disinclination toward me.

Gerarda. What has Laurencio been filling your ears with? Poor Dorotea! Chained to her needlework all the livelong day, making shirts for you—and this is her reward.

Bela. Forgive me, I did not mean to make you cry. Give her another four *reales.*

Gerarda. Which makes twelve. Such a lovely number. I have a special devotion to the twelve apostles.

Laurencio. And not to the twelve Knights of the Round Table?

Gerarda. Raise the count to twenty-four—and may you become one of the twenty-four aldermen of Seville—since I've a gown in hock for sixteen *reales.*

Bela. Let her have them, Laurencio, provided she tells which of the beaux courting Dorotea she inclines to most.

Gerarda. It's you, ninny.

Bela. How do you know, mother?

Gerarda. Because 'none but the bridegroom may enter the bride's room.'

Bela. See that none of this gets back to Dorotea.

Gerarda. Then give me another six *reales.*

Bela. Let her have them, and goodbye. I'm going to Mass.

Laurencio. Mother, that makes twenty-six for you.

Gerarda. Well, you might contribute something. Bring it up to thirty and I'll give you seventeen sweet springtimes with rosy apple cheeks, no paint, no wiles, and no strings attached.

Laurencio. Right you are, auntie. 'A woman should be fresh as a daisy, sweet as a breeze, and never lazy.'

Gerarda. You'll see that I know how to return a favor.

Laurencio. And how do you know the girl you mention will be willing?

Gerarda. Because she's one of the fillies in my stable. She has need of me, can't you see?

Laurencio. And you're quite sure she's seventeen?

Gerarda. You're a queer one! Must I produce a baptismal certificate? They're all as old as they look. I swear you'll find women gadding about in patent leather shoes and flapping their mantillas coquettishly, who gave up baby talk forty years ago. With wimples fixed to encircle the face and hide telltale wrinkles and hair ravaged by the pox, in hoopskirts and their gaudy faces, they're transformed into gay young things through sheer brazenness and a glib tongue.

Laurencio. I am sorry the girl is married.

Gerarda. But her husband is the loser, not you.

Laurencio. If the affair goes on, I'm bound to run a risk.

Gerarda. 'With errant wife, or salad, in clover, take two nips—then it's over.'

Laurencio. What if I fall in love?

Gerarda. Just steal in when the husband is occupied elsewhere.

Laurencio. 'A thief who steals on the loose forgets the hangman's noose.'

Gerarda. 'Nothing ventured, nothing gained.'

Laurencio. I have always respected matrimony.

Gerarda. Excellent, especially if you plan to marry. For many who cuckold others are cuckolded themselves in due course.

Laurencio. If he who takes the sword shall perish by the sword, then he who takes horns and plants them on another may well fear a similar fate. I'd prefer a tumble with someone not totally innocent, free of dust and straw and of all subterfuge.

Gerarda. You set so many conditions—are you aspiring to a knighthood?

Laurencio. Glance through your directory and find the page for girls who involve no risk, look meek and humble, with the face of a novice, covet not a thing, and are totally discreet.

Gerarda. I thought you New World Spaniards were only tight in your giving. I see the same applies to what you receive.

Laurencio. Why do you suppose we're so cautious?

Gerarda. Because you've had to work like slaves.

Laurencio. Not at all. It's because we're so sensible.

Gerarda. Now then, I should like to make you happy.

Laurencio. You must be scraping the bottom of your barrel.

Gerarda. In the Casa del Campo there's a fountain of Neptune, and a niche on each side with a white marble nymph. Let's meet there this afternoon and you may pick whichever you fancy.

Laurencio. If I hadn't already given you those last four *reales,* you'd never get them now.

Gerarda. If you've any regrets, here—take this.

Laurencio. Making the fig at me?

Gerarda. Well, what did you think, you stinkard of a squire?

Laurencio. You shameless old witch, I'll skin you alive.

Gerarda. Wait till this affair is over, we'll see who ends up skinned.

Laurencio. All right, but it's you who are in peril.

Gerarda. Of what, my chuck?

Laurencio. Of sporting the witch's miter, my love.

Gerarda. If doing it were so perilous, you wouldn't find so many aiming to sport one.

Laurencio. 'The cheat who's been to school still can play the fool.'

Gerarda. Easy, now, Laurencio. Men ply my trade, too.

Laurencio. He who must obey is no procurer—he's a servant.

Gerarda. I know a chap with prescriptions for precociously deflowered maidens, not to mention other nostrums, concoctions, and herbs.

Laurencio. You must have been his mentor.

Gerarda. You patched-up excuse for a lackey and a steward, respect my years or I'll . . .

Laurencio. Gerarda, my skin's too tough for vampires.

Gerarda. Scoundrel, I'm a Christian from way back and my unguent is bacon fat. I hail from the hills of Burgos.

Laurencio. That's just where the witches come from.

Gerarda. Like you, from the hills of Judea, you scum!

Laurencio. And you, you mildewed old crumb. I'll have you know I'm the great-grandson of a Persian ambassador.

Gerarda. All right, go stick his turban on your head.

Laurencio. I have a patent royal scroll in gold letters to prove it.

Gerarda. Gold letters? The best your gold could buy, you mean.

Laurencio. I am not one to assume a descent he has no right to.

Gerarda. Let a man's father be a foreigner and he'll immediately be dubbed a gentleman until base conduct shows him up for what he is.

Laurencio. Scurvy words from a scurvy tongue. I've a mind to . . .

Gerarda. Easy now, because, when it comes to taking shots with rhymes, I have a poet-slanderer friend who neither fears the living nor spares the dead.

Laurencio. And I know a woman so crafty she'll stand you off in scurrility anytime, even two hundred lashes' worth.

Gerarda. Steer clear of my venerable years.

Laurencio. Even if you offered your venerability in public, everyone would steer clear of it.

Gerarda. I well know why you hate me.

Laurencio. Why do I?

Gerarda. You lackeys are like dogs snapping at the poor for fear of losing their measly handouts. When Don Bela required my services, you know very well you were not so insolent to me.

Laurencio. And, as you well know, procurers are like jokers in a deck of cards: when you start to play, you discard them.

Gerarda. That I know, Laurencio. I know too that a man's ingratitude for services rendered always equals his obsequiousness preceding delivery and his meekness during courtship.

Scene 3

CÉSAR · DON FERNANDO · JULIO

César. Don Fernando is tuning his instrument. I don't want him to stop, so I'll stay here and listen to his singing.

Fernando. These treble strings are defective.

Julio. Like women, they string you along.

Fernando. Mind what you say. Some do, some don't.

Julio. Are you drawing a lesson from this?

Fernando. It's Dorotea's fault.

Julio. So now Dorotea's your faulty one.

Fernando. You know very well she is.

Julio. Till you stop speaking ill of Dorotea, I refuse to believe you have forgotten her.

Fernando. In that case I'll say she's an angel.

Julio. That's going too far.

Fernando. Well, what should I say?

Julio. Nothing either good or bad, for if you have truly forgotten someone you loved, there's nothing good or bad to say about what's no longer on your mind: nothing good, because she's no longer beloved; nothing bad, because you're not retaliating.

Fernando. Then isn't retaliation part of loving?

Julio. No, it's despair masked as love. Remember what Ovid writes about Medea, how when Jason married another, Medea killed that woman and her own two children, then set their houses on fire.

Fernando.

> If your mood, lass, only
>> matched your looks, then surely
>> you'd be the village queen
>> and all your vassals noble.
>
> But when your eyes' round sun
>> dispels your lunar charm,
>> on that unyielding ground of yours
>> eclipse and shadow swarm.
>
> Fetching as you are
>> (fetcher, they should call you,
>> of all you gaze upon),
>> you're jealous of the breeze.
>
> If your own beauty, Amaryllis,
>> cannot reassure you,
>> how can my love suffice
>> to quell your jealousy?
>
> Fair village lass, on any day
>> that you descend from hill to vale,
>> eyes of envy but confirm
>> your beauty and my words of love.
>
> The maids who watch you pass
>> say they can hardly tell

where your feet alighted,
     the footprints are so tiny.
From envy of your bearing,
     your radiance in dress,
     they all become concerned
     at the unconcern you show.
You seem the very springtime,
     when birds and flowers all
     waken to find they're beckoned
     by the sunlight of your eyes.
A pox on all the rivulets
     that when you step across them
     fail to cry in wonder
     that you should be so jealous.
So why demean yourself
     by thinking I could like
     a lass who envies you
     and mimics your every step?
Oh do not squander pearls,
     cease weeping, do not slay me,
     lest those stars in your eyes
     shatter into fragments.
Forget your anger, Amaryllis,
     come out now, do, and hear me—
     let my song suffuse your darling
     pupils and so soothe them:
"Oh, darling eyes, desist;
     if one can slay with love,
     it makes no sense to weep
     from jealousy alone.
For someone who can slay
     should not seek to die
     when one laugh can do
     more than all her tears.
If you would avenge
     the victims you have slain,
     why not now begin
     by showing me compassion?

Oh, darling eyes, desist;
> if one can slay with love,
> it makes no sense to weep
> from jealousy alone."

César. Don't put down your instrument, Fernando, I beg you.

Fernando. The words have by now given the strings permission to rest.

César. It's no less well sung than written.

Fernando. One's taste is no judge of the skills of friends.

César. Assume I'm not one, in your case.

Fernando. Music is a divine art.

César. Some say it was invented by Mercury; others, by Aristogenes. The truth is that love invented it. Because harmony is concord, and concord, the agreement between low and high notes, and such agreement was established by love; because from that mutual attraction there follows the effect of music, which is pleasure. This union in love Marsilio Ficino called the lord and master of music; thus beautiful Lamia drove the great Demetrius mad with love.

Fernando. What have you been doing these days?

César. I've been away, and concerned about your affairs. How does it stand between you and Dorotea? Unless the stars have deceived me, during this absence of mine from Madrid, matters must have gone remarkably well between you two.

Fernando. You mean your conjectures rely upon the planets? I have never been inclined to credit that branch of learning.

César. At least, it is easier to find out directly from you.

Fernando. My love for Dorotea is no more.

César. I'd sooner be convinced there is no further movement in those two luminaries presiding over day and night. Because you and Dorotea share the moon in the twelfth sign, Pisces, with Venus in the preceding sign, rather than contrariwise, if Venus were in the following sign, behind sluggish and frigid Saturn, and both of you shared the moon in the same sign.

Fernando. Well, the latter must have occurred and you failed to see it clearly. For the understanding of which, I beg you not to consider it a discourtesy if I ask you to yield your attention. You will perhaps consider the listening well spent. There will be revealed to you, as one so painstakingly inquisitive about every sort of subject, the remarkable effects of the laws of human nature and the strange channels taken by inconstancy to prevail over our firmest resolves.

César. Not only will it please me to listen attentively, but for that favor I shall offer you infinite thanks.

Fernando. Julio, remember: to all friends except Ludovico I am not at home.

Julio. It would be much better if you went to the window and said so yourself, as that philosopher did. But let them knock and go away. If I'm here to answer, and not in your company, they will be led to suspect you've refused to see them.

Fernando. César, my friend, before leaving for La Montaña, you and Ludovico had already heard what transpired between Dorotea and me one morning last April in the Prado.

Julio. With such a lapse of time, you again infringe upon the rules of tragedy.

Fernando. My excuse is the story itself, which on this occasion chose to be wedded to fact.

César. I well recall your jubilant return from so joyous a triumph, like some Roman consul bearing in the chariot of love Dorotea's pretended disdain as your spoils of victory.

Fernando. Oh Love, if ever you seemed the child, as you are depicted, this occasion immeasurably surpasses all others. César, scarcely had I discovered that Dorotea still loved me as she had before my departure for Seville, when I felt my peace of mind return, my throbbing heart subside, as all the sensible ways a prudent man habitually behaves came home to my mind, from which the anxiety of imagining myself abhorred had evicted them. Because such ways were like the parts of a disassembled clock: once put back in working order, the whole resumes harmonious functioning.

César. How strange love is: so ardent when abused, so indifferent when gratified!

Fernando. In short, as Dorotea bit by bit revealed her heart to me, my own grew easier, and the more she burned in my embrace with old desires, the icier I grew in hers.

César. According to Marsilio Ficino, commenting on Plato, there are two means of curing love: one through Nature, the other by a concerted effort. Nature achieves her cure by allowing a given amount of time to pass, as is generally the case with all illnesses. Concerted effort means distracting the mind with other occupations or other love objects. The lover's disturbance will continue as long as the contagion of the blood—infused as if by sorcery into one's deepest being—keeps oppressing the heart with its heavy weight of care. For it passes from heart to veins, from veins to limbs—hence the distress in which lovers live cannot cease till the contagion is fully moderated. All this requires a certain amount of time, greater in the melancholic than in jovial and cheerful men, and even greater if they have Saturn retrograde with Mars or opposed to the sun.

Fernando. How quickly you turn professional!

César. Anyone who at birth has Venus in the house of Saturn, or who gazes at the moon most fixedly, will be slow to recover from the sickness of love.

Julio. Though I am not in love with Celia, I would be glad to know how the blood of love is let.

César. Read the whole chapter in Ficino, Julio. It is one of the most extraordinary things I have ever come across. You'll find yourself advised, among other things, to think about the failings of the beloved; to take pains to prevent light from coming too close to the eyes; to apply the mind to sundry grave matters; to try reducing the volume of the blood; to use wine to produce new blood and spirits; to do exercises until you perspire, thereby opening the pores; and, most particularly, to do what doctors advise for protecting the heart and nourishing the brain, all neatly put in four lines by Lucretius.

Fernando. I decided I could not wait for Nature because I distrusted habit. So I put my trust in a concerted effort.

César. How did you proceed?

Fernando. One day, César, my honor was considering how abjectly I was behaving in loving and remaining with Dorotea, like vile husbands, who, to reap profit from their wives, tolerate others' possessing them, and steal in when the others are away, taking pains not to be recognized. Then I grew so angry I thought everyone was staring at me and scorning me, like one who commits a secret crime and always supposes the talk is about him, even though it's on quite a different subject. And so, affronted by myself—since a respectable man, even though entirely alone, need not be told what he is doing wrong in order to blush—I made two resolutions: to retaliate for Dorotea's liberties, and to try an ounce of prevention so that the disease would not take me unawares. All this I easily accomplished.

César. Easily, when it was so difficult?

Fernando. Marfisa and I were brought up together, as you've heard me
tell before. And while it's true she was the first object of my love in
the springtime of my years, her disastrous marriage, along with
Dorotea's beauty, banished all her merits from my mind, as if I had
never laid eyes on her.

César. Such fickleness!

Fernando. The truth is that on returning to our house after the un-
timely death of her husband, she set her cap for me again, but with
none of the effects she counted on from our previous love. One
subject, you see, can have no more than one form and no effect is
possible where the potentiality is lacking.

César. All this and more I can believe where Dorotea's charm and brilliance are concerned.

Fernando. I kept up a pretense with Marfisa, but to no avail, for she
quickly recognized the deception, feigning ignorance to make me
believe she was unaware of my disaffection. So that our friendship
continued, thanks to our long-standing familiarity and to our having grown up together.

César. A woman of prudence, or at least not a jealous one.

Fernando. After what I have related, César, and considering that art is
the result of much experience, and that I had had an abundant
share of it, what with my five years as a prize student in the university of love, I determined to love Marfisa without abandoning
Dorotea, till the effect of the relationship and the desired consequence of my good intentions should bring about a complete cure.

César. Odd stratagem, decreasing love by distributing its pleasures!

Fernando. Dorotea could tell my feelings were less keen and that the
old urge to be with her constantly was abating.

César. Perhaps you mean the urge Plato describes in the *Symposium* in
that long fable about the divided halves, which originally were one,
seeking to be reunited.

Fernando. Since Dorotea failed to grasp the reason, her jealousy was
not aroused, misled as it was by the injury my honor incurred
through her unjustified friendship with Don Bela. And to some
extent she was right, because this was the reason I was trying to
hate her and was taking curative measures by shifting attention to
the beauty and discernment of Marfisa, who, though lacking Dorotea's charm, was more discreet and ladylike. Dorotea would have

been quite happy to love me only. But that was now out of the question, nor would her self-interest allow it.

Julio. Especially with those two bloodhounds, Gerada and Felipa, in the picture. For women are led astray through the urging of their women friends more than by their own weaknesses.

Fernando. I've no complaint against her mother, Teodora, whose only fault was to assent, while the othe women were parties to the solicitation.

Julio. If you still need to be told, Gerarda is the quintessence of wiliness, the last word in trickery, the ultimate headmistress of assignation, which the vain desires of old age, following upon a lascivious youth, have ever produced. Her daughter, Felipa, is a chick of the old owl, whose budding career bids fair to reach the same degree of achievement.

Fernando. Dorotea used to see me unbeknownst to that trio, trusting in Celia, a considerate lass who understood the situation and willingly gave up all thought of profiting from it.

Julio. She certainly was considerate, in view of all she ever got out of it.

Fernando. Dorotea resolved to supplement my wardrobe with a stipend, and I abjectly took a chain and a few coins of Mexican origin, as if we were accomplices in fleecing the overseas Spaniard, or at least dividing the spoils.

Julio. The device she employed has defeated many a husband, not to mention lovers. I wouldn't add judges—that would not be true.

Fernando. Since we only met intermittently, we were compelled to write each other—another reason being to keep Don Bela from noticing anything. I had wounded him one night when he took exception to my voice, as I to his hands, and he desired to display his swordsmanship before Dorotea, though she was so opposed to swords that she used to sing to the harp:

　　Bring on your gifts, I say,
　　but put your swords away.

In order to exchange letters—indispensable to maintaining our connection and avoiding Don Bela's vengeance for his wound—I went to her door nightly at ten dressed as a poor beggar. Celia, the servant I mentioned, came out and gave me alms, placing inside the bread or the alms-money the letter she had for me and taking the one I'd brought for her. This with the blessing of Teodora—in fact, they even called me the house pauper. And they were right, since Don Bela was the rich man. And that's the way the transmutation worked.

César. Ah, if you'd only paid as much attention to that love for divine beauty that dwells in our minds and by whose grace we pursue the offices of piety and the study of justice and philosophy!

Fernando. How taken you are with the higher Socratic love! The baser of those two Platonic loves was what fell to my lot. But if everything living loves—and the thing that seems most to repel another does so naturally through love, not hate—why wonder at this power which the Philosopher himself calls demonic? Love is the eternal knotter and coupler of the world, the unmoving controller of its parts and the solid basis of its mechanism. Fire does not flee water out of hatred but out of self-love, refusing to let itself be killed by water's coldness. Nor does water put out fire from hatred but from a wish to expand it seeks to convert fire into its own substance.

Julio. Good Lord, drop the irrelevant paradoxes. Surely Don Fernando is aware that touch is neither part of love nor a feeling on the lover's part, but a desire for beauty and a baser impulse in man.

César. Go on with the story and forgive me for distracting you.

Fernando. My playing the pauper, instead of Julio, must be an objection your mind is tacitly raising. My reply is that this enabled me to speak to her often by lying flat on the ground beneath her window grille, which was just far enough off the ground for a man to stretch out under. This I did, pretending to be asleep. Then Dorotea would come out, filling the whole window, and talk to me, as I lifted my face to her effulgent beauty.

Julio. So the universal enemy is depicted at the feet of the angel.

Fernando. Some nights Don Bela would find me in this location and, taking no heed, would proceed to knock confidently and enter. Consider what my fortune had reduced me to. At a house where I'd been sole master for five years, the paving stones barely granted me room to stretch my bones, the grillework serving as the merest canopy.

César. What a victory for Dorotea: holding you underfoot as Tamburlaine held Bayazid, only poorer, sorrier, and more humble.

Julio. The grillework being the prison bars, with Dorotea's feet upon the bars.

Fernando. Along with other dangers, the situation was so threatening to my life that on one such night the guard, in passing, prodded me and hauled me off to jail. This, despite Dorotea's protestations that I was the favored pauper of their house, which Teodora and Celia, Felipa and the slaves, attracted by the commotion, all confirmed. But the constable, being cruel (and few are anything else) ... For, ever since spider webs began catching the lowly fly while letting larger creatures through, some officers of the law (though not all) have exercised their authority over the poor, but groveled and prostrated themselves before the powerful. So the women could make no impression on the constables, having passed them no purse. Thus they were dragging me off to the Toledo Street jail as a common thief. When they removed my old hat and the ragged cloak which made me look the pauper, signs appeared of my being well-to-do, however much my outer garb belied it. But stopping off at a mead shop, they called on servants to guard the exit; and as soon as their turn came to drink, I left it to my fleetness of foot to put danger behind, and to my wind power to preserve my reputation.

César. Quite a risk for one so well known and so eager to keep out of Don Bela's way.

Fernando. So superbly did wind and feet perform that the constables, like Ganymede's dog, were left behind gaping at the eagle. But to return to my tale after this digression—for no tale lacks its episodes, nor do they contravene sound rhetorical practice if they are not overextended—you should know, César, that Marfisa took a notion to make me a shirt, which ultimately resembled beautiful Deianira's dipped in Centaur's blood, though my fate was to be different from Alcides'.

César. What did she have in mind then?

Fernando. To have me sport something dyed with mastic and in yellow lace—the latest fashion, you must have noticed. All this she explained to me in a note: "Unless you're afraid that Madam Dorotea will ask you to account for the surprise shirt I am finishing, allow me to send it to you, Fernando. Surely I have earned the right to be granted this wish, in view of all the blood my needles have drawn each time my mind wandered off and imagined you in it. But if this means disrupting your peace, I shall leave the shirt unfinished. Because I do not wish to be the cause of any quarrel between you only to find myself jealous of the lengths you go to in making up with her." In reply I expressed some reluctance about arousing such jealousy and wearing the fashionable shirt. I do dress well, of course, yet not garishly, I hope, though youth excuses anything. But not in the eye of envy, which would as soon snap at one's suit as at one's mind—to which misfortune men possessing some attainments are unhappily subject, the more so if they are handsome—because envy, as its own worst enemy, cannot abide good looks in those with good minds, nor good minds in those with good looks.

César. Only too true, and add that envy prefers to see them deformed and misshapen, as if you could expect souls by their nature to operate perfectly with imperfect instruments.

Julio. It will be argued that harmony, as the Philosopher says, is composed of contraries.

Fernando. He also affirms that to know the nature of the soul, its substance and accidents, is most difficult. Thus we cannot know with any certainty the conditions under which it operates.

César. If only he told us, when he calls philosophy the perfection of the soul, what the body should be like, we'd know in which bodies the soul operates with greatest virtue, since virtue unified is the most powerful.

Fernando. It's not a question of quantity but of proportion.

César. Proceed with your story.

Fernando. Although I kept insisting I would not take the gift, Marfisa prevailed. And when it left her hands, the beauty of the shirt vying with the needlework, she had it brought me by a slave girl with a note, which, after reading and replying to, I carelessly stuffed in my pocket. Oh, the caution love notes require!

César. They are the common pitfall of men.

Julio. As the Castilian proverb has it: "Doctors' mistakes, notes misplaced, and women without shame, put men in the grave."

Fernando. That same day at nightfall, I wrote Dorotea a note and stuck it in with Marfisa's. When handing it to Celia, I gave the wrong one, so that she took Marfisa's and I came away with Dorotea's.

César. Forgive me, but that showed extraordinary ignorance on your part.

Fernando. I have never counted myself among the wise.

Julio. Which means you are. Because if you weren't you'd think you were.

César. The other day I saw a book in a friend's study entitled *Established Truths*. I opened it and on the second page found:
Catalogue of the ignorant:
many.
List of the wise:
few.
Along with various other truths put just as laconically.

Fernando. I admit my mistake but thank my lucky stars for making it. For as the heart is first in showing life and last in dying, so love starts with desire and ends with revenge.

César. I thought you were going to say, along with clever Boscán:
I was right to lose my heart,
my misfortunes gladden me.

Fernando. César, you shall now see whether it was a lucky mistake or not. Scarcely had I gone to bed to await the morrow on which Dorotea, in that note Celia gave me when I handed her Marfisa's, promised to see me, when at the same time Julio and a knocking at the window advised me Celia and Felipa were there. I thought I'd dreamed the night away dreaming such thoughts and that Dorotea had now arrived for our rendezvous. But just the opposite was true. The two women came in and showed me Marfisa's note, claiming I'd done it deliberately, not mistakenly, and adding every insult their anger could invent and my tolerance permit.

Julio. Oh, if only Nature had fashioned us like cicadas, whose females never sing.

Fernando. Who says so?

Julio. Aristotle, for one.

César. And what should we men do, if we alone spoke and they were always mum?

Julio. Take their meaning from their gestures.

César. That would be worse. When they grew angry, they'd gouge our eyes out.

Fernando. I acknowledged, César, that I'd committed an error, not a crime. But when I could not convince them, I was consoled that good fortune had so deviously allowed me vengeance on Dorotea.

César. How could you consider it vengeance?

Julio. Your question smacks of that Aristotelian conundrum about why men are not born with tails. His answer is, they're animals who sit down.

César. Who'd imagine Aristotle would give such an answer!

Fernando. Notes went back and forth, and Dorotea became so impassioned she promised to forgive and forget, provided I gave her the shirt or tore it to pieces in her presence. I found these conditions unworthy of my obligation to a woman as decent as Marfisa. And there being no other way of making up, which in any case I was less concerned to do ... Oh, time! Oh, love's revenge! Oh, vicissitudes of fortune! Oh, human nature! Luis de Camoëns, the renowned Portuguese, had just this in mind in that sonnet of his:

> Mudam-se os tempos, mudam-se as vontades,
>> muda-se o ser, muda-se a confiança;
>> todo o Mundo é composto de mudança,
>> tomando sempre novas qualidades.

In short, I wore the shirt on the most festive day of the year. From a window where she sat, Dorotea was unable to tell the color of the lace. Suddenly, in a jealous rage, she came down into the street and, pushing her way through the crowd who were admiring the decorative images and hangings, approached me as I walked along with several friends, behind Marfisa and without a thought for Dorotea. I shan't bore you with our exchange. She spoke from jealousy, I answered with indifference. She went off infuriated and I had my revenge—especially as I watched her tearlets, pearls no longer, begging her eyelashes not to let them drop upon her countenance, which was jasmine no longer, carnation no longer.

César. From no one else would I believe this. And are you still in full pursuit of Marfisa?

Fernando. With all the love I can summon, she receives my gratitude as the temple of my salvation, the holy image of my restoration, and the final refuge of my misfortunes.

César. Can it be that no vestige of love for Dorotea remains?

Fernando. Not even the scars commonly left by wounds.

César. Take care you do not let the joy of vengeance deceive you and wounds unhealed flare up again. Start up with her again and there's no havoc she won't wreak. You'll be her Troy, her Numantia, her Saguntum. No stone will be left standing in the edifice of your life.

Fernando. I'll be on my guard. But I do not believe she would be so cruel, even if I sank so low.

César. Euripides says there is only one thing certain about women.

Fernando. What is that, César?

César. Once they're dead they cannot return to life.

Fernando. The law, you know, calls woman a most avaricious breed. Dorotea will not forgo her New World riches, nor I put up with her retaining them.

César. Don't disparage her or I shall think you love her still.

Fernando. You are right, for as the common saying has it, lovers' quarrels lead to love reborn, which in my case you need not fear.

César. But is Dorotea not pressing you still?

Fernando. She is as demanding as Pompilius.

César. What has your answer been?

Fernando. A letter murkier than a poem by Lycophron, something to be read by her and not understood, like the poetry of our own time, least understood by those who write it. But do me a favor, and may you fare better with Felisarda than I with Dorotea.

César. Any favor this side of profanation. What shall it be, my friend?

Fernando. Cast a horoscope and show us the outcome of this affair.

César. Asking questions is prohibited, and with good reason. But I have already cast a horoscope of your birth, and was waiting only to interpret it. I'm off to my quarters, and if I don't return this afternoon, I'll come tomorrow. Because I must deliver a sonnet I have written on that most felicitous occasion, the marriage of Her Excellency, Donna Vittoria Colonna, to the Count of Melgar, the son of the Great Admiral of Castile, Don Luis Enríquez de Cabrera. As you know, she arrived yesterday in this Court city. Her reception drew such acclaim that never has Madrid seen so bright a day nor such gala attire. The Prado was a garden of ladies and gentlemen led by the brilliant figures of the Duke of Pastrana, the Prince of Ascoli, and the Count of Castañeda. And there, most striking among the ladies, were the Marchioness of Auñón, Doña Antonia de Bolaños, and Doña Isabel Manrique.

Fernando. You have named the three Graces, daughters of Jupiter and handmaidens of Venus. If one were to add a fourth, as Homer and

Statius did, put Marfisa in Pasithea's place. Indeed, those other three are the goddesses of the Judgment of Paris.

César. Let us also give Marfisa her prize. I doubt you'd still wish Dorotea to have one.

Fernando. I assure you she was not absent from the Prado that day. Aside from ladies of the first rank, she'd yield in no way to Roman Lucretia or Trojan Helen.

César. She was there, eager, I suspect, to pique your jealousy with new finery.

Fernando. It's too late for that, César. But to return to Donna Vittoria, how does it happen you've been asked to sing her praise?

César. Aside from her great nobility of heart, which is reflected, like the fairest sun, in the mirror of all Italy, His Most Illustrious Eminence, Cardinal Ascanio Colonna, her brother, when studying in Alcalá and favoring talented students there, thought well of my ignorance.

Fernando. You'd have a vast field for endeavor if you were to treat the noble deeds of his father, His Excellency Marcantonio Colonna, and of the latter's mother, Doña Juana de Aragón, who displayed such courage on the occasion of the Pontiff's anger. To counter this, our Catholic King, himself angered, came to her defense and showed Rome on its very walls the banners of the Duke of Alba. These remained peacefully respectful of the holiness of the place, and prevailed without violence, despite the gravity of the affront. Now recite the sonnet:

César.

> Great, ever lofty, powerful *Colonna,*
> > upon whose shoulders there did firmly lie
> > the glory of the Caesars, whose first cradle
> > had been the storied seven hills of Rome,
> who, thwarting envy bred of favoring fortune,
> > did follow eastward in the sun's gold path,
> > generous fortune halting her wheel for him,
> > wrapped up his every *victory* in one.
> And she, the glory and the honor of
> > this sacred city, more noteworthy still,
> > is moving to the manor of Enríquez,
> where in sublime succession she'll uphold

the arches of its golden frame, and be
the *Column* of immortal *Victory.*

I shall leave now, to avoid hearing what you think of it.

Julio. Now that César's left, tell me, what makes you waste your time
on horoscopes? Even if the ancients thought so highly of the sci-
ence, many others have disparaged it as reckless, like all else concerned with future contingencies.

Fernando. Simply the faith the ignorant masses put into it, as though
it were an infallible oracle, for things they consider infallible usually
turn out to be the opposite of what men expect. You will find all
this in Cornelius Tacitus, who calls soothsayers deceivers and non-
believers. The examples are as numerous as their equivocal interpre-
tations are unbelievable. Yet for all that, Seneca, in speaking of the
reign of Claudius, does not disparage them, as Favorinus does at
great length in Gellius. Astrologers predict either favorable or unfavorable events. If favorable, and the events prove otherwise, what
could be unhappier than living in such expectation? If unfavorable,
and they prove mendacious, what more wretched than living in fear
of them? If their predictions are ambiguous and doubtful, and they
then take advantage of such trickiness to interpret the events after
the fact, it's just as if they'd not said anything at all.

Julio. Everything you're saying, along with quantities of other authorities, I have seen mentioned in Levinus Lemnius' *Book of True and
False Astrology.* And considering that you regard it as pure fable,
why persist in asking questions of it?

Fernando. To join the infinite multitudes intent on learning something about the vices and virtues of human nature.

Julio. What the Philosopher had in mind was the scientific and not
the fabulous.

Fernando. I tell you I don't believe in it, so why do you keep after me?

Julio. To protect you from what you don't believe. Along the lines
you yourself propound, I'd have you read Cicero's *On Divination,*
Book Eleven, on obfuscations in predicting future events and later
rearranging the facts arbitrarily to fit what has been said in ignorance. Which must also be why Virgil, speaking of the Sibyl, said
she left her verse hidden in a cave.

Fernando. What connection is there, Julio, between such astrologers
and the men Ambrose calls *fanatics* or *phythians?* Ammianus Mar-

cellinus said of them that the sun, as soul of the world, suffused
through their souls certain powerful sparks by means of which they
prophesied. I believe only in divine truth, which has always disap-
proved of them.

Julio. That shows discernment, all else deception. The days are gone
when the Sibyl gave answers in Delphi, she from whom, as Diodorus writes, Homer stole so many lines for his epics.

Scene 4

DOROTEA · GERARDA

Gerarda. Have you lost your senses, Dorotea? What is this? You,
weeping all day? You, tossing all night? What can have brought
this about? What sad event has the power to blight the flower of
your youth and the pleasure of your company, once the delight of
your house and of your friends? You, still unkempt? You, with hair
so disheveled? You, with face unwashed?

Dorotea. Let me be, aunt. There's no lotion for the face like tears.

Gerarda. For sins, child, not for what is merely human.

Dorotea. Those *are* the sins.

Gerarda. True. Still, I well know your weeping is no sign of repentance, but of failure to repent.

Dorotea. And is that not repentance?

Gerarda. I know why you're feeling so.

Dorotea. Why, Gerarda?

Gerarda. For having made such poor use of so much beauty, so rich a
mind, and so many talents. But thank God for bringing you to recognize this at last.

Dorotea. My talents would not have been so poorly used had they been
properly appreciated.

Gerarda. To be sure, he's the *very last* man alive! Yes, yes, after him
Nature's hand went limp. Did she need a model for him? Did
making him require special pains? A fine Narcissus! If only you
could see him with my eyes. What was so remarkable about him?

Dorotea. You mean Don Fernando is not a handsome man at all?

Gerarda. Of course he's not, child, taking his features one by one. But all you young women are taken in by high talk, humbug, effeminate tears, half-choked sighs, like a boy just whipped who can't catch his breath.

Dorotea. As long as a man has no mustache, tears do not seem unbecoming. Don't think men have gone to pieces when they weep; they are merely making a show of being tenderhearted.

Gerarda. Either way, it's effeminate.

Dorotea. The soul is neither male nor female. Tell me, why did Jacob weep when he saw Rachel?

Gerarda. Child, child, women's business is not laying on the learning or discussing tears; it's making openwork hems.

Dorotea. I've never seen any hems you made.

Gerarda. What are you up to now? What are you taking out of the desk? It looks like a portrait. I can tell you whose, too. Let's see, let's see it.

Dorotea. Gerarda, you'll see it soon enough. Now be a dear and go comfort my mother. She's weeping because I'm so unhappy. Keep her company while I write a few lines.

Gerarda. I'll do as you say, since it appears she needs as much comforting as you.

Dorotea. Come out, come out, you faithful likeness of the world's most faithless man. Come out, because I'm about to strike back at you, like the bull taking it out on the cape when the man escapes him. Can it be you whose tender years, here displayed, deceived me, and I so confident that your original would remain unchanged as you grew up? Why do you look back at me now with that false smile which Felipe painted into those eyes of yours? What have you to say? Why don't you speak? Why don't you answer? Anyone who looks out that way might very well reply. With those eyes you look at Marfisa, and with that mouth you deceive me. Little wonder that she loves you and I am left to suffer. Here it says, "Dorotea's slave." Not slave, but runaway. Why am I reading this? Why do I keep looking and putting off my just revenge for all those deceptions and betrayals, those cruelties and poisons so sweet to my senses? Where were my wits when I put my trust in a seventeen-year-old? Why did I go on nourishing a viper in my bosom? So that when it grew it could serve me as the asp did the Queen of Egypt for the sake of Mark Antony? Does that mustache nurtured on my lips by the sweet sighs of my loving breath now serve to flatter Marfisa's lips as he makes love to her, mocking my true love? Was it to such a one I brought the hair my mother pulled out because of him? Oh, Mother, how right you were! Between the locks you pulled out and these I pull now, there'll be none left on my head, because you liked my hair, saying nothing so beguiled desire in you as to see it tousled. And calling me your dawn when heaven's dawn broke, with your loving serenades, like sweet birds from the portals of their nests, you bade me good morning, imitating their voices. Oh, the pity of it all! How can I be thinking of such things? Does he perhaps imagine his portrait will serve this Queen Dido like the sword of some Aeneas? Can anyone ever have been so stupid as to fondle the poisoned goblet proffered? Did he speak like this? How could he so bashfully win happy sway over so free a will? Oh, wretched me! I seem beautiful only in my misfortune, while Marfisa seems uncomely in her good luck. But why call someone happy whose fortunes men's inconstancy soon must alter? For if victory now incites her to laughter, even as it peals forth, I bid her share these tears. Oh, if only, as I can tear this portrait up, I might punish the original engraved in my heart! Lord, how it defies me! Resist, then, will you, you cur! But no, it is only my weakness which lacks the resolve to tear it in two, since these hands are hands of love, and love is but a child. This time I *will* tear it—I'll turn my eyes away! There, I have done it. Victory! This is but a token of what I shall do to the one in my heart. Celia! Celia!

Scene 5

CELIA · DOROTEA

Celia. Madam, madam!

Dorotea. Victory, victory! I've torn Don Fernando's portrait in two.

Celia. You're Charles the Fifth killing the Moor who was trampling that Sevillian gentleman.

Dorotea. So you think there's nothing to it?

Celia. Is there really so much in tearing a card in two? What a powerful Céspedes you are; he tore up four packs at a time!

Dorotea. Well, isn't tearing a man something more than that?

Celia. You might vie at hurling the iron bar with Don Jerónimo de Ayanza or the mighty Don Félix Arias.

Dorotea. Well, I should think Hercules did no better when he broke the jaws of the Nemean lion that was terrorizing the whole countryside. Or Samson, snapping the ropes that bound him, or when barehanded he pulled down the Doric columns of that famous temple, their porphyry bases and bronze capitals, all designed to rival the poles of heaven to the end of time.

Celia. I have read that Milo knocked a bull down with one blow.

Dorotea. I did more in tearing this card apart. I pulled out the tongue of the lion of Lysimachus. When I die, they'll find the heart of Aristomenes in me.

Celia. Where did you ever read so many classical instances? We have Fernando to thank for such edification.

Dorotea. What are you examining? What are you fingering there?

Celia. These halves can still be made to fit together.

Dorotea. A better way to fit them would be not to have torn them apart.

Celia. Why are you tearing up those papers?

Dorotea. You're right. Bring me a candle.

Celia. I'll light the candlestick.

Dorotea. Oh, deceptive slips of paper, oh clever lies, falsehoods masked, poisonous words, vipers lurking in the flowers, and promissory notes with nothing to back them—counterfeit contracts of love binding intentions you never had! Why were you the procurers of my ruination? This time you shall repay me for all the lies you told me, for all your deceptions. I shall turn you into ashes, so that no memory remains of my fire nor any relic of your deceit. Bring on the candle, Celia.

Celia. Put them to the flame, hurry. Why are you still staring at them?

Dorotea. Listen to this one only: "Celia has brought your note, in which you blame and excuse me both. You blame me for not coming to see you and forgive me because of the night's inclemency. I did go to see you, Dorotea. No Alpine snow could dampen the fire of my love. I sat down on the stone where I always sit. Celia came to the window and when I thought she was opening it for me, she must have been telling you she hadn't found me anywhere, so covered was I with snow. Still I waited there half-expectantly, more to suffer on your account than because I thought she would return. And to prove that this is true, look at the top pane of your window where you'll find your name. I wrote it with a piece of plaster I cut out of the wall with my dagger. The cold was overwhelming. It battled my love, but my love won out, and I waited so long I thought I'd die simply to keep you from missing me. I returned home to be scolded by Julio, who was dozing by the fire, as if he were the snowy servant and I the dozing master. It took all sorts of treatment to restore me, and if it hadn't been that I failed to see you, placing you in my debt would have satisfied me. Fido stayed with me all night. Reward the dog's faithfulness with a special treat, even though I paid for his company by sacrificing a good share of my cape. Oh, if you'd only seen me—more truly the snow-mantled shepherd I am always pretending to be in my verse, with a flock of thoughts and a sheepdog beside me." Can that man have gone through so much for my sake?

Celia. Heavens, don't take on so. I'm in a hurry.

Dorotea. Oh, if only there were life in you to feel my righteous vengeance! Bring the candle closer, Celia. Hold it and I will burn them one by one.

Celia. Though the paper be snowy, into the fire it goes.

Dorotea. Into the fire. But here, listen.

Celia. If you stop to read them, we won't have a fifth of them burned by nightfall.

Dorotea. Only the first few words.

Celia. How does it go?

Dorotea. "How fetching you looked as you went out today, heavenly Dorotea, to slay both men and women, the former with love, the latter with envy! And as my portion of that death, you dealt me jealousy—such jealousy, indeed, that I was sorry to see you look so beautiful." Into the fire with it.

Celia. Into the fire it goes. You're not reading another one? When will we ever be done?

Dorotea. Put your trust in men!

Celia. They say the same of us, and both are right. But how did you expect a love to end, whose end was not marriage, where possession finishes love or life itself?

Dorotea. This one looks like a sonnet.

Celia. Reason enough to burn it.

Dorotea. You are hostile to poets.

Celia. To those of wicked tongue and pen, not well-bred and learned poets.

Dorotea.

> The flowers have a grievance, Dorotea:
>> they claim you've robbed them of their every hue.
>> The frosty snow is also heard complaining:
>> it says it holds less iciness than you.
>
> Love is put out because a swarm of Cupids
>> has taken refuge in your frigid breast.
>> The very sun rekindled in your eyes
>> disdains victorious bays at your behest.
>
> Nature herself complains it is not fair
>> for one so fair to be so inhumane,
>> so hard of heart, so deaf to every plea.
>
> Would she have given you beauty beyond compare,
>> had she foreseen such obduracy in you?
>> Pray, then, more gentle or less perfect be.

Celia. So beautifully written and so clear! But the poet would not have made a good woman.

Dorotea. Why?

Celia. Because he was too fluent and easygoing. But how is it, if you loved him so much, that he complained of your attitude?

Dorotea. He was angry at the time.

Celia. And, though angry, praised and extolled you! That's a genuine poet and none of your ignorant fabricators and satirists who dishonor the very persons who praise them.

Dorotea. The honorable ones, Celia, act as mirrors for the infamous. And the latter, seeing how ugly their reflection is, befoul with their dirty breath the brightness which offends them. But listen to this one.

Celia. You're in no hurry. Oh, mad lovers, glorying even in their pain!

Dorotea. "God grant, my precious, if I know the woman you refer to . . ."

Celia. Not jealousy?

Dorotea. And with good reason. Into the fire with it.

Celia. Into the fire it goes.

Dorotea. Only this one, this last one.

Celia. One would think it was yourself, not the love notes, you were setting aflame.

Dorotea. "The dawn broke but not for my eyes. And I asked the dawn why it was breaking."

Celia. For heaven's sake, stop reading that foolishness. Love turns rancid too, like hams.

Dorotea. Into the fire with it.

Celia. Into the fire. But mind now, the candle's burning out.

Dorotea. "Felipe de Liaño says he'll go to paint your portrait today, and I ask him where he'll find the colors. No need to remind you to look beautiful—it's a foregone conclusion at any hour. I regret the painter is himself so handsome that you may leave portraits in each other's hearts." Oh, Celia, could I really have liked this once? How incredibly silly! Into the fire.

Celia. Into the fire. But you should know, madam, that nothing seems so silly as a love letter out of season, or when the game is over. But bless you, do let's burn them all up together. I must starch a number of chain-lace ruffles or your mother will be scolding.

Scene 6

GERARDA · DOROTEA

Gerarda. Water, water! Good Lord, what is this fire?

Dorotea. Is that you, aunt, asking for water? What's come over you?

Gerarda. Letters! I could have sworn it, child.

Dorotea. Troy is aflame.

Gerarda.

"Fire, fire!" is what everyone exclaims.

But Paris says, "Burn, Helen, in those flames!"

Dorotea. Is that a new song?

Gerarda. The musicians of the Duke of Alba are singing it these days.

Dorotea.

Burn, lies, burn away,

expect no help from me.

Gerarda. I know what lies behind this punishment.

Dorotea. This spells the end of the story.

Gerarda. 'Hell knows no fury like a woman scorned.'

Dorotea. Since I destroyed the portrait, what's so remarkable about burning the letters?

Gerarda. 'If you can't stand the heat, stay out of the kitchen.' I'll wager anything that you're sorry.

Dorotea. I feel much relieved already.

Gerarda. 'You may paint your face but not your feelings.'

Dorotea. Aunt, I need not pretend with you. It would be pointless and ungracious. I admit this is killing me. But what can I do? A traitor deluded me, led me on, made me love him—all of it deceitfully—until he found a chance to get back at me for the Don Bela affair, which you know all about.

Gerarda. 'Beware the wolf in sheep's clothing.' What can you possibly regret, considering how poor Don Fernando is?

Dorotea. His figure, his mind, his caresses, his love. All these fit like another skin. To remove them is to be flayed alive.

Gerarda. There's no end to the sophistries he's implanted in you! But, child, if your feelings are as you describe, take the matter into your own hands.

Dorotea. My own hands? But how?

Gerarda. What would you give if I produced him at your very door, meek as a lamb?

Dorotea. Gerarda, if you use the wrong means, may God prevent my undertaking such a thing. Besides which, no self-respecting woman resorts to sorcery. It's a great offense to seek by force what one cannot accomplish on one's merits.

Gerarda. Listen, Dorotea, child, 'every man for himself,' et cetera.

Dorotea. May that et cetera burn in hell. I've already told you, aunt—if you'd only listen—that quite aside from the offense to God, which is of first consideration, I've no wish to do myself the injustice of denying my looks, my mind, my appeal, and my youth by such base means. Of the two courses, begging would be better than forcing him to come. Nor do I know of anything more insulting than calling a woman a sorceress to her face.

Gerarda. Be careful now, I'm listening.

Dorotea. Then are you one, aunt?

Gerarda. I've dabbled a bit, out of curiosity. But now I wouldn't think of it for a moment. I swear in all honesty, I haven't taken the beans in hand for a week.

Dorotea. Don't you dare to, Gerarda. Let the punishment of someone you know be a lesson to you.

Gerarda. Listen to me, child. One can force the will naturally enough with herbs and stones.

Dorotea. Oh, aunt! You are deluded indeed if you believe that powers in things corporeal are capable of influencing the faculties of the soul! This is what you ignorant women are tricked into thinking by those who instruct you for their own advantage and nefarious practice, to the great misfortune of men.

Gerarda. Ah, child, child. You can't build a house with tiles. Take love as it comes, for better or for worse. When all is said and done, ugly you die and beautiful are born. 'Better red-faced than black-hearted.' 'Don't break a leg in the stable.' 'Better make up with enemies than beg from friends.' Don Bela is jealous. There's something he has heard and confirmed in your sad looks. If he leaves you, and that little Fernando of yours sticks with his Marfisa, what will you do—'fold hand in hand and put your neck in the sand'? When I was a girl I read something in Garcilaso about gathering your rosebuds while ye may. Do you think time sleeps when we do? Well, child, you're wrong. Three things never pause to sleep at all.

Dorotea. What are they, Gerarda?

Gerarda. Troubles, taxes, and time.

Dorotea. Hush, mother, here comes Laurencio with some message from Don Bela.

Gerarda. 'Some news is better than no news.'

Dorotea. He's bringing me reproof, no doubt.

Scene 7

LAURENCIO · DOROTEA · GERARDA

Laurencio. What's all this smoke? Ah, such delightful incense! And this, Madam Dorotea, in your house, which my master calls the perfect picture of paradise, the quintessence of every East Indian scent, the home of clove and cinnamon, and the place where amber breezes are wafted about more subtly than over the seas of Florida!

Gerarda. Brother Laurencio, we've been burning a bit of old brocade to get the silver out of it.

Laurencio. Gerarda, you've been reading Bernard of Treviso's *Alchemy,* I think. But, truth to tell, I really thought you were charring one of those animals the prodigal son kept. That's all the *alchemy* you need to wet your whistle.

Gerarda. Laurencio, Laurencio: 'better a good loud fart than all the doctor's art.' Let men thank their lucky stars they weren't born with our complaints.

Laurencio. We've a few of our own.

Gerarda. Men have? What are they?

Laurencio. Putting up with yours when you get started. What can be more exasperating than seeing you through a fainting fit, screeching louder than a peacock opening its tail, servants in a tizzy, neighbors alarmed, treating you with burnt partridge feathers, while searching everywhere for rue, especially if it's midnight?

Gerarda. Insolent, arrogant brutes that you are, what's the reason for it if not the miseries you lay upon us when you return from the gaming house, or that other kind of house, hats pulled down over the eyes like Burgundian visors, and the first thing you do is pick a quarrel over the way the meal is cooked, turning everything topsy-turvy, then throwing your capes on again and going back where you came from? But let's not try to decide who's to blame. Instead, tell us what brings you and if your master is still fretting. It's a crime, isn't it, for our Dorotea to speak a word to an acquaintance! Ah, yes, it's so much better to have people call her discourteous, make rude remarks to her face, or write scurrilous verse about her.

Laurencio. My master is not angry. He's heavyhearted.

Dorotea. What about?

Laurencio. He'd promised certain gentlemen his horse, Ironfoot, for tomorrow's tourneys and the blacksmith put a nail in the horse's hoof. Then when he begged to be excused, they wrote him such an arrogant note that he's beside himself. Here's one I've brought for you, and I've something to tell you.

Dorotea. Let me see it. I don't believe we can be friends.

Gerarda. 'Beware of Greeks bearing gifts.'

Scene 8

DON FERNANDO · CÉSAR · JULIO

Fernando. You mean my horoscope foretells such disasters you won't even tell me what they are?

César. Exactly.

Julio. Don Fernando knows well enough he need not believe them.

Fernando. Look up that place in Jeremiah: "Learn not the way of the heathen, and be not dismayed at the signs of heaven, for the customs of the people are vain."

Julio. Isaiah says the same of those who took to scrutinizing the stars: "Let now the astrologers, the stargazers, stand up and save thee from these things that shall come upon thee. Behold they shall be as stubble; the fire shall burn them."

César. Of that I'm well aware, Julio, I know and believe that the very Truth Himself tells us not to be inquisitive about future things, and I assure you, I've always been suspicious of rashly predicting what our inscrutable God in his eternal mind has foreordained. In my early years I studied all this with that most learned Portuguese gentleman, Juan Bautista de Lavaña, and only occasionally do I cast a birth horoscope, and then out of curiosity, not otherwise. In no instance do I furnish answers to queries. Man was not created by the stars, nor can his free will be made subject to them.

Fernando. Augustine said that astrology and similar branches of knowledge exist more for exercising men's wits than for enlightening their minds with true wisdom.

Julio. You may encounter his abhorrence of them in his first volume, and in his eighth find an invective against false astrologers.

César. Granting all this, simply as a matter of curiosity, let me say what I make of this horoscope, eschewing whatever a proper respect for the Almighty demands. You, Don Fernando, will be severely accused by mother and daughter in the prison where Dorotea will have you confined. After your incarceration, exile from the realm awaits you. Shortly before this, you will court a maiden attracted by your reputation and person, and you will marry her against the wishes of both your relatives and hers. She will remain most loyally at your side during your trials and exiles and show constant strength of character in all adversity. After seven years she will die, and you will return grief-stricken to Madrid, where a recently widowed Dorotea will want you for a husband. But she will not succeed because your honor will triumph over her wealth and your persistent antagonism over her love and blandishments.

Fernando. What weird nonsense!

César. According to your horoscope, you are to be most unhappy in love. Know that tremendous trials await you in this regard. Beware of a woman who will cast spells on you, though you will come through it all by praying God for His help, in a dispensation different from your present one.

Fernando. Dubious as all this sounds, if it should come to pass, I will avail myself of that divine remedy, because it alone is true, while those of men are vain and unworthy of any trust. For, according to Divine Truth, trust is not to be placed even in princes.

César. One there is, however, who will esteem and favor you greatly. His love you will retain until the end of your life, which here appears to be a long one.

Fernando. What toilsome life was ever short?

Julio. The goal of speculative learning is truth, and of practical learning, action.

Fernando. So the Philosopher teaches in his *Metaphysics*.

Julio. César tells us what the reading of this horoscope indicates, and Don Fernando will use his free will to find a way of contravening such harsh predictions.

Fernando. There is a law—and even if there were none—saying that when truth and hearsay occur together, one must maintain that reverence for the truth which is owed it by right, human and divine. And according to another law, it is impossible that a finite cause should produce an infinite result. You grasp my meaning, I am sure.

César. I reply with what is said elsewhere.

Fernando. And what is that?

César. That what can be tacitly understood may be considered already stated. I know you are fully determined to place yourself beyond all thought of Dorotea. You thus convince me that as the cause ceases to exist, so will the effect. But Aristotle in his *Physics* says that purpose comes first in intention and last in execution. God grant, Fernando, that you bear yourself in such fashion that your stars will give way before the power of your free will, against which nothing prevails except itself. For no theory of the planets can overcome an invincible virtue, powerful curb that it is against the disturbing incursions of appetite, whose effects so many philosophers have conquered by its exercise. But if Madam Marfisa is to be your refuge, and your defense conditioned on inciting reckless jealousy in Dorotea, I will never consider you safe. For even if Juvenal had failed to observe it, it is beyond question that no creature, however fierce, delights more in revenge than woman.

Fernando. I am well aware that my peace of mind depends on leaving the country for a while. And so I intend to exchange the art of letters for that of arms in this campaign our King has undertaken against England. But since you mention Marfisa, how is it you tell me nothing about her from your reading of the horoscope?

César. I marvel that curiosity leads you to inquire about something which right reason will not allow you to believe.

Fernando. We are all aware that anything you may find in the stars is subject to the first cause of causes, and that what is first can admit nothing preceding it, as the Proem to the *Digest* has it. Tell us about Marfisa, and—as the true law we profess enjoins upon us—leave the future to Divine Wisdom and its disposition to Omnipotence.

César. With that understood, Fernando, I may say that Marfisa will be married a second time to a man of the law, who will depart from this realm with an honorable position. She will soon be widowed, and on marrying a soldier of our country, will be most unfortunate.

Fernando. In what way?

César. He will murder her through jealousy of a friend.

Fernando. How tragic and bloody you are! How implacably you have set the aspects of this quadrilateral! Will no aspect prevent this from happening? Does none show up triangular and benign? Never in my life will I ask another thing of you. Lord, what gloom you've cast upon me! Marfisa murdered and in a foreign country, too?

César. You may now understand how human desire sooner embraces false flattery than certain truth. I do not say this is true, but only that if I should tell you that you were to inherit a hundred thousand ducats and Marfisa a title, you'd be grateful to me, even though you considered it untrue.

Julio. I once knew a gentleman, a man already well advanced in years, who, on going out one day splendidly attired—as he thought (because he was of those persons wishing to conceal their age)—asked a young page in his employ if he did not think him well appareled. The page—true to form, since a master's bread produces in servants as many fawning words as there are stomach worms in children— told him: "I may assure Your Grace he looks as dashing as a man of twenty-two." To which the gentleman replied: "My boy, I know quite well you are lying, but, on the King's life, I do enjoy hearing you say so."

César. Julio's point is well made. So let's bless the gypsies, who've never predicted anything untoward: everyone's going to be rich; everyone greatly loved by his lady; everyone lucky; everyone will receive a sum of money from the New World; and everyone will live forever.

Julio. Then you have the glib almanac astrologers who predict storms for certain days. When they predict rain, the sun comes out; when they promise a fine day, you have a downpour. And then, after predicting many illnesses and many quarrels over women, as if there were anything new about either, and that the year will be a good one for lentils and sugarcane, and that some Turk will pass away (there being an infinite number of them), they'll casually add, "God's will be done!" If they spoke as truly in all else as they do in this, one would feel at fault not paying a thousand ducats for a prognostication.

Fernando. Though I know it's far from certain, I keep reverting to the tragic fate César has in store for Marfisa. So cowardly is the heart in love and so powerful the forebodings of misfortune. Jail for me— and exile? And Marfisa, murdered?

César. Fernando, forget those empty imaginings. Now let us go to Mass to ask God's divine assistance in mending your ways, and so free yourself completely. Thank Him for the understanding he has bestowed on you by loving and fearing Him, since the crown of wisdom is the fear of God. Stop and consider how many friends of yours have died, so many your own age. To avoid returning to

Dorotea, do not take up with Marfisa, for a danger is not averted by seeking a greater one. To learn what both women seek to gain from you, read carefully the seventh chapter of Proverbs.

Scene 9

DOROTEA · CELIA

Dorotea. Give me the harp, Celia.

Celia. You arise in good spirits. May the sailors' saying about the weather, 'Red sky at morning, sailor take warning,' not apply to you.

Dorotea. There's no need to worry that the weather will change on my account. My love turned to jealousy, jealousy to frenzy, frenzy to madness, madness to rage, rage to a will for revenge, revenge to tears, and tears to expelling the heart's poison through the eyes. Let the ungrateful wretch keep his Marfisa, because if Don Bela will sponsor me, now that the news of my husband Calidonio's death in Lima is confirmed, I'll exchange this finery for a habit and prudently surrender what men call graces to the Author of them, who neither can deceive nor be found wanting, nor fail to respond. For, looking back on what is past, Celia, what have I to show for my friendship with Don Fernando but repentance of my ignorance: all those love notes with their burnt-out characters, white against the blackened paper, frightening me so, and those five years of my life cast out the window of my appetite into the street of my dishonor? Beauty cannot return; the years move ever onward. Our life is a hostelry, time a courier, youth a flower, birth a debt incurred. The creditor demands, illness forecloses, death collects.

Celia. Adversity, they say, often leads to the mending of our ways. In this, one sees the providence of heaven shining forth, and understands how greatly the Divine Maker desires to direct our footsteps into the pathways of His service. Ah, madam, how greatly we are deceived by beauty! Women have always been led astray more through what they hear than what they see. More harm has always been done them by hearing their praises sung than by gazing on handsome features. Fortunate indeed is she who, like yourself now, makes provision for her death early in life. I can picture you, one veil over another, your face lit up by the glow of your virtues, as far removed from the world as you are now bound up in it.

Dorotea. You servant girls are extraordinary. You agree with everything, keep flattering words in readiness for any occasion, going along indifferently with whatever is proposed to you, good or bad. How odd that flattery too should have its sacred version! If I now proposed to go and rouse Fernando, you'd already have tied on your skirt, drawn a cloak around your shoulders, put on your shoes for creeping up and stealing off, and have taken to the street obediently.

Celia. If you want us to go, why not say so directly?

Dorotea. I go there, Celia? May God fail me if I ever . . . !

Celia. Don't go flailing about and swearing if you expect me to believe you. You've been torturing those poor pegs for an hour, not tuning the harp strings so much as your own unstrung thoughts.

Dorotea. I removed a few because they did not ring true on the flat notes.

Celia. Those must have been your thoughts of Don Fernando.

Dorotea. You're quite right, Celia, for the genius of music, as my master Enrique used to tell me, lies not in skilled fingers nor in a voice well trained, but in the soul itself—so the theory of music teaches. But tell me, what is my mother doing?

Celia. She's inside with Felipa seeing to the sale of those slave girls. She says they're everything you could wish, but are too ostentatious for a household such as this.

Dorotea. And what does Felipa advise her?

Celia. Not to do it, that it will make Don Bela angry.

Dorotea. At last the harp is tuned.

Celia. I could wish that you were too.

Dorotea.

> If all things end in time
> > why does not my torment end?
> If all the many griefs
> > my constancy has suffered
> > leave loyalty unshaken
> > and fail to grant release;
> > if my persistence welcomes

loneliness and pains;
if hope's a mountain born
and dies a puff of wind,
why does not my torment end?
Trials and valor both
are honor-bound to learn
which first must reach an end,
my torment or my love.
All-consuming time,
to whom they both appeal,
wonders, since such feelings
claim to be immortal,
why my torment is unending.
Although ill-used by them,
I take the ills so well,
I invoke my soul immortal
should the torment kill me.
I'd wrong my hellish pangs
if I thought them less a heaven.
Nor would I love, if I sought
to discover from my feelings
why my torment is unending.
For these ills I suffer,
what can passing time avail
if each moment it is fleeting
my love stands in its way?
For if, in living or in dying,
I give license to my ills
to continue endlessly,
I never shall discover
why my torment does not end.

Celia. This is where all those things that happen in the shepherd books
would fit in perfectly: how the sweet breeze stops blowing, the
flowers release their petals tightly packed, and the mother-of-pearl
breaks out of budded green confinement to perfume the air, the
tinkling glass of streams grows silent, and the Philomels of the forests learn to trill their dulcet airs. But, ma'am, I had never heard
you perform those verses or that music. Who composed them?

Dorotea. The verses, Celia, are my own, the music by that excellent musician Juan de Palomares, rival supreme to the famous Juan Blas de Castro; the two of them, with Apollo as judge, won equal laurels for mastery of the lyre.

Celia. And you wrote the verses?

Dorotea. Could anyone but a woman have expressed them?

Celia. I must now believe that love first invented poetry.

Dorotea. Anger and love are the principal human passions. So tell me, Celia, if the ancients held that anger created poetry, why should it not be more accessible to love, which laments its sufferings in the sweetest of harmonies?

Scene 10

GERARDA · DOROTEA

Gerarda. Can it be you singing, Dorotea—you so gay, you all dressed up? Can it be you with green ribbons in your hair, the locket and jewelry, really you? What change is this? What's come over you? Is there something new on the horizon, child? You're so different from what you were of late. You positively sparkle in that costume. 'Thank God for bread and the lass it nourishes.'

Dorotea. Aunt, the weather does not stay the same, day after day. From cloudy skies the sun comes forth, from storms fair weather.

Gerarda. Has some meek note arrived from Don Fernando? Does he wish to come and see you? Has he explained away his peccadillos with Marfisa? Are there *décimas* packed with conceits, some stupendous sonnet or flashy ballad with its tag line again and again, or some tearful refrain that goes, "Phyllis, I am slain by thee"? They'll restore your honor, to be sure.

Dorotea. Your taste is so common, Mother Gerarda. Come, sit down, and tell me where you've been.

Gerarda. You're changing the subject. I arose, my darling child, in fine fettle. I thanked God for my health and for being born in Christendom. Suppose I were some Jarifa Rodríguez or Daraja González, the wife of Zulema Pérez or Zacatín Hernández, whatever would become of me? Why, the misfortune would surely take me straight to hell, wrapped in one of those Moorish robes. Then I donned my cloak and went off to Mass. I haven't missed a single day when I've been well since I reached the age of reason. From Mass I went on to Marina's house—she's a tough old crony of mine—to save putting my own stew pot on. There she was planting valerian for certain female friends, and tying gold thread with pearls around the roots.

Dorotea. What strange and silly humbug!

Gerarda. She washed her hands, prepared a few fat chunks of bacon— of the four-slices-to-the-pound variety. And, if you must know, breakfast started at seven, and here I am, coming only now because she had a fine little wineskin there holding a gallon and a half and, as there was no water in the house, no drop could be spared.

Dorotea. Come now, not a single drop?

Gerarda. We left the skin wrung drier than a rawhide squeezed with rope to remove the turpentine. What's more, if memory serves, we sent across the way for another little swallow—one to cap it all, as they say. Because Marina always lives close to someone who keeps taverns, not tabs. There are never any windows in taverns, and everyone leaving them has left his eyes behind. I told her to save you a black kitten from Moronda's litter. She's the animal most sought-after in Madrid, worth more than any civet cat.

Dorotea. Bring me no such thing, aunt. Houses become suspect with black cats about; besides, they're the dirtiest things.

Gerarda. How dainty you are and squeamish, my pretty! The truth is, a thousand of us girls were avid for that cat's litter.

Dorotea. To tell how often she went astray.

Gerarda. Now, suppose we pick up our yarn again. We've paused longer than weavers do in mending it. Give me news of Fernando, tell me all that's happened—you may be in my debt for some kind words I've put in for you. Why do you look at me that way and laugh? All right, all right, put the harp aside and let us share the good news. As long as you're happy, may Don Bela go hang—'a poor thing but mine own,' I always say. And I'll wager that our silly little ninny, that grab-all cock-chick, wishes he'd remembered 'grass always looks greener on the other side.'

Dorotea. Trying to worm something out of me, are you, auntie?

Gerarda. No, child, I am advising you to live and enjoy yourself, for

the wisest thing is to trim your sails to the wind. Love whatever
strikes your fancy, not what fills your purse, for, as they say, 'see
Occasion going by, catch it on the fly.'

Dorotea. Don't worry, aunt, I've had no note from Don Fernando, nor
do I wish any. Go with God and leave me, for this show of cheer is
a coating on the pill and the quince in the cough syrup.

Gerarda. I did not mean to nettle you with what I said. It's perfectly
possible to keep Don Bela happy and also love Fernando. Rich folk
are just the sort not to heed what's going on, while the poor accept
whatever goes. 'Some fancy fat, some fancy lean.'

Dorotea. One must be so constituted, Gerarda.

Gerarda. You can learn anything, child. There's nothing easier for us
than deceiving men, and it's their own fault. Since they've deprived
us of frequenting various fields of knowledge, to busy our subtle
minds we study only one: how to deceive them. And since there is
only one text, we all know it by heart.

Dorotea. I have never seen it.

Gerarda. Well, it makes excellent reading; its chapters are unforgetta-
ble.

Dorotea. Give me some of the titles at least.

Gerarda. "How to feign love for the rich without spurning the poor.
   "How to faint on the spot and jerk out the tears.
   "How to ask for one thing by praising another.
   "How to tickle the monsters and take in the fops.
   "How to offer mere pennies and take in the pounds.
   "How to kindle jealousy out of the thin air and cool the hot-
tempered.
   "How to have doors on two streets.
   "How to teach maids to keep mum when mistresses stray.
   "How to hide the flaw and play up the fine feature.
   "How to train your aunt to barge in opportunely.
   "How to keep mother in the dark while lover thinks her a men-
ace.
   "How to give out that you are more sinned against than sinning.
   "How to make friends in high places and give no cause for slan-
der.
   "How to change your name and flee the poets.
   "How to rouse hopes straight from the start.
   "How to delay the sweets till the price is no problem.

"How to train half-breed maids and spread spice and perfume.

"How to have eyes in the back of the head and laugh like a charmer.

"How to use fancy words and dance to all tunes.

"How to slip in a story and work up a pedigree.

"How to wear a low dress and be clean as a hussy in Holland.

"How to ride in a coach and look like milady."

And "How at all events to avoid falling in love, because that's absolute ruination"—to say nothing of other chapters of the greatest importance.

Dorotea. I assure you it's a hearty laugh you've given me, even though my spirits are so low that I've put on these bright things to escape from myself.

Gerarda. Well, nobody can say of you that 'women and pippins don't need painted cheeks.'

Dorotea. Ah, Gerarda, to speak plainly, what does this life add up to but a rapid road to death? If Don Bela will be my sponsor, you'll see these feet you praised exchange amber-scented pumps for rough rope sandals, these curls shorn off, and these gay colors and gilt lace trimmings exchanged for drab sackcloth. Can anyone know on rising in the morning whether he will live through the day? All of life is a day. Yesterday you were a girl and today you dare not pick up the mirror lest you be the first to despise yourself. One must prize disillusionment above beauty. Everything runs its course, everything palls, everything comes to an end.

Gerarda. Oh, Dorotea, my child, that you should be telling me this, when I'm not even sure I'll wake tomorrow. You've brought tears welling to my eyes straight from my heart. Late though it is, I recognize the error of my ways. God put those words in your mouth.

Scene 11

LAURENCIO · DOROTEA · FELIPA
GERARDA · TEODORA · CELIA

Laurencio. I do not know where I shall find the eyes to look at you in so lamentable a tragedy, or the strength to speak to you in so wretched a season, or breath to tell you, Dorotea, of the greatest misfortune that has befallen any unfortunate since the world began and the arrogant thrusts of anger brought arms to bear against innocence, power against humility, and turned honor vengefully against itself.

Dorotea. Dear God, Laurencio, if I did not see the tears in your eyes, more bloodshot than the finest purple dye, never would I believe your words were not deceiving me. But have men's words ever failed to be true when watered with tears? Remove the handkerchief from your face, catch your breath, and, as you address us, Gerarda and I shall weep in your stead.

Gerarda. Weep we shall indeed! Speak, son, for our lives are hanging on the watery thread of your tears.

Laurencio. Alas, Dorotea! Alas, Gerarda, may my life end when I have ended this report of the cause of which I am the tragic and unlucky messenger, one more dolorous and with more reason for grief than he of Seneca's *Hippolytus*. As I informed you earlier, my master, Don Bela, had promised two stern gentlemen his Ironfoot, a horse more luckless than Sejanus'. The blacksmith put a nail in its hoof, thereby incurring the first black mark in this affair. For this reason the horse could not be used in the tourney. They wrote my master that he had done it deliberately to avoid lending the horse, and had thus shown disrespect for the petitioner and dishonored his word, which for Spaniards is the gravest dishonor of all. Modesty answered the note and honor was silent; weighing offense against fear, honor made an error of judgment. For, wrath remaining unmollified by an explanation of blamelessness, two brothers came to our house and sent a page up to summon my master. Don Bela went down to the patio, clad only in the jerkin and hose he was wearing and with no protection for his person other than the truth of the situation. Oh, how great an error to disregard the arrogance of anger, from confidence in the justice of a cause! Not because doing so is wrong, but because human nature is so given to reckless violence. In short, after addressing a few words to him—I do not know how any of mine can now be spoken, unless the confused upwelling of sobs and heavy deluge of tears make way for tongue to utter them. But how can I hesitate, in view of your distress?

Dorotea. Speak, Laurencio, you are killing me.

Laurencio. Drawing swords, the two of them murdered him.

Dorotea. Merciful God, such cruelty!

Gerarda. Ah, Laurencio! You might have dispensed with grandiloquence in relating a misfortune; words suffice without tears; feelings, without sobs. Take her hand, her heart fails her. Keep her up, hold her, or she'll fall over and be injured, while I go for water.

Laurencio. If water can bring her to, what could be more life-giving than this stream flowing from my eyes onto hers? Oh come, Madam Dorotea!

Final Scene

TEODORA · FELIPA · CELIA
LAURENCIO · FAME

Teodora. Who is that crying out, Felipa, and what is that noise? Has someone fallen down the cellarway?

Felipa. Alas, ma'am, that voice is my mother's. She went to fetch water for Dorotea after Dorotea fainted.

Teodora. Was there nowhere closer to get it? Curious way to revive someone in a faint!

Felipa. You go down, Celia. I haven't the heart.

Celia. Nor do I. Oh, lamentable spectacle! Gerarda is dead. But who could have imagined it happening as she went for water?

Felipa. Joking, are you, Celia? She deserved better of you.

Celia. God only knows I'm sorry. Rest in peace, professor extraordinary of love, sage Seneca of assignation, grand counselor of wheedling, consultant in gift-giving, and the world's greatest trafficker in women and fleecer of men.

Felipa. What are you muttering down there on the stairs, you heartless woman? May you squeal those words, mounting stairs to the gallows! Alas, my sweet mother!

Celia. Until now she was salty.

Felipa. Oh, the sorry sight that saintly headdress makes!

Celia. It's the head that's a sight, not the headdress! But it should console her that she died in a fall, like those whom Fortune has upraised.

Felipa. Sententious, are you? May someone sentence you!

Celia. Never was I more convinced of Gerarda's saintliness. The jug that was to hold the water remains unbroken.

Teodora. I am so distraught, Laurencio, I never thought to ask the reason why Dorotea fainted. My child, my little girl!

Dorotea. Oh God, all these calamities!

Celia. What woman, hearing herself called a girl, would not come back from the next world?

Dorotea. What is there to say, Mother? Behold the tears of this grief-stricken youth and you will know that his master, Don Bela, is dead.

Celia. And that Gerarda followed after to see if he was leaving her any money.

Teodora. Your master dead, Laurencio? That Alexander of the New World, that munificent and most gallant gentleman, that wise and cultivated courtier?

Laurencio. The very one, Teodora. So you see how much trust is to be placed in this life, so called, for no one, as one of the wise has said, could imagine it so brief as to expect death the same day he was imagining it. Nothing is less certain than knowing where death will overtake us nor anything wiser than expecting it everywhere.

Fame. Audience, this is LA DOROTEA, and this the fate that befell Don Bela, Marfisa, and Gerarda. Beyond this were the trials of Don Fernando. The poet refused to amend the truth, since this was a true story. If he has been faithful to the name of poet, heed the moral for which it was written, and applaud it.

> *Chorus of the Moral Ending*
> Reckless youth, behold the end
>   all your restive follies boast.
> Jealousy is bred of love;
>   envy, vengeance follow close.
> Heaven thus contrives to blast
>   each and every sanguine hope.
> The greater the example is,
>   the more punishing it proves.
> Sensual joys all lead to grief;
>   anguish is the fruit of love.

266

Even the heart that fondest is
begins to hate, and ends up cold.
When I think how wanton love
must always take a tragic turn,
even as I entertain,
I would have my reader learn
how all appearances deceive,
exemplify what he must spurn.

Lectionem sine ulla delectatione negligo. (Cic. 2. *Tusc.*)

Everything contained in *La Dorotea* is subject to correction by the Holy Roman Catholic Church and to the censure of its elders, from first letter to last.

Brother Lope Félix de Vega Carpio

THE ACTION
FOR LIBEL
A CONVERSATION
BETWEEN THE
TRANSLATORS

The Action for Libel

On 29 December 1587 Jerónimo Velázquez, the father of Elena Osorio, Lope's mistress, entered against Lope a charge of libel which accused him of having "insulted and defamed" Elena, her parents, her brother, and a female cousin in scurrilous verse. The ultimate sentence on 7 February 1588 incorporated penalties stemming from additional verse and a forged letter signed "Elena," all launched by Lope against the plaintiffs from his prison cell. The abundant testimony taken in the intervening period from witnesses and participants, including Lope himself, enables us to view in vivid detail the climactic stage of Lope's relations with Elena and her family—a stage crucial for the artistic afterlife. The slice of life exposed reveals attitudes, traits of character, patterns of behavior, recurrent emphases which, molded artistically, will reemerge in *La Dorotea*.

Lope's character, revealed under stress, stands out in sharp relief. What emerges is the picture of a young man, impetuous and slightly unstable, yet capable of calculation and showmanship. The connecting link between impetuosity and calculation is an extraordinary self-suggestibility, sometimes kept under control, sometimes not, and a highly vivid imagination. The pose of casual unconcern is repeatedly upset by bursts of anger or surges of vanity, but even these at times seem calculated. Piercing these postures are certain disarmingly frank avowals.

Lope's capacity for dramatic projection coexists with an overriding egocentricity which dooms any chance for consistency in the attitudes he assumes to hide his guilt. One sees him hatching unrealistic schemes more suggestive of stage intigues than of the everyday world, where they inevitably backfire. Such is the stratagem of the compromising letter, forged in Elena's name, which he entrusts to a friend of Elena's. This was to be communicated to her with the threat that, unless she called off the case against him—pardoned him, as Lope significantly said—the letter would be sent to her husband "so that he [would] cut off her head." Technically husbands had such a right over adulterous wives, but it was rarely invoked, save by outraged husbands in stage plays.

Though involuntary admissions of guilt may have escaped Lope, there is no evidence of any feeling that what he had done was reprehensible. His entire production attests to his belief that offenses occasioned by love are, at the most, venial ones. He does not wish to be thought, his angry words say, "a man who would write such things" (as the libelous verse), even if he can't suppress the knowledge that in this instance he happens to have done so. It is wounded vanity—his honor or reputation in the eyes of others—that stirs his anger. His self-esteem is not impaired by feelings of culpability. Indeed, as the hearings dragged on and Lope's prison stay lengthened, the testimony of jailers indicates that he came to feel himself victimized.

What he said in six surviving vituperative poems is scathing enough, however. Elena, her cousin Ana, and a third woman are presented, amid obscenities, as a trio of prostitutes; there are allusions to previous lovers or clients of Elena. Her father, mother, and brother are branded her go-betweens, the latter two being advised to give up their professions (the brother is a law student) since Elena is quite willing to support them. One sonnet presents Elena being auctioned off, with her father as auctioneer and her mother as hawker. There is particular interest for us in the nature of the payments offered. "Ten songs, five sonnets, and a fine little goat" are preferred by Elena to bids of clothing and dress fabrics, but in the end a friar carries the day with his offer of thirty doubloons. This is not the only hint of Elena's weakness for poetry. Other verses faintly allude to the world of pastoral poetry and suggest a contest between material and poetic riches. One senses Elena's inclination to give her relation with Lope a literary flavor, probably incited and reciprocated by him.

The glimpses afforded by texts and documents into the lives of those involved with Lope and their milieu reveal a demimonde of theater people and loose women, frequented by students, aristocrats, and others, a milieu where Lope and Elena seem quite at home. In this world Elena evidently took adultery as a matter of course.

The record of the hearings, together with other documents that have come to light, supplies a plausible reason for the violent breakup of the affair—the advent of a wealthy and aristocratic suitor, a certain Francisco Perrenot de Granvela, nephew of a cardinal and member of a powerful family well connected at both the Spanish and the Austrian Hapsburg courts. Such a figure is obliquely alluded to in the libelous verse; only by hindsight can we identify an allusion by Lope, in the transcribed testimony, to his advent on the scene. Lope clearly preferred to avoid tangling directly with such a personage. According to other sources, Francisco Perrenot was a man of considerable cultivation, with artistic inclinations. There is no way of knowing whether Lope ever actually came into contact with him. Anger and pain at being superseded would well account for Lope's outbursts. The record makes clear that a few months before the hearings Lope had ceased to supply Velázquez with play scripts and he subsequently persuaded himself that this was the real reason why Velázquez was pursuing him. The record offers no evidence of any conflict of interest between Elena and her family in regard to her choice of lovers.

A Conversation between the Translators

EH: A play that is hardly a play and a novel that is not a novel—what are we to make of *La Dorotea?* How can we discover what Lope was trying to achieve in this work on which he spent almost a lifetime?

AT: We ought first to see where Lope stands with respect to his material. The question of irony at once arises. Here we have an artist looking back on a figure of himself as a youth, with mixed feelings: a certain indulgence and considerable impatience. Nothing so obvious as self-love or censure. This is the mixture we need to assay for what it may disclose of Lopean irony.

EH: Because one thinks differently in old age, irony seems an appropriate mode of self-appraisal. But now that three hundred and fifty years have passed since *La Dorotea* was published, I can't help but wonder how common such an author-protagonist relationship may be—I mean this seeming portrait of the artist as a young man, in premodern literature, say since the Renaissance. Montaigne's *Essays*—not fictional, of course—wouldn't fit such a mold. Perhaps in the eighteenth century we come closer to it, with Rousseau's *Confessions,* and then there are Goethe's fictional self-portraits at different stages of his life: *Werther, Wilhelm Meister,* and *Dichtung und Wahrheit.* What comparable masterworks have been created in the past by major authors using this mode? And if Lope's is such a masterwork, why has it gone unrecognized all these centuries?

AT: In Lope we have *Dichtung* built upon *Wahrheit,* but not so much in an attempt to recapture as to refashion the past in order to meet subsequent expressive aims.

EH: Well, the first thing you notice in the pattern of events between Fernando and Dorotea is the reversal of what actually happened between Lope and Elena Osorio. While Lope was clearly rejected by Elena and her family, it is Fernando who in the end rejects Dorotea. *La Dorotea* is one long falling action temporarily suspended when the lovers' quarrel is patched up, only to be resumed subsequently and brought to an end. There's no question of libelous verse. The affair is already seen as running out of momentum. What interests Lope is not an apportioning of guilt between the parties, but a dispassionate presentation of the dynamics of love. So the work engages not so much the putative facts as the substance of a whole lifetime filtered through the re-creation of a particular stage of it—a year or so, actually. The action has been made over by a creative intelligence full of years, though not necessarily wisdom.

AT: No, you can't really think of Lope as a sage. He did not stand away from the world and judge it. He was at home in it from the beginning; he trusted it to the end. As Professor Amado Alonso used to say: Lope never abandoned the world—he only regretted its abandoning him. His genius as poet and playwright remained remarkably fresh.

EH: Well then, I'd say that he treats the world of this work not as a novelist but as a dramatist.

AT: Yes, you feel the author's presence behind each character. In their different ways, the characters become expressive instruments for Lope's temperament.

EH: To read aright what the characters are saying we should know how the irony works as the fiction develops.

AT: I'm reminded that readers have taken Lope himself to be the *eiron* of this work. The closest equivalent of the type in Spanish drama is the *figura del donaire,* or wisecracker.

EH: Since Lope's feelings are mixed—maybe even at this late stage—we need some way of understanding the workings of irony without misunderstanding his *set* toward the work. If we read it straight we can't take seriously Dorotea's effusions and Fernando's counter-effusions. We see them throughout as fluctuating between holding onto and breaking out of a love affair in its last stages. This condition strongly colors the irony. And the protracting of the affair suggests that the old Lope is finding it hard to let go of the most decisive experience of his life. So his irony must be indulgent as well as unremitting.

AT: His ideal reader would probably react half-critically, half-benevolently, to his heedless young lovers. Lope wouldn't wish you to disparage the often melodramatic way they suffer their experience and glamorize it at the same time. Yet he wants the reader to see how self-destructive it is to view life in purely literary terms. But how *does* he bring this across?

EH: As in any drama, the characters set each other off through the dialogue alone, and in the process emerge as distinct persons. Characterization of that sort is not even attempted in narratives of the period.

AT: It *is* in *Don Quixote,* but there the narrative mode marks a totally new departure.

EH: Though *Don Quixote* doesn't seem to belong to any period, a work propelled by a central narrative voice *is* a crucial innovation. Later, with the development of the novel, the absence of such a central voice would constitute a grave limitation on the storytelling. Yet here for Lope the lack of one seems distinctly advantageous. After the immense success of Cervantes' fiction, he must have sensed that the world was moving toward the novel. And his way of keeping abreast of that current . . .

AT: He always wanted to be in the swim.

EH: . . . was to approximate the novel in dramatic form, since drama was what he naturally did best. The result is a work sui generis.

AT: Lope never seems comfortable writing narrative, whether pastoral romance, adventure fiction, or verse epic. He says as much not long before *La Dorotea.* In 1621 and 1624, on publishing some short narratives to please his mistress, Marta de Nevares, he protests that he just isn't cut out for this sort of thing.

EH: By the time he'd finished *La Dorotea,* he was writing pretty much as he pleased, wasn't he? I mean, he is having his say as a past master of dramatic characterization. The ironic tone inherent in the dialogue is sounded at once, in the very first speeches.

AT: As for writing as he pleased, remember, *La Dorotea* is dramatic but not meant for the stage. Although Lope provides the usual dramatis personae at the start, he intended the work for leisurely private perusal. He thus bypasses the restrictive demands of the acting companies he habitually wrote for. He is not confined to character typing or to the pacing of stage dialogue.

EH: By the same token, the talk and creeping action of *La Dorotea* would never have come across to a theater audience. That's because the talk moves associatively and not purposefully with dramatic revelations in mind. Still, for all the surface drifting, the work is clearly being directed at a deeper level by a craftsman who knows where it is all tending. You see this quite well in the opening scenes. Though at first Gerarda seems to be rambling as aimlessly as Teodora, she is actually bringing Teodora around to the subject she has aimed at from the start: a new lover for Dorotea. Still, Gerarda, like the other characters, is in no hurry. In successive scenes the focus on Dorotea keeps sharpening. So, by scene 3, Dorotea's sense of entrapment is crucially fixed in the reader's mind.

AT: We can't go into all the scenes, but let me add that Julio, the manservant, becomes a specific *eiron* figure in the next one: he keeps at Fernando relentlessly, playing along with all his master's evasions, until he succeeds in coaxing out the subject of the other's dream. All this points up Fernando's insecurity, his misgivings about the future, just as the earlier scenes show Dorotea's lack of resolve, her basic helplessness.

EH: If you think of such scenes as illustrating a developing consciousness, Lope's associative technique comes strangely close to what's been called stream of consciousness.

AT: Yes, and Lope the poet naturally works by means of association and analogy. When he plays the intellectual, one of those in the know, the effort is only too patent, and he grows pompous, pretentious, like his own characters.

EH: Even so, his own foibles become grist for his mill. A good deal of self-revelation goes on here. Behind all the name-dropping, the backing and filling of the talk, he is showing us aspects of the literary life. If the substance is recondite, the movement is vital and brisk. Though the talk rambles, it also displays his rhetorical virtuosity.

AT: Incidentally, before we take up rhetoric, I can think of one medium besides the the printed word to which *La Dorotea* could be adapted.

EH: To television, of course. It focuses the action, the way a video drama does, on image and speech—like, of all things, the television commercial. The unsuccessful attempts to stage *La Dorotea* at least show that Lope's "action in prose" does not lend itself to the streamlining procedures of the conventional theater.

AT: Now doesn't the rhetorical element have a good deal to do with that? If you don't give rhetoric free play, you squeeze the life force out of the "action in prose."

EH: I'd say that Lope's rhetoric and style have broken up the hierarchy serving the old decorum. There are no noble characters, socially speaking (despite the "Don" always attached to Fernando's name), nor are there any real plebeians around. It takes place in a world between, on the way to becoming bourgeois, a reflection of that offstage world which Lope himself was living in from day to day.

AT: So the usual high and low styles are not correlated with characters socially conceived. A mixture of styles permits individual character to be seen in psychological terms. When characters are released to speak their minds, psychological realism may displace the stratifications of traditional rhetoric. Here the high style expresses literary status-seeking, ambition, and a need to confer dignity on experience. The low style emerges when the surface is scratched, and unembellished feelings or bare cynicism show through. And so the low style serves to throw the others into relief.

EH: Garrulity may be contagious among the characters but it allows a vital dimension of the work to emerge. As the principal figures self-consciously try to discover themselves, to articulate what is happening to them, we get a sense of private experience. In the fiction of the dialogue, no one has the answers, as, say, sly Socrates does, nor is there anyone truly to the manner born, like the graceful interlocutors of Castiglione's *Cortegiano.*

AT: Well, there is certainly no serious dialectic here nor is there any strict pursuit of values. The sense we have mentioned of an underlying direction is more subtle. An effect of the artist's overall design, it pursues self-understanding, the meaning of experience itself.

EH: Call it the existentialist pursuit before the fact.

AT: Casting off system and formula, Lope imparts greater liveliness and richness to the dialogue. Characters suddenly alight on what they have been groping for, but even so their tentative and approximative formulations do not give them satisfaction.

EH: The reader sees that all attempts at self-analysis or analysis of another are blocked by the very emotions a character is trying to fathom. Still, there are scenes in *La Dorotea*—particularly in the last act, and between Teodora and Gerarda earlier—devoid of any groping for meaning. In those places Lope spins out free-floating conversation for sheer pleasure. The talk seems to have no other function than that.

AT: Even so, you could hardly call otiose the bickering between Teodora and Gerarda or Laurencio and Don Bela, and the sparring of Dorotea and Marfisa. If it doesn't advance the action, it does underscore a situation. They are almost Chekhovian, those slack periods when time merely passes, momentarily forestalling the inevitable.

EH: Surely the conversation, for all its randomness, should not be taken for ordinary speech. Lope has calculated his effects and drained off the incoherencies of everyday talk. The talk coruscates with false gems of poetic and learned allusiveness, going far beyond the customary practice of the period. The language suggests Lyly's *Euphues* or Burton's *Anatomy of Melancholy,* but certainly exceeds the affected idiom of Shakespeare's bookish fops in *Love's Labors Lost.*

AT: Density of allusion brings up again the subject of rhetoric. Actually, we've been discussing a more superficial kind of rhetoric: talk strewn with exempla and sententious sayings, with tags and anecdotes from ancient and modern writers—"wise saws and modern instances"—and a tendency to manipulate exotic and recondite lore and the toss-away allusion to myth or history. It's a kind of humanistic name-dropping.

EH: So the idiom is set up mainly for show, ornamental display, quick laughs. Call it part of the baggage of would-be literati and intellectuals. Fernando is both poet and, along with Julio, a "perpetual student," and what they spout is learning that has lost its bearings.

AT: It's also Lope indulging a foible of his own—the patter that smacks of one-upmanship. Characters vie at showing off what they know, how well-versed they are in all the canonical authors and many others besides. They disdain the tried and true; they want to shine and dazzle. And Fernando is much more adept at the game than his rival, Don Bela, the difference being as marked as the disparity of their wordly fortunes.

EH: Doesn't Lope also go in for rhetoric at crucial moments? There's that occasion again (act I, scene 4) when Julio coaxes Fernando's dream out of him by invoking a battery of authorities and curiosities at every stage of the process. Fernando is both exasperated and flattered at Julio's overplaying, and you can feel a fine edge of authorial irony in the sequence.

AT: The basic mechanism at work is a shuttling between the particular and the general. I say "mechanism" because the usual humanist recourse to ancient paragons for guidance is here faltering. The paradigms no longer furnish ideal role models; they have lost their drive and turn into reflex actions in pursuit of self-enhancement. The characters go through the forms—at times feverishly—but the values have faded away.

EH: Is it because what's missing, except in certain key moments of authenticity and insight, is a genuine code of moral conduct?

AT: Yet it's here precisely that Lope's resourcefulness emerges—in the constant variation in the shifting between the specific present and the established generality. Remember Dorotea's distraught contention with Celia (act II, scene 2): will Fernando in Seville find that absence makes the heart grow fonder, or will it be out of sight, out of mind? Only the matter is not put in terms of simple adages. It turns into a debate on who are more inconstant, men or women. Camoëns, Petrarch and Laura, the river Lethe, Arabic etymologies, a series of pastoral heroines, the Minotaur, are all drawn in willy-nilly. Dorotea keeps coming back to the assertion that, as far as she and Fernando are concerned, none of Celia's generalities holds. Even the repeated arguments between Gerarda and Teodora show a similar casuistry.

EH: Displays of virtuosity, tours de force, are what they come down to, all leading to the ludic aspect of *La Dorotea*. What may seem mere virtuosity ultimately sets serious limits on the all-absorbing erotic and literary games. While these in the end are the limits prescribed by God, the Christian backdrop is only occasionally glimpsed. The game palls of itself. Remember what you said before, Alan, about slack periods when time merely passes. This is human time—time felt in one's bones; it produces an effect of sameness, fatigue, overripeness, decay. However earnestly the game has been played, however high the stakes, the players are eventually worn down. The moments of lucidity, when they see through it all, grow more frequent, making it harder to go on. Gerarda has seen through it from the beginning, though her gusto shows no signs of abating until the last act.

AT: Once you realize time is the enemy, you understand why Lope has taken such pains with chronometry. The time of day and the time of year—clock and calendar time—are always in the characters' consciousness, as their words so often remind us. We are thus able to gauge the subjective experience of time's slowed or accelerated passage—or even its coming to a standstill.

EH: Isn't this related to their wish to deny time's passage? "It takes so little away each day, you're not aware of it," says Don Bela. But if you look closely, you can see dust on the furniture, the undone housework, the meat gone bad—all the little touches of *tempus fugit*.

AT: Such acuity is the fruit of the last years, not the youth, of the author. It's hardly by chance that the oldest character, Gerarda, is the most aware of passing time.

EH: She is and she isn't. I mean, she readily tosses off the go-between's typical injunction to gather ye rosebuds—and with a new twist each time. She also looks warily toward the hereafter, and thinks nothing of putting exhortations and pieties to work for her. All this suggests that Gerarda's perceptions of time and mortality are merely epidermic. They never dampen her spirits.

AT: It also suggests some special affinity between Gerarda and her creator. I'd say Gerarda is both the play-spirit in Lope and his yea-saying to life.

EH: And add that his own visceral awareness of life's evanescence catches up with Gerarda only just in time to ensure her salvation.

AT: Yes, Lope indulges her to the end; her accidental death will not mean hellfire. In his eyes her sins are peccadillos. In his own crowded love life he never needed a go-between. Could he really take one seriously?

EH: Gerarda appears innocuous compared to that distant forebear of hers, Celestina, and that bawd's chilling power to bend others to her corrupt will. Certainly Gerarda corrupts no one; everyone's in on the game.

AT: The most you can say is that she is a convenience, a furtherer of plot—what little there is. She opens the way for Don Bela's wealth to work on the only too susceptible Dorotea. Beyond that, she embodies the ebullience of Lope's own spirit.

EH: We've moved into the realm of characterization with our high-spirited Gerarda and weak-willed Dorotea. Curious we should begin with Gerarda, the one character of any importance who is a free-floater—I mean, who presumably did not originate in Lope's private life.

AT: Not so curious, really. The other side of it is that in responding to her gratuitousness, we realize he needed her for rounding out his testament with his own enduring traits. Though I suppose that makes it all sound too neatly intentional.

EH: Put it as you will, it's hard to separate the characters, the kind of nature Lope endows them with, from their assigned roles in the overall design. He has moved away from the living prototypes toward characterization growing out of the work itself. In discussing the characters let's remember these three aspects—the roots, the design, and what they express of Lope, their overlord.

AT: What about his tendency to pair them off? Teodora and Gerarda, like two peas in a pod, are actually versions of one type—the go-between as mother. The only trace of the social distance that traditionally obtains is that Gerarda's daughter, Felipa, is also Dorotea's maidservant. The linking of the mothers may have to do with the fact that in Lope's libelous poems Inés Osorio, Elena's mother, is charged with acting as procuress for her daughter. In shifting such activities to Gerarda, created out of literary whole cloth, Lope has not entirely dissociated them from the maternal figure, who thus can be both a sparring partner for her crony and her intramural collaborator.

EH: Meanwhile Felipa and Dorotea collaborate to thwart their mothers and promote the reconciliation with Fernando. For that matter, this figure of the maidservant is itself duplicated, as Felipa keeps vying with Celia for Dorotea's favor.

AT: So the pairing device involves rivalry as well as collaboration. In either case the biographical roots of the affair lead Lope away from the conventions of his stage. There, where the social distinctions are more clearly marked, no mother actually appears, let alone one so receptive to a go-between. In fact, the go-between rarely shows up on Lope's stage.

EH: Although, in giving each of the principals a domestic as a sounding board and facilitator of the intrigue, Lope follows a convention going back to Plautus and Terence, maybe even farther, to the Attic New Comedy. Also, as far forward as Henry James, who notably provides his heroes with female interlocutors he calls *ficelles*.

AT: But again, the social relationships are blurred. You see Laurencio, Don Bela's servant, pushing his way up from menial to friend—and being pushed down again. In Julio you have a rather special *servus fidus* whose wit and learning rival his younger master's; who, despite a pedantic streak, plays the tough deflator; who can draw tears from his master when he recites verse—and even turn a fair sonnet himself.

EH: There are probably traces in the secondary figures of actual persons in Lope's entourage during the 1580's. Take the soubrettes. Each stands out

distinctly: Celia touchy, sulky, and envious; Felipa pert, forward, witty;
Marfisa's servant, Clara, often bizarrely caustic.

AT: The far sharper relief in which the four principals are cast does
surely point to actual prototypes in Lope's past . . .

EH: Even if, as the characters now appear, subsequent experience and literary practice have refashioned them. Take Marfisa: no one has ever been
able to come up with an actual prototype, though some woman of forceful
character and emotional intensity must survive in her. She's blunt and direct, honest with herself, and presents almost no façade to others. Though
spurned by Fernando, she remains constant, without loss of dignity. Emotions just beneath the surface are always ready to flare up—remember the
excoriation of Fernando in act IV.

AT: All in sharp contrast with the picture of Dorotea. The pairing
through opposition underscores the differing appeal of the two women.
Marfisa's love is steadfast and quasi-matrimonial, and not as Dorotea's is,
maternal.

EH: Dorotea's temperament is not so easily described. It's a matter of "I
have been faithful to thee, Cynara, in my own fashion." She obviously
never stops loving Fernando, yet cannot withstand the pressure to accede
to Don Bela.

AT: Still, you don't feel that Lope censures her for it. The first four
scenes of the opening act, as well as Fernando's version of events (act IV,
scene 1), show plainly that she has resisted all kinds of pressure for five
years, and even demeaned herself to the point of materially supporting her
young lover.

EH: Yes, Lope is remarkably understanding of this last avatar of the
Elena who had once roused his fury and provoked his scurrilous denuncia-
tion. But when the picture is complete and she is reconciled with Fernando
she remains compromised by her inability to give up Don Bela.

AT: Compromised perhaps in Fernando's eyes, not in Lope's. You sense
that the act of creating her has exorcised any lingering bitterness. He has
lavished attention on her as on no other character. She is never far from
center stage. When not physically present, she is in the thoughts of
others—thoughts which provide a series of physical and moral portraits of
Dorotea. We know what she looks like, her mannerisms, her ways of
reacting—the sensitivity beneath the sometimes aggressive exterior. She is
bold in laugh and look, forward in initiating the affair with Fernando and
reckless in the confrontation which ends it so bitterly. Traits of Elena
Osorio as she appears in the documents surive in the picture, even in the
suggestions of Dorotea's "remarkable mind" and literary aspirations.

EH: And her artistic accomplishments recall Lope's last mistress, Marta de Nevares. It is not just that these biographical strains show through but that Lope intends to make Dorotea a more idealized figure, a courtesan of refinement.

AT: Would "courtesan" be the word for someone whose love exacts such continual self-sacrifice?

EH: I mean a courtesan on the Italian Renaissance model or the *hetaira* of antiquity. She may live for love but her highest values are feeling and imagination, like the heroine of Thornton Wilder's *Woman of Andros*. Fernando lifts her above her tawdry surroundings by re-creating her life poetically as part of his own. That gives him his hold over her.

AT: Besides her indecisiveness, she is also morally obtuse and never understands how taking up with Don Bela can offend Fernando. Being irresolute and insecure, she doesn't command events or even take advantage of them; events overtake her.

EH: The picture is rich in nuance. Vulnerability adds to her humanity and keeps her within reach of the reader. But how are we really to think of her in relation to Lope?

AT: The eternal feminine. She embodies the appeal of particular women who have come and gone in his life. Like Goethe, too, he tended to view woman as a mothering force, a supporter of poetic genius.

EH: If not his muse, then the object of the cult of the poet.

AT: She incites to love and to poetry because she is beautiful. But the beauty is ephemeral and particular despite Fernando's attempts to proclaim it eternal and ideal. It exists in time, the only medium in which it can be sensually enjoyed. Being transitory, it fades, as Fernando ultimately acknowledges. In Dorotea Lope has symbolized the beauty of this world— the world of nature and of art—as he now feels it, slipping through his fingers.

EH: Isn't there some distinction here between a beauty whose fading one experiences, and a beauty that may not be fading but simply ceases to be accessible?

AT: A fine point—the distinction corresponds to the distance between the young Fernando's experience of Dorotea and his aging creator's perspective on her. Fernando loses a mistress to whom he has become indifferent; Lope is losing a world that has not ceased to appeal. The distance helps account for the surprising fact that Lope as a creator stands farther away from Fernando, the persona of his youthful self, than from any other major figure of *La Dorotea*.

EH: "Stands farther away"?

AT: I mean that Fernando is the character into whom Lope has entered least empathically, a circumstance which he even seems to underscore on occasion. The first selection sung by Fernando (act I, scene 4), "To solitude I go," is expressly introduced as "a ballad of Lope's." Julio is surprised that his young master should sing something that we know stems from the mature Lope's melancholy.

EH: You could say the same thing of the two "piscatory idylls" which Julio recites in act III, scene 1. He presents them as written by "a gentleman you know who has lost his lady," that is, the Lope of 1632 mourning Marta de Nevares. Didn't she die shortly before *La Dorotea* was submitted for the censor's approval?

AT: Yes, just a month. Lope apparently did not want Fernando meddling in that sorrow. So he presents him totally absorbed in Dorotea's disaffection.

EH: But what about those mixed feelings you spoke of when we began? There's no denying that, whatever the distancing, Lope is reflecting in Fernando certain of his own permanent traits—egotism, impulsiveness, a histrionic streak, insecurity, subservience to power and rank, and so on.

AT: You've left out the most important—morbidly possessive jealousy. But you're right, of course. Lope is far from eschewing links with his own temperament.

EH: Don't you think there's a confessional psychology at work sometimes? You can imagine the old Lope, having taken holy orders, wanting to make a clean breast at last of his base behavior with Elena Osorio. Think of the instance when Fernando surreptitiously accepts some of the take from Dorotea's connection with his wealthy rival. The specificity of detail is hard to account for otherwise.

AT: If I stress the distancing, it's in reaction to much of the earlier criticism which read *La Dorotea* as straight autobiography. Actually Fernando is less Lope's self-portrait of the poet as a young man than of the young man as poet. Lope pushes to extremes both the youthfulness and the poetic profession, expressly confusing the rival claims of living and creating that he managed to reconcile in his own life. Fernando subordinates experience to expression, or confounds the two, as Lope had never done. As we have said, poetry is the center of his being and the basis of his appeal to Dorotea, though it is no match for Don Bela's gold as a source of livelihood, and Fernando has no other. Lope did have his marketable plays and his secretaryships to nobles. In this reshaping of the original experience, we see a deeper interest: probing the interaction between vital and aesthetic experience, which has become central to Lope's own *poiesis*. Fernando's embracing of art as a vicarious form of experience deliberately overstates the question now fundamental to Lope: how in fact does experience become poetry and can poetry be taken as a more compelling form of experience?

EH: Lope surely knows the answer in advance.

AT: No doubt, but this does not relieve his need to work through to it.

EH: I suppose you could say, then, that in making Fernando four or five years younger than himself when the *éducation sentimentale* began—seventeen as against twenty-one—Lope is widening the distance between them.

AT: I think so, although I would not say he sets out to increase the distance. Rather, he discovers how unbridgeable the gap is—greater than with any of the other characters.

EH: I don't find this so surprising. A person writing an autobiography knows that in delving into the past, the self proves harder to recover than the figures surrounding it. The memory retains some semblance of these figures as originally perceived—that is, from without. To rediscover whatever remains in him of Fernando, Lope must plumb his deepest self; this is a far harder task. And it is in fact what allows him now, the old dramatist, to view Fernando largely from without. The result is a mixture of incredulity and amusement: Fernando treated more ironically than any other character. He doesn't have to avoid partiality toward Fernando; the temptation just isn't there.

AT: In fact, he goes to the other extreme. He relishes overwriting the part of Fernando, who in the course of the action proves frivolous, vain and touchy, unprincipled, narcissistic, moody. His jealousy today would be called neurotic.

EH: In any case, if *La Dorotea* embodies Lope's late conception of the workings of love, that view is certainly more sympathetic to the woman than to the man.

AT: Yes, whether the woman is Dorotea or Marfisa. It's a point we should return to. But we haven't yet considered possible links between Lope and Don Bela.

EH: Let's first determine Lope's attitude toward the figure who stands for his onetime rival. Why should Don Bela be the only character to show some moral growth? When last seen (act V, scenes 1 and 2), he appears distinct from the person we left at the end of act III huffily crossing swords with Fernando.

AT: It's true. Earlier he was the fatuous nouveau riche trying to establish himself at court and buy his way to preferment, and not failing to display a beautiful mistress.

EH: And yet by act V, having fallen deeply in love with her, he struggles to extricate himself, in his own way, from the labyrinth of carnal desire. How? By ascending the Neo-Platonic ladder of love. That is the burden of his newly composed madrigal and his earnest explication of it to Laurencio.

AT: One might imagine that Lope's old hostility toward his powerful rival, Perrenot de Granvela, still colors the Don Bela of the earlier acts. But more probably, with nothing personal at stake, Lope is now showing up Don Bela's inadequacies in order to prepare the ground for his seeing the light.

EH: So the distance between earlier and later is less emphatic than it seems. Perhaps there's an echo here of Lope's own experience with Marta de Nevares. Lope would have sympathized with Don Bela for having to put up with a younger rival, though with Marta the rival happened to be her husband, while Lope was an ordained priest. And with an urgency on which Don Bela's is patterned, Lope had eventually tried to model his love for her on the Neo-Platonic ideal, a recurrent subject of his compositions in the 1620's.

AT: External factors help us see the shift in perspective. But one must still ask whether the shift is internally plausible and whether it serves an artistic function in the design of the work.

EH: The two questions are not quite the same. I'd say yes to both, though. If you think of Don Bela in the earlier acts, you can make out under the complacent surface indications that he's not the simpleton the others play him for. There's a simple strain of decency in him anticipating the developments of act V. This attribute builds into the work an alternative to Fernando's egotism. Young Fernando is certainly no candidate for growth of this kind. If in the end *he* decides to exchange letters (and love) for arms, and to join the Armada against England, it's the need for respite that drives him, not any change of heart. But Don Bela's examination of conscience precipitates a fit of melancholy, like those Lope himself suffered in later years. The sublimation sought through Neo-Platonic harmony— the dazzling vision attained in his madrigal—has brought only temporary relief, as the dialogue surrounding the poem makes clear (act V, scene 1). Still, Don Bela is spared a fate Lope had himself so greatly feared—dying before his conscience was clear and atonement for every sin in the offing. Lope makes Don Bela's death a deliverance by assuring that it does not catch him unconfessed. Don Bela is genuinely contrite, and, the last time we see him, he is bound for Mass. When we hear of his murder, we know he has died in a state of grace.

AT: So Don Bela is led to God by the orthodox route, yet the Neo-Platonic way is not thereby eliminated.

EH: And with Don Bela aspiring to love Dorotea Platonically, as Lope had ultimately loved Marta de Nevares, worldliness is crowned with spirituality. At least some note of this sort does complement the clearly non-tragic tone of the work's ending.

AT: Looked at another way, Lope is broadening the action of *La Dorotea* so that it spans a lifetime of experience in love. The urge to take in his full seventy years would account for his intruding the story of Fernando's earlier life (act IV, scene 1) and the horoscope of his future (act V, scene 8). As Lope implies in the Prologue, he is turning into poetry the history of his life. As for the non-tragic ending, Laurencio's overplayed announcement of Don Bela's death and Celia's awful quips regarding Gerarda's accident strongly suggest that neither by impulse nor temperament do the characters fit Lope's understanding of tragedy. Even so, it is curious that the two lives snuffed out so casually should be those of the characters physically closest to the author.

EH: Is it really so curious? Isn't Lope saying something about his own mortality in this dispensation? He doesn't grant them the spare time he himself enjoyed following the crises of his later years. Some lines in his "Eclogue [i.e., Epistle] to Claudio"—his lifelong friend, Claudio Conde—shed light on the whole question, particularly as this retrospective poem is contemporaneous with *La Dorotea*. Lope, you remember, tells his friend that, as he goes down the path to death, his thoughts center on the afterlife. To this he wryly adds: "I have never yet seen anyone live hereafter who did not die before he died." The epistle concludes: "Begone, hope, if ever I had any: for I no longer have need of fortune." So what do you think is being expressed here if not . . .

AT: Gratification at self-survival: God has allowed him enough time. Whatever remains will be a welcome bonus, but neither sought after nor needed.

EH: And so to deprive Don Bela and Gerarda of such a bonus is not depriving them of anything essential. The trivial ways they die accord with the everyday character of the world they live in. Such deaths bring the work to the only kind of stopping point possible. They bring to a halt yet do not violate the artistic process of winding down that goes on in the fifth act. Anything more solemn would have been out of place.

AT: Well, if that illustrates some of the interweavings of life and art, I'd like to look more closely at Laurencio's overplaying the announcement of Don Bela's death. This might be a good way of going on to matters of style.

EH: Go ahead, Alan.

AT: Laurencio, you remember, actually calls himself a "tragic and luckless messenger ['nuncio,' *nuntius*], with more reason to weep than in Seneca's *Hippolytus.*" In the offstage world of the "action in prose" (where literary posturing is nevertheless the rule), such zealous role playing, especially by a menial, is still ludicrously inappropriate. Laurencio's histrionics outdo Seneca's grandiloquence, impelling Dorotea and Gerarda to join the act with their copious tears. When Laurencio blurts out the naked truth, the top-heavy rhetorical structure collapses and we are at the beginning of the end of that world. When Gerarda falls noisily down the stairs to her death, Celia overplays the deflationary servant-wisecracker as insistently as Laurencio hams up the tragic messenger.

EH: So then what is Lope getting at?

AT: First, he intends to end in a buoyantly spirited coda, without tears—in "upbeat" fashion. Second (to move beyond our original point), there is the usual disjoining of style from decorum, which here functions presentationally.

EH: What?

AT: I mean that style becomes a signifier in its own right. It underscores the sense of the action, here the toppling and breakup of the characters' world, just as earlier the upsurgings of rhetoric had signified their intimate aspiration to live in a high poetical fashion.

EH: Then you could also say that the impending fragmentation has been built formally into the scenic structure of the last act, since, unlike the others, this act is a succession of tenuously connected scenes, eleven in fact, mostly brief. And behind Gerarda's unexpected reproof of Laurencio's overplaying, I can also see an author breaking in to plead for a sounder, more natural stylistic norm: "words . . . without tears, feelings without sobs."

AT: Yes, the statement climaxes many such flashes of lucidity throughout the work.

EH: Is it enough to call these "flashes" interventions of Lope? Appropriating characters as masks for himself goes beyond stylistic considerations. He seems to be signaling us here that language and rhetoric, word- and thought-patterns, collectively constitute a distinct persona, a silent character in the work behind which stands the authorial craftsman. We feel an autonomous presence embracing all the characters in their ludic habit of mind, feeding on and playing with words as subterfuges for emotions.

AT: I have always felt that the craft of literature, both in itself and in relation to living, is a principal subject of *La Dorotea*. And there is more to be said on this subject than anyone has said so far, so go ahead. Perhaps we can pin the matter down more precisely.

EH: Persona might be seen as a way of raising or lowering one's perception of character. To impersonate is to muffle a sense that the tragic or comic aspect of things is what's most important. We can say, can't we, that in *La Dorotea* the characters' helplessness in action is the obverse of their inventiveness in language. And, if so, it would be missing the point to claim that there is not enough action in this action in prose, because the fact is that the action occurs in the sphere of language. Speech style is not exclusively a function of character type. We are constantly aware of the self-generating energy of language. Since little of this is found in his stage plays, perhaps it points to another reason why Lope had to fashion a different kind of dramatic vehicle for *La Dorotea.* With rare exceptions—and I think of Ben Jonson and Jonathan Swift—dramatic interest in language for its own sake is highly uncommon before the Symbolists. It is not so uncommon in our century—think of Shaw, Beckett, Ionesco, and the others. Take Shaw: he may tend, in his plays, to fall back on stock melodrama, but he is constantly focusing on the language in which the characters explain their foibles. *Pygmalion* is only the most obvious example.

AT: But isn't Shaw's indulgence of language more ideological than stylistic—directed toward the social rather than the aesthetic ramifications of the characters' speech?

EH: The emphasis varies but the distinction isn't as sharp or significant as you suggest, Alan. Another case in point is James Joyce, a master of style, like Lope, in love with the whole ludic gamut of language. With him, too, persona takes over as an aspect of style. You could trace the evolution of linguistic and literary stylization from its beginnings in *Dubliners* to its culmination in *Finnegans Wake,* where all language, down to the smallest syllable, becomes a momentous character. The example may have something to tell us about Lope's linguistic maneuverings.

AT: What shall we name the phenomenon? How about logomorphism—by analogy with anthropomorphism?

EH: At the rate we are going, we may well need the term.

AT: To return to *La Dorotea,* the two opening scenes convince us that words have a life of their own. As bawd, Gerarda is the literary sophisticate of all time, though in point of fact she's illiterate. She soaks up words wherever she goes, along with the poetic and learned paraphernalia that sets them off.

EH: Soaking is what she does, all right. Remember how Lope blends the go-between's characteristic thirst for wine with Gerarda's peculiar fondness for words (act I, scene 7). Teodora remarks on Gerarda's use both of obsolete terms and of modish jargon: "Our language has become a brew of white and red vintages," says Gerarda. There's logomorphism for you!

AT: Teodora in scene 2 flings Dorotea's terms *literally* and *ironies* back at her like worthless coins picked up from her impoverished lover-poet.

EH: It's an early hint of a contest already under way between poetry and gold, which runs right through the work.

AT: Gold and poetry, that is, materialism and art: the very dilemma which the impecunious Lope had felt in his bones. Its ubiquity in *La Dorotea* needs no pointing up by us. The fact is that this conflict also facilitates the role of language as a persona. Being basically inert, gold and diamonds make the vital life of poetry stand out more sharply.

EH: From the moment Fernando is upset by a dream (act I, scene 4), you realize that the contest is already staked out between the New World Spaniard's precious metals and fabrics and Fernando's precious words and rhetorical riches. Gerarda in the following act makes herself Don Bela's speech coach, finding his "hyperboles and *enargias*" as exotic as "bananas and alligator pears." By the end of Don Bela's first visit, his sallies and bons mots, however rough-hewn, have supplied the margin of victory in winning Dorotea. Now she even avows she'll be obliged to regard his love as pure poetry.

AT: Words lull her away from realities.

EH: Even though Don Bela's heavy-handed wooing can't stand up to Fernando's agility with words. Language had everywhere intervened to seal the relationship of the indigent Fernando and the logophilic Dorotea. Remember his account of their affair (act IV, scene 1) and her self-confrontation (act I, scene 3). He relates how she sacrificed for him the gifts of former lovers and how in his mawkish frustration at "being unable to cover those lovely hands with diamonds, I bathed them in tears, which she deemed finer stones for rings than those she had scorned and sold." She does her best to live up to his hyperboles by giving substance to the conceit that equates sparkling tears with the sparkle of diamonds.

AT: It is only too plain that their willful confounding of poetry with materiality is bound to come to grief.

EH: Meanwhile, every character carries his own version of the poetic idiom beyond anything found in Lope's dramatic production.

AT: Lope does not actually discard the typology of his stage plays; he moves beyond it.

EH: Seeing language in the context of the speech and behavior peculiar to the individual enables you to pin down personal variations from the start. Take Fernando: his cool histrionic sensibility goes with an obstinately poetic attitude and diction. These traits show up in his cadenced responses to Dorotea's visit and her fainting fit (act I, scene 5), and again in his expertly staged deception of Marfisa (scene 6). Both scenes demonstrate Fernando's verbal sway over the two women in love with him. When each rises to the occasion, she dovetails her response to his rhetoric, though neither can equal his chilly detachment. Dorotea's sympathetic nature makes her rhetoric poignant. Marfisa, though less prone to self-delusion, still allows herself to be taken in.

AT: Not completely, or rather not immediately. Before succumbing, she notes the overdone performance, the inflated poetic diction. But once her emotions are engaged, she does fall right in with Fernando's verbal pyrotechnics. Unlike Dorotea, she is all of a piece: beautifully clear-sighted and blunt at one moment, totally swept away the next. And unlike Dorotea, again, she never plays for effect.

EH: How about Don Bela? His style isn't hard to pin down, is it?

AT: He's the clumsy outsider in this charmed circle, as we've seen. Only his largesse lets Dorotea overlook the inadequacies shown at their first meeting. Lope underscores the rivals' differences in style when they woo her at her window.

EH: I'm struck by Don Bela's viewing metaphorical riches as if they were real, and pouncing on conceits as if they were possessions. You might say he deconstructs standard metaphors. He has no faith in sumptuary imagery unless backed by real gold, diamonds, and rubies. It turns out that Dorotea needn't shut her eyes or ears to anything. For all his verbal shortcomings, he manages to use words as catalysts for his gifts.

AT: We are back to the viability of language as persona. But we've yet to mention the scenes where preoccupation with language takes over as an issue in its own right.

EH: You mean the session of the literary "academy" (act IV, scenes 2 and 3), when Fernando's friends comment on that cryptic sonnet.

AT: The sonnet is in the "new" *culto* idiom, which means that our silent character, language, gets embroiled in contemporary literary polemics. The term *culto* (cultured, cultivated) was appropriated to denote the practitioners and apologists of Góngora's Latinate style, and also the style or idiom itself. The attempt was to acculturate Spanish to the modus vivendi of the ancient languages. You might say the *cultos* prized cultured pearls over natural ones, while their adversaries—descendants of Petrarch—thought natural pearls had already refined the literary language sufficiently. What's more, they regarded the *cultos* as literary heretics and called them *culteranos,* on the analogy of *luteranos* (Lutherans). This term doesn't figure in *La Dorotea* but the implication is there when César speaks of "this new poetic religion."

EH: The climate of conformity during the Counter-Reformation would of course affect literary polemics.

AT: Lope had been feuding with the followers of Góngora and is now having one last go at them. Their way of putting Spanish on a par with Latin and Greek was to use Spanish lexicon, grammar, morphology, syntax, and so on, as if they were those of a classical language. The movement carried to an extreme point of Baroque artifice the naturalistic conventions of the Renaissance. In the major poems of Góngora—the *Soledades* (Solitudes) for instance—this brought dazzling results which both impressed and put off the uninitiated reader. Lope is a case in point. Though dazzled himself, he reacted adversely, seeing in this aesthetic a challenge to his own. He had never abandoned his Renaissance allegiance to nature as the supreme norm for art. His own literary language, rooted in the native rhythms and usages of the vernacular, was close enough to everyday speech to remain comprehensible.

EH: Which the sonnet is *not*. Fernando's literary chums aren't simply imitating the Gongorine style; they do a bizarre parody of it, deftly working in its stylistic clichés.

AT: Their running commentary also parodies the Gongorists, especially José Pellicer, who had published an annotated edition, in 1630, of Góngora's major poems, dubbing it "Solemn Readings." Solemnity of that sort Lope could not abide, and it provoked his ridicule no less than the sonnet does. What we have then is a parody of a parody.

EH: And no small hurdle for the reader! Oh these word-mongers! Remember Swift's *Tale of a Tub*. It presumably parodies an apologist of religious enthusiasm; but the nature of the material is so alien to readers who are neither divines nor hermeneutists that they are soon antagonized and give up. I hope our own readers have less trouble penetrating the bristly exterior and reaching the succulent comedy at the core of these scenes. The commentators go to work with such alacrity . . .

AT: You'd better say "go to play," because it's all a game played according to the letter of certain ridiculous rules. The ludic spirit of the whole work reaches some sort of apogee here.

EH: But with serious intent. As César remarks when Ludovico begs him to be less earnest: "As you please. But should some serious or scholarly matter turn up, you must forgive it [my earnestness]" (act IV, scene 2). Lope evidently takes the underlying issues to heart.

AT: Yes, we are given his own broader, more naturalistic understanding of *culto* as against that of Góngora and his followers. What starts as a spoof ends up as an airing of the literary questions, large and small, which Lope felt most strongly about. The controversy led him to serious reflection on the premises of his own art. And in mocking the monumental irrelevance and ostentation of the *cultos'* literary erudition, he seems aware that his own is not immune to criticism. You certainly feel that the helter-skelterness of the session is not uncongenial to his own way with learning.

EH: He lets himself go—doesn't he?—all the more because Góngora, whose learning awed him and whose devastating wit scared him, was safely dead by the time the scene was written. The sonnet, only just composed apparently, turns up in a letter of Lope's probably written in the summer of 1631, four years after Góngora's death. The impression is that the distinction he usually made between Góngora and the Gongorists—and makes obliquely on introducing the sonnet—grows more and more tenuous as the commentary proceeds.

AT: Yes, there are quite possibly jabs at Góngora himself. Whatever the case, it's clear that the academy scenes are not so adventitious as might appear. Through the reductive power of parody they crystallize the issue of art versus nature implicit in the entire action. Just as these scenes show that stylistic artifice may be reconciled with naturalness, so the whole action suggests that culture, as a refining force, should not lose touch with the original energies of nature.

EH: Can we move on, Alan, and say something about the persistent use of proverbs in *La Dorotea?* Wasn't it Erasmus who set the vogue by presenting the proverb as a distillation of natural wisdom, a practical guide to conduct? Here there is evidently a good deal of artifice in its usage. Many of Lope's proverbs are irrelevant, even incomprehensible. So is Lope again suggesting that there's a line to be drawn between extremes?

AT: Well, if so, not very seriously and mostly by reverse example. I think he is offering a *reductio ad absurdum* in stylizing: turning proverbs into artifacts just as he does other set forms of language—words, figures, tropes; indulging his inventiveness at the reader's expense.

EH: The tradition of the proverb-spouting bawd from *La Celestina* would be his point of departure. But while Celestina's proverbs are purposeful, a part of her arsenal, Gerarda's are bubbles on the surface of her garrulity.

AT: Since she embodies the ludic spirit, she is naturally the principal spouter of proverbs. And it's also remarkable how she infects the others. Teodora, Celia, Dorotea, Laurencio take them up in turn, bandy them about, engage in tradeoffs and endurance contests with her. This development is peculiar to Lope. We watch as he cavalierly undermines their raison d'être. The proverbs are like the exuberant tracery on the walls of those unbelievably ornate Baroque chapels.

EH: If Gerarda is the key to the ludic strain and the proverb, she is also the focal point of one more concern of Lope's.

AT: What's that, Edwin?

EH: The championing of women.

AT: We've already seen that Lope is closer to Dorotea and Marfisa, Fernando's victims, than to Fernando himself. His appreciation of their situation confirms the tendency of all his work to view the condition of women through women's eyes.

EH: That's true, and it's not just a literary stance, either, because the attitude shows up even in his private correspondence. As the Duke of Sessa's secretary he sometimes had to play pander, as we know. In a late letter Lope actually reproves the Duke for his callousness in summarily dropping a former mistress.

AT: Something approaching feminism is noticeable in other ways. It is there when Gerarda says (act V, scene 10) that because no other opening is allowed for women's "subtle minds," they concentrate on deceiving men.

EH: The remark suggests a certain natural solidarity among women in the face of the treatment they receive.

AT: On the other hand, the traditional male view is echoed often enough by Fernando and his companions. As for Lope himself, there is strong compassion for women as inveterate sufferers. Besides, the women in *La Dorotea,* as we have already said, do not accept their lot passively. They stand up for themselves: Dorotea most eloquently in her letter to Fernando (act III, scene 6), and Marfisa most powerfully in her confrontation of Fernando (act IV, scene 8).

EH: Even Celia's burlesque panegyric on the dead Gerarda, in the final scene, points out that as an expert at fleecing men Gerarda merely gave them their just deserts.

AT: Gerarda articulates the women's case. True, taken simply as a go-between she is something of a joke, and though she does cater to men's pleasure in women she always gives women the final word.

EH: We're back to Gerarda—and it's time we said more about her. In her gratuitousness, we've agreed, she practically becomes the author's surrogate. She turns up in every act, insinuates her opinions and advice into every conversation, making herself at home everywhere. Her versatility expresses Lope's many-sided nature. She absorbs all the vagrant energies around her and tries to focus them as an omniscient narrator might do.

AT: The author's sense of her as a literary type even allows her to act coy at times about her accomplishments as a bawd.

EH: The yea-sayer in her reminds me of Falstaff. Though almost never a central character, Falstaff's comic energies keep him at stage center wherever he appears. Both are timeless characters: Gerarda the high-spirited bawd, Falstaff the braggart soldier with a streak of the tragic in him.

AT: Gerarda clearly considers herself an entertainer—leaven for the more ponderous scenes.

EH: Though she can employ poetry tactically—I mean actual poems, not just a poetic idiom—she has no urge to compose it, reserving her verbal high jinks mainly for proverbs.

AT: Remember how she brings Dorotea a poem, purportedly written by Don Bela, to set the scene for his entrance (act II, scene 4).

EH: That's also one way Lope has of weaving poems into the dialogue.

AT: The poems figure so prominently, we should look at them more closely.

EH: My first question: why did he include so many?

AT: A quick answer: he had them on hand and needed a ready outlet. Most of them stem from his later years, having been written mainly for Marta de Nevares, the Amaryllis so often mentioned. Putting them into *La Dorotea* memorializes his love for this last mistress—pointedly elegiac in the four long boat-ballads of the third act. Other poems appear to reflect phases of the relationship—courtship, separation, jealousy, and, in the case of Don Bela's madrigal, a yearning for Neo-Platonic sublimation.

EH: To weave Marta so many times into a work built around the first love affair of his life requires some dexterity. Rather than try to hide the seams, Lope blandly lets them show.

AT: Yes, he turns potential defects to advantage by working listeners' responses into the dialogue surrounding the boat-ballads (act III, scenes 1, 7, 8). Fernando envies the forlorn lover in contrast to himself, the forsaken lover. At the end of the act Dorotea's jealousy is inflamed by the thought that the Amaryllis of Fernando's song is a new love of his. Since the lady in question is clearly dead, the supposition is irrational—but such, we are made to feel, is the nature of jealousy.

EH: Later Lope turns the disparity between the two loves into a laughing matter. Remember Clara's naive question (act IV, scene 8), after Marfisa reads her a poem of Fernando's, mentioning Amaryllis: "But tell me, ma'am, since when has this lady been called Amaryllis? Dorotilis is what he should have said. You being Marfisa, the name Amaryllis was always reserved for you." All of which only confuses things further, since, whoever Marfisa may once have been, she was surely not Marta de Nevares. Lope may not actually be throwing the reader off the track but he's not beyond having his joke at the reader's expense.

AT: Another way of fitting in the lyric poems is to have a few mementos from early in the affair turn up among the lovers' papers. This way the poems supplement the action with glimpses spanning the affair during its full five-year course. One is reminded of the flashback in modern films.

EH: This may be subtler. The poems highlight with great visual immediacy scenes out of the lovers' past converted into pastoral and Petrarchan stylization of the actual past. Hence the poems embody an idealized world where the lovers can take refuge with an impunity denied them in their everyday lives.

AT: Speaking of pastoral, it was in the "shepherd books," in vogue since the mid-sixteenth century, that Lope found a precedent for setting lyrics in a prose work. The connecting link is his own pastoral, *La Arcadia* (1598). But in pastoral romances the ability to sing, play, and improvise verse is automatically given every inhabitant of Arcadia. In the Madrid of *La Dorotea,* on the other hand, it becomes an attainment of particular individuals, and the instruments themselves are more refined: Dorotea's harp and spinet, for example, or Fernando's "classical" guitar. As for poetic composition, that of course is the prerogative of Fernando. But as we have seen, Don Bela and Julio—not to mention Dorotea—can achieve it on occasion. And all the characters except Don Bela prove to be connoisseurs of poetry and music, and aficionados of painting and *objets d'art,* reflecting incidentally, without pose or artifice, Lope's own taste.

AT: It's clear, then, that Lope goes well beyond the usual rationale for inserting poems in prose works: that is, to give pleasure through variety and to afford a respite from *longueurs,* reasons he mentions in his Preface.

EH: Has it ever struck you, Alan, that the most impressive poems are given to Don Bela, Dorotea, and others, while those of Fernando, *the* poet, though more numerous, are of no exceptional quality? He's evidently facile, rhetorically skilled, and competent, but nothing more.

AT: A description which does not fit Lope himself—another instance of the gap between youthful protagonist and old creator.

EH: We've been stressing, from the beginning, the many-sidedness of *La Dorotea* in substance and form. Perhaps we should begin to think of it as an organic whole. Multifariousness does not mean heterogeneity; inclusiveness is the formative principle.

AT: Yes, the whole becomes more than the sum of its parts. You have the conventions, with the generic and specific technical features we've been discussing. What Lope does by making them interact is to leave them free to seek a new and more appropriate form. Pastoral conventions are reenergized through entering the lives of these city dwellers. Senecan drama, which never produced anything vital in Spain, gains new life in this vaguely middle-class milieu. The new way of integrating verse with prose outdoes the rather perfunctory manner in which the two are combined in purely narrative forms.

EH: What does it all add up to?

AT: Well, the slight action, being entirely a falling one, is set at odds with the formality of the external classic framework. The disparity points up the incongruity between the aspiration to a stylized order of living and the shabbiness of the agents, bound by everyday laws of time, space, and causality.

EH: Isn't this a case of tragedy being made to touch base in ordinary living, where it immediately ceases to be such?

AT: Well, we haven't quite hit the age when Melpomene takes note of the death of a salesman.

EH: Yes, I know, but I am speaking broadly to make a point. Take the choruses at the end of each act. Ostensibly offering grave injunctions against love, cupidity, jealousy, revenge, at first glance they appear distinctly out of place. But then you find solemnity undercut by a note of expediency, the tone of Ovid's *Art of Love* and *Cures for Love*. The warnings Lope is giving are based on practical experience—his own, of course—devoid of genuinely moral, let alone Christian, overtones.

AT: Isn't that the old wisecracking voice of his stage plays surfacing again? You know, sometimes *La Dorotea* affects me like Ravel's *La Valse*. You begin in what seems a world of familiar, reliable conventions and mores—like the Vienna of Johann Strauss—where you can count on everything reaching some harmonious resolution, and then precisely the opposite happens. Everything goes awry with dissonance, things fall apart, and the whirling grows feverish, as that charmed world disintegrates before your eyes . . .

EH: Or ears. Good point. The world that disintegrates is a more private one in *La Dorotea,* with signs of collapse visible from the start. And the ending somehow has less finality.

AT: The analogy may help define the differences. You feel at the end that the air has cleared and that life will go on willy-nilly as before. Fernando goes off to join the Armada, Dorotea is left to accept the inevitable. And if the choruses do not truly edify, one glimpses beyond them just enough of what we've called the backdrop of Christian verities to mitigate the pathos of the ending. Earlier, in the final act, César summons Fernando to Mass to ask for God's divine assistance in mending his ways. His *memento mori*—"Consider how many friends of yours have died, so many of your own age"—strikes a sudden note of gravity. It anticipates the concluding Senecan admonition, more Lope's than Laurencio's: "Nothing is less certain than knowing where death will overtake us nor anything wiser than expecting it everywhere."

EH: Remember the similar forebodings from the beginning—those lines of Fernando's ballad: "The world we live in cannot last,/they say—that's true undoubtedly;/it rings like shattering glass/about to break in bits" (act I, scene 4). Then recall other lines from the ballad where Lope, who is expressly identified as author, excoriates the venality and opportunism of his age, something he rarely does elsewhere. So you might say that the disillusionment—*desengaño*—evoked is not just personal and religious, but has social and secular implications. Along with life's fragility and the ephemerality of men and women, it suggests how flawed human institutions and values have become. It also lets us see that the resilience of the spirit prevailing in *La Dorotea* is hard won; it is nothing Lope takes for granted.

AT: Lope wants to set the microcosm of *La Dorotea*—its cherished frivolity and pathos—against that divine truth beyond the limits of worldly games.

EH: We began by discussing what Lope's irony is made of. Maybe we can now see how it affects all the qualities that make *La Dorotea* a masterwork. Keeping Cervantes' masterpiece in mind for comparison, should we say that irony limits or that it liberates the author in composing this unprecedented memoir of the self? If irony *is* the key to Lope's accomplishment, how do its effects on the action differ from those observable in *Don Quixote?*

AT: Granted, the main force of each work is its irony. Still, there can be no question that the range of Lope's vision is more restricted than Cervantes'. Ultimately the lyric temper which shapes Lope's expression makes *La Dorotea* a work conditioned more by sensibility than intellect. It is in the quality of feeling which Lope infuses into the artistic cosmos that he makes his appeal to the reader properly attuned.

EH: What do you mean, "properly attuned"?

AT: I mean possessing the ability to penetrate the cultural idiom of the Baroque without being put off by its pyrotechnics, arabesques, and bristliness.

EH: As against the Cervantes of *Don Quixote,* I see Lope here as a different sort of chronicler of the age. In his fondness for invoking the mores and minutia of his times, Lope brings to mind the furnishings of the naturalistic novel of the later nineteenth century—and even Joyce's *Dubliners.* A chronicler of this sort gives social overtones to the voices of his characters and, like Lope, takes particular interest not only in the news of the day, but in customs and, especially, language. You know, everything the wind blows in from the New World, what's afoot at Court, who is staking a claim to what, the fashionable speech and bons mots. The universe of *La Dorotea* always somehow takes the active world into account, but makes its presence felt somewhere outside, like noises and shouts from the street.

AT: True enough, but for me what really stands out is Lope's stake in this artistic universe. Lope is impelled to come to grips with his own traumatic experience, to transcend and make it over: is impelled, that is, not only by thoughts of literary fame but by an urge to convey the very taste of life—his living—the sweet and the bitter. This is not what Cervantes set out to do in *Don Quixote,* though in effect he achieved as much and more. In Lope, the motivation is unmistakable from the start.

EH: Was Lope trying simply to please himself, in his own way and in his own good time? If so, the difference would be that Cervantes is a novelist with a story to tell, which draws him on and on, even if he is not at first sure who will listen . . .

AT: Yes, the central narrative is the seam binding the whole together from beginning to end.

EH: Then each work fulfills, with the originality that marks a lasting achievement, the creator's most intimate destiny, the *Dichtung und Wahrheit* of a lifetime.

AT: In Lope with more premeditation, in Cervantes with less.

EH: What makes for the two different readings of the age? Cervantes' is evidently a tale of the open road, inns, plains and forests, villages and country manors. The innumerable characters we meet from the greater world, from city and Court, being individuals in transit, reveal themselves in their central, their unconditional humanity. The world of Lope's characters, though only on the fringes of Court society, everywhere reflects its atmosphere and conveys the feel of city life surrounding the Court. Lope reveals the hold it has on its inhabitants, its worldliness, its ceremoniousness, its pettiness and gossip, the urban details which stamp it, its linguistic sophistication and artistic rivalries. We are not drawn in from outside that world, as in the paintings of Velázquez; we are witnessing from the inside the tensions between the unusual liberty of individual lives and the pressures of the social milieu. In the process, we observe the Spaniard's inclination toward love of spectacle, ornament, and display, abiding formalisms in public and private spheres and in verbal discourse. These traits dominate but do not overcome proclivities toward informality and casualness; the pleasures of plain, everyday things; a capacity for homely truth and directness in speech and manner. Somehow arising out of such a contrast are a strong ego and confidence in the irreducibility of one's person—also eminently Spanish.

AT: Speaking of enduring Spanish traits, remember how, a few years ago, while working on this translation in our little Valencian village, we kept recognizing around us the personal and social ethos of *La Dorotea*. The houses huddled together wall to wall and flush with the street—almost conversant with it—showed how firmly the communal impinges on the individual and intensifies the need for privacy. And remember how, in Valencia itself, we kept seeing shops marked "Passementerie"—where still in demand were the silver and gilt tassels, fringes, flounces, lacework so prized in *La Dorotea*.

EH: In another connection, I recall how the touch-and-go situation of the almond blossoms threatened by frost kept the whole village on edge for days. Suddenly the seemingly disembodied repartee on the subject (act II, scene 6) became as grounded in experience as it had been three hundred and fifty years ago.

AT: We're straying from the main concern: irony. Looked at squarely, Lope's irony, you must admit, lacks the prismatic richness of Cervantes'. It does not express a multidimensional reality emanating from some unreachable core of being, but a reluctance to surrender any possibility. The resulting ambivalence does not make Lope uncomfortable because it is one of affirmation, not indecision. As an avid response to the manifold possibilities of life, his irony unquestionably operates closer to the surface than Cervantes'. Irony ends by subserving his ludic sense. It is to this last faculty that one would look for something approximating the irony of Cervantes.

EH: The irony we've been speaking of in *La Dorotea* belongs more to drama than to narrative fiction.

AT: But *not* exclusively to it, considering the mixed generic character of *La Dorotea*.

EH: Would you expect a dramatist, for whom everything tends toward rapid assertion and repartee, to resort to lengthy exchanges in pursuit of some central matter? No, but you would a novelist. This difference in degree and in kind complicates comparison between *La Dorotea* and *Don Quixote*.

AT: And to give literary history its due, you can't speak of *La Dorotea* as signaling a watershed in the development of any later form, as you must of the *Quixote* in the genesis of the novel. Both works mark important points of arrival. Both gather in and blend features of many preceding literary species and kinds. Only the *Quixote* is a point of departure. If *La Dorotea,* as you say, does anticipate developments to come, it does not prefigure them as the *Quixote* prefigures most of what was to come in the modern novel. Both works bring romance down to earth, but the appeal of Lope's formula for doing so must always be to the cognoscenti while Cervantes' readership, broad from the start, has become even broader.

EH: True enough, Alan. By all means let literary history have its say about the past. But let me bring up something about which literary history normally says little: those sudden shifts and transformations in literary art that sometimes lead to a revolution in taste. It's always the deviant and eccentric work that history, bent on keeping the past in place, will reduce, put aside, then consign to one great cul-de-sac. *La Dorotea* has suffered such a fate. Largely unacknowledged for three and a half centuries, its aesthetic possibilities await discovery as—what was your term?

AT: A "point of departure."

EH: I want to say that *La Dorotea* belongs with a masterwork like *Finnegans Wake*. It is an experimental work, an art monument, which demands to be admired for its own sake. Being self-sufficient, it insists on supplying the theoretical basis on which it is to be appreciated. It also invites explicators and proponents to restore its luster, and translators to rediscover its unique topography. Works of this sort usually shape themselves in some encyclopedic form where the author deposits all his learning, experience, and craft, so that we keep returning to the work in order to discover some special insight, aspect of diction, or reference, missed on a previous reading. Think of Burton's *Anatomy of Melancholy,* Blake's *Prophetic Books,* Sterne's *Tristram Shandy,* Melville's *Moby Dick*—long neglected works of psychological complexity. To the imaginative writer, temperamentally attuned, who comes along with quickened perception, they offer totally unexplored country, together with a map on how to proceed. This is how Borges took to Stevenson and probably Montaigne, producing a new kind of *ficción* thereby. Joyce pillaged numberless writers from every age, reshaping and parodying them in his prose epic about a legendary dead man's wake. For similar undertakings Pound is linked to Dante, Eliot to the English Metaphysicals. And we already know what Lope's own *bête noire,* the equally neglected Luis de Góngora and his *Soledades,* did to revitalize Spanish poetry in the 1920's.

AT: Yes, and you cannot imagine Lorca without him.

EH: So the boundless associative range of the art monument implicitly challenges the theme-bound tale of most narrative fictions. It seeks nothing less than to re-create the world in one book, and since experience is not simply classifiable as tragic or comic, it offers a microcosmic panorama, a teeming spectacle, circus, masquerade. In such a work the artist, with a voice so recognizable at the start, gradually fades, as Yeats's dancer into his dance, and Joyce's artificer into his fabulous artifice. This is where *La Dorotea,* by nature and fate, fits in. And if our translation brings it to prominence, the day may come when young writers will seize its invitation to build new structures on its foundations. With its long-delayed promise as a point of departure fulfilled, perhaps *La Dorotea* will find its place somewhere near *Don Quixote* in literary history.

NOTES
GLOSSARY

Notes

ened to kill the boy unless the father surrendered the fortress, Guzmán sent him a dagger and witnessed from the ramparts the beheading of his son. The Infante, who was fighting to regain the small kingdom of which the King had deprived him, failed to take the town.

3 Francisco López de Aguilar (1583–1665): A humanist of considerable attainments and a minor writer who was a close friend of Lope's. However, there is critical consensus, based on the existence of a draft in Lope's hand, that Lope, not López de Aguilar, is the author of this prologue. With numerous literary enemies, Lope must have preferred to avoid incurring the charge of self-praise.

4 and Terence in the *Eunuch:* In both plays mentioned the action turns on the love of harlots.

4 as Bernard says: Reference to a passage in St. Bernard's ninth sermon on the *Song of Songs.* (The location in St. Augustine's writings of the passage paraphrased at the end of this prologue has not been determined.)

4 the irrelevant laws: Lope is referring to the famous Neo-Aristotelian unities of time (twenty-four hours), place, and action, which his stage plays largely ignored. This brought him bitter attacks from traditionalistic preceptists.

4 as Horace puts it: *Ars poetica* 60–62. Horace was born in 65 B.C.

6 Dramatis Personae: The bracketed words have been added by the translators.

10 across your face: This proverb marks the starting point of a strain peculiarly characteristic of *La Dorotea.* All proverbs have been enclosed in single quotation marks.

12 game of bowls: The frequent use of a "five" in the scoring of this game had given rise to colloquial expressions, on which Teodora and Gerarda are here ringing changes.

18 the Philosopher: "The Philosopher" is normally Aristotle; in this case, *Problems* XXX.xiv.956b–957a.

18 Amphitryon was the first: Misled by an intermediary source, Lope writes "Amphitryon" for Pliny's "Amphiction" (*Natural History* VII.lvi). From the latter work come also the references to the chameleon (VIII.li) and to Cornelius Rufus (VII.l).

20 Ovid says: *Metamorphoses* I.141–142.

20 Leo Suabius' instructions: Leo Suabius is author of *Theophrasti Paracelsi Philosophiae et Medicinae utriusque Universae Compendium* (Paris, 1591?), a compendium of the philosophical and medical writings of

Paracelsus, the Swiss alchemist and doctor (1493–1541), from pp. 16–17 of which the ensuing formula is taken verbatim.

21 Diogenes forgive you: The evidently commonplace remark about gold attributed to Diogenes the Cynic (fourth century B.C.) by Diogenes Laertius (*Lives and Opinions of Eminent Philosophers* VI.li) could have been relayed to Lope by any one of various intermediaries, for instance Pedro Mejía, *Silva de varia lección* (Miscellany of Divers Matters: Seville, 1540), in *Bibliófilos Españoles*, ed. J. García Soriano (Madrid, 1933–34), I, xxvii, 164. Similarly Fernando's subsequent commonplace, ascribed by Julio to Socrates, although originating probably in Seneca, *Epistles to Lucilius* XVII.xii, could well have been found by Lope in the *Polyanthea novissima* of Domenico Nani Mirabelli (Venice, 1630), 376a. In subsequent notes, except for those indicating a given compendium or miscellany for the first time, intermediary sources will be pointed out only when some particular interest attaches to them.

24 The same cross: The cross is an insignia of membership in an order of knighthood, a distinction largely honorary by Lope's day but still prized.

26 Prince of Love: Cupid.

26 in a *búcaro:* The *búcaro* was a kind of mug made of a clay which became fragrant when wet. It was used for serving beverages. It could also be broken up; pieces of *búcaro* were a favorite with women for chewing, and sometimes eating.

26 Titian the great: Titian's *Andromeda*, now in the Wallace Collection, London, was originally in that of Philip II.

27 Leënas of secrecy: Leëna is mentioned by Plutarch in *De garrulitate* (On Garrulity; *Moralia* 6.viii), but Lope's source is probably a miscellany much frequented by him, the *Theatrum poeticum et historicum sive Officina Johannis Ravisii Textoris* (Historical and Poetical Showplace or Workshop of Jean Tixier, seigneur de Ravisy; Paris, 1520 and later editions). In a section headed "Those who stood firm in adversity," one reads of Leëna, a prostitute of Athens, whom no torture could force to betray Harmodius and Aristogiton, killers of the autocrat Hipparchus (514 B.C.)

27 that Egyptian crocodile: The crocodile and the serpent probably originate in Pliny, *Natural History* VII.xxxvii and VIII.xliv, respectively. What Lope erroneously ascribes to the serpent, Pliny relates of the hyena, however.

31 great physician Dryvere: Jeremias Dryvere (1504–44) was a widely

read physician, author of a posthumously published *Method . . . of Universal Medicine* (Leyden, 1592).

31 *Nosomantica* of Moffett: Thomas Moffett (1553–1604) was the compiler of a digest of all the prognoses of Hippocrates, the *Nosomantica Hippocratea* (Frankfurt, 1588).

35 Seneca said it: The commonplace originates in Seneca, *Epistles to Lucilius* XX.

38 Claudian said: Lope or some secondary source mistakenly attributes the line to Claudian; it is from Martial, *Epigrams* I.iv.8 ("Lasciva est nobis pagina, vita proba").

38 Virgil's Damon said: In *Eclogues* VIII.41.

39 a poet said: Self-quotation from Sonnet 73 of Lope's *Rimas* of 1602.

44 those of Garrovillas: Julio is expressing a preference for cured meat over the scented earth of the *búcaro*. The most desirable scented earth came from Portugal, whereas Garrovillas, in the Spanish province of Cáceres, was famous for its bacon and ham. These of course spur a thirst for wine.

46 high and mighty: Although an allusion has been seen here to Virgil ("to spare the downtrodden and bring down the overweening," *Aeneid* VI.853), there may be a biblical echo: "He hath put down the mighty from their seats, and exalted them of low degree" (Luke 1:52).

48 hymnody Sapphic: The reference is to the metric structure of this chorus itself. In fact, only in the pattern of line lengths is there any approximation in the original to the stanza of Sappho and later of Horace.

50 and La Membrilla: Coca (province of Segovia, northwest of Madrid) was famous for its red wine, San Martín de Valdeiglesias (province of Madrid, west of the capital) for its white. Manzanares and La Membrilla are located close together in a more southerly wine-growing region of La Mancha.

50 *Omnia vincit amor:* "Love conquers all," Virgil, *Eclogues* X.59.

56 *eu não tenho:* "My hopes he cannot take from me, / for how can he take what I have not?"—lines 3 and 4 of the sonnet beginning *Busque Amor novas artes, novo engenho* ("Let love devise new arts, new skills"), *Obras completas,* ed. Hernâni Cidade, 3rd ed. (Lisbon: Livraria Sá da Costa, 1962), I, 205.

56 the Guadalete: River in southwestern Spain emptying into Cadiz Bay. Celia is capriciously punning on its purely Arabic name.

56 "Star of Venus" ballad: A popular late sixteenth-century ballad, doubtless by Lope.

56 stage of suffering: This verse tag was a favorite with Lope. Quoting it in 1630 in his *Laurel de Apolo,* he attributes it to Alonso de Ercilla y Zúñiga (1533-95).

57 in summer: Lope is quoting inexactly from a sonnet by his contemporary and rival, Luis de Góngora (1561-1627). At the end of the sonnet Madrid's Manzanares River speaks: "Yesterday an ass drank me up and today he has peed me out again."

57 its St. John's Eves: Many traditional practices centering on maidens' prospects in love were associated with St. John's Day, June 24. Plucking vervain (verbena) that morning, for example, forwarded a maiden's chances of finding a husband to her liking.

57 sorely lacking: These lines figure in a composition attributed to Pedro Liñán de Riaza (d. 1607), an associate of Lope's early years, little of whose work has survived.

57 what another poet said: The identity of this other poet is not known.

63 I am Julia: For "Julia" read "Fulvia," the first wife of Mark Antony, remembered for her cruelty in mutilating Cicero's severed head.

64 safe and sure: The sense is that judges knowingly let tavern keepers give them wine undiluted so that it may pass muster, then leave them free to degrade and water it down.

65 jealous thoughts: Lope thinks of pansies and violets as blue, which was the color of jealousy.

65 *habitantibus in ea:* "And to all its inhabitants." True to type, Gerarda, whose literary ancestry goes back to Plautus and Terence, will be characterized by her Latin, usually more defective and macaronic than here.

66 figs for you: Usually apotropaic or defiant, the sign of the fig—holding out the hand with the thumb between the index and middle fingers—could also be used inversely as a compliment.

66 I turn friar: A version of the episode alluded to is contained in a ballad dating from the 1580's and possibly Lope's. The anecdote is older; the refrain quoted here is already proverbial in Lope's day.

67 by pious decree: Gerarda's "day" probably goes back to 1546, the year in which a decree of the Council of Trent forbade reading the Bible in the vernacular. The Indexes of 1551 and 1564 repeated the prohibition.

67 clog and scissors: Practicing a form of sorcery, Gerarda has thrust a pair of scissors into a clog while pronouncing a spell, and observed whether the clog then veered left or right.

68 St. John's Eve: Prayer to be addressed to the Baptist on St. John's Eve by young women eager to learn whom they will marry.

70 athirst for lamp oil: Witches, taking the form of owls, were commonly believed to drink up the oil of lamps.

73 Don John of Austria: Spain and the central Mediterranean were preserved from the Muslim threat when naval forces led by Don John of Austria, illegitimate half-brother of Philip II, defeated the Turks at the Battle of Lepanto (1571).

74 airborne: Flying was a prerogative of witches, in the company of, or to a sabbath with, the devil, the "rooster" mentioned a little further on.

74 did you rent: Plays were presented in innyards and, along with bullfights, in public squares. Adjacent window space was rented by viewers. Celia is understandably treating Gerarda's presence at the Battle of Lepanto as a joke.

76 that shepherd: The shepherd is Argus. After Mercury had put his hundred eyes to sleep and slain him, Juno placed the eyes on the feathers of her peacock (Ovid, *Metamorphoses* I.622–688; 713–723).

77 something impermanent: Plato, *Symposium* 183b.

78 So Plutarch writes: "On the Virtues of Women," *Moralia* III. 249B–D.

82 Abindarráez, prisoner: The ballad refers to the central event of the Hispano-Moorish tale *The Abencerraje and the Beauteous Jarifa*—the generosity of the noble governor of Antequera, Rodrigo de Narváez, toward his captive, the Moor Abindarráez of the illustrious Granadine Abencerraje line. Set in the years just before the capture of Granada (1492), the anonymous tale first appeared in the mid-sixteenth century.

85 White blooms and red: In the color symbolism of the period, white usually signifies purity; red, joy. Purple, three quatrains from the end of the poem, signifies love.

86 ditty beginning with "Mother": The apostrophe to Mother was a hackneyed formula of traditional poetry frequently ridiculed in the Golden Age.

88 assigned St. Agnes: That Gerarda should associate St. Agnes (*Inés* in Spanish) with herself is not only transparently comical. It also hints at an association of Gerarda, the go-between, with Inés Osorio, Elena Osorio's mother. Lope is quoted in the trial record as calling her "Santa Inés" and accused her of procuring for her daughter.

90 *in corporibus nostros:* In contrast to Gerarda's earlier brief snatch of Latin, this one wobbles between Latin and Castilian. The plain

sense is: "Lord, bless us and what we are about to eat; may God bless it in our bodies."

93 seven princes of Lara: The number seven leads Gerarda capriciously to recall these Castilian heroes of medieval epic and legend, betrayed to the Moors by their uncle and avenged by their bastard half-brother, Mudarra. Lope dramatizes the story in his play *El bastardo Mudarra.*

93 without touching stones: Dorotea's pedantic remark originates in a treatise of Hippocrates. *Airs, Waters, Places,* VII.49–50, 63–66.

94 gumdrops to Guinea: The seventeenth-century Spaniard associated black people primarily with Guinea because of Portuguese traffic in slaves from there. In the original, Gerarda's remark is mainly a spontaneous play on sound: "Gragea a Guinea!" *Gragea* was actually sugar-candy in very small drops.

95 blue eyes: Blue eyes and eating sweets were taken as signs of effeminacy.

95 *dicamus el santificetur:* Now even more uncertain, despite its rhymes, Gerarda's macaronic Latin says approximately: "What we have eaten, may it be blessed by the Lord of Lords and for friends [there is an untranslatable play on "monkeys"] and for you, may it never fail, and now let us say the blessing."

96 satyr's brawny grasp: No ancient source is known for this anecdote. It corresponds quite closely, however, to an emblem entitled (in Latin) "Money Makes the Faun Handsome," found in Hernando de Soto, *Emblemas moralizadas* (Madrid, 1599), fol. 13v, and reproduced in the modern emblem anthology *Emblemata . . . ,* ed. Arthur Henkel and Albrecht Schöne (Stuttgart: J. B. Metzlersche Verlagsbuchhandlung, 1967), col. 1836.

97 how slight it seems!: Lines quite probably by Lope himself, in a ballad of ca. 1594.

98 Heliodorus: Author (second to third century A.D.) of *Theagenes and Chariclea,* one of the earliest Greek romances, a tale of adventure and love. "Heliodorus, in our own tongue" presumably refers to the translation by Fernando de Mena (1587, 1614, 1615).

98 hands of a madman: In the *Emblematum liber* (Emblem Book; Augsburg, 1531) of Andrea Alciato (1492–1550), an emblem frequently reproduced, *Insani gladius* (The Madman's Sword), shows the maddened Ajax wielding his sword against some pigs under the impression that he is slaying Agamemnon and Achilles.

104 Franceliso's brush: The identity of this Franceliso has not been established with certainty.

106 *Procreation of Animals:* The statement in question does indeed appear in *The Generation of Animals* (I.xviii.722a), but Lope—or his source—has erred in taking a place name, Helis, for a woman's name.

112 Thisbe transformed: Lope "metamorphizes" Thisbe—who died invoking the mulberry tree under which Pyramus already lay dead—into a lyre, presumably since she was the "instrument" on which Pyramus' amorous inspiration played.

113 ashes of his Amaryllis: A reference to a tradition that Artemisia, widow of King Mausolus of Caria (mid-fourth century B.C.), mixed his ashes in her daily drink.

113 by the priests: The source of this information about India and Hindus has not been determined. Julio's presenting himself as eyewitness to this practice, which he can scarcely have been, carries to an extreme the fondness of the characters of *La Dorotea* for tossing off exotic lore in their conversations.

113 observed in Horace: *Odes* I.xxvi.

113 in his "Cyclops": See beginning of Theocritus' Idyll XI.

113 as Anacreon says: A reminiscence of the second quatrain of the poem traditionally numbered 39, "When I drink wine."

114 in his *Philography:* A reference to the third of the *Dialogues of Love* of this exiled Spanish Jew (1460–1520), an exponent of Neo-Platonism. In the Spanish translation of the Italian by Garcilaso de la Vega Inca (Madrid, 1590), reproduced by M. Menéndez y Pelayo, *Orígenes de la novela* (Madrid, 1915), 4.425a.

115 Garcilaso took from him: Fernando manages to drop three names to authorize the helplessness he feels in his passion: Ovid in *Heroides* 4 (Phaedra to Hippolytus) 154: "No lover can see what is fitting"; Seneca, *Hippolytus* 177–178: "The things you call to mind, I know to be true, Nurse, but my furious passion forces me to pursue what is worst"; and Garcilaso de la Vega (1501–36), Sonnet 6.

116 far side of Morocco: This incident appears in Diego de Torres, *Relación del origen y sucesso de los Xarifes . . . de Marruecos . . .* (An Account of the Origin and Fortunes of the Sherifs . . . of Morocco . . .; Seville, 1583), p. 83. This is an account of the Sa'adi dynasty of Morocco whose sherifs (nobles) took power in 1524.

116 Aristotle worshiped Hermia: A somewhat garbled version of an anecdote appearing in Diogenes Laertius, *Lives and Opinions of Eminent Philosophers* (third century A.D.), 4.1. Lope's source is probably Ravisius Textor in a section entitled "Various Harlots."

117 Marsilio Ficino's explanation: The reference is to Ficino's *Commentary*

on Plato's *Cratylus*, included originally in the edition of Plato's complete works in Latin published in Paris, 1522. In the Basel edition of 1561, 2 vols., 1.1313.

117 Quintilian said: *Institutio Oratoria* 2.xv.9.

119 due to Venus: Don Bela's medical terminology has its source in the *Occulta naturae miracula* (Hidden Wonders of Nature; Ghent, 1559) of the Dutch doctor Levinus Lemnius, pp. 330–332.

121 has not got bells: The sense is ambiguous: emasculation or discreet confidentiality in a lover.

121 red cross of St. James: The still-prized symbol of the Order of St. James (*Santiago*), originally a medieval association of knights formed to protect pilgrims traveling the Way of St. James across northern Spain to Santiago de Compostela.

123 The Queen of Rhodes: Polyxo, who, according to Pausanias in his *Description of Hellas* 3.19, had Helen killed for having caused the death of Polyxo's husband in the Trojan war.

125 Love holding a fish: The iconography suggests an emblem in Alciato's *Emblematum Liber* (D8 in the original edition) entitled *Potentia amoris* (The Power of Love) and showing a blindfolded Cupid with flowers in one hand and a dolphin in the other. The emblem is inspired by the description of a statue of Eros in the *Greek Anthology* 16.207.

125 Arnaldus de Villa Nova: A Catalan physician and alchemist (ca. 1240–1311). Although Ludovico translates accurately the title of his Latin work, the information is in fact derived from Leo Suabius, *Compendium* of Paracelsus, pp. 297–298.

125 the cuttlefish: Lope is confusing the cuttlefish with the stingray, concerning which this superstition was of long standing.

125 according to Leo Suabius: The references to Plato and Virgil reach Lope third-hand, again via Leo Suabius' *Compendium* of Paracelsus, p. 51.

126 according to Levinus Lemnius: Like Don Bela in Scene 3 of this act, Ludovico is here drawing on the *Hidden Wonders of Nature* of Levinus Lemnius, p. 240, as is Julio also two speeches further on in regard to curing the "French disease," that is, syphilis. Julio's subsequent remarks about Archimedes' mirror come from the same work, p. 158. Lope is known to have owned a copy of the work.

127 an epitaph of his: Ariosto's Latin epitaph on Hernando de Avalos, Marquis of Pescara (1489–1525), commander of the imperial forces victorious at Pavia (1525), was still enjoying a considerable vogue in Lope's day. (Text in Ariosto, *Lirica*, ed. Giuseppe Fatini [Bari,

1924], p. 231.) It is not known where it is quoted by Girolamo Muzio (1496–1576), called "The Justinopolitan" after his birthplace, Capodistria, founded by the Byzantine Emperor Justin II in the sixth century.

129 flower of Apollo: Clytie, loved by Apollo, pined away at his unfaithfulness and was changed into the heliotrope or sunflower.

131 Fernando de Herrera: The quoted lines are the first tercet of Sonnet 25 of Fernando de Herrera (1534?–1597), leader of a late sixteenth-century school of Sevillian poets.

131 third book of Xenophon: The work of Xenophon referred to is the *Cyropaedia,* based on his experiences in Persia. This and the subsequent anecdote are drawn, respectively, from *Cyropaedia* III.i. and VI.i. There are slight inaccuracies in both references.

132 the chameleon loses color: The datum on the chameleon stems from Pliny the Elder's *Natural History* VIII.li.; the subsequent lore on the *centum capita* (literally, hundred heads)—eryngium or sea holly—from XXII.ix. The identification with the mandrake is incorrect.

132 one of Ovid's *Epistles: Heroides* XV.

133 in his *Banquet of Love:* Plato, *Symposium* 183b.

133 Pallas Athena's piping: This episode is the subject of the 165th myth in the collection (*Fabulae*) of Hyginius (ca. 64 B.C.–A.D. 17).

133 Duke of Alba: Fernando Alvarez de Toledo (1508–82), general of Charles V in Germany and Italy, and Philip II's commander in the Low Countries, known for his cruelties. It was his descendant, the sixth duke, Fernando Alvarez de Toledo, whom Lope served as secretary in 1590–95.

133 Marquis of Santa Cruz: Alvaro de Bazán (1526–88), naval commander of Philip II in operations throughout the Mediterranean, including Lepanto (1571), and in the expedition against the Azores (1583), in which Lope participated.

133 the beauty of Angelica: An allusion to Lope's poem of this name—*La hermosura de Angélica* (1602)—an imitation of the *Orlando furioso.* Lope claims to have begun it while serving in the Armada in 1588.

133 as Ovid says: *Heroides* II.85.

133 the Philosopher in his *Physics:* Aristotle, *Physics* II.ii.194a.

134 *Dari,* or Donor: There is a play here on *dar* (to give) and *Darii,* a form of syllogism.

135 writer of sacred verse: An allusion to the twentieth sonnet of Lope's own *Rimas sacras* (1614).

135 such different blossoms: Allusion of a type frequent in the period, to the contents of chamber pots emptied from house windows at night.

135 Plautus says of lovers: In *Asinaria,* 184–185.

136 he sweated pure amber: It was Plutarch, in his *Life* of Alexander, who originated this legend.

141 lovelorn nonsense: Dorotea's letter is modeled on the seventh epistle of Ovid's *Heroides,* Dido to Aeneas.

142 poison of its diamond: When worn, the diamond was considered to repel poisons; when swallowed, to become itself a deadly poison.

144 Cacus belched: *Aeneid* VIII.255.

144 Don Luis de Góngora said: In an early sonnet (ca. 1588) recording the Cordovan poet's first impressions of Madrid and beginning, "Grandes, más que elefantes y que abadas" (Grandees greater than elephants and rhinoceroses).

144 picture of Ariadne: Philostratos the Athenian (fl. ca. A.D. 210) describes a picture showing Dionysus, "drunk with love," approaching Ariadne.

144 once age dissolves: In four speeches of his two interlocutors—this remark of Julio's, Fernando's preceding question, and, three and four speeches further on, Fernando's comparison of his heart to the sun and Julio's reply to it—Lope has incorporated almost verbatim successive concepts from the fourth chapter of the seventh speech in Marsilio Ficino's *Commentary* on Plato's *Symposium,* included in Ficino's Latin edition of Plato's *Opera omnia* (1482) and also published separately in Italian.

145 Am I perchance in love: Fernando's two instances of disordinate love, much repeated elsewhere in Lope, are culled from sixteenth-century miscellanies: the first from Pedro Mejía, *Silva . . . (Miscellany)* III.14; the second from Ravisius Textor, *Officina,* the section called "Lovers of animals and other things."

145 According to Paracelsus: While Paracelsus is the acknowledged source of Julio's statement, the actual source is Leo Suabius' *Compendium* of Paracelsus' writings, p. 30.

145 Melusinas: The original Mélusine, subject of a medieval legend related by Jean d'Arras in his *Chronique de la princesse,* written in 1387, was the tutelary fairy of the house of Lusignan in the Poitou.

145 salamander of my heart: Pliny (*Natural History* X.lxvii) says the salamander is so cold that it puts out fire by mere contact, as ice does. The animal next mentioned by Julio is described by Pliny (XI.xlii),

who calls it *pyrallis* and *pyrocolon;* Aelian (*De natura animalium* [On the Characteristics of Animals] II.2) calls it *pyrigonos*.

145 Hesiod says: The surviving works of Hesiod (late eighth–early seventh century B.C.) do not contain this statement. Its source is a fragment quoted by Plutarch in *On the Obsolescence of Oracles* (*Moralia* V.xi.415).

146 who saw Tritons: The information about the sighting of Tritons and Nereids comes straight from Leo Suabius' *Compendium* of Paracelsus, pp. 29–30. The direct or indirect source of the ensuing anecdote is Peter Martyr, *De orbe novo . . . decades* (Decades . . . of the New World; 1530), Decade VIII, ch. vii.

146 Guazzo's *Dialogues:* Allusion to the *Civil Conversazione* (Brescia, 1574) of this Italian moralist and critic (1530–93). The allusion is probably to the following passage: "But Lord Hercules said, 'All women are not comprehended in this kind of qualitie [i.e., prone to love beardless youths] . . . Some wise gentlewomen, and that are of riper judgment have disdeigned those Bereni [i.e., Birenos, referring to a young lover in *Orlando Furioso*] with their painted faces, and friseled hair, knowing that perfect love cannot take deepe roote in an unstable minde, and in a light head' " (*Pettie's Guazzo* [the Fourth Book, trans. by Barth. Young, 1586], The Tudor Translations, Second Series [London: Constable, and New York: Knopf, 1925], II, 203).

146 *troppo maturi:* "overripe," *Orlando Furioso* X.9.

147 in Lactantius' phrase: Lactantius (b. ca. A.D. 250) was a converted pagan and church father, author of *De ave phoenice* (The Phoenix), a poem from which Lope here quotes lines 57–58, and goes on to cull from lines 77 and 83–88.

149 Phaëthon of boatmen: Rather than "green bays" it is poplars along the Eridanum (Po) that mourn Phaëthon, Apollo's son, struck down by a thunderbolt of Zeus in his disastrous attempt to drive his father's chariot. Lombardy poplars are his mourning sisters transformed.

150 mother-of-pearl: By Lope and his contemporaries, mother-of-pearl was often seen as having a pink cast.

156 your blind eyes: Lope's last mistress, Marta de Nevares, went blind in her final years.

157 These new terms: Felipa is suggesting, approvingly, that the poem is written in the *culto* style—Latinate in lexicon, syntax, and erudition—of Góngora and his followers. This Fernando, speaking for Lope, firmly denies.

162 As in those verses: Both these and the ensuing lines are self-quotations, from *La hermosura de Angelica* (Angelica's Beauty) XI.158 and *Rimas* (1602), Sonnet 88, respectively.

164 King Ahasuerus: Petrarch in the third chapter of his *Trionfo d'amore* points to King Ahasuerus' cure for love: using a new love to drive out the old, as one nail drives out another. In Esther 1 and 2, King Ahasuerus thus replaces Vashti, the queen who disobeys him, with Esther.

165 I, dear ladies: What follows is a freely fictionalized account of Lope's own youth.

165 I had already acquired grammar: Grammar and rhetoric were the subjects of the first two years of Latin study in schools.

166 not the oldest of advocates: In one of Lope's plays, *Del monte sale quien el monte quema* (freely rendered, "The Burnt Child Fears the Fire"), a character remarks, "Love always was the greatest [oldest] advocate." (The adjective used in each case, *mayor,* has both meanings.) The general sense here is that Marfisa was not marrying for love.

166 my soul is Portuguese: The Portuguese were considered by Spaniards highly prone to sentimental effusions.

167 vassals of Aragon: The vassals of Aragon are a proverbial example of subservience under any condition—good or bad.

170 Antiochus Magnus: Antiochus III (223–187 B.C.), of the Seleucid dynasty, heir to the Asian territories of Alexander the Great, whose life was spent in battles of consolidation and conquest. Lope's source is an entry in Ravisius Textor's section "Men of wealth," the wording of which he follows closely.

172 wine, women, and truth: The debate is related at length in the apocryphal book of Zerubbabel (or III Ezra), chs. 3 and 4. (The book was excluded from the canon by the Council of Trent but was still printed in some Spanish Bibles into the seventeenth century.) Three guards of King Darius debate before him as to which is strongest: wine, the King, women—but above all else, Truth. The third, an Israelite, prevails (with Truth) and, asked what reward he wishes, holds the King to his promise to rebuild Jerusalem.

172 addressed it in these words: Undoubtedly a self-quotation, though so far not specifically identified.

172 heroic shield of Charles V: The emblem of Charles V consisted of two columns with the legend PLUS ULTRA, i.e., more worlds to conquer beyond the Pillars of Hercules.

177 small hearts: It was widely believed, on the authority of Pliny (*Natu-*

ral History XI.lxx) and others, that the smaller an animal's heart, the greater its courage.

177 coruscations and iridescence: The description closely follows Pliny's in *Natural History* X.ii.

179 I shall be the lioness: A tradition of long standing held that lion cubs were stillborn, or nearly so, and that their parents' roars brought them to life.

181 Hercules and Antaeus: Dorotea's "book of fables" may be the *Philosophia secreta* of Juan Pérez de Moya (Madrid, 1585), a compilation of Greco-Roman mythology, which in Book IV, ch. 8, relates the story of Hercules and Antaeus. Dorotea tailors its "application" to fit her own situation, making the "moral meaning" of Antaeus— carnal desire in Pérez de Moya—the compelling power of wealth.

182 in Taurus and in Libra: The meaning is that the aspect of Venus at Fernando's birth was unfavorable and that he has seen her "today" in the two "houses" of the Zodiac in which such unfavorable influence becomes strongest. The stars are thus compelling him to break his vow.

182 using will power: Julio's two examples underscore an affirmation of the freedom of the will that was *de rigueur* in Counter-Reformation Spain. Scipio Africanus Major, the Roman general (ca. 236–ca. 183 B.C.) victorious in the Second Punic War, was the subject of a widely diffused story (e.g., Ravisius Textor, *Officina,* section entitled "The very chaste") emphasizing both his mercy and his will power in respecting the chastity of a young female captive. The reply of Plato embroiders on a passage in Diogenes Laertius (*Lives and Opinions of Eminent Philosophers* III.29–31) concerning his love of young men.

183 one of my acquaintance: Lope is carefully distinguishing between Góngora and his followers. His attitude toward Góngora was ambivalent; he recognized his genius, wanted his approval, feared his sharp pen, and could sense the appeal of his *culto* aesthetic, even though his fundamental reaction to it was hostile. Toward Góngora's followers and commentators the hostility was unmitigated.

183 Pullulating with *culto,* Claudio: *Culto* (or *cultismo*) denotes the erudite seventeenth-century style of which Góngora was the leading exponent. Its complexity is enlivened by brilliant word play, conceits, verbal ingenuity—in a word, by wit as the term was then understood. The practitioners of the style are themselves known as *cultos.* The Claudio addressed in the sonnet is Lope's lifelong friend Clau-

dio Conde. The sonnet was composed in about 1631, when it appears in Lope's correspondence. With Góngora dead, Lope has no inhibitions about parodying his followers, especially an editor and commentator, José Pellicer, in his *Lecciones solemnes a las obras de don Luis de Góngora* (Solemn Readings of the Works of Don Luis de Góngora; Madrid, 1630).

184 Stobaeus or the *Polyanthea:* The *Polyanthea,* first brought out by Domenico Nani Mirabelli in 1507 and constantly augmented in later editions, contained thousands of classical commonplaces arranged by subject. The *Florilegium* (ca. A.D. 500) of Johannes Stobaeus was an anthology of the sayings of 250 Greek writers on subjects ranging from philosophy and physics to poetry and politics. The Latin abridgement of this work by Conrad Gesner (1516–65), *Epitome . . .* (Basel, 1557), is also alluded to.

184 many serious poets: The list which follows contains names of poets known in the period in which *La Dorotea* is set (1587–88). Some have survived: Espinel, Herrera, Cervantes (though not as a poet), Ercilla, the Argensolas, Góngora, and, of course, "this Lope de Vega just starting out." Other names, presumably familiar then, are unknown now except to scholars. Still others, especially those of noblemen, were probably included for reasons of flattery.

185 that poetic madness: The reference is to the seventh speech, ch. 14, of Ficino's commentary on the *Symposium.*

185 examination of the plays: On various occasions commissions were named to examine the morality and the moral influence exercised by plays of the then burgeoning theater. Philip II, in the last year of his reign (1598), had closed the Madrid theaters by royal decree. The prohibition was lifted by Philip III the next year, at which time the conditions under which they could legitimately be staged were specified by a commission of theologians and the Council of State. They included prior censorship.

186 The second law: Lope has combined concepts from different sources in these words of Ludovico. In Justinian's *Digest* a testamentary law states that "whatever in a will is so written as to be unintelligible is thereby the same as if it had not been written." Similar concepts are found in Aristotle's *Rhetoric* and Cicero's *De oratore* (On the Public Speaker). In the latter work (III.xiii), intelligibility is considered the second most desirable characteristic of good composition, the first being correctness of usage.

186 *sail-bearing doves:* Góngora uses *velera paloma* to describe a "winged vessel" in a ballad.

186 a *flying sword: Aeneid* VIII.694. Lope has gleaned the example from Macrobius, *Saturnalia* VI.v.15: "Virgil properly uses ... for an arrow *volatile ferrum.*" César, in his next remark, explicitly follows Macrobius (*Saturnalia* VI.v.4) on *Bucolics* VI.33 as derived from Lucretius, *De rerum natura* VI.204–205.

187 *gentle lymph:* "Then the lymph is gentle, then the earth gloomy and the happy plowman does well to plant the seed thickly" (*The Phenomena of Aratus Translated into Latin by Germanicus Caesar,* lines 151–152). Virgil—"the greatest poet"—in the first line of the *Georgics* announces his intention to sing of "what makes the crops joyous."

187 by Pico della Mirandola: In the first Proem to his *Heptaplus,* in *De hominis dignitate. Heptaplus. De ente et uno* (On the Dignity of Man. Heptaplus. On Being and the One; ed. Eugenio Garin, Florence: Valecchi, 1942), pp. 172–177. Ludovico's reference to Plato in his next remark closely follows Pico, p. 172.

189 "pullulated in their graves": The reference is to Ecclesiasticus 46:12, "et ossa eorum pullulent," in the Vulgate of 1592, the bible officially approved by the Council of Trent. Lope converts a wish in the original ("May their bones pullulate") into a fact. (We thank Father Alphonse Vermeylen for this information.)

189 Hail and well met: Proverbial exemplars of friendship follow: Nisus is killed avenging the death of Eurialus in *Aeneid* IX. 386–444; in Euripides, *Iphigenia in Tauris,* Pylades and Orestes wish each to die to spare the other; Damon offers his life as pledge that Pythias will return to be executed, and the friends' loyalty prompts Dionysius to pardon them (Cicero, *De officiis* [On Duties; III.x]; the intimate friendship between Laelius (b. ca. 186 B.C.) and Scipio Africanus Minor (ca. 185–129 B.C.) is celebrated by Cicero in his dialogue entitled *Laelius de Amicitia.* Lope has evidently picked up these pairs of names from Ravisius Textor's section "Close friends."

189 Virgil asked his muse: The allusion is to the opening lines of the *Aeneid.*

189 a *brachylogia:* The two lines following translate the first of a Latin distich used to illustrate *brachylogia* in a textbook of rhetoric frequented by Lope: Antonio Spelta, *Enchiridion* ... (Manual or Commentary for Drawing up Epistles, and Fundamentals of Rhetoric; Pavia, 1591), p. 222.

190 Salmacis and Trocus: Hermaphrodites are discussed by Aristotle in *Generation of Animals* IV.iii. Ovid in *Metamorphoses* IV.285–379 relates how Hermaphrodites, a son of Hermes and Aphrodite, is, in

spite of himself, made one body with Salmacis, a nymph who loved him. The intrusive, nonclassical name Trocus apparently originates with Jorge de Bustamante in his Spanish version of the *Metamorphoses* (n.p., 1543?).

190 *Tusculan Disputations:* Cicero speaks of conditions for happiness in this dialogue, IV.xxxv.

190 Lucian and Tully: Lucian discusses friendship in the dialogue *Toxaris,* Tully (Cicero) in *Laelius de Amicitia.*

191 horse of Semiramis: According to Pliny (*Natural History* VIII.lxiv), Semiramis was so passionately in love with a horse that she had coitus with it.

191 Ausonius depicted opportunity: In the thirty-third epigram of Ausonius (ca. A.D. 310-ca. 395), Ocasio (Opportunity) is asked why the back of her head is bald. She answers, "So that I may not be caught as I go by."

191 epigram of Stigel: This "celebrated" epigram has not been located in the collected epigrams (Jena, 1569) of Johann Stigel (1515–62), a professor at Jena.

191 Bounder of Marseilles: With the Bounder of Marseilles begins the string of invented authorities parodying many sounding just as outlandish in the *Solemn Readings* of Pellicer.

191 used to irk Michelangelo: Lope's version of the ensuing episode is considerably touched up with respect to the original account found in Giorgio Vasari, *Vite . . . dei pittori, scultori, et architetti* (Lives . . . of the Painters, Sculptors, and Architects; Florence, 1561). See *Vasari's Lives,* ed. Betty Burroughs (New York: Simon and Schuster, 1947), pp. 260–261.

193 Cairasco outdoes him: Bartolomé Cairasco de Figueroa (ca. 1538–1610) was a great practitioner of proparoxytonic lines, as in this made-up example.

194 Leo Hebraeus: The allusion is to the same passage of the third of the *Dialogues of Love* cited earlier. In the Spanish reprint of M. Menéndez y Pelayo, *Orígenes de la novela* (Madrid, 1915), 4.425a.

194 some poet says: The poet is Lope himself. These much-cited lines from a ballad of the late 1580's became proverbial.

194 Quintilian likewise applied the term: In *Institutio oratoria* VIII.vi.

194 the origin of *rhyme: Rimar*—properly *rimor, rimari*—has in Latin the sense given. The ensuing references are to Cicero, *On Divination* I.lvii; Statius; *Thebaid* VII.761.

194 the blottings-out: The play is presumably by Lope, though no such lines have been located in any surviving play.

194 Suetonius Tranquillus: *Lives of the Caesars* VI.lii.

194 that poet says: "That poet" is Gregorio Silvestre (1520–69), whose verse was spared the general censure by Cristóbal de Castillejo (1490?–1550?) of Spanish poets who adopted the new Italianate meters.

195 *thinking-up:* Cicero's term *inventio* (*Tusculan Disputations* I.xxv.61) has the literal sense "coming upon," "finding." The succeeding references are to Cicero, *Orator* (The Orator) lvii, and Aristotle, *Rhetoric* III.viii.

195 The poet Symmachus: To rhyme was considered a vice in Latin poetry. But the Symmachus whom Lope mistakenly refers to as a poet was in fact an eminent Roman administrator and orator (A.D. 345–405).

195 Pico della Mirandola says: In the third chapter of the *Heptaplus* (ed. E. Garin, p. 212). Ludovico in his next speech picks up the paraphrase of Solomon immediately following in Pico's text, without acknowledging Pico as intermediary. The biblical source is Ecclesiastes 1:4.

195 Spelta, in his *Rhetoric:* Spelta, *Enchiridion,* p. 34. It is Spelta (pp. 34–36) who, on the basis of Aristotle, *Rhetoric* III.iii.14056–62, makes the accusation against Lycophron and Alcidamas. The definition of metaphor is in Quintilian, *Institutio oratoria* VIII.i.1.

196 Ambrogio Calepino: Calepino (1435–1511) was author of a famous polyglot dictionary, first published in 1502 and continually expanded by others in subsequent editions to include new languages. In that of Lyons, 1581 (*Dictionarium septem linguarum*), one finds, s.v. *raucus,* the present explication of Virgil's "Dant sonitum rauci per stagna loquacia cycni" (*Aeneid* XI.458: "Hoarse swans make sounds among the lapping pools").

196 Master Burguillos: Tomé de Burguillos is the alter ego invented by Lope in his later years to serve as an outlet for his jocular vein.

197 Aragonese immunity: Fugitives from justice in Castile habitually made for Aragon to evade the law.

197 Alcides' arrows slew: In Greek myth it is the Argonauts who rid Phineus of the Harpies (depicted as birds with women's faces), whereas Alcides (Hercules) destroys the Symphalian birds as one of his Labors.

199 Ovid calls raucous: *Metamorphoses* VI.377: "Vox iamque rauca est . . ." ("Now also their voices are hoarse . . ."). The peasants had sullied a pool, refusing a drink to thirsty Leto and her infant twins, Apollo and Artemis.

200 Aristotle mocks Gorgias: In *Rhetoric* III.iii.1406b. But Lope has picked up the example from Spelta, *Enchiridion*, p. 36.

200 Cyprian reduces them: Cyprian is Cipriano Soarez, S.J. (1524–93), author of a treatise on rhetoric, *De arte rhetorica libri tres ex Aristotele, Cicerone et Quintiliano praecipue depromti* (Art of Rhetoric in Three Books, Culled Mainly from Aristotle, Cicero, and Quintilian; Paris, 1568, and later eds.), a textbook much used in Jesuit schools and probably by Lope himself as a student in Madrid. It lists eleven tropes and is a likely immediate source for certain *loci* from ancient authors cited by Lope in this and the preceding scene.

200 holy bard of Bethlehem: David, Psalms 118:21: "Dormitavit anima mea prae taedio" (Vulgate; "My soul melteth for heaviness," Authorized Version).

200 The man of Uz: Job is "a man in the land of Uz" (Authorized Version 1:1) and "the greatest of all the men of the east" (1:3). Allusions (in the Vulgate) to his *taedium* are found at 9:21 and 10:1.

200 whose monstrous infamies: Cicero directs this remark at C. Verres, a rapacious governor of Sicily, in *In C. Verres Actio prima* (First Speech on Indictment against C. Verres) XII.35: "Et sunt homines quos libidinis infamiaeque suae neque pudeat, neque taedeat."

201 Cicero, in his *Fifth Epistle:* Lope is inaccurate; the epistle in question is the third of Book II.

202 pastures near Cordova: There is perhaps a veiled, maliciously humorous reference to Góngora, a native of Cordova, in this passage.

202 elegant epigram: Lope is alluding to the *Epigrammatum Libri Quinque* (Five Books of Epigrams; Rome, 1556) of Fausto Sabeo (1478–1558), in particular to one beginning, "Demulsi tigres, firmavi flumina et aequor" ("I tamed tigers, I stopped the flow of rivers and the sea"), an epitaph in which Orpheus enumerates the forces he has subdued, only to be himself overcome and torn apart by the Thracian women. Lope had quoted the epigram in full and glossed it in a sonnet published with his mythological poem *La Circe* in 1624.

202 that philosopher: The philosopher in question is Diogenes the Cynic (fourth century B.C.), and Lope's immediate source appears to be Pedro Mejía's chapter on Diogenes, at the end of which the episode is related in words which Lope's closely follow. (*Silva de varia lección* I.xxxvii.168–169.)

204 Read Giovio: Ludovico, "footnoting" the two prior remarks about the Turks, is referring to the *Commentario de le Cose de Turchi* (Com-

mentary on Matters Turkish; Venice, 1530, and Rome, 1532) of Paolo Giovio (1483–1552). César in his next remark is thinking of Giovio's *Historiarum Sui Temporis Libri XLV* (History of His Times in Forty-five Books; Florence, 1550–52) which covers the years 1494–1547, with a marked anti-Spanish bias. The charge of venality, also made by others, apparently has some basis in fact.

204 stands for *cultos:* The figure exemplified by *Roma pro Romanis* (Rome standing for Romans) and *Ceres* for wheat, as Ludovico has earlier remarked, is metonymy.

204 the Heraclitean you were: The contrast between the pre-Socratic philosophers Democritus, who laughs at the follies of mankind, and Heraclitus, who weeps, is a standard Renaissance commonplace.

205 died of sudden joy: With the exception of Guido of Bituria (a source who has not been identified), these instances all proceed from the section of Textor's *Officina* entitled "Gaudio et risu mortui" (Persons who have died of joy and laughing). Fernando's ensuing remark about the 109 years of Democritus Gelasinus (i.e., the Laugher) has no basis in Cicero. Lope found it in the encyclopedic *Plaza universal de todas ciencias y artes* (Universal Meeting Place of All Arts and Sciences; Madrid, 1615) of his contemporary, Cristóbal Suárez de Figueroa (Seventh Discourse, para. 33).

205 according to Gaguin: The reference is to Robert Gaguin (b. between 1425 and 1450, d. 1501), a professor at the Sorbonne and author of the *Compendium Roberti Gaugini* [sic] *super francorum gestis* (Compendium of the Doings of the Franks; Paris, 1514), fol. 91r.

205 John-Who-Waits-for-God: The Spanish tradition has it that John-Who-Waits-for-God, the Wandering Jew, was a cobbler who, upon hearing the commotion as Christ was being led to crucifixion, came out of his workshop and said, "Off you go," to which Christ replied, "I shall go and you shall stay forever." John is, in effect, condemned to roam the earth till the Second Coming. To sustain him, his purse is constantly replenished with five pieces of silver.

205 the daring of Brutus: The reading of the early editions of *La Dorotea* in regard to Brutus's character—*audiencia* (audience, law court)—seems defective. Unlike Morby, we have followed the emendation *audacia* of most later editors.

206 Tully says: Cicero in an early treatise on rhetoric, *De inventione* II.lix.

217 the rose of Apuleius: In the *Golden Ass* of Lucius Apuleius (fl. ca. A.D. 155), the protagonist Lucius is turned into an ass by a magic ointment, and is eventually restored to human shape after eating a magic rose.

217 what Catullus says: The lines are a free variation on Catullus's famous "Odi et amo" (*Carmina* LXXXVI).

219 a madrigal: The verse madrigal, a monostrophic composition free in form, had enjoyed a revival in the sixteenth century. Lope's, slightly longer than the usual twelve or thirteen lines, shows the customary variation in line length, the usual common rhyme of the last two lines, and the amatory subject, which along with nature was the most common.

219 love all soul will be: The Neo-Platonic character of this madrigal, which Don Bela proceeds to explicate, relates it to other compositions of Lope's later years. It is evidently based on direct reading of the *Heptaplus* of Pico della Mirandola and the commentaries of Marsilio Ficino on Plato and Plotinus. The "Philosopher" Don Bela refers to is clearly Plato.

220 the golden thread of reason: There is perhaps an echo here of Plato's *Laws* 645: ". . . the sacred golden cord of reason [that] every man ought to grasp and never let go."

220 that king of Great Britain: Henry VIII, who on his deathbed was said to have sent for a glass of white wine and, turning to one of his favorites, remarked, "Omnia perdidimus," whereupon he expired.

222 a whole *real:* Since there were thirty-four *maravedís* in a copper *real,* Gerarda's accounting is accurate.

222 Here, take this: Gerarda is here making the sign of the fig at Laurencio in mockery, to ward off evil.

224 Which makes twelve: Gerarda intentionally diminishes by four the number of *reales* she has received. Laurencio will also miscalculate, unintentionally, after Don Bela exits.

226 Casa del Campo: Extensive royal park laid out by Philip II on the western side of Madrid, containing a prominent fountain of the God of Waters.

226 a Christian from way back: Gerarda is reacting to the insinuation that she deals in witchcraft or is anything but an old-line Christian of good family, hailing from the pure-blooded mountainous North. By asserting her unguent is bacon fat, she dissociates herself from witches, who were said to anoint themselves with blood sucked from children, as well as from Jews and Moslems, with their aversion to pork.

228 what Ovid writes about Medea: *Metamorphoses* VII.391–397.

230 Marsilio Ficino: In his commentary on the *Symposium* of Plato (III.iii), from which the preceding part of César's speech is also drawn.

230 the same sign: The "preceding sign" is Aquarius, the "house" over

which Saturn presides. The sense is that the stars' influence makes for the continuation of the love of Fernando and Dorotea. A little further along, with Fernando in mind, César generalizes about persons born with Venus in the house of Saturn.

231 as that philosopher did: Cicero's version of this popular anecdote has the Roman consul Scipio Nasica inquiring of the poet Ennius' servant if his master is at home, having already heard Ennius speaking within. Scipio leaves in anger when told Ennius is not home. On the following day, Ennius in turn asks for Scipio Nasica at his residence, and Scipio himself tells him, "I am not home" (*De oratore* II.lxviii.276).

231 According to Marsilio Ficino: César's exposition in this and his subsequent lengthy speech closely follows Ficino's *Commentary* (VII.xi) on Plato's *Symposium*. The lines from Lucretius alluded to at the end of the subsequent speech are quoted by Ficino from *De rerum natura* (On the Nature of the Universe) IV.1057–60.

233 that long fable: *Symposium,* 189–193, discussed in Ficino's *Commentary* IV.i–ii.

235 if everything living loves: Fernando now strings together statements taken from several different parts of Ficino's *Commentary* on the *Symposium:* VI.viii, III.iii, III.v, II.ix.

235 Tamburlaine held Bayazid: As an example of subjugation by force, Lope frequently evokes the humiliating victory at Ankara in 1402 of the Tartar conqueror Tamburlaine (1336?–1405) over the Turkish sultan Bayazid the First.

236 like Ganymede's dog: Fernando compares his flight to that of the eagle of Zeus with Ganymede, which left his dog barking impotently into the air (Virgil, *Aeneid* V.252–257).

236 to make me a shirt: To win Hercules back, Deianira sends him the shirt given her by the Centaur Nessus and stained with his blood as he was dying from a wound inflicted by Hercules' arrow. The shirt causes Hercules' death (Ovid, *Metamorphoses* IX.101–272).

237 as the Philosopher says: Aristotle quotes but rejects the view that harmony is composed of contraries (*De Anima* [On the Soul] I.iv.407b). He remarks on the difficulty of understanding the nature of the soul, (ibid., I.i.402a). César's subsequent remark echoes that work (ibid., II.i.412a).

238 the heart is first: While the statement seems an echo of Aristotle (*Generation of Animals* II. i.734a and 735a), it varies from Aristotle's statement, conforming instead with Levinus Lemnius, *Hidden Wonders* 400, and Leo Suabius, *Compendium* 37–38.

238 with clever Boscán: The lines are in fact attributed to Jorge Manrique (1440–78) and only glossed by Juan Boscán (ca. 1500–42), among others.

238 whose females never sing: Aristotle, *History of Animals* V.xxx.556b, repeated by Pliny, *Natural History* XI.xxxii.

239 that Aristotelian conundrum: *On the Parts of Animals* IV.x.690a.

239 in that sonnet: "The times do change and with them change our loves, / our natures change, with all the trust we hold. / The world consists of change and change alone, / new qualities must take the place of old." First quatrain of a sonnet, *Obras completas,* ed. Hernâni Cidade, 3rd ed. (Lisbon: Livraria Sá da Costa, 1962), vol. I, 199.

239 the most festive day: Corpus Christi Day.

240 cannot return to life: Aulus Gellius (ca. A.D. 130–ca. 180) makes the attribution to Euripides in his *Attic Nights* XV.xx. The remark is diversely attributed by others.

240 Asking questions: Lope is careful to distinguish between the astrology that inquires into future events—prohibited by the Church and prosecuted by the Inquisition as an invasion of God's all-seeing Providence and the individual's free will—and the casting of a horoscope of a person's birth, which could be construed as indicative only of inclinations, corrigible by the will.

240 marriage of Her Excellency: The wedding described here took place in fact at Vich in Catalonia on 31 December 1587, after which the participants, all illustrious personages of the day, came on to Madrid. The Vittoria Colonna mentioned was the daughter of Marcantonio Colonna (d. 1584), a celebrated Italian naval captain who commanded the papal squadron at Lepanto. The bridegroom, after inheriting his father's titles in 1596, on the latter's death, died himself in 1600. Doña Isabel Manrique was the sister of Luis de Vargas Manrique, the companion of Lope's youth mentioned above (act IV, scene 2).

240 the three Graces: The Graces traditionally are three: Euphrosyne, Aglaia, and Thalia. Rather than add a fourth, as here affirmed, Homer and Statius call Aglaia Pasithea.

241 Cardinal Ascanio Colonna: Ascanio Colonna (1559?–1608) became a cardinal in 1586 and Viceroy of Aragon in 1601. He appears to have studied at the University of Alcalá before 1586 and it is very likely that Lope knew him there and saw in him a possible future patron and protector.

241 the Pontiff's anger: Doña Juana de Aragón was detained in Rome with her daughters in a small war between the anti-Spanish Pope Paul IV

(1555–59) and Philip II, but managed a dramatic escape. Philip sent the Duke of Alba in 1557 against Rome; the Duke began storming the city walls but withdrew, for reasons unknown, without carrying through the attack. Philip's victory was not as clear as Lope would have it.

242 *Book of True and False Astrology:* All the information Fernando has been relaying comes straight from Levinus Lemius, *Libelli tres, perelegantes ac festivi* (Three Most Elegant and Diverting Little Books; Antwerp, 1554), specifically from fols. 6–8 of the first, whose title announces that it deals with what is true and what is false in astrology. The same passage will also later provide Fernando, Julio, and César (beginning of scene 8) with three scriptural *loci.*

242 intent on learning: An expansion of the first sentence of Aristotle's *Metaphysics:* "All men naturally desire to know."

242 Cicero's *On Divination:* II.liv.iii. The subsequent Virgilian reference is to *Aeneid* III.445–446. These and the succeeding allusions by Fernando and Julio probably derive from a compendium containing a section on divination, not as yet identified.

242 Ambrose calls *fanatics:* The references are to St. Ambrose's *Commentary on the First Epistle of St. Paul to the Corinthians,* and the *History* of Ammianus Marcellinus (ca. A.D. 390), XXI.i.11.

243 as Diodorus writes: Diodorus Siculus states in his history of the world, *Bibliotheke Historike* (The History Library: ca. 40 B.C.): "It was from her [the Sibyl's] poetry, they say, that the poet Homer took many verses which he appropriated as his own and with them adorned his own poetry" (IV.lxvi).

244 why did Jacob weep: Genesis 29:2.

245 Charles the Fifth: Various accounts of this anecdote all describe the Emperor rescuing a Sevillian gentleman who had lost his mount and was being trampled by a Moor on horseback.

246 Or Samson: Judges 16. The architectural detail is provided by Lope.

246 the lion of Lysimachus: The feat of Lysimachus (fourth century B.C.) stems directly from Ravisius Textor, *Officina,* section called "Men extremely strong or very robust in bodily strength," to wit: "Lysimachus strangled a lion to which he had been exposed by order of Alexander, after seizing it by the tongue." For the same section of Textor come the preceding examples of Hercules, Samson, and Milo and the subsequent one of Aristomenes.

246 the heart of Aristomenes: Pliny (*Natural History* XI.lxx) cites Aristomenes, a traditional hero of Messenian resistance to Sparta (seventh century B.C.), as an instance of the truth that persons born with a

hairy heart are exceptionally brave. After killing three hundred Spartans, he was finally captured; when "cut . . . open alive . . . his heart was found to be shaggy."

249 "Fire, fire!": The lines are the refrain of a ballad, no doubt by Lope, "Ardiéndose estaba Troya" ("Troy was aflame"). It probably alludes to Elena Osorio. As the present context suggests, it would date from Lope's period of service as secretary to the Duke of Alba (1590–95).

249 Burn, lies, burn: Dorotea is appropriating the opening lines of a song then popular: "Arded, corazón, arded . . ." ("Burn, heart, burn away . . .").

251 I read something in Garcilaso: Gerarda, who is evidently illiterate, has picked up this tag from the opening line of the very well known Sonnet 23 of Garcilaso de la Vega.

252 Bernard of Treviso's *Alchemy:* Bernardo Trevisano, an Italian doctor (1507–83), was author of *De Chymico Miraculo Quod Lapidem Philosophiae Appellant* (On the Chemical Marvel Known as the Philosopher's Stone; Basel, 1583), the first part of which went by the title *The Alchemy Book.*

253 that place in Jeremiah: Jeremiah 10:2–3. As earlier noted, this and the two following references to Scripture—Isaiah 44:13–14 and Luke 12:29—are culled from the first book, dealing with astrology, of Levinus Lemnius, *Three Little Books,* fols. 6–8.

253 Juan Bautista de Lavaña: Portuguese mathematician, historian, and cosmographer (d. 1625), with whom Lope probably studied astrology. He became master of cosmography to Philip IV.

253 against false astrologers: The volumes of Augustine mentioned are those of a ten-volume edition of his works (Paris, 1555). The content of the statements comes not from the text but from the wording of items near the beginning of the general index (vol. 10) under the headings *Astra, Astrologia, Astronomia* (Stars, Astrology, Astronomy).

254 Beware of a woman: In this "woman who will cast spells on you" there is probably an allusion to an actress, Jerónima de Burgos, with whom Lope's private letters show him to have had a brief affair around 1607, when she would have been about seventeen. Lope speaks of her as practicing sorcery.

254 trust is not to be placed: An echo of Psalm 146:3–4: "Put not your trust in princes, nor in the son of man, in whom there is no help." The prince referred to immediately thereafter by César is Lope's patron, the Duke of Sessa.

254 So the Philosopher teaches: Here begins a series of six statements
derived from a single unmentioned intermediary source: Mateo
Gribaldi, *De Ratione Studiandi Libri Tres* (Three Books on the Program of Study; Lyons, 1544). Julio's reference to Aristotle, *Metaphysics* (II.i.993b), comes from Gribaldi, p. 201. Fernando's
subsequent two "laws"—ultimately from the *Digest* of the Justinian
law code—come here from Gribaldi, pp. 156, 219; César's response
comes from the *Digest* via Gribaldi, p. 168; his two subsequent
statements on cause and effect and on "purpose"—from Aristotle's
Physics (II.iii.195b, and II.ii–iii and viii, passim)—proceed from
Gribaldi, pp. 152, 200.

255 it is beyond question: Lope is transcribing, practically word for word,
Juvenal, *Satires* XIII.191–192.

255 the Proem to the *Digest:* Though the *Digest* is here mentioned directly
for the first time, the source is still Gribaldi, p. 199.

256 the crown of wisdom: César is quoting Ecclesiasticus 1:22.

257 the seventh chapter of Proverbs: This chapter describes a brazen wife
who entices a young man to her bed, "as an ox goeth to the slaughter," while her husband is away on a journey. It concludes, "Her
house is the way to hell, going down to the chambers of death."

260 some Jarifa Rodríguez: The Moorish first names are traditional in
Spanish literature, with the tongue-in-cheek exception of Zacatín, a
well-known street in Granada. The last names are among the most
common Spanish family names.

261 planting valerian: Valerian was considered a "love flower." Tying
thread or human hair around the roots was a way of winning reciprocation of love. Valerian also figures as an aphrodisiac.

264 he of Seneca's Hippolytus: The *nuntius* of Seneca's play (beginning at
line 991) is no less grandiloquent than Laurencio, without the sav-
ing grace of Lope's irony.

264 more luckless than Sejanus' [*sic,* for Sejus']: This superior horse originally belonging to a clerk, Sejus, brought ill luck to all its owners,
including Cassius and Mark Antony (Aulus Gellius, *Attic Nights*
III.ix).

266 one of the wise: Whom Lope has in mind is not known beyond a
doubt—possibly Horace: "Believe every day that dawns to be your
last" (*Epistles* IV.13); or Martial: "Living tomorrow it too late: live
today" (XV.12). The next sentence is a Senecan commonplace,
found, among other places, in *Epistles to Lucilius* XVI and XXVI.

266 *Lectionem:* "I refrain from reading anything that fails to yield some en-
joyment" (Cicero, *Tusculan Disputations* II.iii.7).

Glossary

Aelian, Claudius (fl. ca. A.D. 200): Author of *On the Characteristics of Animals*, in seventeen books.

Alaejos wine: A sparkling white wine from the province of Valladolid in Old Castile.

Alcalá: Alcalá de Henares, near Madrid, site of a Renaissance university founded in 1508.

Alcaraz: Town and mountain range southwest of Madrid in the province of Albacete.

Alciato, Andrea (1492–1550): His *Emblematum liber* (Book of Emblems; 1531) initiated a trend.

Alcibiades (ca. 450–404 B.C.): An Athenian disciple of Socrates.

Alcidamas (fl. fourth century B.C.): Greek sophist and rhetorician.

alcorza: A sugar-coated sweetmeat containing spices, seed pearl, and other substances considered medicinal.

allemande: An ancient dance of German origin, distinct from a later dance of the same name popular in the seventeenth and eighteenth centuries.

Amaryllis: Lope's poetic name for his last mistress, Marta de Nevares, original addressee of many of the lyrics found in *La Dorotea*.

Anaxarete: A princess loved by a commoner, Anaxarete was turned to stone for her indifference to her suitor's suicide (Ovid, *Metamorphoses* 14.698–760).

Anchises: Father of Aeneas, carried on his son's shoulders from burning Troy, as related in *Aeneid* 2.

anthypophora: A rhetorical figure which consists, among other things, of asking questions with the intention of answering them.

Antiope: The wife of King Lycus of Thebes, who repudiated her and married Dirce, by whom Antiope was treated with great cruelty.

antistes: The priest of a particular cult (Latin).

Apollo Delphian: The principal shrine and the oracle of the sun god were at Delphi.

Aratus (b. ca. 315 B.C.): Greek poet whose *Phenomena* deals with astronomy and meteorology.

Araucanas: See Ercilla.

Archimedes (ca. 287–212 B.C.): Greek mathematician, astronomer, and inventor whose devices helped postpone for two years the capture of Syracuse by Marcellus.

Argus: A hundred-eyed giant, the epitome of sharp-sightedness, whom Juno set up as watchman over Io, a rival she had changed into a heifer.

Arias Girón, Don Félix: A soldier, musician, and poet of noble birth who held various official posts in Madrid and was eulogized by Lope and Cervantes both for his musical accomplishments and for his great strength and valor.

Aristides (d. ca. 468 B.C.): One of the democratic leaders at Athens, known as The Just for his rectitude and impartiality.

Aristogenes (*sic,* for Aristoxenus): Musical theorist and philosopher, a disciple of Aristotle, quoted by Cicero (*Tusculan Disputations* I.x.19) as holding that the soul is the body's harmony.

Artemidorus (second century A.D.): Greek philosopher, author of a treatise on the interpretation of dreams.

Artemisia (fourth century B.C.): Queen of Caria, who commemorated her husband, King Mausolus, with the tomb (Mausoleum) which was one of the seven wonders of the ancient world.

Atalanta: Mythical Greek beauty outwitted in a foot race for her hand when she could not resist pausing to pick up the golden apples Hippomenes dropped along the way (Ovid, *Metamorphoses* 10.560–707).

Atocha: Seat of an ancient shrine of the Virgin who is Patroness of Madrid.

Auñón, Marquis of: Iñigo Fernández de Velasco, minor poet, second Marquis of Auñón by marriage to Ana de Herrera, who inherited the title prior to 1605.

Austriadas: See Rufo.

Averröes (1126–98): Ibn Rushd Averröes of Cordova, Moslem physician, philosopher, and commentator on Aristotle.

Avicenna (980–1037): Ibn-Sina Avicenna, Moslem physician and philosopher whose name was used metonymically for "physician."

Ayanza, Don Jerónimo de (d. by 1617): A musician and a man of great strength known as the Spanish Hercules.

Bandurrius the Shepherd: A fictitious rustic poet and musician.

Bautista de Vivar, Juan: Minor poet, balladeer, and friend of Lope's, about whom little is known; only a few lines of his verse survive.

Bembo, Pietro (1470–1547): Italian humanist and poet who championed the Tuscan vernacular in his *Prose della volgar lingua* (On Writing in the Vernacular; 1525) and used it extensively in verse and prose.

Bernardes, Diego (1530–1605): Portuguese Renaissance poet.

Berrío, Gonzalo Mateo de: Poet and dramatist of repute in the seventeenth century, now largely forgotten.

Betis: Spanish form of the Latin *Baetis,* Roman name for the Guadalquivir River.

Blas de Castro, Juan (d. 1631): Musician and longtime friend of Lope's, he composed music for many of Lope's verses.

Bonamí (1586/7–1614): A favorite palace dwarf at the Spanish Hapsburg court.

brachylogia: Concise form of expression.

Briseis: In the *Iliad,* a slave girl belonging to Achilles, taken from him by Agamemnon during the siege of Troy. The incensed Achilles then refused to fight along with the Greek army.

búcaro: A fragrant clay vessel.

Calepino, Ambrogio: Compiler of a multilingual dictionary first published in 1502 and augmented in subsequent editions by adding new languages.

Calle Mayor: This "Main Street" of Old Madrid was used for parading criminals as part of their punishment.

Camillus, Marcus Furius (fl. fourth century B.C.): Roman statesman and general who reputedly needed much coaxing before assuming the task of driving the Gauls from Rome.

Camoëns, Luiz de (1524?–80): The foremost Portuguese epic and lyric poet.

Campuzano, Doctor: Francisco de Campuzano, a contemporary of Lope's youth, physician to Philip II, and minor poet.

Carmenta: In Roman religion, a deity credited with inventing the Latin alphabet.

Carranza, Hierónimo de: A celebrated swordsman of seventeenth-century Spain, author of a *Philosophy of Arms.*

Carrera: The Carrera de San Jerónimo, a street still in use, leads into the Prado Boulevard from the Puerta del Sol.

Cato, Marcus Porcius (95–46 B.C.): A man unyielding and of absolute integrity, Cato took his life when defeat by Caesar's forces in North Africa became inevitable.

Cato, Marcus Porcius (234–149 B.C.): In the office of censor (184 B.C.), a stern reformer of Roman morals.

Cava, La: See Rodrigo.

Cephalus: See Procris.

Cervantes, Miguel de (1547–1616): Galatea is the heroine of Cervantes' first published work, the pastoral romance *La Galatea* (1585).

Céspedes, Alonso de (d. 1569): Captain famous for legendary strength in his time.

chaconne: A dance in moderate triple time, probably of Spanish origin, considered scandalous when introduced in the late sixteenth century.

Chariclea: See Theagenes.

Chiron: Wise and learned centaur, tutor of Achilles and other heroes.

Cid Ruy Díaz: Rodrigo Díaz de Vivar, national hero of Spain, historical personnage of the eleventh century and subject of the medieval epic *Poema de mio Cid* (ca. 1140).

Claudius: Roman emperor, A.D. 41–54.

Cloelia: In Roman legend, a maiden who escaped the Etruscan king Porsena by swimming the Tiber at night.

Coccaï, Merlin (1496–1544): Pseudonym of Teofilo Folengo, the most gifted practitioner of macaronic Latin verse.

Columella, Lucius Junius Moderatus: Author of *De Re Rustica* (ca. A.D. 65), a work dealing with farming and gardening, and *De Arboribus,* on trees.

Corte-Real, Jerónimo (1533–88): Portuguese poet in whose historical epic *The Shipwreck of Sepúlveda* (1592) Leonor de Sá figures prominently.

Court city: Madrid was commonly referred to as *La Corte* ("the Court").

Croesus (*sic,* for Marcus Licinius Crassus; d. 53 B.C.): A very wealthy Roman statesman killed in the Parthian War, though not from drinking molten gold.

Croesus: The last king of Lydia (560–546 B.C.), whose wealth became proverbial.

Cuenca cloth: Made in Cuenca, east of Madrid, and most prized in blue.

Cueva y Silva, Don Francisco de la (1550?–1627?): Jurist, minor poet, and playwright.

Curtius (*sic,* for Manlius Curius Dentatus; early third century B.C.): Exemplar of ancient Roman virtue and austere frugality, who served as consul several times.

Danaë: The mother of Perseus by Zeus, who visited her in a shower of gold.

Daphne: A nymph who escaped Apollo's pursuit by turning into a bay tree (Ovid, *Metamorphoses* 1.452–567).

Deborah: A prophetess and judge of Israel (Judges 4, 5).

décima: Verse form of ten eight-syllable lines, with set rhymes, also called *espinela* after the poet Vicente Espinel, who perfected and popularized it.

Demetrius: King of Macedonia (294–286 B.C.) enthralled by the flute-playing of the beautiful courtesan Lamia (Plutarch, *Life of Demetrius* xvi and xxxii).

Dino da Mugello: Italian jurisconsult and poet of the thirteenth century.

doubloon: A gold coin formerly used in Spain and Spanish America, originally equal to two *escudos.*

eiron: In Greek comedy, the clever underdog who consistently won out over the dull-witted, braggart *alazon.*

Elysian: Refers to the Elysian Fields, abode of the blessed after death, where only asphodels grew.

enargias: Greek rhetorical term denoting verbal constructs of such vivid intensity that they make the things described appear present to the eyes.

Endymion: A shepherd on Mount Lathmos, put into a perpetual sleep by the enamored Moon, who descended every night to embrace him.

Ercilla y Zúñiga, Don Alonso de (1533–94): Soldier and poet, author of *La Araucana,* an epic poem describing the Spanish conquest of Chile.

escudos: Gold or silver coins of varying monetary value, no longer in use.

Espinel, Vicente (1550–1624): Spanish poet, musician, and prose writer. See *décima.*

espinela: See *décima.*

Euphranor (fl. ca. 360 B.C.): Greek sculptor and painter.

Evadne: Wife of Capaneus, one of the Seven against Thebes, she threw herself on his funeral pyre to join him in death.

Fabius Maximus, Quintus: Roman leader known as The Delayer for his strategy of harrassing Hannibal's forces in the Second Punic War (218–201 B.C.) while evading battle.

Figueroa, Francisco de (1536–1617?): Spanish poet who celebrates in his verse a "Filis," presumably his wife.

Fílidas: See Gálvez de Montalvo.

Francavila, Duke of (1564–1630): Diego Gómez de Silva y Mendoza, a minor poet praised by his contemporaries, forgotten today.

Galateas: See Cervantes.

Galen (ca. A.D. 130–200): Greek physician whose name Lope often uses metonymically for a cure.

Gálvez de Montalvo, Luis (1549?–91?): Author of *El pastor de Fílida* (Phyllida's Shepherd, 1582).

Garay, Francisco de: A contemporary of Lope's youth, much praised by him as poet and historian, of whose works little survives.

Garcilaso de la Vega (1501–36): The foremost Spanish Renaissance poet, whose Camila in his *Second Eclogue* probably represents a lady of the ducal house of Alba.

Gellius, Aulus (second century A.D.): Author of *Attic Nights,* brief essays in Latin dealing with a wide variety of curious points and anecdotes based on readings, conversations, and lectures heard, and preserving many fragments of earlier Greek and Roman writers.

Germanicus Julius Caesar (15 B.C.–A.D. 19): Nephew and adopted son of Tiberius, author of Latin paraphrases of the *Phenomena* and *Prognostica* of Aratus.

Gesner, Conrad (1516–65): Swiss doctor, botanist, zoologist, philologist, and bibliographer.

Getafe: Town in the province of Madrid thirteen kilometers from the capital.

Giralda, La: A Sevillian landmark, formerly a minaret, now part of the Cathedral and topped by a turning female figure which serves as a weathervane.

Gold Tower: Still standing, this originally Moorish watchtower served as a treasure house and is now a naval museum.

Góngora y Argote, Luis de (1561–1627): The most brilliant poet of Lope's age, whose controversial learned (*culto*) style is at issue in act IV, scenes 2 and 3.

Gorgias (ca. 485–375 B.C.): Influential rhetorician and orator who gave prime importance to fine expression rather than subject matter.

Guadalajara Gate: The streets adjoining this city gate, no longer standing, contained the most elegant Madrid shops.

Hephaestion (d. 324 B.C.): Intimate friend of Alexander the Great, and one of his captains.

Hernández de Velasco, Gregorio: Translator of Virgil's *Aeneid* (Toledo, 1557 and 1574).

Hero: See Leander.

Hesperidian apples: One of the Labors of Hercules required him to gain possession of these fruits of a tree far in the west guarded by the Hesperides (daughters of Evening).

Hyblean: Pertaining to Mount Hyblea in Sicily, renowned for its roses.

Idalian dew: Pertaining to Idalium, center of a Cyprian cult of Venus.

Illescas: A Madrid bridge over the Manzanares on the road which leads southward to Illescas and Toledo.

Jarifa: Moorish woman's name, conventional in Spanish prose and verse.

Jehoshaphat: Lit. "whom Jehovah judges," this valley (Joel 3:2 and 12) prefigures the site of the Last Judgment.

John of the White Hose: A legendary dead man said to have left his tomb.

Julia (d. 54 B.C.): Daughter of Julius Caesar, wife of Pompey, who miscarried and died upon seeing her husband's bloodied garments.

Knight of the Burning Sword: Style taken by Amadis of Greece in a continuation (1535) of the romance of chivalry *Amadis of Gaul.*

Laínez, Pedro (d. 1584): Minor poet remembered chiefly because he is praised by Lope and Cervantes.

Lamia: See Demetrius.

Laudomia: Wife of a Greek, Protesilaus, killed before Troy, who took her own life in order to accompany him to the underworld.

Lazarillo de Tormes: In this first picaresque novel (1554), the black offspring of a white mother takes fright at the sight of his black father.

Leander: A youth from Abydos in love with Hero, priestess of Aphrodite at Sestos, drowned in a storm swimming the Hellespont to join her.

Leda: Loved by Zeus who, in the form of a swan, fathered Helen of Troy on her.

Lemnius, Levinus (1505–68): Dutch physician, author of *Hidden Wonders of Nature* (Ghent, 1559) and *Three Books . . .* (Antwerp, 1554).

Liaño, Felipe de: Sixteenth-century portraitist, famous in his day for his miniatures.

López Maldonado, Gabriel: Poet, now largely forgotten, of whom a *Cancionero* (Songbook) of 1586 survives.

Louis the Young: French king who reigned 1137–80.

Lucretia: Roman matron who, according to legend, committed suicide after being raped.

Luna, Alvaro de (1388–1453): A powerful favorite of King John II of Castile (1406–54), he was eventually conspired against and beheaded.

Lupercios: So Lope always refers to the Argensola brothers, Lupercio Leonardo (1559–1613) and Bartolomé Leonardo (1562–1631), both significant Aragonese poets.

Lycophron (b. ca. 325 B.C.): Greek tragedian of the Hellenistic Age who may or may not be the same person as the Lycophron who wrote the *Alexandra,* a dramatic monologue in verse proverbial for its obscurity.

Macrobius Theodosius (fl. ca. A.D. 400): Roman writer and philosopher whose dialogue *Saturnalia* chiefly treats the works of Virgil.

Manzanares: Small river that passes through Madrid.

maravedí: A minor copper coin in circulation until the nineteenth century.

Marcius, Ancus: According to legend, the third king of Rome after the death of Romulus.

Mariamne: Wife of Herod (73?–4 B.C.), king of Judea, put to death at his order. Lope's version alters the facts as put down by Flavius Josephus, the historian of the Jews, in the first century A.D..

Maya jugs: Clay vessels made in Lisbon, probably named after a family of potters.

Mena, Juan de (1411–56): Spanish writer known principally for his "Labyrinth of Fortune" consisting of three hundred stanzas.

Mendoza, Diego de: Little is known of this figure, tutor to the fifth Duke of Alba, the father of Lope's patron in 1590–95.

Mendoza, Don Diego de (1503–75): Spanish Renaissance poet who dedicated some of his poems to a "Phyllis."

Mentor (d. before 365 B.C.): The most famous Greek master of the art of metalworking.

Merced, La: Church belonging to a convent founded in Madrid in 1564 and torn down in the nineteenth century.

Milo (late sixth century B.C.): An athlete of Croton in Magna Graecia who performed legendary feats of strength, such as killing a heifer at one blow.

Minos: A king of Crete whose wife, Pasiphaë, became enamored of a bull and gave birth to the Minotaur, part bull (Gr. *tauros*) and part man.

Mondoñedo, Bishop of (1480?–1545): Friar Antonio de Guevara, prolific and prolix Renaissance writer.

Montalvo: See Gálvez de Montalvo.

Montaña, La: Common name of the province of Santander in northern Spain, a region never conquered by the Moors. Its inhabitants prided themselves on their ancient Christian lineage.

Montemayor, Jorge de (1520?–61): Author of *La Diana,* the first pastoral romance in Spanish (ca. 1558).

Montes Claros, Marquis of (1570–1628): Juan Manuel de Mendoza y Luna, verse writer, army officer, and viceroy of Mexico and Peru.

Moretum: A poem dubiously attributed to Virgil, it describes the domestic routines of a peasant farmer on a winter morning.

Mucius: See Scaevola.

Myron (fl. 460–440 B.C.): Celebrated Greek sculptor.

Naaera: A servant of Cleopatra who killed herself following her mistress's suicide.

Nemean lion: An invulnerable monster which Hercules choked in the first of his twelve Labors.

Nicander (second century B.C.): Greek didactic poet who wrote on poisons and their antidotes.

Nuestra Señora de los Remedios: A hermitage honoring the Virgin, established in the sixteenth century on the banks of the Guadalquivir downriver from Seville.

Numantia: An ancient city in northern Spain, besieged and taken by Scipio the Younger in 134-133 B.C..

Omphale: Queen of Lydia, for love of whom Hercules put on women's clothes and spun wool, while she wore his lion's skin.

Ordóñez, Don Diego de: See Zamora.

Orontes: River in western Syria, celebrated for the production of myrrh.

Padilla, Pedro de (d. after 1599): Friend of Lope and other poets, author in the 1580's of several volumes of sacred and secular verse.

Palomares, Juan de (d. by 1598): Musician of the latter part of the sixteenth century who set some of Lope's lyrics to music but is otherwise not well known.

Pan: God of flocks and shepherds, he was represented with the legs and hooves of a goat.

Panchaean: Pertaining to Panchaea, the fertile coastal region of Arabia, and its incense-bearing sands.

Pangaeus, Mount: A mountain range in Macedonia, noted for its roses.

Paredes, Pablo de: A fencing master who gave lessons in Madrid between 1580 and 1590, possibly to Lope, and was later appointed by Philip II principal examiner and master-at-arms.

Pasiphaë: See Minos.

passementerie: Edgings and trimmings, especially those made of gimp, braid, or the like, often set off with jet or metal beads.

Peñafiel, Marquis of (1554-94): Juan Téllez Girón, later Duke of Osuna, a poet respected in his day.

Pêrez, Gonzalo: Translator of Homer's *Odyssey* (Antwerp, 1550 and 1556).

Pescara, Marchioness of (1492-1547): The Italian poetess Vittoria Colonna.

Pescara, Marquis of (1489-1525): Hernando de Avalos, celebrated captain of Charles V, and victor at the battle of Pavia (1525).

Petrarch (1304-74): Francesco Petrarca, the Italian poet whose famous *Canzoniere* is devoted to his love for the lady he calls Laura.

Phaedra: Daughter of King Minos of Crete and wife of Theseus. Repulsed in her love for her stepson, Hippolytus, she accused him falsely and, after his death, hanged herself.

Phidias (b. ca. 500 B.C.): Athenian artist especially renowned as a sculptor.

Phryne (fourth century B.C.): Famous Greek courtesan whose beauty brought her great wealth.

Pico della Mirandola, Giovanni (1463–94): Florentine humanist and philosopher, author of the *Heptaplus* (1491), an esoteric exposition of the creation.

pie de gibao: A dance in vogue in sixteenth-century Spain, possibly of French origin, about which little is known.

Polyclitus (fl. 450–420 B.C.): Celebrated Greek sculptor.

Pompilius (i.e., Numa Pompilius): Tradition makes him successor to Romulus as king of Rome (715–673 B.C.). He is credited with writing books of sacred law and establishing many religious institutions.

Pompilius (*sic,* for Gaius Popillius Laenas): Leader of a Roman embassy to Egypt, 168 B.C., he demanded that a decision about leaving Egypt be taken by the Seleucid king Antiochus Epiphanes before the latter stepped out of a circle drawn around him by Popillius.

Pontano, Giovanni (1426–1503): Italian humanist who wrote extensively in latin.

Porsena: See Scaevola.

Portia: Wife of Brutus (78?–42 B.C.), one of the assassins of Julius Caesar, who killed herself with live coals on receiving news of her husband's death.

Prado: A Madrid thoroughfare, now a boulevard, site of a royal residence which in 1814 became the Prado Museum.

Procris: Fearful of the love of Eos, the dawn, for Cephalus, her husband, Procris secretly followed him as he hunted and was accidently slain by him.

Propertius, Sextus (ca. 50-ca. 16 B.C.): Roman poet known especially for his elegies and love poems.

Pyramus: In Ovid's *Metamorphoses* (4.55–166), a Babylonian youth who stabbed himself, believing his beloved Thisbe dead.

Pyrrhus I (ca. 319–272 B.C.): King of Epirus, cousin of Alexander the Great, a symbol of humanity for his return of Roman captives without exacting ransom.

Ravisius Textor (1430–1524): Latinized form of the name of Jean Tixier, Seigneur de Ravisy, author of a compendium much used by Lope, the *Officina ... sive Theatrum ...* (Workshop ... or Showplace ...; Paris, 1520 and later eds.).

real: A former silver coin of Spain and the Spanish New World, the eighth part of a peso.

Redbeard: Cheridín Barbarroja, a sixteenth-century Moslem privateer, notorious as a scourger of Christians.

Regulus, Marcus Atilius: Roman commander captured by the Carthaginians in the First Punic War, who returned to Carthage from a peace mission to Rome (250 B.C.) to face death by torture rather than break his word and risk the lives of the other hostages.

Rhodope: Mountain range in Thrace, metonymic for hardness.

Rodrigo, King: The last Visigothic king of Spain, whom legend held responsible for the loss of the country to the Arabs (711) after he seduced La Cava Florinda.

Romulus: In Roman legend, Romulus built his city on the Palatine Mount and ruled as first king of Rome.

rose of Jericho: Also called "resurrection plant," it was used as a talisman by midwives in determining the hour of a birth.

Rufo the Jurist (ca. 1547–1620): Juan Rufo Gutiérrez, whose epic, *La Austriada,* treats the campaigns of Don Juan of Austria against the Moors of Granada.

Sabean: Pertaining to Saba (the Biblical Sheba), an ancient kingdom in southwestern Arabia noted for spices and gems.

Saguntum: A city north of Valencia on the east coast of Spain, besieged by Hannibal in 219–218 B.C.

Saint Agnes (292?–304?): Roman Catholic virgin martyr. That she should allegedly be assigned to Gerarda is transparent irony on the latter's part.

Sanlúcar (de Barrameda): Town at the mouth of the Guadalquivir River, southwest of Seville.

Sannazaro, Jacopo (1456–1530): Neapolitan poet and author whose works in Latin include *De partu Virginis* (On Him the Virgin Bore; 1521) and the *Eclogae Piscatoriae* (Idylls of Fishermen; 1526); in Italian, *Arcadia* (1504), the original pastoral romance, and lyric poetry.

Scaevola, Mucius: A legendary patriotic Roman who thrust his hand into fire to show his indifference to death when taken prisoner by Lars Porsena, king of Clusium, thereby winning his release from the astonished monarch.

Scylla: Beloved by Glaucus, a marine deity, Scylla aroused the jealousy of Circe, who changed her into a sea monster.

Scythia: Name given by the Greeks to the region north and east of the Black and Caspian Seas.

Seleucus (d. 281 B.C.): An officer of Alexander the Great, founder of the dynasty which inherited his empire, and supposed author of the first legal code in Greek.

Semiramis: The legendary Assyrian queen, founder of Babylon, who exchanged her mirror for a sword when advised while combing her hair that an army was advancing against her.

Servius (Servius Tullius): Semi-legendary Roman king, the fifth after Romulus, a man of humble origin who enlarged the city and instituted administrative reforms.

Solitudinous, The: A swipe at Góngora's *Solitudes* (1614), poems in which *cultismo* is pushed to an extreme.

Sophonisba: During the Second Punic War (218–201 B.C.), captive of the Numidian prince, Masinissa, who became enamored of her and assisted her suicide by poison to evade Roman captivity.

Soto, Doctor (1548–95): Luis Barahona de Soto, poet who preceded Lope in writing a sequel to Ariosto's *Orlando Furioso* and was much admired by Cervantes.

Suabius, Leo (b. early 1500's, d. 1576): Name assumed by the French hermeticist Jacques Gohory, author of a *Compendium* of the writings of the Swiss alchemist Paracelsus (Paris, 1591?).

Suleiman, Rosa: Sixteenth-century Turkish beauty painted several times by Titian and much alluded to in the literature of the period.

Tagus (Tajo): The classic river of Spanish pastoral literature, it flows around Toledo and on to the sea at Lisbon.

Tarquin (i.e., Tarquinius Priscus): Fourth king of Rome after Romulus, according to legend, an adventurer of Greek and Etruscan ancestry whose existence may have some basis in fact.

Tárraga, Canon (d. 1602): Francisco Agustín Tárrega, Valencian dramatist and poet.

Teladeus and Theodoros: Teladeus is an erratum picked up by Lope from the *Officina* of Ravisius Textor, for Telecles, father of Theodoros of Samos (fl. ca. 560–530 B.C.), with whom he executed a famous statue of the Pythian Apollo.

Terracina, Laura (1519–77): Neapolitan poetess whose *Rhymes* were first published in 1548.

Theagenes and Chariclea: Greek romance by Heliodorus, 3d cent. A.D.

Thisbe: See Pyramus.

Triana: The old gypsy quarter of Seville, separated from the city proper by the Guadalquiver River.

Triton: Son of Poseidon and Amphitrite, represented with the head and trunk of a man and the tail of a fish; or any of various minor sea deities.

Uchalí: A sixteenth-century Christian renegade and privateer who took part in the battle of Lepanto (1571) and became a legend in his time.

Vargas Manrique, Don Luis de (ca. 1556–before 1600): Dramatist and lyric poet, a companion of Lope's youth.

Vega, Marco Antonio de la (d. by 1622): Minor poet who has passed into oblivion save for admiring mention by Lope and Cervantes.

Vesta: Roman goddess of the blazing hearth, whose temple fire was tended by the vestal virgins.

Vivar, Juan Bautista de: A ballad writer much praised by his contemporaries, Lope and Cervantes. His work has not survived.

Xenophon (ca. 430-ca. 355 B.C.): Athenian soldier and polygraph, author of the *Anabasis*.

Zamora: The siege of this Leonese city by Diego Ordóñez in the eleventh century was a favorite theme of traditional Spanish balladry.

Zulema: Moorish man's name, conventional in Spanish prose and verse.